W9-ADH-909

Winter Park Public Library

Presented by

The
Rachel D. Murrah
Fiction
Endowment Book Fund

Feb. 06   Centra Points   32.95

Winter Park Public Library
460 East New England Avenue
Winter Park, Florida 32789
Renewals: (407) 623-3300
or www.wppl.org

A Grave Mistake

Center Point Large Print

**This Large Print Book carries the
Seal of Approval of N.A.V.H.**

A Grave Mistake

STELLA CAMERON

CENTER POINT PUBLISHING
THORNDIKE, MAINE

This Center Point Large Print edition
is published in the year 2006 by arrangement with
Harlequin Enterprises Ltd.

Copyright © 2005 by Stella Cameron.

All rights reserved.

The text of this Large Print edition is unabridged. In other
aspects, this book may vary from the original edition. Printed in
Thailand. Set in 16-point Times New Roman type.

ISBN 1-58547-692-7

Library of Congress Cataloging-in-Publication Data

Cameron, Stella.
    A grave mistake / Stella Cameron.--Center Point large print ed.
        p. cm.
    ISBN 1-58547-692-7 (lib. bdg. : alk. paper)
    1. Police--Louisiana--New Orleans--Fiction. 2. New Orleans (La.)--Fiction. 3. Large
type books. I. Title.

PS3553.A4345G73 2006
813'.54--dc22

                                                            2005023429

For Julian and Gerry Savoy, proud Cajuns
who answer all those questions.

Laissez le bon temps roler!

3/06

Prologue

Near Chartres Street, New Orleans, Louisiana,
1:35 a.m.

His feet were wet.

Shit, why hadn't he kept his mouth shut back there? Why had he asked for money?

He could still hear it, the jazz in that place, music as old as this town, older, the rhythm thumping, but not as fast or hard as the blood at his temples.

The goons they'd sent after him were too slow to have seen for sure where he'd taken a right off Chartres Street. Deep in a doorway, neon lights laying bright stripes on the soaked street, Pip Sedge couldn't hold the breaths that burned his lungs, hurt his heart, so he pulled up one side of his suit jacket and plastered it over his face, hoping to muffle any noise.

The rain had all but cleared the late stragglers away.

Maybe he'd lost those two guys. He didn't hear anyone running, but two hundred and fifty pounds or so of muscle—and fat—apiece had to make the going tough.

Shut the hell up. Shut up! His brain wouldn't be quiet, it yammered at him, slid into a screaming chorus that went on and on. *I'm a dead man. I'm a dead man. I'm a dead man.* They would put a bullet in him. Chase him closer to the river, farther and farther from any help, shoot him in the back and leave him facedown in stinking mud and garbage.

Help? What help?

Quiet. Hush. Just keep cool.

Moving from the doorway could be suicidal. For all he knew there were eyes watching for his first step into the open.

He felt the air change, the spaces around him contract, and he strained to separate sounds. *I'm a Yankee Doodle Dandy.* It was a horn player's riff somewhere inside an old Dixieland number that could have been the soundtrack from a black-and-white movie. A shutter creaked back and forth, a little slam in between. The rain subsided to a patter.

Shadows gathered before his eyes. He blinked. Shadows shifted on the walls that faced him across the narrow road. Bars on windows shimmered wet. He took in air and held it, and his guts turned to water.

He could stand and wait to die, or he could try to outrun two lumbering punks with guns. And he could hope, just a little, that they wouldn't see him until he was out of range, or that they didn't see him at all.

If he got out of this, he already had a new plan. It had come to him earlier when he'd overheard those jerks congratulating themselves. He should have thought about it a long time ago.

Revenge time.

Pip dared to peer from the doorway, back toward Chartres Street. Nothing. No cartoon heavies hunched together, weapons cocked. Now he wanted to laugh, to scream.

He ran. One downward step and another, and he hit the sidewalk almost brushing the wall as he went. The newspaper blocking the holes in his shoes was sodden—what was left of the thin leather soles, sodden. At least they didn't make much noise.

The rain fell heavier again, slanted into his face, but didn't cool the blinding heat swelling in his head. He opened his mouth and let his breath drag in and out, lengthened his stride, punched the seething air with jabbing fists.

Asking for money, letting it out that he had proof he was owed, had been a crazy move. He'd launched into a diatribe about ruining reputations and putting people in jail, even though their sneers should have shut him up. He had threatened some of the most dangerous people in New Orleans.

His left ankle turned. Pain shot through his foot, up his leg, but what the hell, he could run with no legs if he had to. He ran on. With freedom in your sights, you could limp at the speed of a Jaguar.

The ankle buckled at every step. He stumbled and caught at a street-sign pole. He wanted to be sick.

There could be a bone broken down there.

He was almost on top of a small cross street. He was going to make it. His breaths turned to sobs. His eyes filmed over. He would make it. There wasn't any sound of heavy men running in hard shoes. All he heard through the roaring in his brain was the approach of a car from the left.

He paused, panting, his veins fluttering, and checked his pockets to make sure he hadn't dropped anything. He hadn't. Bending over at the curb, his hands on his knees, Pip waited for the car to pass. Damn them all. He'd taken too long to find a way to get back what he'd lost. He'd owed them big, but not so big they should have taken everything he had.

He had to show Zinnia he was man enough to fix things.

The first shot caught him in his injured leg. He screamed and began to crumple forward.

The second shot punctured his right shoulder, drove straight back. He heard the bones explode, felt the flesh burn, saw red blossoms like flames. He couldn't see.

The third shot . . .

1

Toussaint, Louisiana

Jilly Gable had a man to confront. Maybe this time Guy Gautreaux would keep his big mouth shut and let her finish what she had to say before he piled in and told her what to do and why, and reminded her of his earlier warning that the reappearance of her long-lost mother could be bad news.

Guy had trouble with the concept that a woman could have a change of heart after thirty years of not giving a damn about a person. He didn't believe people changed; he thought that as years went by they became more of what they had always been. In this case, once a bad mother, eventually a *really* bad mother.

Jilly pulled her aging VW Beetle into the forecourt at Homer Devol's gas station—the last gas station on the way out of the town of Toussaint, and first on the way in, depending on whether you were going or coming and which side of the sign you looked at.

Homer usually went to pick his granddaughter up from school in the afternoon, leaving Guy to tend the gas station and the convenience store beyond, where a string of colored lights outlined the roof. The lights stayed on all day and into the evening, all year.

Pots of showy geraniums hung beneath the eaves with ivy trailing to the ground.

Jilly looked around. Nothing on two legs moved. With her head out of the window, she called, "Homer! Guy!" then she screwed up her eyes and listened. No response. She looked quickly toward the road. All day she'd had a sick sensation that she was being followed, watched. Last night she had got a warning, even if it wasn't direct, that someone was watching her movements. Who better to advise her than Guy, a New Orleans Police Department homicide detective on extended leave?

Way to the left, closer to the bayou, Homer's split-timber house stood on stilts with its gallery facing the bayou across the sloping back lawn.

She got out of the lime-green Beetle and went through the useless exercise of trying to take in a breath. Hot didn't cover it. Heat eddies wavered above the burned-out grass and did their shaky dance on tops of the roofs. From where she was she could see cypress trees crouching, totally still, over Bayou Teche. Beards of Spanish moss hung from branches as if they were painted there, and the pea-green surface of the bayou might have been set-up Jell-O. Even the gators would be sleeping now.

She reached behind her seat and hauled out several bakery boxes tied together with string. If she didn't get them inside fast, the contents would be gooey puddles. Jilly owned All Tarted Up, Flakiest Pastry In Town, one of Toussaint's favorite gathering places. Her brother, Joe—a lawyer—had been her partner until his marriage the previous year. She'd been able to assume the loans and she loved having the business to herself.

Guy's beat-up gray Pontiac hugged a slice of shade beside the store, but she saw no sign of the man, either in the gas station or the store. He didn't live out here and mostly stayed away from the house.

A walk toward the bayou ended her search. He stood on the dock, a cell phone clamped to his ear, his arms crossed, and his face pointing away from her.

A door slid open behind her and she jumped, swung

around and barely kept her balance. Homer's fish-boiling operations were housed in this other building, one you didn't see until you got close to the bayou. Ozaire Dupre walked out and turned to slide the doors shut, but not before the dense smell of boiling fish rushed free. Ozaire, caretaker at the church, man of many schemes, also helped out with Homer's boiling and drove the giant pots of fish, and sometimes vats of his part-time boss's own special gumbo, to backyard barbecues or any event looking for real Louisiana cooking.

Ozaire saw Jilly and frowned, shook his big, shaved head dolefully. "Better you keep me company today, girl. That one down there—he's one big, black cloud, him." Ozaire fooled some people with his short, thick, slow-moving body. In fact, the man's strength was legendary in the area, and his speed if he chose to hurry.

A part-grown black mutt with long, silky hair loped around his legs but soon left to investigate Jilly.

"You say that every time I come," Jilly pointed out, scratching the dog's velvet head. "Who's this good-looking fella?"

"That Guy Gautreaux's a big, black cloud all the time, that's why I say it." Ozaire looked smug. His scalp shone in the sunlight and sweat ran down the sides of his round face and heavy neck. "Never got nuthin' good to say. I reckon he's got a curse on him. Bad-luck boy, that one."

"You should be more careful what you say, you,"

Jilly told Ozaire. "A man could get in trouble for saying things like that."

"Get *on*. I'm just sayin' it like it is. Last woman that boy got close to is in a cemetery."

Last year Guy's longtime girlfriend had been murdered in New Orleans. He blamed himself.

"Later," Jilly said, exasperated. She held out the boxes. "We had extra at the bakery. They're fresh. Put them in the store case for Homer to sell."

Ozaire took the load from her and gave a rare grin. "An' I thought you was bringin' me a treat."

Jilly wagged a finger at him. A bug flew into her eye and she dealt with it, then pointed at him again. "You get one. I've counted those pastries, I'll count them again when I come back up. There better be no more than one gone." Give the man the chance and he'd be hauling the stuff off to sell to whoever was using the church hall at St. Cécil's.

"That there's a dog what's a prize, that's what he is," Ozaire said, as if the topic had never been pastries. "Can't keep 'im, no sir. My Lil says four dogs is enough. But this guy's too good, got too much character to drop him at the pound and have 'em put him down in a couple of days."

Jilly had been the recipient of Ozaire's earlier attempts to place strays. "Hope you find a home for him," she said. The man's love of dogs made her feel more kindly toward him.

"Reckon I have," Ozaire said. "With your prickly friend, huh? Put in a good word, huh? For the dog's

sake, and for that miserable son of . . ." He let the rest
trail off.

Jilly shook her head. "You're too hard on Guy," she
told him, and headed toward the dock. She turned and
walked backward a few paces. "I'm going to check on
the pastries, mind."

Jilly hurried downhill.

Guy was leaning over, pushing off one of the rental
boats. A couple of guys with fishing gear started the
outboard and phut-phutted into the middle of the
channel. With the phone still clamped to his ear, Guy
stood up and saw Jilly. He gave her a brief wave and
started meandering back along the dock. They'd met
the previous year when an investigation brought him
to Toussaint and he'd become her friend, her best
buddy, and she needed to talk openly with him about
what was on her mind. He had never attempted to turn
their relationship into something deeper, but Jilly had
seen the hot looks he quickly hid—she wasn't the only
one frustrated by the sexless hours they spent together.

"Take your sweet time," Jilly muttered. How could
a man walk that slowly? "Just let me squirm as long
as possible." *Do I admit I'm scared and I need to tell
you about it?* If she did, he'd probably jump all over
her, say she was putting herself in danger. Get out of
the situation. End of discussion.

Guy stood still, staring up at her, and continued his
conversation. After the death of the woman he had
loved he refused to go back to the NOPD, but they
were holding a place for him. Guy was a darn good

15

detective. Meanwhile, Homer had needed someone reliable and asked Guy if he'd work at his place—just to fill the time until he moved on. Guy accepted the job and gave it his all. He seemed grateful to Homer and treated his own place at the station as a trust, even though Jilly knew he had enough money to live on if he wanted to hang around his rented house and do nothing until he decided on his next steps.

Jilly didn't want Guy to leave his haven in Toussaint, even though he had made it plain he didn't intend to stay for good.

He stuck the phone back on his belt and speeded up. A tall, rangy man, in faded-out jeans and a navy T-shirt with holes in it, he could cover the ground quickly when it suited him. He met Jilly before she could put a foot on the dock.

She looked up at him, at his unreadable, almost black eyes, and wished she hadn't come. Ozaire hadn't been joking about the cloud.

"I wasn't expectin' you," he said, and winced. He almost always said the wrong thing to Jilly, but not because he didn't want to tell her how he felt each time he saw her. He guessed he'd never be polished.

"I'm not staying," Jilly said. Not when he looked as if he wished she was somewhere else and couldn't even manage to crack a welcoming smile.

He cocked his head to one side and took off his straw Stetson, then held it by the fraying brim. "You must have had somethin' on your mind," he said. "No reason to come this way otherwise." And he wished she'd say something he'd really like to hear, like her creep of a mother had packed up and left town again.

"You can make a person feel pretty unwelcome, Guy." She didn't dare say it hurt her when he behaved as if she was a stranger with bad timing.

He ran a deeply tanned forearm over his brow, blinking slowly.

You got used to a man's little mannerisms, got to like them even. Next he'd rake his fingers through his dishwater-blond hair. Yep, that's what he did.

"Guy, can I ask your honest opinion about something?"

He swallowed and rubbed the flat of his right hand back and forth on his chest. *Jilly, you can ask me anything. If I was any kind of a man, I'd get over what I can't change and find a way to be what you need, what you want me to be.* "Ask. Maybe I can be useful— maybe not." He sickened himself. She wanted intimacy with him, the kind that never let her doubt he was on her side. But he was scared to give it to her. Stuff had happened, deadly stuff, to the only woman he'd gotten really close to.

Yeah, Jilly thought, she just wanted him to reassure her that she shouldn't question her mother's motives for being back in Toussaint. And she'd like him to put her mind at rest about one or two things that made her antsy when she visited the old Edwards Place, where her mother's second husband, Daddy Preston, had set his wife up in lavish style. She'd dissuaded Edith from renaming the estate, so Edwards Place it remained, but Jilly didn't like the house much. Too big and eerie, filled with memories and sad stories Edith insisted on relating.

Then there was what happened last night. Guy could help her get through that if he had a mind to. All he had to do was tell her it was no big deal, and that he was on her side.

Jilly gave Guy a little smile, then dropped her face so he couldn't study her so closely anymore.

Would it be so dangerous to give her a hug? he wondered. A brotherly hug to take away some of the trouble he had seen in her eyes? He wasn't the only one who had suffered loss. Jilly's former fiancé turned out to be a felon and was destined to spend the rest of his life in the pen.

Jilly moved closer. She could feel him, always could when he was anywhere around.

"Okay," he said, and put a hand on her shoulder. She wasn't a fragile woman, but he felt clumsy around her. "Tell me about it, cher."

It was just his way to be reserved. He cared what happened to her, the same as she did about him. "You don't like it that Edith came back," she said.

"I never said that."

"You said she'd make trouble in the end. That sounded pretty much as if you didn't think she should have come here."

Had he said that? "I don't think that was exactly what I said, but if you want me to take it back, I will.

She's been here awhile now and she hasn't hurt you so far as I can tell."

"Having her show up was a shock." Jilly rested her forehead on his chest. "I'm still getting used to her. She's not what this is about. Forgive me for being a whiny wuss, but I'm worried about something." Guy looked down at the top of her head, at her thick, blond-streaked brown hair that reached her waist. A yellow ribbon, tied a few inches from the bottom, kept it behind her shoulders. That had been his old partner, Nat Archer, on the phone. Before long he would show up here, even though Guy had warned him previously that he didn't want them seen together in Toussaint. From the sound of Nat's voice, something big was going down. Ozaire was already backing a truck out and would be on his way back to St. Cécil's within moments. Jilly ought to be gone before Nat arrived, too.

A half-grown black mutt with legs too long for its body ran back and forth and Guy made a note to call for the dogcatcher when Jilly left.

Jilly looked up at him. "I said I was worried."

"And I'm waitin' to hear why."

"You are so tough, Guy Gautreaux. You never give an inch and you're the only person I have to share this with."

"You have Joe. I'd have thought your brother would have the best insight on this one."

Hurt, disappointed, she tried to shrug away, but he exerted a little more pressure on her shoulder and she couldn't go anywhere. "Joe isn't objective about this. He hates Edith. He isn't into giving people second chances. But then, he's my half brother. Edith isn't his mother."

"Joe Gable has his head screwed on right."

"Damn it, Guy." She punched his unyielding chest. "I think you'd side with anyone but me."

He shook her gently. "Could it be that Joe and I have your best interests at heart? Could that be it? Joe might remember picking you up when your dad was long gone, who the hell knows where, and the people he hired on the cheap to look after you kicked you out because he'd quit sendin' money. You were fourteen years old. Joe might harbor a grudge against the so-called mother who walked out and left you with that angry son of a gun who fathered you and left you just like she did."

"Yes," she said. "That could be. Sorry I bothered you. Joe and Ellie won't be back from Italy for weeks, anyway. Forget it. It's no big deal." Except that she felt she could choke, and wished her brother and his wife weren't so far away.

Yes, it was a big deal. He could feel that it, whatever it was, could be a very big deal. "I've got a clumsy mouth, you know that? When it comes to your old man, I'd gladly help Joe feed him to a gator."

The suspicious sheen on her light hazel eyes turned his stomach. If she cried, he was a goner.

"I want to hear what you came to say and you aren't leavin' till you tell me," he said in a hurry.

20

Jilly met those black eyes of his and he made a valiant attempt to give her a reassuring smile. "Okay," she said. "No, it isn't okay. It's going to sound stupid. Forget it."

He put his mouth by her ear. "Listen to me carefully. You and I will stand right here until you come clean." He was starting to get a really nasty feeling that this could chew up some time and prayed Nat would take longer than expected to arrive.

"You know there's a live-in staff at Edwards Place?" she said.

"Only because you told me. I haven't been invited to tea yet."

She looked at him sideways. "There's a new man who came from New Orleans a couple of days ago. I think he's a bodyguard."

He didn't know how he felt about that—if he felt anything at all. "Edith and that woman who came with her are pretty much alone. Could be they feel safer with a man watching out for them."

"When this one arrived—he came in on the chopper—I think Edith was as surprised as I was. That he was there, I mean. She knew him, even though they didn't say much to each other. He just went to a room as if he knew it was going to be there, and moved in." There was no reason to mention that Edith's daughter-in-law, Laura Preston, threw a tantrum at the sight of the man.

"Mr. Preston flew in, too," Jilly went on. "I was glad to meet him finally."

"Is that right?" All of Guy's nightmares were coming true. The so-called *happy family* wanted to draw Jilly in, to change her.

"Yes. He's a nice man. He couldn't have been kinder to me. He said he hoped I'd let him think of me as the daughter he never had."

"Did he?" Guy had turned ice cold. Goose bumps shot up his arms. "Is he staying at the house now?"

"He had to go back to New Orleans, but he said he'll be spending a lot of time here. I can't get used to the idea of someone having a helicopter pad in their garden." She held out her left arm to show him a thick gold bracelet with a diamond clasp. "I feel funny about it, but he gave me this. He gave one each to Edith and Laura, too."

Guy felt his nostrils flare. Every alarm bell went off. What could this guy possibly want from Jilly?

"Very nice," he said. "But the bodyguard stayed?"

"Yes. Daddy Preston went back alone."

Had he misheard her? "What did you call him?"

She reddened. "That's what everyone calls him. At least, Edith and Laura do."

"So you call him what? Daddy?"

"*No.* I wouldn't be comfortable—even though he did ask me to. I call him Mr. Preston."

If he had the right, he'd tell Jilly to stay away from that place. He didn't have the right and wasn't likely to. "You were talking about the new bodyguard. Did he seem threatening to you?"

"No-o. Not at first."

He gripped both of her arms. "Explain that."

"I think I was followed back to my place last night. It was getting dark but when I got out of my car in the driveway, a car drove by slowly."

"And you believe this was the same man who just moved into Edwards Place?"

She hadn't been able to see his face, just that he was big. "I don't think so. But the car had those black windows."

If he showed any sign of the sudden panic he felt, she'd be terrified. "That doesn't mean it had anything to do with you, then."

"When I was inside, I went upstairs and looked out of a window. A man was standing close to a tree at the corner, watching my house. I could have missed him if he hadn't drawn on a cigarette."

Guy set his back teeth. "He didn't have to be looking at your house—and he didn't have to have come from the car you saw being driven past."

"No. Except I just knew he was looking at my place and I could see the back of the car around the corner."

Guy put his hands on his hips and expanded his lungs. He felt an artificial calm in the air as if the world was about to split wide open and nothing but filth would pour out.

He wanted Edith Preston, and anyone remotely attached to her, out of Toussaint, preferably yesterday.

"You were right in the first place," Jilly said. "I'm overreacting. I need to head back into town."

And without a word of reassurance from me, ass that

I am. "I'll walk you to your car. Good-lookin' mutt running loose up there. I'll call the pound."

Jilly stopped so suddenly, he'd taken two steps before he halted and looked at her. "What is it?"

"You call the pound on that dog and I'll never speak to you again."

Shee-it. "It's lost, Jilly. Kindest thing to do—"

"Is have it picked up and gassed? Oh, no, sir, not that sweet-natured pooch. Look at that trusting face. He's just what you need to take your mind off yourself now and then."

Guy felt a bit wild. "*I* need that trampy dog?"

"You surely do, Mr. Gautreaux." She clapped her hands at the hound. "Here, boy. Here, boy. Come and meet Guy."

"Damn it, Jilly, don't do that. I can't have a dog."

"Sure you can. What else do you have in that miserable shotgun house of yours? Not furniture, that's for sure."

"I like—whoa." The dog arrived, bypassed Jilly as if he'd never seen her, now or before, and landed against Guy's middle. His long tongue lolled out of his mouth, he slobbered, and looked for all the world like he was grinning.

Guy patted the dog's head and said, "Down, boy," which the critter did. He sat beside the man as if he was giving an obedience demonstration.

"Look at that, he—"

"Never mind the dog. I'll see he's taken care of. Let's go sit at a picnic table. I want you to tell me what

24

you *really* need from me. And you can kick me if I put my foot in my mouth."

She blinked. He was trying to reach out to her. Jilly couldn't find the words she really wanted to say. "The first thing you need to do when you adopt a dog is to get him looked at by a vet. He'll need all of his shots, and—"

Guy's pinched-up expression stopped Jilly. "I said, forget the dog." He took off toward the back lawn.

Jilly followed him. She surreptitiously patted her thigh and the big pup gamboled past her to lope along at Guy's heel. Guy walked easily, his big shoulders and arms swinging.

"I'll get us a cold drink," Guy called back.

Something about him suggested he was in a hurry. "Not for me, thanks," Jilly said, although her mouth felt like sandpaper.

They sat, facing each other across the table, the dog a couple of feet distant with his liquid eyes firmly on Guy's face.

"Let's get to it," Guy said. He wasn't going to grow a silver tongue so he might as well wade in.

"Why don't you like Edith?"

He gave her a long, considered look. "I like you. I don't like anyone who hurts you. That should cover it."

"She's changed."

"People don't change."

Jilly hitched at the thin straps on her yellow sundress. One of the nicest things about Edith's mother having been part black was that Jilly had inherited skin the color of pale gold coffee. Edith had it, too. Guy's eyes flickered toward her thumbs, where they were hooked beneath her straps, then away again. Most of the time he treated her like one of the guys, but there were those moments that let her know he didn't entirely think of her that way. Those moments tended to make her legs wobbly.

"I already told you how I felt about that, Jilly," he said. "People changing. But I understand you wanting to believe something different."

"I don't like to disturb you, Guy, but I am going to ask you something. As long as there's nothing to suggest Edith is some kind of criminal who came here just to ruin my life, could you try to back me up? Give me some confidence until I know, one way or the other, if she wants to make things up to me like she says she does?"

"How do you intend to find out these things?" he asked her. "One way or the other? Do you wait till you get dragged in too deep to get out? Or until the man you insisted watched you from across the street decides to wait for you inside your house one night?"

"Stop it!"

"I can't. I can't pull any punches. What if Sam Preston decides you could be dangerous to him?"

She crossed her arms. "I couldn't be. That's silly."

"You don't know that."

"What have you got against the man? He's married to my mother, that doesn't make him a criminal."

And there she had him. "You're right." He couldn't tell her Joe Gable had already confided that he didn't trust Edith's supposed reason for being in Toussaint, or that he thought all the flash was to impress Jilly for some ulterior motive. Joe had speculated that Edith might know about an inheritance Jilly was about to get—a big one—only between them they couldn't come up with a plausible benefactor. "Preston's an antiques dealer in the Quarter, right?"

"Yes," Jilly said. "I told you that before."

"I guess you did. I can't help thinking about the guy seeming to be stinking rich. I suppose there must be a lot of money in antiques."

"I suppose there must. Guy, all I want is for you to tell me everything's okay," Jilly said, feeling empty. "Just be there for me while I allow it all to settle down."

"Everything's okay," he said, his eyes burning in their sockets.

"No! Please don't patronize me. I know what I'm asking is kind of silly, but I won't find out what happened between my parents, not for sure, unless I can take this chance I've been handed and make the best of it."

He let out a long sigh. The dog, with his long fur shining like sealskin, had slid his head onto Guy's thigh. He stood quiet, like a statue—as if he could be invisible if he tried real hard.

Guy gave the mutt a rub and that earned him a look of adoration. "I don't want to patronize you, Jilly. I'd be a fool if I did, because you're one smart woman." Why would she want to know anything more about the senior Gables' dysfunctional relationship?

"Could you try to be happy for me?"

"I'm happy for you."

"You're doing it again." She blinked and her eyelashes were wet. "Repeating what I say in that flat voice you can put on. I've finally got what I've always wanted, a family. Can't you be glad about that?"

"You've always had Joe. Now you've got a sister-in-law, too, and Ellie's one of the best. You've always had a lot of people in this town. You've got . . ." *Whoa.*

"Yes? What else have I got?"

"I'm not the same as family, but I hope you think of me as a good friend," he told her rapidly, feeling the hole he'd dug open up beneath his feet. He smiled at her and reached for her hand. "Jilly, you're the best friend I've got and you know it. That's why I worry about you so much."

She smiled back. "Thank you. Forget what I said about that man. You're probably right and he wasn't looking at my house at all."

He'd let it go at that, even though the thought of *Daddy* and his expensive gift made him crazy.

Jilly got up from her bench and came around the table. She slipped her arms around his neck, pressed his face to the soft, bare rise above her bodice, and hugged him. She rested her cheek on top of his head and rocked a little.

What was he supposed to do? Be real careful, he

guessed. His hands fitted around her waist and came close to touching at the back. "You are a sweet thing, Miz Gable. You've had too much hardship and it's time for the good stuff to come along for you." If he had his way, it would, even if it probably shouldn't be with him.

Her face dropped to his neck.

This could so easily go further than he had promised himself it ever would.

Lifting her with him, he got up and swung her around before setting her feet firmly on the ground. She smiled up at him and he smiled back, tapped the end of her nose with a forefinger, tried not to stare at her mouth.

Over her head he saw a black Corvette slide past the gas station and come to a stop. The driver maneuvered until the nose of the car pointed uphill.

Ready to get away fast, Guy thought.

Jilly felt his attention move away and looked behind her. A man got out of a flashy black car. A man with a linen fedora tipped over his eyes, and a shirt so white it made him look even darker than he was, especially where the sleeves were rolled back over his bunched forearms. His pants were dark, his tie loosened, and he carried a suit jacket tossed over his shoulder.

Guy waved, shouted, "Some wheels you've got there."

"Hard work and clean livin' pay off," the other man said, walking toward them. "Less vices a man got, the better he lives, and I got *no-o* vices, Guy." The grin was as white as the shirt and he was one spectacular looker. The dimpled grooves beside his mouth only got slightly less defined when he turned serious and looked at Jilly.

"We get good cell reception down here, huh?" Guy said in the most obvious attempt at distracting someone that Jilly had ever heard.

"Yeah," the man said, nodding.

Jilly wished she could sit down again. Guns were a part of life in these parts, but this man wore a shoulder harness with the kind of ease that yelled "cop," and she didn't have to work hard to figure out this was someone Guy had worked with.

She didn't like to be reminded of his other life.

The man's eyes went from Guy to Jilly and back again. "Son of a gun, Gautreaux, you never did have manners. You gonna introduce the pretty lady?"

His easy manner made Jilly grin.

"Jilly's a friend of mine," Guy said. "She was just leavin'. Take it easy as you go, kid."

He might as well have said, *get lost*. A creepy sensation shot up her spine and she felt sick. "Yes, right." She backed away, perfectly aware that the newcomer was just about as uncomfortable as she was. He shot out a hand and she took it, shook it and tried not to wince.

"Nat Archer," he said. "Guy and I go way back. Like I said, he's got lousy manners."

"Jilly Gable," she told him, and waved her hand at waist level before running uphill toward her car.

"Hey, Jilly," Guy hollered. "I'll call you later. Maybe we can get a late bite." And he had to make sure she didn't mention Nat to anyone else.

"Not tonight," she called back. "I've got plans."

2

"**Y**ou might need some new hookup lines," Nat said when Jilly was in her car and driving away. His deep voice was pure, tumbled gravel. "That girl didn't buy your 'get lost now but I may have time for you later.' No, sir."

Guy didn't intend to give anyone the pleasure of seeing how teed off he was, especially smart-mouth Archer.

"Jilly, darlin'—" Nat used his slow, most reasonable drawl "—this is my good old friend, Nat Archer. He's come to discuss a little business. I don't want him sharing a minute of my time with you. Make yourself comfortable awhile, cher, but first say, yes, you'll join me for a sexy little dinner for two later. I'll—"

"Can it, Archer." He couldn't help grinning. "You don't change, do you, partner? Jilly and I understand each other."

Nat pushed his hat to the back of his head. "You don't say? Guy, I think something's breakin'. I didn't want to say too much on the phone, but it may be time for you to come back where you belong. The department needs you."

Where did he belong? Once he thought he knew, but he didn't anymore. "What's up? Last time you called, some girl's daddy was after you with a shotgun."

Nat punched Guy's arm. "Trust you to mangle history. The girl was a woman in her thirties and her brother was the goon on my tail. I spoiled their scam. They thought they had a patsy with deep pockets—me. They're guests of the State."

"Such excitement," Guy said, rubbing stubble on his jaw. "Makes a quiet type like me feel giddy."

Nat quit smiling. "Is there somewhere we can go where we won't be interrupted?"

"It's quiet here," Guy said, "but it can pick up anytime. There's just me till Homer gets back. I could call someone in so we could go to my house. It's the safest place I can think of."

Nat nodded. "I admit I'm tryin' to connect some long wires here. But we could be about to skate over the thinnest ice you and me ever stepped on. That's saying somethin'. I'm not sure—I can't be yet—but it could be somethin' big is about to blow up in Toussaint. And if it does, yours truly is going to be right here with you."

Curiosity strung Guy out tight. "That so?" He had never known Nat to embellish things.

Calling Ozaire back didn't rate high on Guy's list, but he wasn't about to bother Homer, who would be over at Rosebank—a resort hotel owned by his daughter-in-law, Vivian Devol, and her mother, Charlotte Patin. Homer's son, Spike, helped run the place with his wife, while he also kept the Toussaint sheriff's department running. Each afternoon Homer picked up Spike's daughter by a previous marriage, and took her home from school. Only Wendy could turn Homer into a softie.

"You got a bug somewhere he didn't ought to be?" Nat asked. "Looks like you got pain."

Guy's response was to call Ozaire, who was so enthusiastic about returning to work he made Guy suspicious.

"Go on ahead to my house, I'll join you as soon as he gets here," Guy told Nat. Then he had a thought that started him punching numbers on his phone again. "What the hell am I thinking of?" he muttered. "How's she supposed to know if I don't tell her? She needs to know now, not later." He could not wait to tell Jilly to forget she had seen Nat.

"Aw, you know those aren't things you tell a woman on the phone. You had your chance to say the sweet nothings in person. You blew it."

Guy ignored Nat and looked at the sky while he listened to Jilly's phone ring. She wouldn't even be back to town by now and she always kept her cell on.

He hung up and stuck his hands in the pockets of his jeans.

"What's up?" Nat asked.

"You," Guy said without preamble. "I told you I didn't want us seen together around here. If Spike, that's the sheriff and he's Homer's son, if he gets wind that I'm holed up with my old partner, he'll be sure I'm getting ready to leave. He'll tell Homer. Homer will get mad and fire me because he'll want to tell me to go before I can quit."

Nat shook his head. "Why would you care?"

"Jilly needs me here." He needed her. "And I owe Homer."

"She already knows about me, man," Nat pointed out.

"Jilly might not make the connection if . . . Let it go. I don't want people speculating about you, okay?"

"O-kay."

His partner's attitude galled him. "Look, Nat. You come sashayin' in, driving a car people around here will talk about. There isn't always a lot of excitement, see, and they can get pretty imaginative with very little encouragement."

"Whoa." Nat held up both hands. "I asked you if you were on your own and you said you were, or would be in a few minutes."

"I didn't expect Jilly to stay."

"Is it my fault she did?"

"This had better be important," Guy said. "I'll join you as soon as I can."

His phone rang and he looked at the readout. "Hi, Jilly," he said, trying not to sound as relieved as he felt.

"Sorry I didn't pick up just now," she said.

"You had a right," he told her. "I need to ask you a favor. Nat, the guy you just met?"

"Yes."

The sound of zydeco from her car radio made him smile. She loved the music, and she loved to dance. So did he, with her.

"There's a real good reason why he wasn't here."

"Huh?" She turned off the radio. "What did you say?"

"He wasn't here."

"Nat Archer, the knockout guy I just met at Homer's, he wasn't there? The one with a voice like warm, tumbled gravel? For goodness' sake, why don't you just put things so they aren't so confusing? You don't want me to mention Mr. Archer to anyone. Right?"

He blew out a breath in a whistle. "I just don't have your smooth way with words, cher."

"You can say that again," Nat muttered.

Guy reached out and snatched the fedora, jumped on the closest bench, then on the picnic table, and held the hat high.

All Nat did was shake his head slowly.

"You've got my word, Guy, you know that," Jilly said. "But I hope you'll explain the reason to me."

Just what he didn't want to do. "Sure. How about that dinner?"

"Maybe I can fit you in. I . . . *get back! Stop!*"

Jilly screamed and, at the same time, Guy heard the gut-churning sound of a collision, breaking glass, buckling metal—and a cacophony of shouting voices.

"Jilly," he yelled. "Jilly!"

35

She didn't answer him.

There was only one road into Toussaint from Homer Devol's place, so that simplified Guy's rubber-laying drive. You also couldn't get lost in the town and you for sure couldn't miss a car crash, any car crash there.

He saw flashing lights behind him, then heard a siren. "Not now," he said through his teeth, and floored the accelerator. Almost at once he saw his folly, slowed and pulled over. The cruiser screeched to a stop, slewed behind the Pontiac.

One big "ain't I cool?" officer took his time getting to Guy's window. The man's hand hovered over his weapon and he spread his feet. "Out," he said, "hands behind your head, down on your face."

Guy did something he tried to avoid. He smiled at an asshole and said, ever so sweetly, "Afternoon, Officer. I'm Detective Gautreaux, NOPD. Should have put my light on top, but you know how it is with these pricks, think they're smarter than we are. I prefer to sneak up on 'em when I can."

He was on thin ice. "Inactive duty" wasn't a designation that carried weight, and if he told the guy the truth he'd have to run a check. Guy couldn't afford the delay.

The officer looked uncertain. "Yeah, I know what you mean. You got a badge, sir?"

"In the pocket of my jeans. Left front." He put his hands behind his head. Because they expected him back at NOPD he'd never been asked for his badge.

Carrying the thing was a habit. "I'll get out."

The man made up his mind. "You'd best get going. Sorry I slowed you down."

Guy nodded and took off fast enough to reach Bigeaux's hardware store on the outskirts of town and disappear around a corner without ever seeing the cop again. But he had lost at least eight or nine minutes and it was his own fault.

He dialed Jilly's number again. No answer.

There it was. Toussaint's very own talking points for the next few weeks. In the intersection of St. Mary's Street and Main, the only four-way stop in town. A big old burgundy Impala station wagon stood at an angle, one side shoved in, empty holes where the window had been. And a few feet distant where it had come to a stop after bouncing off the Impala, was Jilly's Beetle. The front had crumpled and popped open, and the damage was what you would expect when the engine was in the rear: the front wheels had moved a whole lot closer to the rear ones. In every direction, sun bounced off broken glass. Gas ran all over the road.

With her head in her hands, Jilly sat on a curb. Guy could see the scrapes from yards away. Father Cyrus Payne, pastor of Toussaint's St. Cécil's Parish, owner of the Impala, crouched beside her, an arm around her shoulders.

A deputy Guy hadn't seen before had his hands planted on his hips while he had a face-to-face discussion with a large, thickset man in a dark suit.

Jilly looked up, saw Guy, and burst into tears.

He parked and got out of the car. Immediately he heard the deputy's raised voice. "You've told me what you saw, sir. You'll be contacted if we need more information." The officer's thin face had turned bright red and Guy wondered if this was his first day on the job.

The other man held his hands loosely in front of him and spoke softly, too softly to be heard.

"No," the officer said. "You can't take care of this *little* matter. We've got procedures we follow."

A small crowd had already gathered and every face was familiar.

Guy went to Cyrus and Jilly and bent down beside them. "Who's the guy arguing with the deputy?"

With no warning, Jilly's crying intensified. She covered her face and shook her head, but tears made it between her hands to drip off her chin.

"Cyrus?" Guy looked at the priest. "Jilly's really shocked."

Cyrus raised his brows, widened his deep blue eyes as if trying to send a silent message. He indicated Jilly by inclining his head at a sharp angle.

"Jilly," Guy said. "Jilly, cher, all this will go away. You must have hit something slippery and slid right into Cyrus."

She bowed lower with her hands laced over the back of her head, and Cyrus shocked Guy by grabbing the neck of his T-shirt and yanking him down. "You mean well," the priest said into Guy's ear. "But it would be better if you found out how Jilly is before you analyze the rest of this situation."

Guy squeezed his eyes shut. "You're right," he said. *I am a fool and I never was any good with women. She deserves better than me.*

"How're you doin', Jilly?" he asked quietly. Too bad he couldn't feel noble for never making a move on her. He wanted to.

"You didn't hear the crash?" she said, in a choked voice. "I don't know what happened. Maybe the brakes felt mushy. I don't understand why you didn't hear all that noise."

He blinked a few times. "Of course I did. We were talkin' on the phone."

"Then why didn't you come right away? If you cared . . . Friends look out for each other." She brought her left hand down and looked at her watch. "If it had been you, and I knew something bad had happened, I wouldn't have taken my time getting to you."

Cyrus actually gave him a sympathetic look. Honesty was the only way of saving his tail here. "I did, Jilly, but I speeded like a fool and got stopped by a cop. If he hadn't decided to be reasonable, I'd still be there."

"Oh, Guy." She looked at him reproachfully. "You shouldn't have been speeding."

Cyrus said, "I think I'd better help out the young deputy. I don't know who the other man is, but he's making nothing into something. Uh-oh, here comes

Patti-Lou, or Lee I guess her name is when she isn't writing her gossip column." He got up, slapped Guy's shoulder and walked away.

"C'mon," Guy said, taking hold of Jilly's free hand and pulling her up. "Do you hurt anywhere? Hurt bad like something's broken?"

She shook her head and leaned to look around him. "I don't want anything in the *Trumpet* about this."

Guy turned enough to see Lee O'Brien, cousin of Reb O'Brien Girard, Toussaint's medical examiner and only doctor, pushing a tape recorder under the deputy's nose. "Forget it. Whether you like it or not, you're in the paper. Can't really blame the woman— most days she doesn't have a whole lot to write about."

"Except gossip." Jilly groaned, touched the side of her head and mouthed, "Ouch."

"You did hurt yourself," Guy said. "You hit your head."

"A bump. It's nothing."

"I expect someone already made it over in the aid car to check you out."

Jilly shook her head again.

"Hey," Guy yelled. "Officer, get over here. And you can get lost," he added, pointing to the suit. He ignored Lee O'Brien, her tape recorder and her expression of breathless anticipation.

"Guy," Jilly whispered, "that's the bodyguard from Edwards Place—the new one I told you about."

"I don't give a shit if he's Darth Vader." He cleared

40

his throat. "Pardon me for the language, please. He's interferin' where he's got no right to be."

Cyrus had reached the pair. He said a few quiet words and the deputy followed him back toward Guy and Jilly. The bodyguard also approached, his flat, freckled face impassive. He walked slowly and ignored Lee O'Brien, who trotted beside him and talked cheerfully.

"You didn't send for an aid car?" Guy said to the deputy. "You've got casualties. Who did you call so far?"

Again the man turned red. "I got real busy, sir."

"First day on the job?"

"Second. Nothing happened yesterday, and—"

Guy checked out the youngster's name tag. "Tell the gawkers to move on, Hall. Cyrus, Jilly, do we want the aid car?"

They both said, "No."

"Dr. Reb's going to expect a visit from the pair of you."

"Later," Jilly said.

Deputy Hall had developed a much bigger voice and he herded citizens on their way. "Look," Guy said. "You need to give a report to him, exchange particulars with each other, make sure pictures are taken and get the tow truck here. Call your insurance companies. Either of you have a problem with sending the cars to Mortie's?"

"Mortie's is the only body shop in town," Cyrus pointed out, and Jilly actually smiled.

"I'm Caruthers Rathburn." The bodyguard had arrived. "I think I can make this a great deal easier for everyone."

"Excuse me?" Guy looked the man in the eyes. Standing so close, he could see that rather than freckles on his round face, he had open pores where oil mingled with sweat. "This is a routine traffic accident. No need for anyone to make anything easier."

"How are you feeling, Jilly?" Lee O'Brien asked. She had the kind of blue eyes that suggested she'd never seen anything worse than a piece of eggshell in an omelette.

"Good, thank you, Lee," Jilly said. "Give my best to Reb and Marc. We're finished here."

Guy coughed.

Caruthers Rathburn reached inside his jacket and Guy's hand went instinctively for the gun tucked into his belt.

"Wallet," Rathburn said with a knowing sneer. He pulled out the wallet and eased out a fan of big bills. "I work for Miss Gable's stepfather. I've spoken with him and he insists she's to go to her mother immediately. Please take this, Father. Use what you need for transportation until we deal with things. I know—"

"No, thank you." Cyrus looked at the fistful of money pressed against his middle as if it were maggots. "I'm sure things aren't as bad as they look. We'll fix any little problems."

"Father," Lee said, her blond ponytail flipping as

she looked from one person to another. "You don't have any *little* problems with that car of yours. How does that make you feel?"

They said she was sharp, Guy thought. You could have fooled him.

Cyrus smiled at the woman and said, "I'll be glad to talk to you about this, and I'm sure Jilly will, too. But we ought to deal with the formalities, first."

The way very pretty Lee O'Brien gazed at Cyrus reminded Guy how hard it might be for a priest who looked the way this one did. Women invariably sent longing glances in his direction.

"I don't think I heard your name," the bodyguard said to Guy.

"No reason you should. Excuse me." He turned back to Jilly.

The bodyguard didn't figure out that he was supposed to get lost. "I have my orders. This is yours." He gave the bills another push against Cyrus, and when he wouldn't touch the money, let it slide and flutter to the ground at their feet. "I'll drive you to your mother, Miss Gable."

"Thank you for the offer, but I'm going to my shop now," Jilly said, her face white. "Please tell my mother I'm fine."

Rathburn only hesitated a moment before walking away, leaving the four of them standing in a heap of money.

"Cyrus," Jilly said. "We can do this between us. It was all my fault."

"You don't say that when you have an accident, Jilly," Cyrus said.

"You would."

She didn't get an argument from Cyrus. When she glanced at Guy he was smiling. Darn it all, anyway, he had the clumsiest mouth in the South, but he also had the best heart—if he'd ever stop burying it in a hole and piling body armor on top.

Wally Hibbs, fifteen-year-old only child of Gator and Doll Hibbs, who ran the Majestic Hotel, arrived on his bicycle, which he stopped by slamming his sneakers on the street. He'd outgrown the bike a long time ago.

"Everything's okay here," Cyrus said at once, and Jilly felt good just knowing Wally had the priest and the folks who worked at St. Cécil's to give him the warmth and welcome he didn't get at home. Wally hung around with Cyrus whenever he could, and the man had become almost a surrogate father to the boy.

"Who is that man?" Lee asked, her eyes on Rathburn's back. "He's got a nasty attitude. He said he worked for your stepfather, Jilly?"

"Yes," she said, pretending not to see the faces Guy made at her.

Wally's bike crashed to the ground and he stooped to gather the money. "Can't just leave this here, Father," he said. "I saw that man give it to you. Is it true your dad's the richest man in all Louisiana, Jilly?"

What were folks saying to make him come up with a question like that? "I'm not sure where my father is," she told him. "I haven't seen him for years."

"Your *new* dad," Wally said, sitting on his heels to carefully face all the bills the same way. "This is a lot of money," he said, his eyes round. He started counting, licking the tip of a grubby forefinger now and again.

"I don't like to ask you," Cyrus said. "But would you get that money back to Edwards Place?"

"No way," Wally told Cyrus. "I told you, I saw that man push the money on you."

"I don't need or want a stranger's money."

Wally looked smug. He wiggled his nose and sniffed. "Is there anything says a stranger can't give money to the church?" His smile grew wider, showing the space between his two front teeth. "I don't think the Lord would be pleased with you discriminatin' like that, not when the church needs new bingo boards and there ain't—isn't enough money."

A frosted beige Jaguar convertible slid to a stop, and a woman wearing large sunglasses and a pink baseball cap over curly red hair trailed her left arm and hand over the top of the driver's door. Dazzling prisms shot from whatever jewelry she wore on her fingers.

"Jilly?" Laura Preston said, amazement dripping from the single word. "What are you doing here with these people?"

"For those of you who don't know," Jilly said, "this is Laura Preston, my mother's daughter-in-law. Laura and Edith live together at Edwards Place."

Silence met the announcement. "Laura, please let

45

Edith know I'll be over to see her later. I'm not hurt at all."

"Where do you think you're going with that?" Cyrus said, laughing at Wally, who remounted his bike with a determined expression. He took the money from the boy and walked toward the deputy.

Wally shrugged. "I knew he would do that, but I had to give it a try. Wait till I tell Madge how Father turned down good money when there's never enough to pay the bills at St. Cécil's."

Guy made a grab for the rear of the bike, but Wally shot out of range, heading for Bonanza Alley and the rectory. "Don't you go mixin' it up," Guy yelled. Madge Pollard worked for Cyrus. She kept the parish running and watched over Cyrus, although not like a mother hen. Jilly tried not to think about the complicated friendship Cyrus and Madge had, not often, anyway. Some people just didn't have much luck when it came to falling in love, and Jilly guessed she and Madge had great men in their lives, only they were the wrong men.

Without another word, Guy walked away. He approached the rucked-up Beetle and looked down through the broken passenger window, at the seat, Jilly assumed.

He dragged open the door and stooped to pick something up from the floor.

Lee said, "Guy's a nice man but he's too difficult to read. Too quiet. He's real easy on the eyes, though." She cleared her throat and turned a little pink. "You already noticed that, Jilly?"

"Uh-huh."

On the way back he only broke his stride for a few moments when he passed them. He gave Jilly her cell phone and said, "I'm relieved you're okay. Take care, y'hear. I'd better get back to it." His down-turned mouth and narrowed eyes turned him into the stranger she'd seen before and she didn't like him.

Well, she'd taken all she intended to take from Mr. Gautreaux and she wasn't taking any more.

3

"What d'you think you're doin', Jilly?"

She had run to catch up with Guy and get into the passenger side of the Pontiac. Let him stew over *her* silence for once.

He dropped down beside her, slammed his door shut and rested his head back. "You heard me. Why are you following me? You aren't finished back there."

"You mean-mouthed, insensitive son of a bitch," she told him. "Drive. I don't want all those people watching us. Especially Laura. I might have known she'd hang around just to see if she could pick up something to worry Edith with." She laced her fingers in her lap. There went another promise she'd made to herself—that she wouldn't say anything negative about the people at Edwards House.

"You better get out," Guy said. He felt something he thought he had finally left behind, that mix of fury and arousal that ought to worry a woman. It worried him.

Jilly turned sideways in her seat. "I told you to drive. I'll get back soon enough—not that there's much to do but make phone calls."

"They're going to blow this into something. The two of us taking off in my car when I'm supposed to be goin' to work and you're supposed to be hangin' around to deal with the formalities. I said goodbye in front of everyone."

"Nobody in this town has a reason to think we're havin' a lovers' tiff, if that's what you mean. It's pretty clear we're not lovers. But if you're worried about your reputation, the sooner you go where they can't see us, the better. Behind the old laundry is close enough, and it's private."

He puffed up his cheeks, blew the air out and gunned the car. If she wanted him to drive, he'd drive. And she'd better not complain about the result. The tires shrieked forward, went into a spin on a patch of gravel, then lurched on and flew.

"Slow down," Jilly told him. "If you're tryin' to be cool in front of the gallery, you just blew it. There's nothing like the sight of a man and woman arguin' to make folks think they're more than friends on the outs."

Guy gritted his teeth. His heart pounded. He had a monkey on his back and its name was guilt. If he couldn't buck it off he was no good to anyone—surely not to this little woman with a big mouth but a gentle heart. "That's the last order you give me. Got it?"

"Got it," she said, and laughed, she couldn't help it. "If I thought you were as mean as you sound, you wouldn't have to tell me to get out again. I'd do it now, moving or not."

"Just tell me what's goin' on."

"You're the one who's going to do the explainin'."

He swung the car hard left down an alley and Jilly landed against him. He ignored her pressure on his shoulder. When they straightened out again she buckled her seat belt fast. The abandoned laundry stood against the searing blue sky like an empty prison block, its windows boarded up. Guy drove the perimeter, through tall, crackling weeds and grass that flattened under the front of the vehicle and scratched against the windows.

Into a neck-jarring, hidden rut, then out again—and he stopped with the bleached and brittle stalks reaching the roof and beyond.

"There—I brought you where you wanted to go." Darn it all, he was behaving like a spoiled kid whose date didn't put out after the prom. Too bad. This was Jilly's idea.

"You make me so mad," she said, and her voice broke pretty much as he'd feared it might.

"I don't want to. Just can't seem to help myself." He faced her, one knee pulled up and clasped in both hands. "You're impetuous. You did the first thing that came into your head back there and walked off after me. And you know that wasn't a good idea."

"Why? Because someone might think there's something new going on between us?"

He didn't like what he was feeling. Or did he? If they didn't go their separate ways, and soon, something was going to explode around here.

"Why do I attract men who leave me convinced I'm not meant for love?"

She could have said just about anything but that. He buried his head in his hands. "Am I supposed to answer that?"

"Damn you, Guy." She grabbed hold of his short sleeve and pulled on it. She pulled and pushed, gave a final shove and thrust open the door.

Guy caught her by the arm, but anger could give even a fairly small woman a lot of strength. Jilly wrenched free and all but fell out. She marched around the back of the car and took off into the dead grass jungle, slapping herself a pathway as she went.

"Damn it, Jilly," Guy muttered, crossing his arms over the wheel. She hadn't been thinking when she'd suggested he was attracted to her, but she was so right. She was wrong about the rest, about not being meant for love.

He turned his head to watch her go—but she'd gone so far, so fast, all he had to follow was a line in the white brush that got a little wider, then waved together again in her wake.

"You'll break your fool neck," he said, and burst out of the car on his side. He started walking fast, pushing straight ahead with his hands and forearms in front of him. He needed to run. One leap to look ahead and he saw he was right on course to catch up with her.

Jilly choked on the dust and dry ends of grass gone to seed. They filled her nose and mouth and she coughed, then wiped the backs of her hands across her face.

Get busy, get so busy you don't have time to think about that ornery man. She didn't have time for men in her life, anyway. She had a business to run and a house to keep up. And now she had to fix her car, if it could be fixed. That was an expense she hadn't planned on and she didn't want to think about buying another one.

That Impala of Cyrus's was a fixture in this town and he'd kept it alive—or friends had kept it alive years after it should have gone for scrap. The frame must be bent now. All her fault.

This was getting her nowhere fast, this anger and rushing away toward nothing in particular. She turned and headed back, veering off toward the side of the building, figuring out how she'd get back to the café without having to see anyone on the way. She'd deal with reports later.

Guy slammed into her so hard, he couldn't stop them from falling. The best he could do was use his arms to stop her from taking his full weight. "Don't you do anythin' but *cry* anymore?" He snapped his fool mouth shut.

"I'm not crying," she told him, mortified, "the dust is getting in my eyes."

51

"Yeah, well, I'm sorry I walked into you like that."
He made a move to climb off her but she shoved her
hands up, between their chests, and pummeled his
shoulders. And while she hit him, she struggled to get
up.

Neither of them went anywhere.

"Hey!" He caught hold of her wrists. "What's gotten
into you? The way you are, I don't even know you."

"Why? Because I've got warm blood runnin' in my
veins and when it gets heated up I do somethin' about
it? How would you understand a person like me when
you've got ice water runnin' through you?"

His insides hummed. Looking into her eyes, he said,
"Are you trying to goad me, cher? Are you lookin' for
me to take you by force right here under the sky, in
this stickery stuff where anyone might happen along?
Does that thought excite you?"

She felt her cheeks throb. "Don't flatter yourself."

He clamped her between his thighs and there was no
escape. "I don't think I'm flattering myself at all. I
think you need sex as much as I do. Difference is, I
have control of myself and you don't."

A kind of excitement closed her throat and scared
her out of her mind. "Let me up." Wriggling did her
no good unless it was a good thing to feel hard evidence that he'd just lied about being in control.

"Sure. Go right ahead. Get up." But he wasn't going
to help her. Hell, no, not when he was in some kind of
painful heaven with her right where she was.

She went limp. "What was it all about back there in

town—going to my car and rooting around for the cell phone so you could throw it at me? Then talking to me like I was the enemy?"

"You'll argue, but I caused you to have the accident. I upset you out at Homer's because I behaved like a roughneck. Then I called you and you got more upset until you called me back. Crash. End of story. Except I didn't throw the cell at you."

"You have it so wrong. I think my brakes went out. My foot went down and it felt soggy, then there was nothing." She had the worst timing, but she wanted him badly. "Nothing to do with you."

He'd relaxed a little. "When's the last time you had the Beetle checked?" He tugged out a handkerchief to wipe his face, pulled his shirt over his head and ran the cloth around his neck and over his chest. "When did—"

"I don't remember." Jilly spread a hand on each of his thighs and he quit moving. All but for the flicker in his jaw—and strong signs of approval against the inside of her thigh.

They watched each other's faces.

"Gimme a break, cher."

"Give *you* a break? But you're the man who's in control. The only one we have to worry about is me. I'm a loose cannon." She raised onto her elbows and splayed a hand on his hot chest. She just happened to catch a flat nipple between two of her fingers—and squeeze.

"Oh, my . . ." He shut his eyes tightly but it didn't

53

stop him from feeling what she was doing. He knew what he wanted to do. "That's it. Up you get before someone comes lookin' for us."

He took her by the shoulders and stood, a foot on either side of her knees, to haul her up.

"I didn't know you were so shy," Jilly said. A small but important piece of her reserve hadn't just stretched, or cracked—it had completely blown away. Without giving him time to figure out her intent, she grabbed him by the neck and pulled his face down to hers.

In the breathless second before they kissed, she opened her eyes and saw that his were closed. Jilly moved her hands to the sides of his head and pushed her fingers into his hair.

The kiss was about taking. She took him and he took her and Guy locked his knees. If she could see inside him now, she wouldn't find ice-cold anything. He should stop this, stop her, but damn it, he'd already tried and she wouldn't take no for an answer.

He held her on either side of her ribs, his thumbs just beneath her breasts, and she forced herself against him so hard the thin little sundress wasn't enough to stop him from feeling her peaked nipples on his chest.

Jilly's mouth opened wide. It was like drinking him in. She wanted her bare breasts touching him, but even with a dress on, the contact sent hot, mad-making sensation into her nipples. Elsewhere she was wet and throbbing.

He couldn't think straight. But he couldn't do this here, not to her and not to himself. Not the first time they made love. "Jilly, no!"

She cupped him and squeezed. "Make me stop."

He held her shoulders and looked down at her, down the gaping front of the dress at her round breasts, and he paused, dragging in air. Sweat shone on her golden body. Naked, they would slide together.

This was her moment. There wasn't enough room inside his jeans to allow the zip to move easily, but she was strong. He made a pretty feeble attempt to dissuade her from pulling him free of the jeans and working over him.

"Cher, no, not like this. Aw, hell, it feels so good. You feel so good."

"I want it this way."

"If we're going to be together it ought to be where we can take our time."

She showed him she'd taken control and didn't intend to give it up. He'd never been forced—he'd been missing a lot.

"Help me," he said, and bit down on the soft flesh at the side of her neck. They fell into the grass again. "Stop . . . don't stop."

4

Well, hell, he hadn't expected Jilly to do what she did, to make love until he never wanted to stop, then rush away refusing to even talk to him.

He had tried to hold her. She'd warned him off with a glare and outstretched palms. So he'd backed off and let her go, and got into his car to drive home. He couldn't think of anywhere else he could go to find some peace.

Guy swung into the overgrown lane leading to his house.

Get rid of Nat. Figure out what just happened with Jilly—apart from the obvious—and decide how in hell you're going to fix things.

He should be making her go somewhere quiet and talk to him right now. The longer they waited, the harder it would be for either of them to make any sense.

Unfortunately the lady had made it clear the next call was hers.

He wouldn't wait very long.

Nat's Corvette looked out of place in front of Guy's wood-sided shotgun house. True to type, the building sat lengthwise on the lot, the front of which should have been a gable end, with the entrance leading to a passageway against the left wall and a single window to the right. Inside, four rooms stacked one behind the other opened onto the passage, which ran the length of the house. If you had a mind to shoot from the front door to the back door it was no big deal. Just stand in line with the front door and hold that shotgun steady.

Concrete pilings stood high enough that you could have put a second story under the only one the place had. He'd parked his car down by the gravel road, as was his custom. He preferred to walk quietly up the lane to the house in case someone he didn't want to see was waiting for him.

He dipped his hat farther over his eyes and ran up the steps to the gallery. A single bentwood rocker, weathered to silver-gray, rested where he could sit, prop his heels on the railing and look at the sky through a dogwood tree.

"Is she all right?" Nat called from inside as soon as Guy touched the screen door. "I called the emergency number to see if she'd been taken somewhere but they said she hadn't."

"You did *what?*" Guy yanked open the screen door and strode into what passed as his living room. "How many times do I have to—"

"I gave a phony name. Get over here."

"Did you use my phone?"

Stretched out on the couch—a queen-size tweed sofa bed—Nat reached for a can of beer he had set on the brown shag rug. He took his time over a long swallow before he said, "I'm sorry you think I'm a moron. Now, drop it. How's Jilly?"

He probably shouldn't say *fantastic.* "She's good. Bit shaken up but it was mostly a fender bender. A hummer of a fender bender, to be truthful." He tossed his hat on the TV antenna. The TV sat on the floor and the room was otherwise unfurnished.

A paper bag lay on its side near Nat with papers spilling out—and photographs, the kind Guy recognized as the artwork of NOPD.

Nat saw him angling his head to look and sat up.

57

And then the dratted, leggy black mutt from Homer's place came down the hall, loped into the room and flopped down at Guy's feet. "Where was he?" He didn't want to tell Nat how Jilly tried to foist the dog off on him.

"*She* was sleepin' on your bed. Tired out, poor pooch—and hungry. I had to give her that steak out of the refrigerator. You're out of dog food as far as I can see. I cooked the meat just in case. She was really hungry, Guy." Nat gave him a disapproving look. "You left her behind so I brought her home for you."

Jilly had called the dog "he."

This was his day for being outmaneuvered by females. He would take the dog and dump her on Jilly. Meanwhile, he'd act as if there was nothing unusual about a big mutt wandering around his house, eating Guy's own dinner and sleeping on his bed. "Thanks for bringing Goldilocks home," he said, and the dog put her head on his boot.

Dump the dog on Jilly, which means I'll have to go see her. He smiled.

"I won't ask how you came up with *Goldilocks,*" Nat said.

"Good idea."

"A man called Pip Sedge got murdered in the Quarter."

Guy waited for Nat to continue.

"Any bells ringin'?" Nat asked.

He wanted to sit down but didn't like to disturb the dog. "No bells."

58

"He was shot—three times."

"Hoo mama, that's a first." As soon as he grinned, Guy knew his mistake.

"I didn't come down to this morgue of a town because I needed your wisecracks." Nat's white teeth came together with a snap. He held his head by the top and the chin and snapped his neck in each direction. "You're makin' me tense."

He'd always been good at doing that. "Give me something that makes sense. This isn't the first DB found in the Quarter with three bullets in it." Carefully, he pulled his foot from beneath the dog's head and took a seat beside Nat. "If I can help you, I will."

Nat leaned over and shuffled among the mess of papers on the rug. "I wanted to see if the name meant anything to you first. Take a look at this." He gave Guy a photograph of a man in shirttails, shoes and socks, holding what looked like his balled-up pants to his chest. The legs were on the skinny side, very white, and defensively bent at the knee. He stood outside a closed interior door.

Guy flicked a fingernail against the shiny paper. "This was pinned up somewhere. Quite a few places at different times." He indicated a scatter of thumbtack holes.

"Yeah, it was. Oliphant still had it on his bulletin board—under just about everything he's collected forever. I recalled seeing it sometime ago—Sedge hadn't changed much facially. He could still look like a kid caught with his hand in the cookie jar."

"Sedge is the vic?"

"Pip Sedge, yeah. Forty-nine, divorced."

The guy in the photo could be midthirties or older. Pleasant-looking in a nondescript way with wavy, mussed-up blond hair. He stared into the camera lens as if he'd been blinded by high beams on a one-way street. "This used to be on the wall in the squad room. Jeez, Nat, how long ago?" He glanced at the date. "Eleven years? I was a rookie."

"That's what I figured. I knew it was a long shot that you'd remember much. I wasn't on board yet."

Nat found another photo—this one of the all-too-familiar crime-scene variety. A close-up of the vic's face. Bits of hair were still blond, the rest was caked with blood.

"Shot through the back of the head?"

"Top," Nat said.

"I'd like to know how that happened. It's the same man. You've got a good eye—but we've always known that."

Nat flashed him a quick smile. "This was a dirty crime. Sedge might as well have been executed. He *was* in a way. But you can read all about that."

"Maison Bleue," Guy said, suddenly remembering Detective Fleet, who owned the case. "On Chartres Street. Underage prostitution ring. Or that's what they thought. The place had belonged to the Giavanelli family, but it was under new management."

"Bingo. But they were looking for a missing girl that night. Someone thought they'd seen her there."

"Had they?"

"Seems so, but she was found at home later—dead."

Guy murmured, "Too bad," and pinched the bridge of his nose. "Fleet, God rest his soul, he thought this photo of a bare-legged Sedge was hilarious. Laughed every time he walked by. He used to say, 'The douche bag got kicked out by a sixteen-year-old while she took a call from her boyfriend.' Then he'd remind anyone who'd listen that, thanks to him, the guy in the picture 'never did get his rocks off.'"

"He also didn't get arrested," Nat said. "Comin' up with anythin' at all on him was dumb luck. I worked for Oliphant a few times. He was Fleet's partner."

"I was just one of Fleet's water boys." Back in the days when he still thought the good guys always won in the end. "I don't even know what happened to the case."

Nat aimed a long forefinger at the papers. "Reckon it's in there. You may want to read it. If you lose any of that stuff, I'll be sharing a drawer with Pip Sedge. Don't ask me why, but none of it's been entered."

"I'll make sure you get it back before it's missed."

"I'll make sure I take it with me in the mornin'," Nat said. "It may not have a thing to do with anything, not now. But we need to be sure."

Guy didn't comment on the fact that Nat intended to spend the night. "Look, maybe I'm obtuse, but I don't get why you came to me with this. Sedge's murder doesn't have to be connected to the Maison Bleue case, and I know almost nothing about that."

Nat took a folded file card from a pants pocket and handed it over. "The original is in the evidence room. I copied what was on it."

"Jazz Babes," Guy read aloud. This was Nat's evening for guessing games. "Okay. Is it a club?"

"Affirmative. It's the club that used to be Maison Bleue. Sedge had a matchbook from the place in his pocket when he died. Look at the back—most likely scribbled there by Sedge."

Guy looked. "Toussaint?" he said, meeting Nat's innocent eyes. The rest said, "Backs on Parish Lane—wall—gate unlocked."

"Is there a Parish Lane in Toussaint?" Nat asked. "I didn't find it on a map of the town."

"Parish Lane is behind Main Street on one side and Catfish Alley on the other. You think Sedge was coming here with stuff on his mind? Like going through an unlocked gate and getting to someone's place?"

"That's what I think. I sure don't have anything else."

"This is your case?"

"Right on, Mr. Holmes. You can do what I can't, not without half the town finding out there was a stranger creeping about. But you can wander along Parish Lane and figure out where this might be. You're part of the scenery. You won't get a second look." He took back the card.

Guy stared at the dog. The dog stared back. "Just about all kitchens are in the backs of houses."

Goldilocks heaved to her feet and settled again—with her head on his left boot. "There's a wall down both sides of Parish Lane. All the way down. And a lot of gates."

5

Losers only have themselves to blame.

Sometimes you can't help sliding toward the gutter, but if you don't dig your heels in before you reach it, you deserve what you get. And if you once win your way into a place where you want to be, you never let down your guard because someone is always waiting to take away what you have.

And if someone stands in the way of you getting everything you've set your sights on and you can't take it anymore, the answer is simple. Get rid of the obstacle.

Tonight is the perfect night. Too hot, too breathless, too still. The kind of night that woman can't stand.

Nothing has been forgotten, and nothing will be forgotten when it's over. No one will cry for her—they all hate her guts—only most are afraid to do anything about it.

This is going to be so easy, like drowning a paralyzed rat in its own blood.

She'll come soon. Stupid fool. All blubber and sniffle, then the hysterical laugh and fluttering touch.

She might as well say, "Kill me, I'm so lonely I want to die," only she never would because she's invented her own rosy lie of a life.

Good thing she's got a someone who reads her mind and gives her what she's begging for.

This closet smells like her, like bruised camellias and used skin no man wants to touch anymore.

Makes me want to puke.

But the closet is the perfect hiding place.

Footsteps on the carpeted stairs. Unsteady footsteps and a thud each time she falls against the wall. She's stopped. Don't let her pass out down there.

Glory, glory, she's moving again.

There's a soft pink light, turned down real low, by the bed. Of course the silly bitch won't have anything but all white on that bed. What do you call that old-fashioned stuff where they cut holes and embroider around them? Cutwork. That's it. And she has the coverlets made for her. They cost a fortune. She's a drain, a waste, a user of what she's got no right to—and she is in the way.

Not for long now.

Come right on in, whore. Look at you, you're too drunk to stay on your feet, but you're still drinking. Just make it to the bathroom, sweetie, that's it. Shit!

Great. Flat on your face. Gin all over the rug. Makes me want to laugh. That's right, up you get, hold on to the bed—that's it. Now, into the bathroom with you.

You can't clean up the rug. That's right, you pick up

64

that glass and see if there's a drop left.

Hurry up.

More than a drop, huh. But you don't want anything in the drawer. Just go in that bathroom. We'll get you all clean and white.

What the hell is she taking? Lordy, Lordy, it could be the painkiller from when she broke some ribs. The stuff that sent her to la-la land. Quite a story about that. Got a headache, baby? Drinking doesn't pay, not when you can't hold it. You made that gin go a long way. Forget the pills. Mixture like that could kill you. . . .

Everything's ready. The box of razor blades. They'll say you bought them for the job. Unwrap a blade. Careful.

It's getting hotter. I hate it like this—unless I'm in a pool—or skin to skin and getting it off.

Don't just stand there, crying. You're even uglier when you cry.

Move, damn it, move!

That's . . . shit, shit, shit. Why'd you have to pass out on the bed?

I'm going to walk right up and see just how out of it you are. Lock the door and go look at her.

Out cold. And she's sweating like a pig. Let's get this done, piggy. Wake up too soon, and I'll tell you I'm saving you from yourself.

I've got to make sure she doesn't bleed on me. Push her arm above her head.

She's out of it.

I'll keep down and make one tidy slit. No, not too tidy, it ought to jerk around a bit like she's having trouble aiming.

My hands are shaking, dammit. Chill out. Nobody's going to interrupt you.

See how easy the blade slides. The blood wells, then pours. All over the white coverlet—such a shame. Whoa, good job I got myself out of the way.

Now the other one, Miss Piggy.

Damn, she's heavy. No falling off the bed. That's it. Cool. I wish this had been in the bathroom.

If she cut one wrist here and got to the bathroom for the second, would it look strange?

Stay there, baby doll, while I take a look and decide. Oh, yeah, the shiny white bathroom. You'd bleed everywhere on the way. Best finish it where you are.

What was that? She's fallen off the bed. Just like her to mess things up. Nobody else to have heard her bump onto the floor like that, but I've got to get out of here. Hurry.

She looks dead already.

Used razor in left pocket. Can't risk leaving it. Could have marked it somehow. Quick, got to leave the weapon. Another razor. Rip paper off one side. Finger and thumb, and squeeze. There you go, Miss Piggy. Now, stick it in the wound. Hah, it's going to stay there, like an ax in wood.

It's perfect. It feels like sex. The rush. Ride it, go with it.

I'm outta here. Next stop, a great fuck.

6

Father Cyrus Payne sat on the stairs inside the rectory. Using an old, broken-bladed but extremely sharp knife, he peeled an apple, the skin falling in one long, unbroken strip. He glanced repeatedly at the front door. From his right came the muted click of Madge's keyboard as she worked late in her office. Madge always worked late. He gave a satisfied sigh at the thought. She was his assistant, the best he'd ever had, but she was also his best friend and he liked having her where he could see her when he needed to.

He couldn't settle to do anything, so he'd given up and planted himself where he could see when Guy Gautreaux approached. Cyrus would have volunteered to go to Guy's place if the Impala hadn't been out of commission. Gator Hibbs had shown up at the accident scene and left Cyrus with a small, rusty pickup. It ran. That was about the best you could say about it. The lights dimmed without warning and Cyrus didn't want to drive the vehicle at night, or in isolated places like the location of Guy's house. Cyrus was still grateful for Gator's kindness.

Madge's keyboard stopped clicking and she put on one of the hundred or so zydeco CDs she owned.

The wallpaper in the hall and up the stairs, "ducks in flight" folks called it, had finally turned yellow, mostly along the seams. He'd like to strip it and paint instead, only the place was so old Cyrus feared he'd be knee-deep in crumbling plaster if he tried.

The doorbell rang. Cyrus saw a tall man's shadow through a pebble-glass panel in the front door.

"Coming," Madge called, and shot from her office to let the visitor in, noticing Cyrus as she took off the bolt. "I didn't know you were there." She smiled with her dark eyes. So much warmth came from the way she looked at him.

"I'm expectin' Guy Gautreaux."

She opened the door and Guy stood there, hat in hands, around a foot taller than Madge. "Come on in," Cyrus told him.

"I'll get you something to drink," Madge said. "What would you like? I'll bring it up to the sittin' room. Are you hungry?"

"There's no need, ma'am," Guy said. "Thank you."

"There's fresh coffee in the kitchen," Cyrus said. "Okay with you if we sit out there?"

"Like your taste in a tune, ma'am," Guy said with a nod at Madge. He set off down the hall toward the kitchen and Cyrus followed him.

Guy made straight for the big oak table in the window that overlooked the yard and Bayou Teche. "No coffee for me," he said. "Madge is dedicated to you. She's here late and she's still got quite a drive getting home to Rosebank."

Madge rented rooms from Vivian Devol at Rose-bank Resort. A floor in one wing of the hotel was dedicated to long-stay guests. Cyrus did his best not to show how much he worried about Madge making that drive alone. "I don't know what I'd do without her. I'm going to have a glass of wine, how about one for you?"

"Red?"

"It can be."

"Thank you, then."

The man looked even more buttoned-up than usual. Cyrus glanced at him between pouring glasses of wine. Guy's palms were pressed together and he tapped his joined small fingers on the table. Right about now Cyrus would guess Guy had forgotten where he was.

Carrying the wine, and with a can of nuts clamped beneath one arm, Cyrus approached, and Guy went right on staring straight ahead. "Something on your mind?" Cyrus asked quietly.

"Nope." Sometimes you had to lie. Guy focused his eyes on his host and rested his hands on the table. "You called and asked me to come here."

"I know. I'd have come to you, but—"

"The Impala's in the shop and you're waiting for the verdict," Guy finished for him. "Don't worry about it, I like a drive at night." A drive with Goldilocks, who had followed him down the lane to the Pontiac and jumped in as if she belonged there. *All the better to get you to Jilly's house.* Shoot, that was the Wolf in Little Red Riding Hood.

Cyrus sat at the end of the table and put down the

wineglasses. "I stopped to see Jilly on my way home. I'm concerned about her." He took the lid off the nuts, searched for a pecan, and put it in his mouth.

Guy paused with a glass in midair. "Why?" She'd looked collected the last time he'd seen her—mussed, pink and tight-lipped, but in control. In fact, truth was she'd been the most beautiful thing he'd ever seen.

His physical reaction was predictable. Everything constricted.

"She never came back to answer any questions the deputy had," Cyrus said. "Not that it matters as long as she called her insurance company."

Jilly had said she was going back to Cyrus and the deputy, and to tell Laura Preston to get lost. There had also been mention of nosy reporters.

"You're closer to her than anyone," Cyrus said. "She and Joe have always stuck together, but his marriage had to change that some and he isn't here, anyway."

Guy wanted to get up and go to her at once. "The accident shook her up, but she should have answered any questions the officer had." This was his fault. Not because of what they'd done in the afternoon, although the circumstances should have been so different, but because he'd sent her mixed messages for the better part of a year. Right after Billie's murder he hadn't wanted anyone else, then he met Jilly and got scared spitless of falling for her on the rebound. He still wasn't sure he was ready to be what she needed. But he'd driven her to act the way she had and now she would be embarrassed.

"She didn't answer her door until she figured I'd keep on ringing the bell. I saw her shadow move in the upstairs window."

Still nervous at the possibility that some goon had followed her home last night, Guy thought. "It's good for a woman alone to be cautious, but I'm glad you didn't give up," he finished hurriedly.

"Yes," Cyrus said. He fell silent and drank some of his wine.

A round clock ticked on one of the white walls. The room smelled of homemade bread and Guy saw loaves on a wood cutting board with a red-and-white cloth over them. He doubted there had been any changes made around this place for years, but he felt comfortable surrounded by the ceiling-high cabinets with thick glass fronts.

On his own minute back porch, a turquoise refrigerator shaped like a capsule of some kind crowded most of the space. The refrigerator came from the same era as the mottled-gray appliances in the rectory kitchen, and they didn't make their kind anymore.

"I've never seen Jilly the way she was when I went to her house. First she tried to be all buttoned-up. She said she forgot to go back and talk to the deputy. Then she cried, and Jilly should never feel so badly she cries like that. She said she was all muddled up. Those were her words. I asked what she meant, but all she could say was that caring too much could mess you up."

Guy was well aware of Cyrus's hard stare. He was watching for reactions. "I don't like to think of Jilly being upset," he said, and felt lame. *Caring too much? Did she care more than he did?* "What do you think she meant?" He knew the question could be dangerous.

Cyrus didn't hesitate to say, "You. What else could she be talkin' about? There's no one else she cares a lot about who treats her badly."

"Damn it." Guy shot to his feet. "You may be a priest, but that doesn't give you the right to make guesses like that. I wouldn't treat Jilly badly." But he hadn't treated her as well as he should have.

"I didn't mean you abuse her." Cyrus scooped out a handful of nuts and started popping them. "You asked a question. I gave my best answer."

Guy let out a long breath and sat down again. "Sure you did. Sorry I piled on like that, but don't you see how dangerous it could be for Jilly and me to get more involved?" *We already have, and look how much damage we've done.*

"I think I do," Cyrus said. "You're both worried one of you will decide this is a rebound thing and you'll get badly hurt again. I think the difference between the two of you is that Jilly, bein' a woman, needs the lovin' enough to take the risk. Bein' a man, you don't think you do. Not that kind of lovin', anyway."

Guy scowled at the priest. "You don't know what I think." He'd better make up his own mind about that. "And you're out of line pinning Jilly's behavior on me. How is it my fault she didn't make sure and talk to the deputy?"

"The two of you drove away in your car, arguin', and she didn't come back afterward. What would you think in my position?"

No answer was expected. Guy stacked his hands behind his neck. His job was to go to her now.

A rapid knock on the kitchen door startled both of them. L'Oiseau de Nuit burst into the room and Goldilocks shot in behind her.

Guy pointed at the dog. "Dogs don't belong—"

"Not a word, you," Wazoo, as the whirling, plan-a-minute woman was known locally, said. "Later, I tell you about dogs, N'awlins."

Gritting his teeth, Guy ignored the nickname Wazoo had adopted for him over the past months.

The dog saw him and her tongue lolled from her mouth. She high stepped to flop down beside his chair and nuzzle a foot.

Black-haired, flamboyant, shimmering with energy, Wazoo had blown into town a few years back according to Jilly, to attend the funeral of a friend— and stayed. She lived at Rosebank and helped out there to keep her rent low, worked many mornings at Jilly's place and was currently filling in at Hungry Eyes, the bookstore and café owned by Jilly's sister-in-law, Ellie Gable. Wazoo also insisted she dabbled in "the arts," and considered herself a fine animal psychologist.

"I come to see you, God Man," she said to Cyrus. "And you knows I don't do that so easy. But I'll be talkin' to you, too, N'awlins. So don't you try sneakin' away. I'll take some of that wine, me."

Wazoo made great sport of pretending not to like Cyrus, to be afraid his Christianity would get her darker side all stirred up.

Without complaint, Cyrus went and poured her a glass of wine, and put it on the table. Wazoo sat down facing Guy. She saw the nuts and helped herself.

The wild mane of black hair that used to reach Wazoo's waist remained a mane, but much shorter now and kind of pretty, Guy decided, all tight, springy curls that accentuated her white skin and dramatic features. There used to be long discussions about Wazoo's age. Was she forty, fifty? Then she'd started making something of herself and the latest conjecture put her in her thirties.

"You're gonna know me if you see me again, N'awlins," she said, raising her face and laughing her full-throated laugh.

He grunted. "It's not my fault you're a fascinatin' woman. You'd make any man stare."

She laughed some more and the look in her black eyes was actually one of liking. "God Man," Wazoo said to Cyrus. "You know everything that goes on around here. They reckon you saw Jilly early this evenin'. She ain't seein' no one else. What's up with her? And I wouldn't ask if I didn't love her."

"Jilly's lovable," Cyrus said. He looked at Guy, who looked away, unwilling to have more conversation with Wazoo than he had to.

"You know Joe and Ellie Gable went off on some

74

fool trip," Wazoo said. She wore her usual black clothing, but today the dress was simple, with a belt, and it would be hard not to notice her nice figure. "I open up at Hungry Eyes. The café, anyway. Elsie from the dime store does the books. She's in a book club so she's good with recommending. Jilly sends Missy Durand over from All Tarted Up in the afternoon when they aren't so busy. That's so I can get back to Rosebank and do my chores there."

"I know," Guy said. "Jilly told me."

"Missy Durand couldn't come today because Jilly never got back to the shop so Missy had to stay there." Wazoo cast an accusing look at Guy. "That meant I couldn't leave so I'll have to make up my chores at Rosebank real late. I can't expect Vivian to keep my rent low if I don't do what I'm supposed to."

An urge to tell Wazoo to get to the point tensed every muscle in Guy's body. The fact that he couldn't tell her made them ache.

"Wazoo," Cyrus said gently. "It's too bad you were inconvenienced, but—"

"I don't care about no inconvenience," Wazoo said, her voice rising. "What I care about is Jilly. She doesn't let people down. So there's somethin' real wrong with her and I figure I'm in the right place to find out what."

"Your intuition is failing you this time," Cyrus told her. "You're right. I went over to see her because I was concerned. But I can't tell you what's happened to her because she didn't tell me."

75

Wazoo turned her attention completely to Guy. "But this is the one who knows," she said. "I'll bet you— er, Father, I'm sure you got him here with you because you know he's no good for Jilly, *and* he's finally done somethin' to mess her up but good. You're goin' to tell him to move on."

"Wazoo—"

"If he was any good at all," Wazoo said, interrupting Cyrus, "he'd be with her now instead of steppin' out in her hour of need to go drinkin' with the boys."

"A glass of wine with the local priest isn't exactly drinkin' with the boys," Guy said, looking at the grain in the old oak table.

"That's better," Wazoo said. "You feelin' miserable now. You should be. And Father here is most likely feelin' better. He don't care what you do as long as you have a bad time doin' it—includin' drinkin'."

Cyrus, in the act of emptying his glass, laughed until tears popped in the corners of his eyes. "Can I use that in my next homily?" he asked.

"Not unless you want me to sue you." Wazoo narrowed her eyes but her mouth twitched.

"I'm glad the two of you are havin' such a good time," Guy said. "I've got things to do." He'd gone over the top. What was he thinking, speaking to Cyrus like that?

"You mean you're goin' over to try and sweet-talk your way into Jilly's good graces. Well, don't hold your breath, N'awlins, she's got her head screwed on right and I can tell she's made the right decision.

You're out. Time you crept away."

Understanding how Wazoo had burrowed her way into the hearts of the folks in Toussaint could be tough to understand. Guy liked her, too, but didn't know why. She had an acid mouth when she wasn't being outrageous and she pushed herself into the middle of anyone's affairs. And they accepted her as if she was meant to be there. Bottom line was most likely that she'd do anything to help anyone.

In a low voice Guy said to Cyrus, "Sorry for snappin'. I was out of line."

Cyrus gave his shoulder a light punch and turned to Wazoo. "You have no reason to behave that way."

"It's awful," Wazoo said suddenly. She gripped her glass in both hands and raised it to her mouth, at the same time staring ahead at the dark window. "I see it now. I got it wrong. All wrong, me. That's gotta be 'cause I ain't practicin' like I ought to these days. Oh, so much pain and sufferin' I see and—and—you the only one who can stop it." She pointed at Guy but continued to stare with unfocused eyes.

With a sigh, Cyrus reached to pat her but she pulled back and slowly turned to Guy. "Death," she said. "Maybe. Then maybe more death. Don't you stop listenin' to someone who knows things or evil will descend on this town and we'll be too late to stop it."

Wazoo was given to weighty predictions.

From the hallway, Spike Devol came into the kitchen. "Evenin'," he said, his blue eyes crinkled at the corners and his blond hair standing on end in front like it always did. For years a deputy, now he was actually the elected sheriff in these parts, but he still worked all hours.

Wazoo gave no sign of having seen him. "There's blood," she said. "Blood everywhere. And poison—voodoo." Her shudder visibly moved her flesh.

Spike tossed his Stetson on the table and adjusted the belt around his trim waist and flat stomach. His marriage to Vivian Patin and his move to Rosebank Resort had been good for him. He was one healthy-looking lawman who made his khaki uniform look like a must for a *GQ* spread—with Spike in it.

"I know where some of this is comin' from," Wazoo said, the focus back in her eyes. She pointed a long, red-tipped finger at Cyrus. "You can make a difference. You let those charlatans park their trailer on church land for free. You don't know what they do, or where they come from. I heard they got all kinds of voodoo goin' on. And your parishioners won't tell you, but when they're sure you won't catch 'em, they're linin' up for that nonsense."

"You've been known to dabble in a little voodoo yourself," Spike remarked. "Who is she talking about?" he asked Cyrus.

"A very nice couple who earn their way by doing odd jobs. They're willing and prompt. They were on hard times so I let them hook up their trailer over that way." He pointed vaguely in the direction away from the church. "Ken and Jolene, their names are."

"You sure that was a good idea?" Spike asked.

"I feel ever so much safer when you're around," Wazoo said to him. "You've got a level head, Spike Devol, and it's one of the few in these parts."

"They're fine people," Cyrus told them. "Don't go makin' up stories about them because you think they could take away some of your business, Wazoo. And remember they grow vegetables and sell them. That's probably their primary source of income. They do a good business."

Wazoo gave one of her memorable frowns. "In case you've forgotten, animal psychology is my thing and there's many who'll tell you how good I am at it. You ask Spike's Vivian—and Joe and Ellie Gable. I've got plenty to speak for me—includin' Dr. Reb. Her Gaston was one mixed-up poodle before I straightened him out." She looked under the table at Goldilocks. "If you've got the sense you was borned with, N'awlins, you'll get that sweet thing to me quick, too. I never saw a more obvious case of low self-esteem."

Guy resisted the temptation to check on Goldilocks.

Spike stood at the opposite end of the table from Cyrus, but looked at Guy. "What's going on?" he said. "You've been behavin' different—so Homer says— and Jilly's locked herself up in her house. If you don't want to discuss it here, we can go somewhere private."

Guy's stomach made a slow revolution. "You're overreactin', everyone is."

79

"Gator reckoned I'd find you here. You left Homer's and never went back."

"I left a few hours early and Ozaire covered for me. But Ozaire must have passed along the good news to his buddy, Gator."

"Some man with a flashy car was leavin' with the dog when Ozaire got back to Homer's. He gunned it out of there as soon as he saw Ozaire. Who was that?"

"Why the interrogation, Sheriff? Am I under arrest?" he said, trying to lighten things up, but failing.

The atmosphere had a slow, darkening pulse.

"Don't be a smart-ass—I'm lookin' for answers, and help." Spike pulled out a chair at the table. He declined wine or beer but got up again and poured coffee. "Vivian's on the warpath. Reckons it's all my fault Jilly's upset."

Guy looked to Cyrus, who crossed his arms on the table and waited for Spike to continue.

"Ozaire said he saw a black Corvette leave Homer's place just as Ozaire was getting there." Once again Spike's expression pinned Guy.

"I have a friend from New Orleans who owns one of those," Guy said. He might as well spit it out. "He stopped by to see me. I thought he would leave before Ozaire got back."

Red fingernails flashed and Wazoo made shooing motions at Guy. "Leave. Go. You don't want to be here."

He had to ask, "How does Vivian know Jilly's upset?" He would never get used to the way gossip traveled in this town.

"There was an accident," Spike said. "Corner of Main and St. Mary's Street. You know that, anyway. You were there."

"You weren't," Guy told him.

"Half the town was," Cyrus said, grinning and tipping up his glass.

"Vivian's on my case because Deputy Hall's a new recruit and he let things get out of hand." Spike shook his head. "He didn't take down anything about the mobsters who showed up and hassled Jilly."

Wazoo sat forward, all eyes. "I told you bad stuff was goin' to happen here."

Cyrus and Guy shared a blank glance, then Guy remembered. "You mean a man called Caruthers Rathburn? Just one man, not a gang, and he works for the man who married Jilly's mother after she left Toussaint."

"How about an altercation between Laura Preston and Lee O'Brien? And all the threats that were tossed around? The way I heard it, Miz Preston made a threat against Miz O'Brien's life. Told her if she wrote about Jilly or herself in the *Trumpet*, Lee's body would never be found."

"That's exactly the way it went," Guy said, getting up and retrieving his hat. The fib felt justified. He made for the door to the backyard with the pesky hound at his heels. "Didn't anyone tell Vivian the war-

81

lock from the wood was there, too, with his witch partner? Could be it was all the chicken innards they threw around that really got to Jilly."

He let himself out into a night that still steamed and closed the door behind him—and Goldilocks. The whole situation had gotten blown out of proportion. Nothing funny was going on, not a damn thing. If he had to guess he'd say Nat's New Orleans murder case had nothing to do with this town, either.

The dog wouldn't get in the back of the car. Instead she settled herself on the passenger seat, and each time Guy tried to put her in back, she climbed up front again.

"So sit there," he told the critter. "This is our last ride together, anyway."

Guy got in the driver's seat and switched on the engine. Bonanza Alley separated the rectory from the church and graveyard. He ducked his head to look at the old white building glowing in the moon's cloud-stained light. Shadows rippled across the glimmering facade.

The windshield fogged up fast. He found a cloth in the glove compartment and swiped at the glass. Wazoo's van stood close to the Pontiac on the gravel parking strip outside the rectory. He noticed she'd left the dome light on. Shutting the dog in the car, Guy strode to the van and tried the passenger door. Locked. He walked around the hood—and collided with Wazoo on the other side of the vehicle.

"What you sneakin' around for, N'awlins?" she said, leaning inside the van to put off the light.

"I was goin' to steal your wheels—after I made sure the battery was still charged. Night."

"You was goin' to turn off my light. I know that. You got a nice dog there."

Guy mumbled nothing in particular.

"Don't leave her in the car, you. She could suffocate in there. When I got her out she was pantin'."

"Night," Guy said again.

"Yeah. Jilly Gable's too good for you but maybe you'll improve. Don't you hurt her no more, you."

Guy watched her return to the rectory kitchens before he got into the Pontiac once more.

Goldilocks barked.

Guy whipped his face toward her. "What's up with you?"

The dog barked again, and set up a whining that made the hairs on the back of Guy's neck stand up. That was the moment before he smelled something burning, something foul burning. Black smoke forced itself from the engine compartment and between the spaces around the hood.

He switched off, grabbed the fire extinguisher from behind his seat, the flashlight he kept in the pocket beside him, and shot from the vehicle.

He threw up the hood and took several steps backward from a blast of heat and acrid smoke laced with particles that stung his eyes.

With the light trained on the engine, he started a

stream of foam from the extinguisher, but stopped. The smoke had thinned already.

If you liked your meat really well done, the gutted chicken, its blackened innards tidily arranged beside the carcass, was scorched to perfection.

7

Guy parked the Pontiac several houses away from Jilly's. He said a small prayer, "Let her be reasonable," and roused Goldilocks, who snored beside him.

The chicken was a joke. People didn't really believe in all that voodoo hooey these days—they just liked to pretend so they could support Louisiana's reputation.

"C'mon, dog, this is our fond farewell." He couldn't help wondering if the burnt offerings were Wazoo's idea of being funny and she'd come outside for a good laugh at his expense.

If she'd done the chicken number she would have expected him to drive away as soon as he got in the car and not see or smell anything until he was on the road and his engine heated up. She couldn't have known he'd hang around a bit too long.

Who else would go to so much trouble? He was darned if he knew.

Goldilocks climbed sleepily over his seat and jumped out. She leaned against his leg and yawned. It didn't cost him anything to scratch her head. She wasn't so old, maybe a year, and she still tired herself out.

"Now, do as I say," he told her, walking in the shadow of a tall hedge and holding the scruff of the animal's neck.

Up the driveway to Jilly's front door they went, and Guy knocked softly.

The house was in darkness.

He knocked harder. She'd never hear otherwise.

Goldilocks whined and Guy gripped her muzzle in one hand while he whispered in her ear, "It's real important you don't get on the wrong side of Jilly, so be very quiet." As soon as he let go, Goldilocks whined again.

This time Guy rang the bell—three times—and stepped back. He heard the slightest scrape and looked up to see a curtain blow where a window had been opened an inch. The window hadn't been open when he arrived. He'd checked.

He stood beneath the window. "Jilly," he said hoarsely, trying to project a whisper. "Jilly, it's Guy. I need to talk to you."

He waited and watched. Nothing moved and there wasn't another sound. The curling in the pit of his stomach was too familiar. He was getting frustrated and that wouldn't help a thing.

"Please, Jilly." He glanced around to make sure no one else saw him grovel. On his cell phone, he dialed her number and heard the phone ring five times inside the house, then fall silent. No answering machine came on.

"Okay, I don't want to do it, but I'm gonna have to get tough."

Kneeling beside the dog, he said, "Bark. Go on, just bark."

Guy's ear got a thorough cleaning but not one peep did Goldilocks make.

He put an arm around her and made what he hoped were good imitations of low barks, then he growled for good measure.

The only thing his attempts bought him was a passionate face washing.

Guy filled his palm with pieces of gravel, stood up and shied one gently against the open window. After a few seconds he tossed another and another.

"Sheesh," he muttered, "why can't women be sensible—like men?"

After what felt like minutes he said, louder, "I've got that mutt here and I'm not taking her with me when I leave. Come on down and get her. Unless you just want her to wander off and get . . . lost." You had to be careful with Jilly over some things. Most things.

He lobbed more pieces of gravel, being careful to make sure they barely touched the glass. She'd have to hear them.

The next one he tossed a little harder—and he winced. The pane cracked. He blew up his cheeks and stared upward. What kind of luck was that, dammit? A piece of gravel thrown underhand and gently shouldn't break a window.

Aw hell, he had broken her window. And he was a bit old to run away.

He kept on looking up but there was no sign of Jilly. She was in, he'd stake his life on it. Admittedly her car wasn't around to prove it, but that didn't mean a thing since the Beetle was in the shop.

Kneeling beside the dog once more, he told her, "I give up. The woman is totally unreasonable. You stay here and bark whenever you feel like it. If you leave it could be curtains—for both of us. But she'll show eventually and take you in—she's too soft to turn you away." He lifted one ear flap and growled softly. "Do that. It works every time."

Jilly had opened the front door a couple of inches while Guy had been throwing rocks at her bedroom window. She couldn't believe a grown man would kneel there in the dirt giving a dog instructions as if the poor animal understood and would do as she was told.

"Only you would try to frighten a sweet dog like that," she said.

He started and looked at her over his shoulder, and she did believe that if there were any light she'd see he was blushing.

"Why didn't you let me in?" he demanded.

"Before you broke my window, you mean?"

"There must be something wrong with the glass for it to break like that. It's your own fault, anyway. I need to talk to you and you wouldn't let me in."

"I'm letting you in now. Get up and move before I call the sheriff and have you hauled off to jail."

Guy could see the glitter in her eyes but very little else. "You can be so annoying," he said.

"Thanks—maybe you don't need to come in after all."

"I thought you were upset. Crying."

She swallowed. "Why would I be? If you're coming in, come, and don't leave her outside or you'll be back with her before you can check your fly," Jilly finished with her mouth open. She never, ever said things like that.

Guy decided against suggesting she had a fly fixation. He stood and went inside. Neither of them needed to worry about whether Goldilocks would join them.

"Do you always break people's windows if they don't answer the door?" Jilly said. "Do you have any idea how bizarre that is?" She led him into her small sitting room and turned on the lamps.

Ignoring her, he went directly to the windows and drew the drapes.

"You," she said while her insides shook. "You don't get to come in here and do as you please."

"We'd rather not be seen," he said. Bareheaded for once, he'd found the time to change into clean jeans and a white shirt.

"You're right," she told him. He looked good—much too good.

Now that he couldn't give her the manly, calming hug he'd practiced in his mind, Guy scrambled for a way to make conversation. "Someone put a dead chicken on my engine block." *Great. He could have said anything but that.*

She narrowed her eyes. "When?" The thermal cotton pajamas she wore wouldn't have been so appealing on any other woman.

Guy's throat dried out. "Not long ago. I was getting ready to come here and left the engine running a bit. The smoke and smell were my first clues."

Suddenly, she dropped into the corner of an orange suede couch and he realized she had turned pale. "That's something to do with voodoo," she said, pulling up her knees. "You're making it up, of course you are. People don't do those things anymore."

"Right," he said. "I'm makin' it up. Get dressed and I'll take you to see the mess it made. I'm goin' to be smelling burned barbecue for weeks."

She wrinkled her nose. "That could have been a warning."

"What kind of warning?"

"Not to do something you're doing. To keep your nose out of people's business, maybe."

"Did you put it there?" Sometimes the devil made your tongue loose.

Jilly gathered her voluminous hair behind her head and gave him the kind of steady, sharp hazel stare intended to make him back off.

"No, of course you didn't. I'll have to follow it up,

because unless it was put in my car by mistake, someone's following me around and looking for opportunities to be a pain in the neck." He smiled at her. She didn't smile back.

Time for a new angle. "Jilly, Cyrus told me you were real upset. He's worried about you."

Jilly couldn't stand thinking she'd troubled Cyrus. "I don't know why you thought coming here would make a difference."

"Because," he said, standing over her, "Cyrus told me it's my fault if you're unhappy. He said I don't treat you well. In fact, he said I treat you badly."

"Sit down," she said. "My neck's starting to hurt."

Rather than retreat to either a dark blue chair, or a love seat, he sat down right where he was, on the couch beside Jilly with his hip touching her drawn-up bare feet.

Goldilocks jumped up at his other side, but before she could make herself comfortable, he ordered her down. "Dogs need a lot of attention," he said. "They need a home where there's more than one person to make sure they do what they're supposed to."

"Millions of people on their own have dogs."

Silence lengthened. He slid his hands behind his neck and squinted at the ceiling. *Let her be the one to start talking.*

Finally he glanced at her—and found she'd closed her eyes.

Well, *hell.* "Do you keep the kitchens and the back gate locked at the café?"

Her eyes popped open and she frowned. "Of course not. People are coming and going all the time. And the garbage is out there. D'you like chocolate?"

She was changing the subject. "Yeah." He thought about the next thing he needed to say.

Jilly scooted to her knees and bent over the side of the couch. Her bottom stuck up in the air and he heard her open a drawer in a cabinet. She puffed and struggled and slowly pulled and pushed herself back where she'd started from.

She took the top off a box of pralines and held them out.

Guy looked into the box but his vision glazed. He still saw Jilly's bottom, tidy, round, curvy as a bottom should be curvy, and the way she crossed her feet to get more purchase while she all but stood on her head.

"Take one," she said, sounding irritable.

"I thought you said chocolate." He felt a little disoriented and the idea of the lady's nether regions had awakened other parts of him.

"That was just a question," Jilly told him. "I was thinking about the pralines all along."

He took one and put the whole thing in his mouth.

"You're supposed to bite off a piece," Jilly said.

Guy couldn't speak so he savored the sweet maple-nut-sugar explosion in his mouth.

"I bet your mother would be pleased with manners like that."

He finished but continued sliding his tongue over his teeth. "My mother," he said, "would laugh, just like she always did. And she'd eat one the same way and the whole thing would be a private joke."

Jilly saw the smile of remembrance on his lips and dropped the subject. Finally she knew one more little thing about him that she hadn't known before. His mother was dead and he'd had a close relationship with her. Good.

Eyeing the box of pralines, he reached for another, then changed his mind and looked at her instead. "Please do something for me. I know it'll be a hassle, but lock the kitchen door at All Tarted Up, and the back gate. It's important or I wouldn't ask."

She rubbed the side of her face and he saw uncertainty flood her. "Why?"

"I can't tell you exactly why, only that it could be real important, Jilly. To your safety and to Missy Durand's." Had he thought she would meekly do as he asked without wanting an explanation? He shrugged his shoulders and prepared to be grilled.

"You have proof that someone intends to come in through the back way and kill us?"

"You do beat about the bush, Jilly. One day you'll learn to come to the point. It saves time."

She poked a sharp finger into the hard flesh beneath his thigh.

A little thing like that shouldn't bring a man so much pleasure.

"Most of the time you don't say enough and when you do speak, you're a smart-ass." Her mouth turned down. "Sorry, but it's true."

A few hours earlier they had come together in a field of sunburned grass, violently, passionately. Yet they sat here sparring and avoiding the topic.

"Someone died in the Quarter. Shot three times. There's the vaguest chance there's a connection between that killing and Toussaint. Only I don't know what it is yet."

"Except I ought to lock my back door?"

"Sounds strange, but yes. A lot of people in town should probably lock their back doors. I just don't have enough to go on to make a broad suggestion like that. Would you do it for me—because you'd make me a happier man?"

He would say that to anyone, Jilly thought. A kid who wouldn't give up an Uzi, someone he was persuading not to jump off a bridge. She didn't need to make anything personal out of it.

It was personal. "Why would it make you happier?" *You know you don't dig for sweet talk, not from Guy Gautreaux.*

"Your safety is important to me. I shouldn't have to tell you that."

No, but she enjoyed hearing every word. "I'll make sure it's done. Thanks."

"First thing in the morning?"

He was serious about this. "Yes."

She nodded and her face puckered into a deep frown. He wouldn't be surprised if her mind had already moved on—way on.

"We can't avoid the subject forever," she told him,

and her throat moved sharply. She bit into her bottom lip and he didn't like the sheen in her eyes.

When he didn't react to her opener, she said, "I shouldn't have done it. It was wrong and I don't understand what came over me."

"What exactly are you talking about?" *Dumb response.* Quickly, he added, "I know you're talking about this afternoon. Forget it."

Jilly blinked. She wouldn't allow him to make her cry. "I intend to. But not without admitting I jumped the gun."

He grinned, actually grinned. She felt like slapping him.

"Interesting choice of clichés," he said. The grin gradually slipped.

"You can be so mean, Guy. And you think you always win discussions, but this time I'm going to come out on top."

"You already did." He pinched the bridge of his nose.

Think longer, speak slower. "I'm ignoring that," Jilly said. "I'm a big-enough person to face up to my short-comings. You didn't do a thing toward what happened today. I forced you."

His grin returned. "Don't beat yourself up. It wasn't so bad."

Now he'd done it, Guy thought. Jilly's very shiny, damp-lashed eyes had narrowed to slits.

Guy rotated his shoulders and turned his grin into a warm smile. "Those pajamas look hot." He was in a minefield. "I mean they look as if they make you hot."

She put a hand over her mouth.

"I'm not suggesting you should take 'em off."

Jilly put a single finger to her mouth, shushing him.

"Oh, come on," he said. "Gimme a break. I'm a challenged man. Whenever things get serious I say something that's supposed to be funny. It's usually inappropriate."

"Nothing's getting serious here," Jilly said.

Guy moved even closer to her. She saw something new in his eyes, need—and uncertainty. He kept on coming and she gasped when his lips met hers. His mouth was firm but gentle, for the first few seconds before it turned hard and he showed the things he could do with his tongue. She crossed her arms and kept them there, tightly. This time he had to make the moves.

He kissed her for a long time and there was no doubt the man had kissed at least one woman before. His hands settled around her neck with his thumbs pushing her chin up. She fought to breathe evenly—and failed. From her lips to her closed eyes, he moved. There was no way he wouldn't feel and taste the tears.

His mouth stilled and she knew he had discovered she was crying. Her brain told her it could not be a good idea to show any vulnerability around him, but her heart wouldn't cooperate.

"Jilly," he said quietly, "we'd better make sure no one gets permanently damaged here. You'll have to help me figure out how to do that." His lips touched her cheek and she felt him lick away a tear with the tip of his tongue. He rested his face against hers.

She sniffed and didn't dare open her eyes. "You're right. We wouldn't want anything to get messy." Jilly opened her mouth on his skin. Her breathing turned shallow. "I blame myself for this, but I've already done the mea culpa routine."

"If anyone should be blamed, it's me," he said, barely above a whisper. "How are you supposed to know what I'm thinkin' if I don't tell you?"

What are you thinking? That was a question she wouldn't ask.

She didn't put distance between them, but she did sit up straight, with her feet on the floor. The top of her head didn't reach his chin and he felt clumsy all over again.

What the hell. The way she makes you feel is too good to lose. See if you can get this back on track. Waiting for her to push him away, he slipped an arm around her shoulders. Jilly stiffened but she stayed put. "We can't turn the clock back," he told her. "What happened, happened, and I'd be a liar if I said I regretted it."

She held her tongue.

He eased her face back toward him. "I care about you."

And that would have to be enough. "Thank you. I care about you, too." It was more than she'd had up till now.

His free hand settled over one of hers, a large, warm,

work-roughened hand. When he threaded his fingers through hers he seemed unsure of himself for a moment, but then he raised the back of her hand to his lips. He kissed her there, lightly, and again on one knuckle after the other, before he rested his beard-stubbled cheek in her palm and shut his eyes.

God help her, he mattered so deeply to her, yet she didn't have a clue whether there was any chance of a future together for them.

"I don't want to lose you," he said, and Jilly longed to hold him so badly it hurt. "We don't know . . . Who does know what's likely to happen next year, or tomorrow? Don't ever quit bein' my friend, okay?"

She said, "Okay," and dared to hope he really meant what he said.

"Even when I'm an ass, try to be kind. Kick me if it makes you feel better, but be there for me." He felt like a drowning man, but the feeling wasn't all bad.

"I'll be there for you," Jilly told him. "I can't forget the way I behaved with you. I'm not even sure why I did it, except maybe I wanted to shock you out of being angry with me for no reason."

"Like I've said, I have trouble with feelings. I was angry at myself, not you. And you don't have to forget we made love—I'm not going to. Kissing you was a high, too. I can't promise I won't do that again." He couldn't promise anything and he wouldn't tell her he wanted to make love to her again—now. "Could we have breakfast in the morning?"

"I work," she said, wishing she could pretend he'd

meant breakfast after they woke up together in the morning.

"So do I. Early." He didn't look forward to Homer's wrath, or his suggestions that Guy intended to sneak off. If Homer fired him, he wasn't sure how he'd react, but he'd better not laugh if he didn't actually want to look for work. "I could stop by while y'all are bakin'. Coffee and the first two sweet rolls out of the oven sound good to me."

This time she grinned. "With Joe away, Cyrus runs on his own, and now he heads right over for the first marzipan tart of the day so you'd better not be late. Why Cyrus is all muscle, I'll never figure out. He has some sweet tooth."

"If necessary, you and I will eat in the kitchen," Guy said. He would have gone on, but Jilly's phone rang and she picked up.

"Yes, Laura," she said.

In seconds she was on her feet. "Of course. I'll be right there." She hung up. "I've got to get dressed and get to Edwards Place. Something's happened."

Guy got up, too. "What is it?"

She paused in the act of speeding from the room. "It's Edith. She's been seriously injured. They brought medical personnel in by helicopter and Laura said Edith's going to make it. But she's very weak and she's asking to see me."

"Injured how?"

"Don't slow me down. She got cut by something and lost a lot of blood."

8

"Come in," Mr. Preston said, turning away as soon as he saw Jilly on the doorstep. "I could have lost her, it was that close."

In her peripheral vision, Jilly saw Guy enter Edwards Place behind her and shut the massive front door. He'd insisted on coming with her, and even if she'd wanted to refuse, she didn't have a car to get there on her own.

She was glad he was there.

"Laura's in the salon. Wait with her until the doctors say Edith can have company."

"What happened?" Jilly asked.

Preston stood still, although she felt his need to keep moving. He covered his face and held out an arm to her. "It was a stupid thing," he said, clamping Jilly to his side when she reluctantly went to him. "She was shaving her legs and managed to cut herself really badly. If she hadn't been found fast, she wouldn't be with us."

Guy sized up the other man, who had made no attempt to acknowledge him. "Good evening, Mr. Preston," he said. He hated the way the man pressed Jilly against him. "I'm Jilly's friend, Guy. I drove her over."

Preston lifted his head and his gray-streaked dark

hair shone. He was solid, maybe an inch under six foot, and although he had to be in his late fifties, his palpable vitality, his powerful aura, made him seem ten years younger. It didn't hurt that his suit had been tailored to show off a hard body, or that he had the face of a man made to be on a screen.

"Who the hell are you?" he said, continuing to hold Jilly. He moved his arm down and rested his hand at her waist. The green shirt she'd changed into rode up from low-rise white pants and Preston's fingers splayed on her bare skin.

"As I told you, I'm Jilly's friend. Her car's in the shop so I drove her here." He extended a hand. "Guy Gautreaux." *And I don't want you or any man touching her like that—unless it's me.*

"Nice of you," Preston said, ignoring Guy's hand. His face showed little emotion, but his eyes made up for that. Mr. Preston didn't want a friend of Jilly's around—particularly a male friend. "Would you mind seeing yourself out?"

Guy was still holding back the first words to his lips and deciding the safest thing to say when Jilly cut in. "Guy, I'd prefer you to wait for me," she said. "Would that be okay?"

When she looked at him like that, with a certain intimate confidence, he wanted to get her away, alone. "You've got it," he told her.

"You'll want to stay here with your mother tonight," Preston said, and he brushed his jaw against Jilly's hair. "She needs you."

Manipulative bastard.

"I don't want you to worry, mind," Preston said. "I won't let anything happen to any of my family."

Guy couldn't take it. "Jilly, if you want me to wait, I will. Otherwise just call when you're ready." If he had to watch Preston maul her much longer, he might lose it and punch the guy.

"If you can stay, I'd like it," Jilly said. "I do need to be at the shop early."

The woman with the explosion of red hair, the one who had turned up at the accident scene that afternoon, came into the marble-tiled hall. She leaned a shoulder against a wall and held her hands together in front of her. Once more he caught the flash of large diamonds on her fingers.

She said, "Come and sit with me," with her violet eyes on Guy's face. "This has been a terrible night. I'm all wrung out. Jilly, I wanted to call you earlier but Daddy wouldn't hear of it till Edith was more stable."

Laura wore gray sweats with pink stripes in various places. He'd bet there was a fancy workout room somewhere in the house, where the lady paid homage to her body.

Jilly wanted away from Preston. He kept his cologne light but it still sickened her. She also wished Laura weren't turning her charm on Guy—and that he wouldn't look her over with more than a spark of interest.

She patted a lapel on Preston's silver-gray suit jacket and moved smoothly away from him. "Thank you for

101

taking such good care of Edith," she said. "Can't I go up now?"

He let out a slow breath. "Better wait till they say it's okay. She's had a transfusion."

So why isn't the lady in a hospital? Guy thought. With a chopper on the pad in the grounds, how hard could it be to take her in where she could get any care she might need.

Preston went to Jilly again. He looked deep into her eyes and rubbed circles over her back. The man was grooming her, Guy thought, appalled. And Preston had complete confidence in himself—he thought his efforts were too subtle to be noticed.

At last the man walked toward an ornate, gilt-trimmed staircase but turned yet again to draw Jilly into his arms. He hugged her, rocked her. "You'll learn to trust me," he said. "Just like your mother did. She was so much like you are now when we met—beautiful enough to turn my knees to water." He released Jilly and laughed. He laughed while he ran upstairs with the springy step of an athlete.

"He's such a sweetie," Laura said. "Let's have a drink."

She led them back the way she'd come, past ivory flocked walls heavy with paintings and lined with marble busts on plinths. Deep-piled celery-green carpet in the hall covered the floor until they reached what Preston had called "the salon." Guy guessed that was code for "fancy room." He'd been in plenty of those along the way and they had all been more welcoming than this crystal palace of Preston's.

"Sit down," Laura said, assuming the lady-of-the-manor role.

Jilly watched Guy while he passed his eyes over a vast chandelier dripping with clear prisms and too big for the room. She caught hold of his hand and pulled him over white marble tiles shot with gold veins, to soft white carpets. Later she'd tell him she also disliked the ostentatious decor at Edwards Place.

"Are you hungry, Guy—Jilly?" Laura asked. She appeared tired and marks of strain showed around her mouth. "I think I finally am. I couldn't have eaten anything earlier. What a shock."

"You must have felt helpless," Jilly said.

"I did." Laura spread her arms. "Blood everywhere and poor little Edith in the middle of it. I feel light-headed again."

"You sit down at once," Jilly said. "I'll go see if I can make some sandwiches."

Laura put her hands on her hips. "You'll do no such thing, stepsister-in-law." She giggled. "Is that what we are? I've been trying to figure it out."

"I guess," Jilly said. She had to look at Guy, whose expressionless face gave away how much he disliked this house and the people in it.

"Well—" Laura tapped the toe of a pink leather sneaker "—I do believe I like that idea. Now, both of you sit down here." She stood behind a white damask couch, one of several similar pieces in the room, and patted the cushions.

Jilly felt the slightest resistance from Guy as she followed Laura's instructions. They sat down and Laura went to a blond marquetry desk to pick up a phone and press a button on the intercom. "Pizza, please," she said, smiling. "I know, Mrs. O, this is late, but it's one of those evenings when you get a craving. It's all been such a strain. There are three of us. Maybe there's a little somethin' sweet for after the pizza? Bye-ee."

When Laura put the phone down, Jilly smiled at her. For the first time she felt some warmth toward the other woman.

Guy caught sight of gold ribbon tucked into the folds of looped-and-fluffed floor-to-ceiling draperies —white naturally. At least with everything the same color he guessed they didn't have to worry about stuff clashing. What he'd expected was a display of antiques; after all, that was Preston's specialty.

Guy put his booted feet on the edge of a glass-topped table covered with crystal and porcelain. He smiled a little at his dusty toes. Sometimes the devil got into him.

Jilly gave his hand a hard squeeze and sent him a ferocious stare.

He sighed and put his feet on the floor again.

"Edith really did almost die," Laura said. "It was terrible. I'd already gone to sleep and it was the thuds and then all the running footsteps that woke me. Caruthers saved her. He charged in there and applied pressure or whatever to the bleeding and he shouted for me. I wouldn't have known how to help if he hadn't been there."

"Where did she cut herself?" Guy asked. "She must have got a vein."

"I had to call Daddy. He went mad, I can tell you. Then, before you could think straight, he'd flown down here with an entire medical team and they went to work on her. She's lost a lot of blood, but I suppose the transfusion will help with that."

Jilly hadn't missed the way Laura had avoided Guy's question. "So you were there," she said.

"I sure was. And I stayed there holdin' her hand while Caruthers worked over her. I had no idea just how capable that man is."

"Did she slice the back of her knee?" Guy suggested. "Or a vein in her groin?"

Laura checked her watch. "No," she said. "They think the razor bounced and caught her across the inside of her left arm. I've never seen anything like it. All that shiny blood on those white covers of Edith's. I kept on talkin' to her, tellin' her to stay with me. I kissed her cheek and begged her not to leave me." Tears welled in her remarkable eyes. "Edith's the closest to a mother I've ever had."

A young, blond man built like a middleweight boxer came into the room with a tray. Guy could smell cooked onion and garlic from where he was.

"Mrs. O said to tell you she heated these leftovers in the microwave—just to tide you over. She's making fresh." He slid plates and napkins on the table, put the tray down in front of Guy and Jilly and made for the door again.

"Thank you, Michael," Laura said as he disappeared. She had a slightly different kind of smile on her face and Guy decided she liked Michael.

"Leftovers," Laura said, drawing her lips back from her lovely teeth. "Not very hospitable, but I suppose Mrs. O's right. They'll tide us over."

The front doorbell rang, followed by the sound of voices in the vestibule, mostly excited voices.

Michael returned with a man and a woman in tow.

"That's Ken and Jolene Pratt," Jilly murmured. "They're the ones who live in a trailer on a piece of St. Cécil land. They grow produce to sell. Some folks say Cyrus shouldn't have them there, but you know how he is. If anyone says a negative word he tells them the Pratts tithe. Which means they do."

Guy bit into a piece of pizza and said, "Mmm." He thought about cooked chicken innards and put the pizza down while he watched with interest as Michael tried to apologize for letting the couple in. At the same time the two of them talked very fast about how they'd only come to pay respects to Mrs. Edith and they'd leave as soon as they'd seen her.

Guy realized he hadn't considered that they might have been the ones who put dinner in his car. They were allegedly the most sought-after voodoo merchants in town.

"Thank you, Michael," Laura said. "Are you the people who sell flowers to Mrs. Preston?"

"That would be us," the woman said. She slid her eyes toward Guy and Jilly and said, "I've seen both of you but you wouldn't know us. Ken and Jolene Pratt. Father Cyrus is so kind to us, letting us put the trailer on church land."

Ken did a lot of nodding. The pair wore jeans and T-shirts and had similar, long, angular faces. They wore their dark brown hair pulled back into rubber bands at the nape and both looked at the world with large, darting, light-colored eyes.

Voodoo or not, Wazoo didn't have to fear for her reputation as the wackiest woman in town. These people were ordinary, except for their childlike, luminous eyes. Each of them held large bouquets of mixed flowers and Jolene had a plastic bag filled with lumpy shapes.

"I don't think you'll be able to see Mrs. Preston this evening," Laura said. She appeared uncomfortable and Jilly liked her for not just brushing these people off. "She's lost a lot of blood and we're told she'll take a few days to get her strength back."

They looked at each other. "I told you," Ken said. "It's a blessing we came."

Jilly's skin tightened and she felt cold. "What are you talking about?"

Two pairs of disconcerting eyes turned on her. "Nothing, really," Jolene said. "Mrs. Edith's been a friend to us and we want to be near her when she's in need, that's all."

Guy startled Jilly by holding the back of her neck

and rubbing with his fingertips.

"She loves your flowers," Laura said, not looking herself at all. "And she says how kind you are." She closed her mouth and her expression suggested she couldn't believe what she'd just said.

Jolene and Ken smiled. "You don't know how much it means to us to hear you say that," Ken said. "We've been more peaceful living here than anywhere else. Could you ask Mrs. Edith if we can go to her?"

"Yes," Jolene said. Her voice was small and thin. "We really mustn't delay. Do you know if she had been drinking?"

A small noise escaped Laura.

Jolene flew to her and patted her arms. "No, no, you must not be distressed. Many people take a drink in the evening. We counted it into our calculations, but we are also prepared in case she did not."

Guy held Jilly's wrist and squeezed to stop her from saying anything.

Again the bell rang from the hall and shortly Cyrus appeared.

Ken said, "Thank you for coming so quickly, Father." The man actually grinned. "Madge said she'd get our message to you. She agreed that there's nothing wrong with covering all our bases. Do you know Mrs. Edith?"

"Yes," he said shortly, with a questioning rise of the brows at Guy and Jilly. "Mrs. Preston comes to mass. The late mass, not the early one like you. She comes to your stall when she leaves—or so she tells me."

Jilly felt like crying. Her emotions felt stripped. She hadn't known her mother attended mass. How like Cyrus not to mention a thing about it before.

"Father," Jolene said, "Ken and I feel it's a matter of life and death for us to see her now. She was already anemic and now she's lost a lot of blood. We brought something to help her."

Cyrus bowed his head and shrugged. The two walked to him and he held their shoulders. "Not everyone understands or accepts natural medicine," he said. "The man who let me in said the doctors are with her now. She's had a transfusion. We would have to get their permission before intruding."

"It's important!" Jolene's eyes shone. "Tell him, Ken. We can help her."

"How did you know she was anemic?" Laura asked in a breathy voice.

Jolene shrugged. "We've studied these things. We can tell. And we don't use anything that isn't natural, Mrs. Laura, so you don't have to worry."

"How do you know my name?"

"Mrs. Edith loves you. She talks about you."

Laura subsided to a couch and sat, doubled over. "It's all too much," she said.

"She loves you, too, Miss Jilly," Jolene went on. "She's never been so happy as she is knowing you're safe and well."

"Even if she did—"

"You make her happy," Jolene added quickly, cutting off Ken.

"I'll go up and see how things are," Laura said, and left the room abruptly.

"You must have sold a lot of produce this week," Cyrus said to the Pratts. "The collection box had to be emptied earlier today."

"We're not happy about what's happened to Mrs. Edith," Ken said, shifting the topic. "There are a lot of elements shifting in Toussaint—and beyond. It could be that all we can do here is keep watch until the source of evil is brought to justice."

Cyrus crossed his arms. "We talked about tolerance," he told them. "But we also agreed that meant we must be careful about forcing our beliefs on others. Sometimes you can frighten people by saying things they don't understand."

"Sorry," Jolene said promptly. "Let's sit down and wait, Ken." When he joined her she looked at him and said, "It's not getting better, is it," and put a hand over her mouth.

Cyrus smiled and sat on another couch. Tonight he was still in black and wore his collar. Jilly loved to see him like that. She knew how good a man he was, but when she saw him in his "uniform" as she called it to irritate him, she realized how committed he was and how much he liked to let people see he was a man of God. An errant thought about the unusual affection between Cyrus and Madge rushed in and her stomach turned over. They worried her so.

"Are you brother and sister?" she asked the Pratts suddenly, and felt foolish. "Of course you are. I can see it now. You have exactly the same eyes and hair color, and you wear matching clothes. Twins?" *What an idiot. They had to be in their late twenties and most unlikely to choose matching clothes.*

"Ken and Jolene are married," Cyrus said, the corners of his mouth twitching.

"We know we look a lot alike," Jolene said. "That's what brought us together." She looked at her husband with open affection.

"Someone's coming," Guy said. He heard squeaky running footsteps.

Laura arrived. "Daddy doesn't like it one bit, but Edith wants to see all of you. She says you're all some of her favorite people."

Guy didn't point out that he'd never met Edith Preston. He wanted to size up what had happened in this house a few hours earlier.

The Pratts rushed from the room at once. Guy and Jilly followed with Cyrus, and much more slowly. Laura didn't join them immediately. "I tried to reach you at your place," Cyrus told Guy. "When you didn't answer, I drove over there. That mess in your engine bothers me."

"It sickens me," Guy said.

"There's a friend of yours there," Cyrus said, keeping his eyes on Guy's. "The one with the black Corvette. Nice man, but pacing around waiting to hear from you."

"Yeah," Guy said. He'd all but forgotten his uninvited houseguest. "I'll give him a call in a bit."

"He's staying at your place?" Jilly said.

"Uh-huh. Cyrus, can you get a few hours off later tomorrow?"

"I'll try."

"Good. I'll let you know when we'll pick you up. It'll be late morning."

And she, Jilly thought, wasn't supposed to ask what Guy was talking about. "Pick him up to go where?" she said. They'd reached the bottom of the stairs.

"It wouldn't be wise to tell you," Guy said. "If that changes, you'll be the first to know."

"I hate it when you treat me like a child."

"I'm not treating you like a child." He fought to keep his voice down. "I'm protecting you, dammit. That's my job." Surely Cyrus would back him up.

"*Protecting* me? Whatever may be happening around here, and we could be imagining the whole thing, whatever happens I'm part of it. So back off with the protection and include me in everything. You got that?"

Guy looked to Cyrus, who turned away and started up the stairs. "You're right," Guy said to Jilly. "There's probably absolutely nothing to worry about. Pack up your imagination, stop jumpin' at your own shadow and get on with your life."

"You condescending son of a bitch," Jilly said, and enjoyed it. She left him and ran to catch up with Cyrus.

Guy closed the space between them and whispered, "Sorry for that." This would be a bad moment to turn

Jilly against him, not that there would ever be a good moment.

She led the way from the top of the stairs, to the right along a corridor. Guy noted there was a second corridor to the left. When she reached closed double doors, she tapped, turned the handle and peeked inside.

In she went, leaving the door open.

Cyrus and Guy followed her with Guy expecting to be thrown out at once.

"Jilly, darlin'," a woman in the bed said, smiling wanly. "Come close so I can see you." Frosted streaks probably covered gray in her long, thick hair. Just as Preston had said, she was beautiful with Jilly's exotic air of mystery.

Jilly went to her and kissed her cheek. She smoothed mussed hair away from Edith Preston's pure white face. "What's happened?" she whispered.

The Pratts stood on the other side of the bed and Mr. Preston sat in an overstuffed gray chair, watching and chewing the skin around his nails. His face remained immobile, but his eyes shot fury at the group around the bed, then at Cyrus and Guy.

Guy could hear voices in a room that opened off the bedroom and presumed the medical personnel were gathered there. One male nurse remained nearby checking monitors and drips.

"Edith," Jilly said, "this is my best friend, Guy Gautreaux. He drove me over and I'd like you to meet him."

"This isn't the time," Preston snapped.

"Hello, Guy," Edith said with what could only be described as a knowing smile. "Come closer and let me see you."

Jumping to conclusions (he didn't think he'd ever mention jumping the gun again) seemed to be a family problem. The lady had decided Guy and Jilly were an item, he could see it in her eyes.

Who knew? They might be heading in that direction—if they hadn't actually arrived without knowing it.

He held the dry hand Edith offered and looked into a face that could only belong to someone closely related to Jilly. This was how Jilly would look in her late forties—and very beautiful she would be. He hoped life would be kinder to Jilly so she wouldn't carry the fine lines of worry Edith had, or the darkness beneath her eyes that he thought would be there even if she hadn't lost blood. She was too thin, although from what he could see of her beneath the covers, Edith remained very feminine.

"How do you do, Guy," Edith said in a whisper. Her hand felt like a small bird in his own. She smiled up at him. "No wonder she's fallen in love with you. You'll be able to make sure she's happy and no one spoils her life. I'm glad."

He didn't dare look at Jilly, but he felt squeezed inside. If he could, he'd do those things for Jilly. "How are you feeling?" he asked Edith. Regardless of what he thought of her, he felt sympathy for the frail woman.

Jilly felt so tense she ached. Guy's jaw worked and she felt a strong connection between them.

Cyrus came to stand beside him. "Hello, Mrs. Preston," he said. "Are you feeling better?"

"I'm not sure," she told him.

Ken moved forward. He placed his bouquet on the foot of the bed and the nurse promptly removed it. Next Ken took Edith's other hand, even though a taped-down catheter remained in a vein. He closed his eyes and grew quite still.

"Jilly's the only one who should be here," Preston said suddenly, getting to his feet.

"Hush," Edith said, but she smiled at her husband. "This is good for me. They're life and I need that. I don't want to die."

Instantly, heavy silence fell.

Ken's eyes remained shut. "Bring me the tonic," he murmured. He looked at Edith. "I made it myself and it will help you grow stronger."

"Look here. I'll get one of the docs," the nurse said.

"You will not, thank you," Edith told him. "These are friends of mine and I absolutely trust them."

From the bag, Jolene removed a round plastic bowl with a lid, which she took off. She gave the bowl and a spoon to Ken, who stirred a thick brown mixture inside. "Just soup," he said. "Made from good, natural foods."

Laura joined them and once again Edith smiled. "This is my other daughter, Laura." Then she let Ken feed her the soup. At first she swallowed tiny amounts, but gradually she speeded up, taking spoonful after spoonful until it was all gone. "So good," she said. "Thank you."

Ken gave the empty bowl and the spoon to Jolene, then placed his hands on Edith's head.

He had to be wrong, but Guy could swear the faintest blush of color entered Edith's cheeks.

"Mumbo jumbo," Preston said. "If my wife gets sicker, you two will wind up in jail."

"Hush, Sam," Edith said. "Ken and Jolene wouldn't hurt me."

"She should rest now," the nurse said.

"I'm going to sit with you, Edith," Laura said. "Jilly has to get a ride back with Guy. She's got to open her shop in the morning—and help with the baking, I should imagine."

"Of course," Edith said. "I love the shop. Pink door and all." She smiled and looked younger.

"Did you try Jilly's marzipan tarts?" Cyrus said. He kissed the tips of his fingers. "My mouth waters just thinkin' about them."

"Marzipan is my favorite," Edith said. "You'd better get some rest, Jilly."

"I'm not in a hurry," Jilly said.

Ken began chafing Edith's arms. First one, then the other, through the sleeves of a silk gown.

As Guy watched the left sleeve slid higher and he saw a heavy dressing on her wrist. She'd been shaving her legs and accidently cut her wrist—seriously enough to almost kill her?

116

Cyrus touched his back, letting him know he'd seen the same thing and had his own thoughts.

"Did Caruthers stop the bleeding?" Cyrus asked. "I should like to tell him how grateful we all are."

"He did it," Edith said. "He's so strong. Laura told me all about it. He did it with his hands and told Laura to call for help. When I started to come to, Caruthers was still gripping my arm. It hurt so much. He's a very strong man."

The very strong man was nowhere to be seen.

"He's on an errand for me," Preston said to Cyrus. "I'll give him your regards when he gets back."

Guy nodded. He couldn't take his eyes from Edith's left arm. He'd been around enough lowlifes to know needle tracks when he saw them. Cyrus's fingers pressed slightly harder on his back.

At least the tracks didn't look fresh.

How had Edith got from the bathroom to the bed without dripping blood everywhere on the light-colored carpets? Surely she wouldn't shave her legs on the bed. If he didn't think Jilly would accuse him of deliberately making trouble, he'd suggest contacting Spike. As long as Edith continued to improve, Guy decided he'd keep his mouth shut.

She kept on smiling, apparently oblivious of a new and chilly atmosphere in the room.

Cyrus's cell phone rang, and as usual, it took him a couple of seconds to realize he'd got a call. "Excuse me," he said, and left the room.

"Father Cyrus Payne here," he said, looking over the

banisters into the hall below, where the front door stood wide open.

"This is Spike. Madge said I should get in touch with you in case you know where Jilly is."

"She's here," Cyrus said, keeping his voice down. "We're at Edwards Place."

"Why?"

"Mind if we discuss that later?"

"No, but we can't put off what I'm dealing with. I wish Joe was in town. I'm at Jilly's place."

Cyrus looked at the door to Edith's bedroom. "Her house? Why?"

"No, All Tarted Up. Folks across the street called . . . oh, shit! Keep her out of here." Spike talked to someone in the background.

"What?" Cyrus said. A man walked into the hall below, his face shadowed by the brim of his fedora. He shut the door and strode toward the back of the house, but not without feeling around in his pocket for a scrap of paper, spitting out his gum and tossing it into a tall Dresden vase.

Spike hadn't answered, although Cyrus could hear voices and shouts in the background.

"You there, Spike?"

He told Cyrus he was, and added, "That Lee O'Brien from the *Trumpet*'s showed up and she doesn't hear the word no." He coughed. "I need Jilly over here. You should come with her. This isn't pleasant."

"Just tell me about it." Sometimes he got irritated

when people tried to soften things for him. "Guy's here, too, by the way."

"Fine. Bring him with you. How about the Preston men?"

"Also here."

"I should speak to Preston himself but I want to wait on that. At least for now."

"Spike, would you spit it out?"

"Right. There's a body in the yard behind Jilly's café. It's pretty fresh."

9

"Did you do it?"

Laura closed the bedroom door and gave a smile her best shot. "I haven't—no, I can't do it." Wes was an angel, a tough angel and her drug of choice. And even after she'd been married to him for seven years he could still frighten her. "Everyone's gone but one of the nurses."

Wes gave her an open-handed slap on the shoulder and sent her sprawling over the shoes he'd taken off and onto the floor by the bed.

She could tell him Daddy would punish him if he knew, and she'd be right, but Wes would only beat her in places that didn't show until she was too cowed to fight back.

The anticipation made her shiver. They danced to

different beats. Wes got off on pushing her around, then turning into a whimpering puppy. Fortunately, Laura preferred the opposite scenario.

The perfect couple.

He kicked her hip. "Don't look at me like that. I gave you one little job to do and, as usual, you let me down. I hate the sight of you. It's about time you stopped dyeing your hair red. It makes you look so old."

"I don't dye it."

"What's so hard about paying someone off and making sure you've got enough on 'em so they never come back—or talk out of school?"

Wes was a looker and he knew it. He swaggered, even at times like now when he was barefoot and wearing nothing but a pair of black bikini briefs.

She made herself look straight into his green eyes. "If it's so easy, why don't you do it?"

He kicked her again.

Laura curled her legs tightly. She'd have blood-filled bruises by morning.

The membership in a high-class New Orleans gym, a personal trainer who worked Wes over every day, and lifetime access to a tanning bed kept him bulked up and bronzed. When he smiled, he flashed white teeth. He kept his dark brown hair cut short and carefully gelled up to camouflage a thinning area.

"Give her money," Wes said. "I already said you could have as much as it takes. It'll be a lot less than you think because there's no way she understands what she could get. You've seen how he is with her. I want her out of our lives before he gets into her pants, and she gets into the will."

"I don't believe she would sleep with him. She's got other interests." And Laura also thought Jilly had a real honor and honesty about her.

"What other interests?"

"Some man who works for Homer Devol out at the gas station."

Wes laughed. He stood close to Laura, close enough that the toes of his right foot slid easily upward, between her thighs to her butt, then forward where he could always get a reaction.

She didn't try to stop him.

"A gas jockey is going to hold her interest when Daddy waves the big green bills in front of her face?" he said. "I don't think so. In fact I'd put money on my Daddy fuckin' her whenever he decides the moment is right. And she'll be good. She's got that thing about her. You can feel it."

Laura stared up at him. "Can you? I think you feel that *something* every time you see a nice ass."

"Could be." He laughed and flexed his shoulders and arms. "But we're talkin' about a piece of ass that Daddy intends to get. This time won't be like the others. He wants her to make him feel like he's gettin' fresh Edith all over again. It excites him. I've seen sweat when she's mentioned and Daddy doesn't sweat."

"Sick," Laura muttered.

Wes snickered. "Yeah, well you might know about that. We're goin' to make a plan, you and me. Our future could depend on it."

Laura grabbed his ankle, yanked his foot from between her legs and jerked it upward. All in one motion. Wes lost his balance and fell backward onto the carpet with a loud-enough thud to bring a "Shush" to Laura's lips.

"Bitch!"

"Bastard."

Wes pushed up on his elbows. "Where's Daddy now?"

"He's got a cot in Edith's room."

"Cute. He's not going to hear us from there."

Laura turned her mouth down at the corners and got to her feet. "On your knees," she told him. She stuck out her tongue and wiggled it.

Under the tan, Wes turned pale. His eyes looked suddenly feverish and moisture glistened on his forehead.

The black briefs didn't stop any movement down there. He was long and thick—that was one of the things she had married him for. That and the money. And she loved him.

With his eyes at the level of her breasts, he pumped his hips up and down from the floor.

"You know what you have to do," she told him. "On your knees, now."

Wes followed orders quickly this time and knelt there demurely with his hands clasped over his crotch.

"Have you gotten better at speaking nicely to me?"
He shook his head. "You'll have to make me."

Laura went into the closet and returned with a box she'd taken from the top shelf. From inside she pulled out a full helmet fashioned like a metal cage and snapped it open from hinges on top. The contraption slid easily over Wes's head—it ought to, it had been made for him. A small key locked the leather neck band on both sides.

"I'm going to have to punish you again. This time I won't stop until you promise to do whatever I ask you to do." She poked a finger through the bars, directly at his eye but stopped just short of jabbing him with her fingernail. "Hiss."

Wes pulled a sulky face but he hissed softly through his teeth. Metal pressure against the lower half of his face made talking a problem.

While she had control, why not take even more advantage than she usually did? She pointed to the bulge between his legs. "Jerk off." He liked this bit—usually.

Wes hissed again, but at the same time he took his briefs down until they stretched around big, flexed thighs. His butt could have been carved in marble. She strolled to drop down beside him and test his flesh there. Nothing moved. His dick sprang up, begging for attention.

"Do it," Laura said.

She watched him go to work on himself and began to undress herself. She shed the gray sweat-suit top that was all she wore over an abbreviated pink bra. Lace along the top of the quarter cups nestled just beneath her nipples. She knew her breasts looked like smooth, white-chocolate truffles. That was Wes's favorite description before he set about "eating" them.

Wes had paused, the veins in his neck standing out in cords and his face red. She heard him pant. Wes could always be relied on to give an outstanding performance. Quickly, she skimmed off her track pants, taking the pink sneakers with them. Very deliberately she bent over in front of Wes to pick up her clothes, then she turned her back on him and folded the sweats on the bed. Her thong was a work of art with tiny, shimmering crystals outlining her cheeks.

"Ah," Wes moaned, sounding drunk. He probably *was* drunk now she thought of it. She could smell liquor on his breath.

She faced him, pointed to his south pole, and said, "I'm getting impatient."

His hand moved hard and fast, jerking him, contracting the muscles in his belly. Faster and faster he went, his teeth gritted, his lips curled back, his eyes glazed.

Laura got ready. A catcher needed to be on her toes. Wes ejaculated in an arc. She had decided this was because he held back as long as he could.

There it came. Exactly in time for her to gather it up with the pants of a suit that cost him thousands. And he didn't even know while he slumped, his head pressing one side of the cage into his shoulder.

His chest heaved and he opened his eyes—and saw the pants she held in front of his face. The fire in his eyes turned to pure evil and he reared up.

And Laura dropped the little key to his head cage inside her mouth.

Evil turned to fear in his face and she fought laughter. "Down, boy," she said. "Whew, is it just me, or is it hot in here?" She did smile.

Wes fell to his knees again. She'd panicked him.

"The air-conditioning can't be working properly." She folded back white wood shutters and wound open the jalousies. Really hot, wet air slipped through the glass slats and she stood there until she felt moisture trickle between her breasts. The moisture between her legs didn't need any help.

"You were very, very good," she told him. "When you're ready for more, just nod and I'll decide what's on the menu."

When she turned back to the room he was already nodding.

Laura walked slowly in front of him and slipped off her thong. "Who's in charge?"

He pointed to her.

"You hit me—you've hit me too many times."

Wes's worried stare centered on her mouth.

"Oh, yes, the key. Don't worry, sweetie, I've got it in my cheek and I promise . . . I'll try not to swallow it."

She walked into the closet again and selected a pair of needle-heeled shoes so high she had to get her balance. *But once Laura has her balance, watch out.* Giggling, she strutted back to Wes and stood with her feet braced apart, rolling her hips. He shoved his hands under his thighs. If she didn't have the shiny little key, he'd have grabbed her by now.

"Look," she told him, jutting one hip to show him the forming bruises. "Whatever I have, I want you to have. I'm like that. I share." One transparent spike heel connected with his solid butt.

He screamed, thrust to his feet and raised a hand.

Laura pointed to her cheek.

Wes dropped his hand to the bloody puncture wound she'd inflicted.

She slapped him until her hands stung, then stopped to catch her breath. "I shouldn't have kicked you like that." She panted. "I hate it when you kick me, Wes. Let's not do that anymore, huh?"

His eyes slid away but he nodded.

"If I unlock you will you come inside me this time? No rubber? No withdrawal?"

She got another affirmative and her heart squeezed. "Oh, Wes. Would it be so bad to have a baby?"

He shrugged and the old puzzled, boyish look hovered.

"Sit on the bed." She fished the key from her mouth and unlocked the helmet. Immediately she popped the key into her mouth and grinned at him while he freed his head.

"Such a clear-headed woman," he told her, grabbing the bra between her breasts and twisting until it broke

126

apart. "Dance for me, baby." He had hurt her again, but she kept on smiling.

This was why she sweated in the gym for hours, for times like tonight when she got to show off for Wes.

"Oh, yeah," he murmured, joining her and rolling his hips in rhythm with hers. He got so close she felt his heat, and often, his skin.

Humming an old swamp pop-blues tune, he moved her with his body and she went willingly. Hands above their heads, they strutted rhythmically, hips doing most of the work, hips that would do a belly dancer proud.

Heat and need built in Laura. She leaned her breasts on him and he smiled down at her with half-closed eyes. Spreading a hand over each breast, he stooped to suck on her nipples. Immediately weak, she held his arms. "Make love to me, Wes," she whispered.

He lifted her and she expected to land on the bed.

Wes clamped her legs around his waist and entered her. He kept right on humming and jerking his pelvis in time. "Time for us to make a plan to get Jilly Gable out of our lives. For good, if necessary."

"Wes." She whined and plucked at his shoulders while he bucked her.

"I'm here," he said. "You're going to offer the bitch money, lots of it."

"Later." Laura whimpered and attempted to kiss him. She tried to switch off the pulse mounting inside her. Wes made sure she didn't have a hope. "Please,

Wes. I'll do what you want me to do. Let's talk about it later."

"If she doesn't take the money, you threaten her. Either she gets lost or you'll spread it around that she's fucking Daddy. That would get rid of the gas jockey and anyone else she thought was a friend." He chuckled. "Might be good for her business, though."

She gritted her teeth and rode with him, helpless, swept away just as he intended. He wouldn't change his mind about Jilly. But he would stop saving himself—stop taking away any chance of Laura having a child.

"You with me, Laura?" He set up a slapping rhythm. They came together harder and harder. "You ready?"

"Yes!"

She climaxed as Wes pulled out of her. His semen hit the wall nearby and he dropped her to stand on the floor, held her wrists and swung her back and forth, his face tilted. He kept on humming.

Laura wrenched away and reached inside her mouth for the key. "I warned you," she said. And if he wanted Jilly out of town so badly, he'd have to do his own dirty work.

Wes laughed, hung his head back and howled at the ceiling. When he could speak, he said, "You fool. What do I care about the fucking key. Keep on holding it, flash it around while you're at it. Does that mean you want me to be a good boy and let you put the helmet back on me?"

10

"Stay here," Guy told Jilly, parking behind a row of official units in moonlit Parish Lane. "I'll bring Spike back to you."

"Hell, *no*." Stay on her own in the dark? Jilly didn't think so.

Of course she would be difficult, Guy thought. The rusted old truck Cyrus drove pulled in behind the Pontiac and Cyrus jumped out. He walked to Guy's door.

Guy rolled down the window. "Do you think it would be a good idea if Jilly stayed here until we find out what's goin' on?"

Cyrus looked unsure. "Is the dog there?" He peered into the back of the car.

"She's at Jilly's place. Can't leave a dog in a car, y'know."

"Of course not," Cyrus said. "Jilly better come with us."

Jilly rolled in her lips to stop herself from grinning at the cross expression on Guy's face. Maybe she was a little hysterical, but she felt jumpy.

"There's a DB in there. That means—"

"Dead body," she finished for him. "Someone killed somebody and—"

"God rest that soul," Cyrus put in. He stood up for a moment while a white van passed.

"Yes," Jilly said. "And there's a killer on the loose. I'd rather be with some big, strong men than stay here like a sitting duck."

"Sittin' chicken," Guy mumbled, and held up a defensive hand when Jilly glared at him. "This is the chicken-in-the-engine car, remember? I wasn't talking about you."

Jilly heard another car and craned to look over her shoulder. She didn't need much light to make out the sleek Corvette belonging to Guy's friend Nat.

"Good," Guy muttered when he saw Nat get out. "That'll save a lot of explanation later."

Nat walked around to his passenger door and opened it.

"Who the hell did he bring with him?" Guy said. "Sorry, Father."

"I need help leaning some masonry fragments against the wall in the graveyard. That'll be—"

"Your penance." Jilly tried to lighten things up but Guy only said, "It'll be a pleasure. Oh, my God. *Wazoo!*"

"Perhaps you could do that little laboring job without my help?" Cyrus said mildly.

Guy wasn't listening. He got out of the car and strode back to meet Nat and Wazoo. He leaned forward to get a better look at her.

"You ain't seen Wazoo before?" She elbowed Nat, who cleared his throat. "See. I tol' you he's got it in for me. Always lookin' for somethin' to insult me about."

Guy turned to Nat. "How did you know to come here?"

"I told him, me," Wazoo said. She whirled around and moonlight shone through the inky lace cloak she wore. "Got on my mournin' duds," she said. "The dead deserve respect."

Guy wasn't giving up easily. "Who told *you?*"

She placed two fingers together and used them like a rifle sight. "I got my ways of knowin' things."

"Who could have died in my backyard?" Jilly said, joining the group. She turned to look at the row of vehicles. Bright white light blossomed from behind All Tarted Up and she shaded her eyes. "I think I feel sick." For the first time she noticed yellow crime-scene tape stretched across the lane and flapping gently in the breeze.

"Find yourself a big log to lean over," Wazoo said. "Keep the stuff off you that way."

"What log?" Guy said, looking significantly up and down the walled lane.

"Lie over the hood on one of them sheriff's cars, then." Wazoo wasn't one to let a little difficulty get in her way. "That would work the same way. I help you."

A deep, rumbling snicker had all eyes on Nat. His teeth shone and the light caught the glint in his eyes. He patted Wazoo's back and said, "I do like a woman who's a problem solver." He chuckled on until he bent over and put his hands on his knees. "Whoo-ee, I needed to laugh. Thank you, ma'am."

"Why, you welcome, killer man."

"Wazoo!" Jilly said. "You can't just call someone that. Not in a situation like this."

That started Nat laughing in earnest. This was serious, serious laughter. He staggered back, catching hold of Wazoo's hand as he went. "You are too much, sistah," he said. "You gotta explain to some that bein' a killer man is what all us manly types aspire to."

Cyrus moved closer to Jilly and Guy. "Let's go. We can't put this off any longer."

Guy didn't point out that for him and Nat, calls like this were routine. "Let's do that. Are you going to throw up, Jilly?"

"No," she told him stiffly. "I've hardly eaten today and I felt a bit dizzy when I got out of the car is all."

You'd say you felt just dandy if you were dying. Guy didn't say anything. He walked ahead, but Jilly caught up at once. "I admit I'm nervous," she said in a quiet voice. "Who could it be? A homeless person, maybe?"

"Spike sounded as if he had some idea who it is," Cyrus said. "He probably only wants to ask you some questions."

They ducked under the first line of tape and arrived at the open gates to Jilly's property—it actually belonged to Dr. Reb O'Brien Girard's husband, Marc. Half the town did—or to his Floridian mother—and Jilly leased from them.

A deputy by the gates stopped them, listened to the explanation that they'd been called by Spike, and went quickly to a group working around a body on the paved ground. Two small vans all but filled the right side of the yard, and a canopy had been erected over a large part of the area.

"Oh dear," Jilly said.

"If you're goin' to be sick, just warn me," Guy said, and one glance at him left her in no doubt that he'd moved into professional mode. "Nat and I can't walk in here without being invited, you understand that? We'll wait for Spike."

"Of course."

"Dem bones, dem bones, dem dry—" Wazoo's voice blasted in full, mournful force but she closed her mouth, then said, "Too soon for that one."

"No singin', please," Cyrus told her, but not before Jilly saw a smile in his eyes. "They're working here and we shouldn't distract them."

Forensics personnel moved deliberately around the area. Cameras flashed. An unattended gurney stood close by. Jilly took a deep, calming breath. She was an outsider looking in and the players went through their paces in what felt like slow motion.

She had to keep her head.

The officer spoke to Spike, who turned and walked toward them. He carried a clipboard. "I know I asked you to come, Jilly, but maybe it's not such a good idea."

"You think you know who it is?" Guy tucked an arm around Jilly.

"It's more a hunch than anything. I wish Joe wasn't out of town, not that I'm too sure he'd know."

Jilly's heart beat heavily. "This is someone you feel

might be connected to Joe and me?" The body was in her yard.

"I don't think so." Spike shook his head. "Jilly, you stay with Cyrus and Wazoo. No reason for you to be subjected to this."

She almost felt the pats on top of her head. She didn't want to go look at a murdered body, no way, but it seemed that she had to establish herself as anything but a wimp. Guy kind of liked to think of her as a wimp in need of protection, or so she had decided.

"I can handle it," she said. "If you can't toughen up in this world, you won't make it. I'll do it. It's not necessary for anyone else to come." She ducked under Guy's arm and hurried toward the body.

"No." Spike caught up. "I just got this idea it was your father come lookin' for you, but why would he after all this time? This guy's too young, anyway."

"Jilly?" Guy said, but she ignored him.

"I need to look," she said. The distance she had to cover was short, but her legs got heavier with each step. A couple of feet away from the body she stood still, swallowed several times and breathed in gulps of air through her mouth. The spotlight turned the blood purplish red and glossy. Reluctantly, she looked at the dead man. "Hard to live without most of your head," she heard herself say.

A titter went up.

Of course these people were immune to sights like this. This was how they put food on their tables.

Her throat contracted unpleasantly. She might never be able to eat again.

"Jilly?"

She glanced around and picked out Deputy Lori, who had recently returned to the department from maternity leave. The reassuring sight of her brought some blood back to Jilly's head. "Hi, Lori. How's Tippy?"

"Wonderful," Lori said of her baby daughter. The deputy smiled but quickly got serious again. "Mostly we wait and do the identification at the morgue, but this is going to take a while around here. Dr. Reb's on her way." She spread her arms and Jill noticed strings of gooey, bloodstained stuff spreading from the corpse's wide-open skull.

Jilly stepped closer and looked down. "Oh, no," she whispered, turning her head away. "That's his brain, isn't it?" The arms and legs lay in an almost natural manner.

"Part of it."

"It's Caruthers Rathburn," Jilly said, looking at the grotesquely wide-open mouth. His broad, pocked face was unmistakable, even in this condition. "That is so bizarre. He saved a woman's life tonight, now he's here, dead."

"Thanks, Jilly," Spike said. He'd taken off his hat and his blond hair stuck up in front. "There's no identification on him, no vehicle that we can find except for your fancy new wheels out front."

With his head bowed, Cyrus knelt beside the body and prayed silently.

Wazoo bent over Caruthers and said, "He was a marked man, him. If I was allowed to look through his brains I'd find the evidence, too."

Silence followed. Wazoo had the complete attention of all present.

She shrugged and looked delighted with herself. "I'd find hair in those brains. His hair what someone fed him in somethin' he ate. Voodoo, that's what that is."

Nat put his mouth to Wazoo's ear and whispered for a long time.

The expression on her face changed from second to second, and in the end, she nodded at him and pressed a hand to his chest. "You a good man. And you right, I shouldn't give my secrets away for free. If they want my help, they can come and ask, then pay for it. I think I'll go sleep at Hungry Eyes so I'm ready to start early. Spike—you tell Vivian I'll be back to Rosebank in good time tomorrow."

She walked away and Cyrus followed immediately. "Wait up, Wazoo. I'll drive you." Partway out of the gate they stopped walking and Cyrus ran back to Spike. "I meant to ask you about Lee O'Brien. I know she was here. She's only tryin' to do her job. You didn't go too hard on her, did you?"

"No," Spike said. "I sent her home and she seemed fine with it."

Cyrus left and caught up to Wazoo.

Jilly touched Spike's arm. "What did you mean about fancy new wheels?"

"C'mon, you don't have to be coy with me. How long have you been plannin' that? Vivian's going to be jealous. She'll want one next, wait and see if she doesn't. In dark green and gold, of course, with Rosebank Resort on the side."

"How did you find him?" Guy interrupted to ask Spike.

"Neighbor on the opposite side of the lane called in because her neighbor's dog was raising the dead. Her words, not mine."

"She didn't say she heard shots?"

Spike shook his head and moved out of the way of a technician. "Nothin'. I've got a deputy with her now. She fell apart when she heard what happened."

"Silencer," Guy said. "Most people don't identify the sounds they make."

"That's what I reckon."

"Why would he come here?" Jilly said. "Maybe he tried to reach me at home and when he couldn't, he came over here."

"That doesn't really make sense," Guy said. "He must have known you were going to Edwards Place."

"They shot him in the face," Spike said. "There's no sign of a struggle. Way I see it, he walked toward the killer because he knew him."

"Or her," Jilly said.

"Could have been a woman," Guy said. "There's no identification at all?"

"Nothin'. I guess we inform the Prestons. They should know who his next of kin are." Spike peered around. A woman wearing green scrubs and a white coat passed by. She was dragging a body bag, and she had another camera. "Looks like they're gettin' closer to moving him out," Spike said, watching the woman take the bag to the gurney.

"He saved Edith's life," Jilly said, with a lump in her throat.

"Mrs. Preston was in an accident?" Spike's back stiffened.

"She's all right."

"She's going to be fine," Guy said rapidly. "Just a little slip."

Jilly looked at him curiously. "That's right," she said. "Thanks to Caruthers Rathburn. I think he was a good person." If Guy wanted to keep quiet about Edith's mishap, so be it.

"Maybe he was decent," Guy said. "Could have been in the wrong place at the wrong time. Maybe he interrupted a burglar."

"Did I say it looks like Rathburn was walking into the yard when he was killed?" Spike said. "If we're right it probably means the murderer was already here."

Jilly put her hand in Guy's. Let him push her away if he wanted to, but she needed human warmth, his warmth. "I want to go inside the shop," she said. "Just to make sure everything's okay."

"We were going to have you unlock it for us," Spike said. "Didn't want to mess anythin' up. It would be easier for you to walk around to the front. Too much equipment to get past on this side. And you'd get in the way," he added, not unkindly.

Guy held her hand firmly and it felt so good.

"We'll let you know if we find something interestin'," he said to Spike. Jilly taking his hand like that was all it took to tighten his heart. "Hey, Nat?"

"If the sheriff agrees, I'd like to hang around a bit," Nat said. "I'll get back with you later."

Spike wasn't the kind of guy who got his feathers in a fluff when an officer from another jurisdiction showed interest in a case. "Sure," he said.

To save time, Guy and Jilly drove to the front of All Tarted Up, crossed the deserted oncoming lane and parked facing the wrong direction. They also faced a Hummer that looked as out of place on one of Toussaint's streets as a tank would.

"Fancy new wheels, you think?" Guy asked. He could be wrong but the thing looked . . . pink?

"Not mine," Jilly said, leaning forward to get a better look. "I never saw one of those in Toussaint before. Guy, it looks pink."

"Uh-huh. To match the front door to the café, maybe?"

She leaned to the right and squinted down the side of the vehicle. Something had been painted there, but she couldn't read it.

"You've got to be wiped out," Guy said. "Why don't I call Spike and tell him I'm takin' you home. I'll come back and let him in—you don't have to be here."

Jilly sighed. "I don't want to be, but I do have to."

She got out and went straight ahead to the Hummer. The closer she got, the pinker it looked. "Will you look at this?" Jilly heard her own voice rise.

He was right behind her and didn't know if he should crack up or get mad as hell. "You didn't order this?"

"Of course I didn't. How could you even wonder if I did? And even if I did like ugly things, where would I get the kind of money these things cost?"

"You got a gift, then. And it's only a coincidence it came the day the Beetle got flattened. You don't order up somethin' like this in half a day."

"The Beetle's not flattened. Don't be so mean. It's a bit bent is all. It'll be just fine when they get through with it."

"You could be right," he told her. *And you could be wrong.*

Emblazoned in burgundy across the doors of the Hummer was the name of Jilly's shop, All Tarted Up. Underneath read, Flakiest Pastry in Town, and a big, shiny picture of Jilly's face smiled out from the dot at the bottom of an oversize exclamation point.

Bemused—and embarrassed—Jilly went to the other side and found the identical layout.

"Somethin' tells me Mr. Preston sent you a present," Guy said, seething. "He must have been plannin' on givin' it to you. Couldn't come at a more fortuitous time."

Jilly stood directly in front of him and stared into his face. "Could you put your dislike of Mr. Preston and

Edith behind you? At least for now? How do you think I'm feelin'? I don't want this thing. I won't have it. It's a joke. You're probably right about Mr. Preston arrangin' it, but he's only bein' kind and tryin' to show an interest in me."

"You can say that again." Now, that comment had been a mistake. "I'm sure you're right," he said in a hurry, but the look on her face let him know he was too late to get out of jail free.

"What did you mean by that?" Jilly said.

"What?"

"Guy, you were suggesting something nasty about Mr. Preston."

"You wouldn't jump to that conclusion if you hadn't felt somethin' weird about the way he is around you." He watched her look down. "Be honest with yourself. He can't keep his hands off you. You should stay away from him. Meet Edith somewhere in town—if you have to meet her."

"You're jealous." She said it in such a small voice he barely heard. "This is what you've been hoping for, a reason for me to brush off the closest thing to family I'm likely to have—other than Joe and Ellie. Why should you care, anyway? You've been pushing me away for months."

He didn't know why he did it. He sure didn't plan it, but he grabbed Jilly and hugged her, wrapped her so tightly against him, he shuddered. "You think I don't understand needin' to be needed? Or wantin' to love without being afraid you'll do someone harm

141

just by gettin' close to them?"

She hung on to his shirt. The tears that started were filled with struggling hope—and with confusion. Was it in her hands at all to influence what happened to them? "I made a terrible mistake this afternoon."

"Yesterday afternoon now," he corrected her. "And you didn't make a mistake. How could you?"

"Because I did, that's why. It was unthinkable and unforgivable. I didn't control myself and I'm not like that." Exhausted, she rested her face at the open neck of his shirt. "The only chance we have is to forget about it and start over."

He pushed a hand beneath her hair to stroke her neck. "You want us to get amnesia? Sorry—I'm not forgettin' one second of it."

She thought for minutes. "Okay, so what does that mean? We don't even get along most of the time."

"Only because I'm prickly. I could work on that."

"Guy. I—"

His mouth cut her off. He kissed her deeply, probing her mouth, sucking, turning her head from side to side with the intensity of his wanting her. Jilly made some tentative attempts to meet his tongue with her own before she grew more confident and stood on tiptoe to get leverage. Guy drew back and looked down into her eyes, reading her. He kissed her nose, then covered her lips with his own and pulled gently.

She fell against him. "Our timin' isn't the best."

"So what—it's working."

"With a murder victim on the other side of this

142

buildin' and a swarm of cops waitin' for us to let them into the café?"

"Look at me," he told her. "It may be late, but when the time comes I'm takin' you home. You need to sleep, then we need to talk. I'm ready for that."

"So am I."

An unearthly moan sounded behind Jilly. They both looked at the shop—and didn't see anything unusual.

"Give me the keys," Guy said.

Jilly went to the door herself. A letter slot below the window clacked and rattled. She turned to Guy. "I think there's someone hurt in there. We've got to be careful how we open the door."

Guy took the keys from her, unlocked the door and pressed it carefully, inch by inch, inward. He met no resistance. "Please get back, Jilly," he whispered. "You understand why."

She stepped away at once, but not very far.

Once the door stood open a little, a yipping, jumping Goldilocks forced her way out and flung herself on Guy, almost knocking him over. She stood on her hind legs with her front paws on his chest and did what came naturally; she leaned on him.

"How can she be here?" Jilly asked. "This is so creepy." She joined Guy to help calm the animal down. Goldilocks licked them both madly and rested her head on Guy's shoulder. She gave a huge sigh.

"She was locked in at your place," Guy said. "Every window was locked—I checked—and the dead bolts were on."

"So someone broke in."

"Looks that way." He patted the dog and disengaged from her. He turned and she tripped over the heel of one of his boots.

Guy trod on something hard. On the floor, right where they must have been pushed through the letter slot, lay a set of keys, and Guy picked them up, already knowing what they were. *Rathburn came here to deliver the Hummer for Preston.* Guy didn't intend to tell Jilly that. Spike was the one who needed to know.

"Guy." Jilly put an arm around his waist and sounded nervous. "Do you think Caruthers drove the Hummer over here for me? That would be the type of thing Mr. Preston would have him do. And it would explain why that poor man didn't have a vehicle anywhere around."

So much for keeping her in the dark. "I'm goin' to let Spike in."

"So you agree with me?"

He felt vaguely peeved. "It's obvious." Now he felt petty. "What we don't know is whether someone followed to take him home afterward."

Jilly nodded. She wasn't keeping score. "I want to know what's happened at my house. It isn't obvious to me how the dog got here—or why."

"Spike will send someone over there immediately."

Goldilocks leaned on his leg.

"She's fallen for you," Jilly said. "Look how she loves you."

144

He scratched between the dog's ears. "It's too bad I can't keep her."

He was being difficult, but Jilly intended to find a way around that.

Guy closed and locked the front door then followed Jilly past the tables and chairs, and the long, L-shaped counter he'd never seen empty before, through the kitchen and to the back door. She opened the door and peered into the yard.

Outside the activity had grown intense again. A woman was bagging the victim's bloodstained hands and Reb O'Brien Girard had arrived. A very pregnant Reb, whose husband, Marc Girard, stood a short distance away watching his doctor wife with a concerned crease between his brows. They were expecting their second child, but Marc was as edgy as he'd been the first time around.

Marc held the family poodle, Gaston, under his arm, and the dog leaped away and executed a graceful, rapid track to the kitchen door, where he pushed inside.

"Oh, no," Jill said. "He sensed there was another dog here."

She needn't have worried. Goldilocks, many times bigger than Gaston, lay on her back with her tongue lolling out of her mouth while Gaston investigated all points. Goldilocks got to her haunches for some face-to-face. Then they dropped down, side by side, and rested their heads on their paws—and closed their eyes.

"We've got a lot to learn from dogs," Jilly said. "We'd better get outside."

"You can lie naked on the floor for me anytime," Guy said. "And—"

"Outside, pervert," Jilly said.

Reb O'Brien Girard didn't even glance up from what she was doing with Caruthers's brains. Her thick red hair slid from a knot atop her head to hang in curly strands around her face.

At her side crouched Spike, who did see Guy. He got up and Nat took his place beside Reb while Spike skirted the canopy over the body. Marc came, too. A head taller than most men present, he followed the route Spike took.

"How does it look in there?" Spike asked, leaning through the door.

"Fine, except someone took Guy's dog from my place and locked her in the shop," Jilly said. "Gaston's keeping her company."

Spike swiveled back. "Turner. Take your partner and go to Jilly's house. Know where it is?"

A deputy called, "Yessir."

"Check for forced entry and watch out for anyone who doesn't belong there. Radio me."

"Someone could have gone in for a look around," Guy said. "Let the dog out and she ran here. It's not far."

Jilly looked unimpressed. "So how did she get inside?"

"Through the kitchen window." He inclined his head

and sure enough a window was open.

Jilly screwed up her eyes. "How could I have forgotten to close that?"

Guy told the story of the Hummer keys and the theory that Rathburn may well have brought the gift from Mr. Preston.

"Yeah." Spike and Marc looked puzzled at that.

Jilly looked away and Guy didn't want to pursue the topic. "Come and look at the vehicle with me. Could be a clue there."

Spike followed him with Marc bringing up the rear and Guy sighed his relief when Jilly didn't come with them. They went to the front sidewalk but didn't attempt to open up the Hummer.

"What is it?" Spike asked.

"Just now you looked as if you were about to say something about the Prestons."

"What made you think that?"

"You know what," Guy said.

Spike leaned his slim rump against one of the tables Jilly kept on the sidewalk. "Does it seem to you like Preston might be involved in somethin' here?"

"For obvious reasons I want to be cautious goin' in that direction," Guy said. "It's touchy business with Jilly."

"Of course it is," Spike said. "More likely to be an interrupted break-in, anyway."

"But the Preston setup doesn't seem quite right, does it?" Guy said. "I also think that man's tryin' to get his hands on Jilly." He wished he hadn't said that.

Marc muttered something negative. He made a slow circle of the Hummer.

Guy got a quizzical look from Spike. "When are you going to do something about you and Jilly?" he asked. "Now you're cookin' up stories about her stepfather being some sort of sexual predator. I think you see threats to her in every direction, and because you can't make up your mind to quit being her buddy and start taking her to bed, you're paranoid."

"Nice of you to pick your words so carefully."

"I think you can take it. Let's get back to the yard. Look how the dog follows you. She's a good-lookin' animal."

Only for Jilly's sake, Guy didn't tell Spike the dog was still a homeless stray.

"Take it from me," Marc announced, picking up Gaston again. "Once you want the woman, waiting to seal the deal can be dangerous."

What, Guy wondered, would they say if they knew he and Jilly had already come together like a pair of wild animals? He smiled slightly. "You could be right," he told Marc.

"I'm goin' to have to follow up on Preston," Spike said.

"Join Cyrus and me in New Orleans tomorrow. We've got some useful connections through Cyrus. His sister's married to a man who saw his father and mother murdered in their pool by the local mob. The dad was one of them, then said he was getting out of the rackets."

"I've met the Charbonnets. Nice people," Spike said. "Helluva story, Jack has. Gettin' away from the mob usually means being dead."

"I know," Guy agreed. "I don't know how much information you've got on Preston. He has a prestigious antiques firm and he's stinkin' rich."

"He's the one who uses a helicopter to get back and forth from New Orleans?" Marc asked.

"That would be the one."

Guy leaned against the Hummer and crossed his arms. "Jilly's house was locked up tight when we left," he said.

"Turner will call if he turns anythin' up," Spike said. "When I can get away I'll go over and take a look myself. I doubt I'll be able to take any time off for the next several days—unfortunately. Keep me in the picture." He went back into All Tarted Up and they all tromped through to the yard.

Guy wrestled with how much he should say to Spike about Edith Preston's injury. There was a lot of wisdom in the idea of not mixing business and pleasure. It made things messy.

"Reb looks great," Spike said, stepping outside again. "How much longer?"

"Six weeks or so," Marc said, glancing at Guy. "Soon enough that I don't want her out here, or anywhere else, alone. She did deliver the first one late, but the doctor says that doesn't mean it'll be the same this time around."

"I don't blame you for staying close," Spike said,

but his face hardened. A few months earlier he and his wife, Vivian, had lost a baby. The couple continued to mourn, even though they tried to put a cheerful face on their tragedy. It was rumored that another pregnancy might not be able to happen.

Jilly wandered in their direction and Guy found it harder to concentrate.

"I saw Wendy with Homer," Marc said, and glanced heavenward. None of them knew what to say or not to say around the Devols these days.

"She's always been his sidekick," Spike said of his daughter by a short first marriage. "I don't know what Vivian and I would do without her. Hey, Reb." He walked away.

"Shit," Marc said. "I mess up every time."

"No, you don't," Guy said, and liked it too much when Jilly arrived at his side. "He took it in stride. Speakin' of kids, who's with your boy?"

"Amy." Marc closed his mouth and appeared so startled Guy knew something was odd. He didn't say anything.

Marc caught his arm. "I'd be grateful if you wouldn't mention that to anyone. I wasn't thinking. Amy's my sister. She's been gone for years and there's too much history for right now. She isn't ready to deal with people in Toussaint, yet."

Guy said, "You've got it."

"Does Wazoo know Amy's here?" Jilly asked. "They were close, weren't they?"

"Yes," Marc agreed. "She'll have to know soon, but

150

we're letting Amy make her own moves. You know what she went through."

Very few people in Toussaint didn't know how the wife of a local businessman had set out to kill Amy Girard several years back. "I do know. It was horrible." Jilly dug her fingers into Guy's arm and felt him stare at her. "Excuse us, please," she said to Marc, and walked Guy away.

"What is it?" he said.

"You made a big deal out of wantin' me to lock the back of this place." Her spine prickled. "Like you knew this was going to happen."

"Whoa!" Guy swung her in front of him and backed her even farther away from the others. "You're absolutely right. I'd be disappointed if you didn't make that connection, but you're also absolutely wrong. I had no idea what might happen here—or if anything would happen at all."

"It looks suspicious to me." She put trembling fingers to her lips. "I don't mean it like that."

"Yes, you do. And it does. But I give you my word I had no idea someone would be murdered here tonight." With his hands on his hips, he bowed his head and tried to think of a way to convince her Rathburn's death was as much a shock to him as it was to her. "Would I have said anythin' to you if I thought it could incriminate me?"

"*Incriminate?* Hoo, you can make me steam, Guy Gautreaux. Did I say anythin' about incriminating you—you *dingbat?* What I meant was that you might

151

have known somethin' was going to happen for sure and you wanted to take care of me. I don't think you killed someone."

He had to smile. "Dingbat, hmm? I admit I've been called worse. I didn't know, but I was told somethin' that makes this death even more significant." He put his own fingers on her mouth. "I will try to keep you in the loop, okay?"

Condescending as usual. "Okay," she said.

"Turner called in," Spike said, joining them. "Living room window ajar in front. No prints except a dog's." He smiled. "You sure you closed that window?"

Jilly grimaced. "I did, but the lock doesn't work right. You can still open it."

"Well, someone did," Spike said. "Doesn't look as if he went in the house, just let the dog out for some reason."

"To bring her over here and make me nervous," Jilly said. "Weird."

Guy's expression was grim. "Why didn't you say the latch was broken? I'd have fixed it."

"Spike!" a member of the forensics team shouted. "Get over here."

The man faced a woman with a camera—the one who had passed with the body bag, Guy thought. She was the only member of the team in a skullcap.

"Yo," Spike called back, and left Guy and Jilly to join the couple.

"What's that about?" Guy said. He and Jilly moved a little closer, but not close enough to be too obvious.

"Now what?" Spike said.

"She doesn't belong here," the technician said, indicating the woman. "I don't know who she is but she isn't one of ours."

Marc groaned and hurried forward to help Reb to her feet. "Hold it," Reb said. "No harm's been done." She sounded tired and edgy.

The tech looked furious. "Someone wanders in off the street and takes pictures of a crime scene and no harm's been done? God knows what she's messed up around here. Gimme the camera."

Spike let out a big breath. "Lee, you know you can't do this."

"The press has a right to be here," Lee O'Brien said, whipping off her green skullcap and revealing her long blond ponytail. "You people are too used to running things around Toussaint and it's not going to work anymore. The people of this town have a right to know."

"Know what?" Spike asked, bending and bringing his face close to Lee's.

She waved her free hand—the other protected the camera she held to her chest—and said, *"Everything."*

11

"I can't see where a shop would have to close for a whole day just because some man got himself shot out back," Doll Hibbs, Wally's mom, said.

Madge Pollard concentrated on stirring her coffee and shifted uncomfortably. While Doll gave vent to her disapproval because All Tarted Up hadn't opened yesterday, Jilly marched around behind the counters wearing a cold and closed expression. Laura Preston seemed out of place, leaning against the tall cupboard where glasses and tableware were kept. She slouched there, all dressed in turquoise Lycra with a matching baseball cap pulled over her red curls, following Jilly's every move.

"The authorities had things to do around here, I expect," Madge said. Her tummy turned over. "It's a real serious thing. They have to look for any clues they can find."

"We know," Lil Dupre chimed in. "You aren't the only one who watches TV. And that man was shot in the head, not the back, Doll."

Doll glared at her. "I said he was shot *out back,* not *in the back.*"

"I don't often watch TV, me," Madge said mildly.

Lil was Ozaire's wife. She was also Cyrus's house-keeper, but that had never deterred her from speaking her mind. The woman also leaked any snippet of gossip she could—preferably from the rectory.

The three of them sat at the same table.

Wazoo popped in and out of the kitchens, making Madge wonder who was looking after Hungry Eyes for Ellie Gable today. She spoke up. "Wazoo, is the bookshop closed today?"

"My, no," Wazoo said. "I'm spending a few nights with Jilly at her place. I come here after and Missy Durand, she lookin' after the other place."

Madge didn't miss the significant look Wazoo sent her way, and frowned. A lot was going on and she decided she was being kept on the outside. She glanced out at the street, at the big pink vehicle parked there. "I like your new, er, car, Jilly," she said, smiling so widely her jaw ached.

"It's not my car," Jilly said, turning her back and slamming a coffeepot back on its burner. "I am so sick of all this messin' about. That thing's got to get moved and I don't care where just so long as I can't see it."

Madge smarted. It wasn't like Jilly to snap.

"You'll make Edith sad if you give back Daddy's present," Laura said. "Are you going to talk to me, by the way?"

Jilly faced her. "I'm all stretched out," she said. "It's been too much and I can feel there're things happenin' around here, only I'm not being told what. Will you please take the keys to the Hummer back to Edwards Place? Tell Mr. Preston he's real kind but I can't take a gift like that."

"He's not there," Laura said, snapping her fingers to the blues Jilly chose to play this morning. "He took Edith to the hospital in New Orleans, just to be safe."

"Safe from what?" Doll Hibbs asked. "She don't need to be kept safe from whatever killed that man out back of here. They'll have moved on by now. There's nothin' unsafe about Toussaint."

"Oh, yeah?" Wazoo said, wiggling her way from the kitchens, stamping her feet and moving to the music. "There never was a smarter woman than you, Doll Hibbs. You got a way of just nailin' things."

"What does that mean?"

Wazoo stopped behind Doll and tapped out the rhythm on the woman's shoulder. "Nuthin', or it could mean I thought one or two folks might already have figured that out."

"I wasn't talking about whether or not the town's safe," Laura said, shrugging away from the cupboard. "Daddy's takin' Edith for a checkup just to be sure she's gettin' better is all. She hasn't been well."

With their usual shy smiles, Ken and Jolene Pratt edged inside the shop.

"Will you look at that," Lil said, not quite softly enough. "Those two comin' in here like they belong."

"Hush," Madge said. "They do belong."

"You ask Wazoo about 'em," Lil said. "Ask her who goes into the graveyard at night and who you can't find there even if you go in right after 'em. You know all about it, don't you, Wazoo?"

"I got nuthin' to say, me." But Wazoo watched the

156

newcomers through narrowed eyes.

"Stop it," Madge said, embarrassed. "People are free to do as they please. If you don't believe me, ask Cyrus."

"He's too gentle," Lil said, but her expression softened. "The Lord should have put a suspicious bone or two in that man's body."

Madge didn't agree. "A person can't be too gentle." She didn't even try not to think about Cyrus the man anymore. They had their friendship with its pleasure and pain, and Madge knew she was maid of honor to the church. Being the bridesmaid rather than the bride didn't stop her from loving Cyrus.

"Mornin' to you," Jilly said to the Pratts. "It's good to see you."

The couple smiled and took a table as far as possible from Madge's group. Ken said, "How's Mrs. Edith?" to Laura.

"Still weak," Laura said. "But gettin' better, thank you. I think that tonic of yours helped."

"Tonic," Doll muttered. "They let a sick woman take somethin' from a pair of—you know what I mean."

"Will you have coffee?" Jilly asked the Pratts, going to their table with a carafe. "What can I get you to eat?"

"Father Cyrus likes the Pratts," Madge said quietly. "If you can't hold your tongues and quit insultin' people, I'll be leavin'."

Doll and Lil stared at Madge, then looked at each

other with the kind of knowing little smirks guaranteed to suggest they knew too much. Or that they were coming to conclusions they had no business to concoct.

Reb O'Brien Girard came in with Vivian Devol. "Hey, y'all," Reb said. "Guess the town's takin' a day off. Everybody's here."

"Almost everybody," Jilly said darkly. She stopped to take a mug from the cupboard and pour coffee for Laura. "Will you settle somewhere, please?"

"Hey, Reb, Vivian," Madge said. How easy could it be for Vivian, having lost a baby not so long ago, to be with very pregnant Reb?

The women pulled chairs from another table and joined Madge's party. "I met Reb on the way over here," Vivian said. "We figured we'd find sympathizers here. You know what I mean, Madge?"

She surely did. "Maybe. Absent friends of the male variety?"

"You've got it," Madge said. "Yesterday Cyrus was busy counsellin' people who were upset about the killin' the night before. Today he's gone on *important business*."

Madge wished she hadn't allowed her tongue to flap. "He's always busy. Just doesn't usually get going so early is all—unless Joe Gable's in town and they go runnin'."

Jilly couldn't contain herself a moment longer. "Can y'all believe this? A bunch of men who should know better, behavin' like silly boys playin' a game? Where were they yesterday? Someone tell me that."

Silence met her questions and she felt her face redden. She should have continued to keep her mouth shut. She still smarted from Guy's failure to as much as call about the breakfast they'd been supposed to have at the shop.

Vivian Devol tucked one side of her short black hair behind an ear. "You never saw such a scurry. I didn't see Spike from the night before last until late yesterday. There was so much goin' on. Other agencies came in and you know what that means around here."

"Spike's good about that," Jilly said. "He doesn't mess around before callin' in help."

"No, he surely doesn't, but it still makes for a lot of stress," Vivian said. "Makes the local guys feel like they're under microscopes. Same story today. Spike's up to his eyeballs in this case and holed up in that disgustin' office of his this time."

She should go in the kitchen and stay there, Jilly thought. "I was told to stay at home yesterday, and wait until I wouldn't be in the way around here. My own place, mind you. *In the way.*" Now she'd started talking and letting her anger out, she couldn't seem to stop. She had really expected to hear from Guy long before this.

"Marc got all involved yesterday," Reb said, easing herself into a more comfortable position. She didn't meet Jilly's eyes.

"So," Jilly said, feeling foolish, "they were just millin' around the place? Where? They wouldn't all be messin' with things here. Except for those who had a right to."

"I'm sure that's how it was," Reb agreed. "But they were all at the rectory with Cyrus for hours, too. In the afternoon. Isn't that right, Madge?"

Squirm. That was the only word for what Madge did. She squirmed and looked as if she'd like to disappear. "Yes," she said finally. "Shut away up there in Cyrus's room."

"You mean in his sitting room?" Jilly said. She'd never heard of anyone being invited into what she liked to think of as Cyrus's cell, up high beneath the eaves at the rectory.

"No siree," Lil said, her voice high and scraping. She could be having more fun than she'd had since they discovered someone was stealing bingo boards from the church hall and she set herself up as head detective. "They was in the Upper Room." She chuckled and tears gathered in the crow's-feet at the corners of her eyes.

"Lil," Madge said sharply. "You know Cyrus doesn't like you calling it that. He feels like you're makin' fun of the Last Supper."

Lil never had discovered who absconded with the bingo boards, and when Ozaire turned them up in one of the church's outbuildings, more than one person suggested Lil had put them there herself.

"They were in Father's own room," Lil said, all proper but not one bit apologetic. "You should be around that Nat Archer. The mouth he's got on him?

Whooee, liquid silk with a sandpaper lining, and as cheeky as you like. I'm glad Guy Gautreaux thinks he's wonderful because I think he's the only one . . . 'cept Wazoo." Lil crossed her arms and the smug expression was back.

Wazoo hugged herself, threw back her amazing hair and closed her eyes. "He's one killer man. And *silk* ain't the way I'd describe his voice, no way. More like rough tweed—or burlap. So-o sexy. Thank goodness I'm the only woman around here who can judge a man by the way he *feels*. Not that he isn't a wicked good-looker."

"What d'you mean?" Doll asked. "The way he feels? You not supposed to be feelin' no strangers, Wazoo. I don't know how Vivian and Spike put up with you, to say nothin' of Charlotte." Charlotte was Vivian's mother and part-owner in Rosebank.

Vivian only chuckled and wrinkled her nose at Wazoo, who gave her a sidelong glance that spelled nothing good. "You know what *feel* means," she said, stroking her upper arms with her crossed hands. "*Feel,* oh, yeah. Dancin' in the dark, skin to skin, nipple to nipple, hips locked together, all the hot fluids runnin', sweet, slick bodies slidin' and rockin'."

The laughter began. Laura Preston fell into a chair at an unoccupied table and held her stomach.

"Mmm, mmm, mmm." Wazoo at her bad best was something. "Oh, yeah, I got to get me more of that sweetness." She looked at Vivian with completely clear eyes. "I still think you're missin' a bet not providing some special extras for unaccompanied females at Rosebank. Remember the stuff I suggested with fans coolin' moist skin, and massage—and feathers, some of that tasty lube in kinky tubes and a dinky diggle thing. Whoo! You'd have those ladies linin' up to be repeat customers."

"Dinky diggle thing?" Madge said, leaving her lips parted.

"You ain't got a dinky diggle, Madge? Well I'm just goin' to have to fix that. You want yellow—like a banana, or plum-purple? They taste to match the color."

Reb rubbed her face with both hands but Jilly saw how she smiled. Jilly wasn't sure what this diggle was but she had a good idea. She took two plates of beignets, fresh from the fryer, and put one on Madge's table and another in front of the Pratts, who were obviously listening but not saying a thing.

"A beignet, Miss Laura?" Jolene asked Laura, offering the plate.

Jilly expected Laura to refuse, but she took one immediately and smiled her thanks. She set the roll on a napkin, then took a bite and closed her eyes in ecstasy. Powdered sugar flew in all directions.

"Café au lait," she whispered as if in a trance. "I'm comin' back there to make some for everyone. On me all around."

"Ooh, fancy that," said Lil, who enjoyed anything free.

Instead of letting fly with her instinct to tell Laura

she didn't have to make anything around here, Jilly smiled at her and let her get to work. The atmosphere in the shop grew almost jolly. Jilly wished she could put aside her own concerns and join in.

"Laura," she said quietly. "I'm goin' into New Orleans to see Edith tomorrow."

"I wouldn't," Laura said, adding hot milk to coffee. "Daddy's angry about everything at the moment so it's best not to get around him."

"That's nothing to me," Jilly told her sharply. "It's Edith I intend to visit. Which hospital is she in?"

The jug Laura held wobbled and milk splashed on the counter. She grabbed a cloth and wiped it up. "I don't think for a moment she'll be in a hospital tomorrow," she said. "She was just going to be checked over then go home."

"Home here, you mean."

"Home in the Garden District. Prytania Street. Real close to St. Charles Avenue."

"An apartment?" Jilly asked.

"Hunsingore House. It's a beauty," Laura responded. "Wes and I live there, too, when we're in N'awlins."

Jilly had no concept of how Edith and Mr. Preston lived in New Orleans. She'd never been to their place there, never been invited. Tomorrow she would find this house, and meanwhile, she'd say nothing more to Laura. There was a big problem to deal with right here before the day was out and his name was Guy.

As if she'd summoned him up by thinking his name,

the man walked into the shop. He looked in the region of her face but didn't meet her eyes. Passing the counter, not bothering to greet anyone else present, he said, "I'll be in the kitchen," to Jilly, and strolled out there as if he owned the place.

"How are you coming with that?" Jilly asked Laura, praying to keep her temper and her voice down. She picked up two cups and walked over to the Pratts' table.

Laura passed her on the way back. "I'm doin' just great here. How about Wazoo and I watch the shop while you go talk to Mr. Sunshine?"

Already toting four cups, her fingers wound through the handles, Wazoo headed to the tables and gave Jilly a smile and a nod as she went.

Okay, curtain time. She found Guy, with his back to her, apparently examining the back door. He looked as if he'd just got out of the shower. His damp hair stood in wet spikes, he was clean shaven, and he wore a gray-and-white-striped shirt tucked into blue jeans. The shirt actually had creases down the sleeves from an iron and she doubted he was the kind to take clothes to the cleaners. On the other hand, she couldn't visualize him at an ironing board.

"What did I tell you?" he said, swinging around. He must have felt her behind him.

"Which order would that have been, specifically? You give so many." *Step carefully, buddy.*

"I told you to keep this door locked and it's not. Didn't you get the picture the other night? A man got shot at point-blank range in your backyard. What does it take to make you wake up? A bullet in . . ." He crammed his mouth shut and glared at her.

Jilly glared back, even if she did feel anything but sure of herself. "A bullet in my head? Was that what you were going to say? Wouldn't that do the reverse of wake me up? You can be so mean."

"You drive me to it. I'm— Shoot, Jilly, I'm tryin' to take care of you."

"Don't bother, I'm not your responsibility."

"The hell you're not. I've made you my responsibility, so get used to it."

"Keep your voice down. You'd better leave. Any minute there'll be people wantin' cooked breakfasts. And the door has been locked. I expect some garbage was just taken out."

"You're mad at me," Guy said, taking a step toward her.

Jilly didn't retreat. "You don't understand me, but that's not your fault."

"This is because I couldn't come back to you the night before last."

"When you arranged for Wazoo to move in with me, you mean? Why would that make me mad? I surely didn't want you clomping in expectin' to be waited on at whatever hour in the mornin' you decided to show up. Anyway, I'm used to being disappointed." She didn't want to think about past patterns.

"See, you are mad. Why try to hide it?"

"You have a dog at my house and she's grievin' for

165

you. Never did understand a dog's loyalties. I'll lend you a key to go over and get her. Lock up behind you, please. Wouldn't want to get shot in the head when I go home."

"Jilly." His voice softened and he looked pained. "I didn't come to fight."

"Why, forgive me for mistaking your shouting at me for fighting words. I should have known you were bein' nice. I don't want to discuss any of this, not now, not ever. Here's the key." She put it in his hand. "Leave it there. I've got another one."

"I worked all through that night," he said quietly. "If I could have, I'd have come to you—that's what I wanted. Yesterday I went with Nat into New Orleans to see if we could find anything on Rathburn. We didn't. Then we got back and—"

"Spent hours shut away with Cyrus," she finished for him. He should have called and if he didn't know it, he was beyond civilizing.

"I intended to call you."

"Intended?" So he thought of calling her and still didn't do it.

"The time got away from me."

"You look well rested to me. You could have picked up a phone at some point. And, let me see, did I forget, or did you bother to mention the breakfast we were supposed to have here?"

"We couldn't have it here." He scrubbed at his hair. "Why do women have to keep pickin'? Wazoo was with you last night and the night before. I didn't want

166

to interrupt and I could hardly have turned up for a romantic evenin', could I?"

"You could have said something about eatin' somewhere else yesterday mornin'." Her eyes prickled and she blinked. "And I'm not interested in any romantic evenings with you. Or romantic anythings." Darn, why did it hurt so much that he could be casual and harsh?

"I wanted to tell you I'm goin' back to New Orleans tomorrow morning and I'll spend the night there."

"You don't owe me any explanations. Just pick up Goldilocks and be good to her."

"She's not my dog."

"Oh, Guy, quit! Take that nice animal and get lost."

He put his hands on his hips and jutted his chin, and then moved so fast she couldn't begin to fend him off. "Not here," she said. But Guy ignored her warning and gathered her up in a tight hug instead. He lifted her from her feet and kissed her until she couldn't catch a breath. Then he set her down and grinned with that pure male satisfaction that could make a woman furious—or helpless.

"Admit it," he said. "You missed me."

She shook her head and smiled, even though she'd rather bite him. "Whatever you want to hear, hear it," she told him.

"Like I said, you missed me." He slipped a hand around her neck and pulled her so close she had to look up at him. "But not as much as I missed you. I'm in a bad place, Jilly—with the killin', and what Nat

167

has told me, and some history that may fit in to all of it if I can just put it together.

"I've got to get out and talk to Homer. I'm worried about how he may be reactin' to me showin' up at all odd hours. He deserves to be able to count on me bein' on a schedule. I know he gave me a job because you were all worried about me being a morose son of— being morose—but he did, and does need help. I told him I'd be around and reliable for a long time, and if I did decide to go back to New Orleans, he'd get plenty of notice. I want to work for him. The job keeps me grounded. Anyway, he may be waitin' to fire me by now."

"Homer wouldn't do that," Jilly said, shocked at the idea. "All you have to do is explain what's goin' on."

He brought his face close to hers and spoke into her ear. "That's the one thing I can't do. And I'm askin' you not to share a thing I tell you."

She didn't understand, but she nodded.

"You are special, Jilly. Probably too special for me." He kissed the corner of her mouth and played there with the tip of his tongue. "I came because I had to. I get so lonely for the sight of you." His hands, covering her breasts, shocked her, but she moved into him. Guy kissed her again.

Jilly shuddered, returned the kiss—quick and hard—and stepped away. "When will you get back from . . ." She mustn't ask when he'd be back. He wasn't even leaving till tomorrow.

"As soon as I can," he said.

She followed him into the shop, where the volume of conversation should be a whole lot louder and said, "Bye," in as normal a voice as she could manage when he left.

Guy opened the door again and beckoned to Jilly. She went to him and he put his lips on her ear. "Any problems while I'm gone, you call Spike, got it?"

"Got it."

"I feel better just seein' you." He looked into her face.

Jilly whispered, "Okay," and he strode away.

When she turned back to the café not a soul would meet her eyes, except Wazoo, who actually looked as if she wanted to cry. With all the equipment humming in the kitchen, they couldn't have heard what she and Guy said.

"The table by the window wants cooked," Wazoo said, rocking back and forth and sniffing. "Muffulettas and hush puppies with red beans on the side. I'll get started."

She swept away to the kitchen, her black-and-purple silk skirts swishing and floating. And the instant she was out of sight, Reb got up and took Jilly aside. "I don't know how Lil knows Marc's sister, Amy, is with us at Clouds End, but she does. And she took pleasure in letting Wazoo know. Wazoo and Amy were friends and now Wazoo's feelings are hurt because Amy hasn't gotten in touch with her."

Wazoo stuck her head from the kitchen door and beckoned to Jilly. "We're bein' made fools of," she whispered. "Every which direction there're secrets and we—you and me—got to dig deep and get the truth. Reb just told you about Amy, didn't she?"

"I don't think it's all that bad," Jilly said.

"Not that bad," Wazoo said. "You plain don't know, Jilly. In case you forgot I sang at Amy Girard's first funeral."

12

"I left the front door open, me," Wazoo said, out of breath more from excitement than exertion, Guy thought. She'd just run from Jilly's driveway and up the street a way to meet him. "Jilly, she think I gotta go back to Rosebank."

Guy bent over her. "You told her that's what the call was? You said my call was really from someone at Rosebank?"

"I did. I wasn't about to risk her refusin' to see you, not me."

Guy whipped off his hat and ran a hand through his hair. "Wazoo, you are a kind woman with a good heart."

"No such thing," she said. "Ask anyone."

He had to smile. "You're right," he told her. "I was tryin' to be generous, is all. But you did an unfortunate thing, my friend. More unfortunate for you than me."

"How you figure that, handsome?"

Guy shook his head slowly. "Because Jilly is going to know you set her up. As soon as I tell her I called to let her know I was comin' over and you said she was in the shower, I reckon your name will be mud."

She laughed, a rich, low sound that demanded smiles. "Hah. I always did say men got a bi-ig handicap. They logical. What they don't remember is we women logical *and* sneaky. Now I gotta go."

He stepped in front of her before she could make a dash for her van at the curb in front of Jilly's. "Sneaky? Did you do somethin' sneaky? Now, Wazoo, you know you don't want to come between Jilly and me. You do that and you might get squashed."

"All you gotta do is tell the truth and shame the devil, Guy Gautreaux. I left to do you a favor. Now, don't you go lettin' on it was you who called me."

"You females can drive a man crazy," he said. *And how.* "All you had to do was tell her I was comin'. It's not a big deal."

"Out of my way, lover boy. You not thinkin' at all. She madder than a gator with rubber teeth at you— even if she does go all misty-eyed when she thinks she's not bein' watched. She's thinkin' 'bout you, but no way you'd get in tonight 'less I helped you. Now *go on.*"

"Get in the van," Guy said, checking around. "Get in and lock your doors."

Her black eyes caught the moonlight and he thought she gave him a quizzical look, but she got into the van and he heard the locks click. She rolled down the window. "I decided I like you after all," Wazoo said. "Come closer and I'll give you some advice."

"Do I have a choice?" He walked to her door.

"No choice at all." He smelled her musky scent and recalled the way Nat looked at her. "What's the advice?"

"You missed out once, lover boy. No!" Her hand shot through the window and she grabbed a handful of his shirt before he could turn away. "Quit runnin' from the past, from the truth. You lost a woman you loved a lot and you been blamin' yourself ever since. How could you have known she'd die lookin' at some piece of jewelry she wished you to buy for her. She never told you about it. It could just have been some other woman left alone in that shop when a crazy man came in. She was in the wrong place at the wrong time. My advice is that you don't put that dear lost girl between you and Jilly. Leave her out here. Let her go. She'll be happy for you."

Guy couldn't take his eyes off Wazoo's face. She held him fast with the challenge she'd made. And, damn it, she was right—but he also knew it was easier to know what a man should do than it was for the man to do it. "Okay," he said at last. "I understand. Thank you."

She let him go, rolled her window up again and drove off.

The walk from the curb to Jilly's front door didn't take long enough. He wanted to keep this visit light and start making Jilly really comfortable with him again. Hey, so that wasn't all he wanted. He might be tired, but he wasn't dead yet, and making love, long and slow, or fast and wild . . . A message came from a southern region. "Down," he muttered, turning away from the house.

Jilly heard a voice outside. The door was ajar and she eased it open. Guy stood there with his back to her.

"Get *down*," he said.

"You get down!" Jilly threw herself on the hall floor and peered up at Guy. "Right now. Omigod, where's your gun? Don't you have a gun anymore?"

He spun around, crouched and reached to pat the top of her head. "It's okay. There's nothing wrong."

"Don't *do* that patting stuff to me," she told him. "Who's out there? *Get in here, Guy Gautreaux.* On your stomach and crawl. Backward. No, forward. Better get shot in the foot than the head."

"Or the rear. Don't you ever change, you," Guy said. He sprang into the hall and landed on his haunches beside Jilly's prone body, stuck out a hand, shut and locked the door. "What a greetin'."

She angled her head to look at him. Jilly didn't look too amused. "Just what do you think you're doin'? Opening my front door and standing outside tryin' to scare me to death."

Wazoo, you did this to me. "I didn't actually open it. Honestly, I didn't. Don't be mad, cher—I had to come and see you." He dropped to sit cross-legged.

His "I wouldn't do anything bad" little-boy expression almost made Jilly laugh. Almost. "Why did you tell me to get down?"

"I didn't . . . Not you . . ."

He was being weird. "Who, then?"

"Isn't the floor hard?"

"I'm comfortable, thanks," she said, but scrambled to her feet. "Who were you talkin' to?"

"*Women.* You never can leave a thing alone." This was funny, but he really didn't have a clever escape route.

She surprised him by offering a hand and then pulling him as if she could lift him from the floor. "Is someone hiding out there watching the house for you?" she asked.

"Nope."

"You can tell me. He was too obvious so you told him to get down so he wouldn't be seen?"

Why was it so difficult for him to explain himself to her?

He could say she was right, but knowing his luck she'd insist on going out to say hi. "I threw a rock at a stump. Looked like it went too high and I was goin' to miss. So I said, get down."

"What stump?"

Shee-it. "Post. Gatepost or somethin'." *Will you let it go?*

"Weird," she said. "The last time you threw rocks around here, you broke a window."

"I'm still embarrassed about that, okay?"

"Forget it." She tightened the sash on her robe.

"Wazoo must have left the door open by accident. She had to go back to Rosebank."

"Good."

Jilly decided to let that pass. He must be as edgy as she was and it wouldn't hurt her to be kind. She wanted to be kind.

"Come on in," she said. "Question is, where? I don't like the sitting room anymore—all I can think of is someone getting through the window and taking Goldilocks to the shop. Weird."

Guy faced her in the hall, turning his hat in his hands. "Who told you they came inside? I thought they just let Goldilocks out."

"I guess Turner didn't come in. But Spike did and he said someone had entered. Does it matter? They got in and out of that window. They'd gone through things but left them more or less tidy and nothing seems to be gone. I feel weird all the time, though."

"*Weird*'s your word of the day, hmm?"

Jilly frowned at him. "The windowsill is scratched, and the wall, but the cops couldn't find any evidence to use."

"I'll put on a fresh coat of paint for you."

"Guy! Don't you think this is weird, standing in the hall talkin' like this?"

Now she mentioned it . . . "Yes. Could we sit in the kitchen?"

"There's a crack where the curtains don't meet. Someone could see in."

"You plannin' on doin' something you wouldn't

175

want anyone else to see?" He closed his mouth.

"We'll go in the sitting room."

He didn't like seeing her so uptight. "Would you feel better in your bedroom?"

Jilly laughed. "Oh, boy, you do have a way with words. This is one weird night. I think Goldilocks followed the criminal around, pointin' out anything he might have missed. Then she jumped out the window after him and followed him to All Tarted Up. I'm grateful he shut her inside rather than shootin' her."

"So am I," he said, and meant it. He smiled at her. "Hey, where is that dog?"

"Asleep on my bed, I guess. She sleeps a lot."

"Damn it," Guy said, then went to the foot of the stairs and shouted, "Goldilocks, get down here, you good-for-nothing hound. *Now*."

The next sound infuriated Jilly. "Idiot," she said, bounding past Guy and up the stairs. "She's scratching the inside of the door to pieces. I thought you were supposed to come and pick her up earlier."

He knew better than to follow Jilly. "I'm sorry," he said. Visions of a romantic interlude grew paler.

Goldilocks threw herself downward to Guy. She rubbed against his legs and licked his hand, then gave a great sigh and leaned on him, panting. "Good girl," he said. Poor mutt couldn't be blamed for her situation. "You're supposed to be a watchdog, though. You're no good snoozin' on Jilly's bed." Oh, but he would be real good snoozing on Jilly's bed—in an hour or so. "And what's this about you helpin' burglars put the goodies in their bag? You're gettin' fat. Don't feed her so much."

"Take your own advice. She's yours."

Jilly sat on the top step with the corners of her mouth turned up and a thoughtful expression in those big hazel eyes. Guy had never seen a more gut-wrenching woman. Her hair, too many shades of gold through blond for him to count, shone thick and a little unruly—like she'd got out of the shower and hadn't dried it.

You are good, Guy Gautreaux. She got out of the shower and didn't have time to dry her hair because you showed up. Jilly held her knees together, and her toes. Her heels turned out. The little pink cotton robe, cinched at the waist and short enough so he could see a couple of inches at the backs of her thighs looked as sexy as a skimpy bra and a pair of tap pants. He never had gotten past finding tap pants paralyzing—mostly paralyzing.

He had come to be with her, Jilly realized. For no other reason. She'd bet her life on it. And if she didn't keep a tight hold on herself, she'd be repeating her attack act. *Not cool, Jilly.* From the way he stayed where he was, she'd say he didn't have anything phys-ical in mind. He just wanted to talk, maybe to ease things between them.

His head tilted to one side, he regarded her straight in the eye and he didn't flinch or blink. He did shift his feet now and then—and he put his hands on his hips, jutted his pelvis ever so slightly. Jilly parted her lips to breathe. When a woman's darkest places almost itched and she knew the only way to scratch that fabulous itch was by taking the only man she wanted inside her, she was the luckiest woman in the world. She was also up a creek without a paddle—that being because the broad-shouldered, tall, all-muscle man looking back at her owned the only paddle likely to do what needed to be done.

Slowly her eyes closed and she heard a crackle, just a little crackle. A bayou night sensation—the kind that happened when the moon went away and the spaces filled up with the snick and rustle of a million invisible critters, and the shush-shush of willow branches dancing a delicate dance in a breeze you hardly felt on hot, moist skin.

"Can I come up, Jilly?"

Hair stood up on the back of his neck. He wasn't subtle.

"If you want to." For months they'd managed to be wary buddies, the sex kept under control even though they knew it was there, begging to get out. She'd opened the door and there would be no going back. "There are chairs." And she wasn't fooling either of them.

He went up slowly, leaving the dog at the foot of the stairs. At least the critter had the sense to know when she wasn't wanted. Jilly remained where she was, sitting on the step at the top. "Does any of this scare you?"

"To death," she said.

Guy stopped. "I don't want to do anything to frighten you. I'd never hurt you."

"I'm scared to death a day will come when I find out you're gone. New Orleans, wherever, but gone and never coming back."

What was he scared of? He knew the answer and he owed it to Jilly to get over it. "Wanting to be with you the way I do, shakes me up, but I do want it. I couldn't just drop out." He tried a smile. "Anyway, you'd track me down and by the time you finished with me, I'd wish I'd stayed put."

This was going to take more than smiles. Sweat popped out on his brow. He flexed muscles turned stiff with tension.

Once more she extended a hand to him, and he continued up to take a firm hold. When she started to get up, he stopped her and raised her face. One by one, he kissed her eyes shut. Kneeling just below her feet, he raised her left hand to his mouth and rested his lips there.

He knew about turning her soft with his sweetness, Jilly thought. His dishwater hair, bleached at the ends by the sun, stood up where he'd run his fingers through it. She smoothed it absently—the center of her attention hovered where his mouth rested on her hand. Starting at the back of her ankle, he smoothed her skin, moving inch by inch to the touchy place behind her knee. With his fingers curled around, he slid the pad of his thumb back and forth. Her bottom shifted forward on the step and she tried to close herself up tight. She was wet and feared for a moment that she might climax. Sitting there, with Guy at her feet and doing nothing more than passing her hand from his mouth to his cheek, and smoothing that erogenous little place on her leg he seemed to know all about, Jilly felt the building pressure. She sucked her belly in tight and held back.

"Jilly," he said. "We fight like pros, but I think we could love with just as much . . . you know what I mean." Her eyes were closed again, her lips pale and parted as if she couldn't breathe. Carefully, he shifted his hand to the back of her thigh and felt her jump. "You do know what I mean, don't you?"

"Yes." She leaned over him and pressed his face to her breasts. "When I'm with you I hardly know who I am."

"You're Jilly Gable. One sweet, sexy woman, and the things you do to me—I don't want you to stop doin' them."

With his palm under her leg and his fingers curled between her thighs, he moved on until he felt her panties and the sensation of thin fabric moving over hair—and dampness.

He had to hold on. Pulling his head away from her, he sucked on her bottom lip, nipped at it, and massaged between her legs. Her cry was filled with pleasure.

The robe gaped. Except for the panties, she was naked underneath. Loathe to leave her begging for release, but drawn on to take her as high as he could,

Guy spread the robe open, and weighted her full breasts. When he stroked around and around, never quite touching her nipples, she arched her back and panted.

Only the picture of pure sexuality that she made kept him from losing everything right then. He wanted to watch her like this for as long as he could hold on.

"Guy," she whispered. "Come to bed."

Wonderful words, lady. "Do you have to go anywhere soon, cher?"

"Not unless you're with me. Do you?"

"No. We've got all night and I think we can use it up, don't you?"

At last he closed his mouth over one of her nipples and she cried out. At the same time, he returned to the hot place between her thighs, slid his thumb inside her panties, along slick flesh, and stroked her there, long and gradually harder.

"Guy!" Her hands fell away from him. She held the edge of a stair and her hips reared up. "This isn't right."

"Oh, yes, it is." He replaced his thumb with his tongue and played out the parody until her release. With his face on her belly, he blew into her navel but stopped long enough to say, "You were ready."

"Oh." She lay flat on the landing with her legs resting on the edges of the stairs. "I don't know what you think of me. I guess I'm a frustrated old maid, huh?"

"Mmm." He started pulling down her panties.

181

Of course he needed more. Jilly unsnapped his jeans but couldn't make more progress with them. She whipped the buttons on his shirt undone instead and he shrugged it off. He raised her bottom and shifted her legs around until he had her completely naked. Laughing, he got rid of his jeans, rolled them up and pushed them beneath her head and shoulders.

"You look like something I ought to eat," Guy told her. He already had the taste of her on his lips and tongue. His elbows beside her shoulders, his knees somewhere or other, he brought the end of his penis to the opening of the place it wanted to go and poked, just a small poke, and withdrew, and poked again, farther this time.

"You get the tease prize," Jilly said. She still throbbed, but she was ready for him. "C'mon, *please.*"

"We've got to savor these moments." He laughed and said "ouch" when she managed to pinch his butt.

He bounced in and out of her, never going so far he couldn't retreat.

"Ooh. Guy! Dammit, my back hurts."

"Romantic," he told her, chuckling and hurting with his own need. "Okay, you asked for it." *And I want it.*

Jilly gasped, and shrieked. Guy picked her up by the waist and ran the last step to the landing, turned and took the steps to her bedroom at a run, almost falling forward with her as he went.

He was afraid he'd kill them both, but what a great death. Turning on a light wasn't an option. Tumbling with Jilly onto her bed, he drove into her. Two strokes and she pushed at him. "On your back," she said, and on his back he went.

With her breasts swaying over him, she finished what he'd started far too quickly. "Jilly," he said, gripping her arms. "Don't move. Please stay right where you are. Just gimme a little time. Just a few seconds."

"Long as you want," she said quietly. "Let me lie on your chest."

He released her arms and she did as she'd said she would, her breasts flattened to his chest, her damp face tucked into his neck. She stayed closed tight around him and he let his arms spread wide on the bed.

Those seconds he'd mentioned passed, tick, tick, tick, and he was going to show her he didn't make hollow promises.

"Mmm," she said, stirring. "I'm getting a message."

"I'm sending you one. I need to get closer to you, Jilly."

She rose up and started to move.

"Hold it, cher," he told her. "Keep still and let me do the work this time. Just don't let go of me down there. Er, yeah, let me go."

"But—"

"We'll both be glad you did."

He moved fast, diving for the other end of the bed. He arranged Jilly on her side, lifted her upper leg and wriggled until they lay threaded together, a leg in front and a leg behind each other's body. Guy smoothed her foot, kissed her toes, reveled in feeling their most sensitive parts rubbing together. "Hold my hands," he said.

She started to giggle but took hold of his hands. "Why are you down there?" she said, choking on her own words. "Oh, man, Guy."

End to end, literally, nothing stopped him from doing his manly best to reach her throat with his penis from a long, long way down. They ground their entwined fingers together and pulled, rocking, moaning.

He filled her up. The man knew a thing or two and so far she liked whatever he chose to share with her. In the semidarkness, with her head on the pillow and his somewhere beyond her feet, they rocked and pressed, released a fraction, and pulled and drove again. Her heart beat so, she heard it inside her head.

She burned up. He touched inner places with sensations she'd never known of, never hoped to feel. She heard his breathing speed up. They banged together.

"Guy!" Again she climaxed, and in the mad, thundering tumble she heard his voice but not what he said.

He dropped her hand but stroked her stomach and gradually maneuvered himself beside her. "Jilly, sweets, we have wasted a lot of time."

She turned her head and looked into his shadowy face. "You're right."

"I don't want to waste any more."

"No." But she wasn't foolish enough to think their

lives were about to become idyllic. "I'm glad you came tonight."

He buried his face in the pillow, surrounded her with an arm and pulled her close. "I'm cold."

Jilly pulled the quilt over them.

"There's more than sex for us," he said. "Not that the sex wouldn't be enough for most people."

"It would never be enough for me. Let's leave it there for now, shall we? Wait and see?"

He raised his head and looked at her. "Okay. Of course." He should feel relieved, so why didn't he?

13

"Are you stiff, Guy?" Nat said when they'd parked the Pontiac in the closest spot they could find to the address they wanted on Chartres Street. "You hurt somewhere?"

"Hell, no," Guy said, and he lied.

Delivery trucks clogged the streets in the Quarter. Drivers yelled at anyone and everyone to get out of their way, just as they did every day—not that startled tourists knew the bad banter was just part of the ritual.

Warm mist pressed down and with it, the sweet and not-so-sweet scents of the place. Guy took in a deep breath and coughed. Moisture filled his nostrils and his lungs felt wet.

They were just around the corner on Conti, and a

five-minute walk would get them to Jack and Celina Charbonnet's home on Chartres. "This guy used to be part of the mob?" Guy said. "The Giavanellis?"

"No, no," Cyrus said. He walked a little ahead of Guy and Nat, probably in a hurry to see his sister, Celina, and the kids, of course. "His father was, and his father was taken out when he tried to quit the family."

Nat barked out a laugh. "Listen to yourself, Father. Those words roll off your tongue like you say 'em every day."

"I've been around," Cyrus said, but his grin gave him away. Cyrus wore his collar today and seemed oblivious to the attention he got from females he passed.

"D'you think women just have a thing for priests?" Guy said. He *was* stiff, dammit, and he had pulled a muscle or two. What he needed was a lot more practice.

Nat elbowed him and drew a hiss. "You are hurtin', bro. But I guess I'll leave that alone. Priests are mysterious." He raised his voice. "Aren't they, Father Cyrus? Women find priests mysterious, and sexy."

"Shut up," Guy said under his breath.

"Absolutely," Cyrus said. "It gets to be a chore fightin' them off all the time."

Nat made explosive sounds and Guy thumped his back. A tall black woman in a rich red robe that showed glimpses of four-inch red heels as she walked, paused in front of Cyrus and said, "Good mornin',

Father," in the kind of full and deep voice a man never forgot.

Cyrus said, "Good mornin' to you."

A beauty with fine features, she wore a red turban and looked, Guy thought, like an exotic goddess. Not that Cyrus would appreciate that idea.

"Father, I'm an honest woman and I got to tell you, I ain't never seen a better-lookin' man than you."

Nat hooked his arm through Guy's. "Let's see him get out of this one," he said.

"I try," Cyrus said. "But we all have to struggle to please the Lord. Could be I look better than I really am. I'm the pastor at St. Cécil's in Toussaint. If you're ever out that way, I hope you'll celebrate mass with us. Good day to you, friend."

With a nod and smile, on he walked, leaving the woman to first gawk, then break into the kind of laughter that might come from a perfectly tuned trombone.

"Sheesh," Nat said, "and I thought she'd manage to embarrass him. Okay, we must be about there." He dodged a kid on a glitter-covered skateboard. Green glitter. The sidewalk being so narrow meant the three men walked almost in single file.

"Some of these places are worth a fortune," Guy said. "What am I sayin'? They're all worth a fortune." Flats, some with wrought-iron-fronted galleries, stacked above ground-floor shops. Massed petunias overflowed from pots and trailed between railings.

A man in silver shoes, baggy jeans held up by his

very round butt and no shirt unfolded from where he'd been curled up on the sidewalk, and danced.

"Man, I love this town," Nat said, tipping his straw fedora over his eyes.

The dancer twirled, tapped, rose to the tippy toes of his shoes and walked like a cat-man on the prowl. Damp air gave his body a shiny glow.

Nat tossed the guy a bill and Cyrus immediately followed suit. Guy looked heavenward, but added to the man's purse.

"This is it." Cyrus stood before a shiny black door with a brass, dragon-shaped knocker—which he used. "Dragon Prince. Named after a stuffed animal. Two years ago Jack and Celina bought the place next door and made two flats into one. They've got three kids now, Amelia is Jack's, Deck is Celina's, and Leah is Jack and Celina's. They're ten, five and two."

"You're sure Jack will be here now?" Guy asked, digesting the idea of stuffed dragons important enough to warrant effigies on door knockers.

The sound of footsteps running downstairs came from inside.

"He will," Cyrus said. "Most nights Jack's on his riverboat till late. In the daytime he writes and helps run a major charity with Celina."

Once bolt and chain were taken off, the door opened and a girl looked out. She didn't waste time on Guy and Nat but launched herself at Cyrus, leaped from the ground and wrapped her arms around his neck. "Uncle Cyrus," she said, covering his face with kisses. "I've been waiting for you since I woke up."

"And I've been waiting to see you since I woke up, Miss Amelia," Cyrus said, hugging his niece back. "Maybe we should be quiet if Leah's asleep." He set the child on her feet.

Amelia's black curls reached her shoulders and she had very green eyes. For ten, she was a small girl, all sharp joints and slender limbs—insubstantial. She was also a striking child with the promise of becoming a knockout woman.

"Quit hogging the company," a woman's voice called from above. "Cyrus? Get up here, Brother."

"Leah's at the park with Tilly." Amelia looked at Guy and Nat and said, "Tilly is our helper. Uncle Cyrus, sometimes it gets hard with little kids around. We got a break today, though. Deck wanted to stay home, too, but he's got to practice for a play at school. He's in kindergarten." When she said "kindergarten," she wrinkled her nose.

Cyrus took the child's hand and walked inside, indicating for Guy and Nat to follow. They climbed steep stairs that turned at the top of the first flight and carried on to where a woman with red hair stood, smiling and beckoning to Cyrus. They wrapped each other in a tight embrace.

"Great-looking family," Nat said into Guy's ear.

"Yes." Guy wasn't feeling so good about this visit. Cyrus and Nat had set their hopes high and insisted Jack and one or two of his friends would be able to talk about the New Orleans club scene. Guy wanted history, the story of Jazz Babes. He wanted to trace Pip Sedge's recent connection to the place, and his reason for having directions to Toussaint and Parish Lane in his pocket when he was murdered.

Each of them shook hands with Celina Charbonnet and stepped inside the flat, an eclectically furnished warren of comfortable rooms. Guy smelled apples baking, and cinnamon, maybe nutmeg, too, coming from his left, and looked into a kitchen at the front of the flat. He raised his face and sniffed, and when he looked at the others again it was Celina's laughing, navy blue eyes that held his attention.

"Tarte aux pommes," she said. "I'm bakin' two. I'll send some pieces home with you. Do you like kirsch—I do get a little carried away with my kirsch."

Feeling no shame, Guy said, "Love kirsch."

"Would you look at that?" Celina said. "Amelia's gone. You can bet where we'll find her. Jack's waiting."

They walked along a central hall and she led the way into a masculine study where a long, lean, dark-haired man with olive skin and eyes the same green as Amelia's, sat in a well-used leather chair with his daughter perched on one knee.

"Cyrus," he said with genuine pleasure. He set Amelia aside and got up to give Cyrus a bear hug. He looked at Guy and Nat, who introduced themselves.

"Amelia," Jack said. "We're goin' to do some grown-up talkin' here—"

"So would I please get lost?" Amelia finished for

him, already on her way from the room. She paused and pointed at Cyrus. "Don't you leave before I see you again, Uncle Cyrus."

When they were closeted away, Celina included, Jack arranged his chair to face a billowy leather sofa and pulled up two overstuffed armchairs. "Pick your places. Coffee, anyone?"

Everyone declined.

"Dwayne's coming over," Jack said, and added, "Dwayne LeChat and his partner are club owners in the Quarter. They're old friends of ours."

"You could trust them to keep quiet about anything," Celina said, glancing quickly at her husband.

"Les Chats," Nat said. "I know the place, and Dwayne and Jean-Claude."

Guy didn't and wasn't thrilled at the idea of getting more people involved.

His cell phone rang and he whipped it from his belt, embarrassed he'd forgotten to turn it off. "Sorry," he said, glancing at the readout. Jilly knew he was tied up with business, but she was calling. "Excuse me."

In the hallway, he walked toward the kitchen and stepped down into the warm, fragrant room. "Jilly?"

"Yes," she said in a suspiciously small voice.

Suddenly it didn't matter if she'd interrupted him "Did something happen?"

"No."

"Spit it out," he told her.

"You always make me feel like a nuisance," she

191

said. "Forget it. I was just trying to be open with you. Doesn't matter."

"You hang up on me, and—" he glanced around and lowered his voice "—I won't tell you what I'll do to you, but be afraid."

"Goldilocks has to go to your place, Guy. At least if she runs free out there she's not so likely to get killed by a car."

"I'm not discussing that now."

"Fine. Goodbye."

"Jilly."

"Okay. I wanted to let you know I'm in New Orleans today. I decided to come and visit Edith. Mr. Preston brought her here for a hospital checkup and now she's staying at their New Orleans home until she gets her strength back."

He took a deep breath through his open mouth. "Why didn't you say something last night, or this morning?"

"I didn't want you to try to stop me."

"As if I could." But he would have tried. "They're in the Garden District. Big fancy house on Prytania Street."

"How did you know?"

"Occupational hazard, I like to know who I'm dealing with."

Jilly sighed. "What has Edith ever done to you?"

"She left you with an unfit father and ran off to chase a fast life."

"Guy, she's an unhappy woman. Did you notice . . ."

He waited.

"Did you think the excuse for her wrist being cut was a bit thin? And why didn't they take her to the emergency room or call in Reb? I don't believe it's as simple as they want us to believe it is."

He didn't want to miss out on whatever the men were saying in the study, but he had to make sure Jilly was safe. "Let's talk about this tomorrow. I don't think I'll get back to Toussaint tonight. I'll call you at home, though."

"I won't be in Toussaint, either. I asked you a question."

He puffed up his cheeks. "And the answer is that I don't think Edith Preston cut her wrist while she was shaving her legs."

"You think she . . . Guy, why would she try to kill herself?"

"That's a deep question, cher. I'll be glad to try to help you work through it. I don't want you staying at their house tonight." He really didn't want her under the same roof as Sam Preston.

"I'll be just fine there. Don't be silly."

His head started to pound at the temples. "Please, Jilly. If you don't want to drive home alone, I'll drive you. How did you get here?"

She was quiet for so long he bit into his bottom lip to keep from pushing her again.

"I'm going to stay. I already told Edith I would. I'm driving that ridiculous pink machine—and I intend to leave it here."

He felt afraid. "I'm stayin' with Nat. Cyrus has to get back to St. Cécil's tonight. You can go with him. Jilly . . ." If he didn't hold back what he really wanted to say, she wouldn't cooperate at all. "Call me later, hmm?"

"Okay."

"Is Preston there?" He couldn't, not even when he really tried, he couldn't keep his mouth shut in the danger areas.

"He will be," Jilly said, her voice flat.

"Lock your door when you go to bed." He bowed his head, expecting her to hang up, or let him have it.

"I'll call you later, and Guy?"

"Yes."

"I'm not a fool."

This time she did hang up and Guy felt panicky. He didn't have a thing on Preston. The man appeared the squeaky-clean antiques dealer he said he was, but the sight of Sam Preston cozying up to Jilly wasn't easily forgotten.

Someone came in downstairs. Guy figured it couldn't be Tilly and the baby because whoever it was ran upward, whistling.

A curly-haired blond man reached the top of the stairs and turned right without noticing Guy. The latest arrival had broad shoulders and a compact body molded to the inside of a black T-shirt. His black jeans were perfectly creased. He walked with purpose straight to the study.

"Hold up," Guy said, striding to catch up. "You

194

must be Dwayne LeChat."

A pair of intelligent light brown eyes gave him a thorough examination. "That's me. And you're one of the policemen, although I don't recall seeing you before. And I would recall it if I had."

"Guy Gautreaux."

"Jack mentioned your name. And your partner's. Nat Archer—and I think I remember that from somewhere."

Guy didn't feel like going into his history with NOPD—or Nat's. "We're all glad you could come. Let's go in."

"If Jack and Celina want something—I'm there. Then there's Cyrus—" he rolled his eyes "—who could turn that man down?" He smiled and raised his eyebrows.

"I'm told that what Cyrus wants, Cyrus gets," Guy said, and went ahead of Dwayne into the study.

More introductions followed before they could settle again. Celina had moved to sit on a deep windowsill and light from outside turned her hair fiery.

"Dwayne," Jack said. "What d'you know about Jazz Babes? It's on—"

"Toulouse Street," Dwayne said quickly. He sat in one of the armchairs and crossed his legs. "Used to be called Maison Bleue. That was some years back. Biggest mystery about that place is its reputation. Elite? High-priced trash more likely. What makes it so interestin' to you?"

Guy shot a look at Nat. They hadn't discussed this

visit in enough detail beforehand. So Jack and Celina thought LeChat walked on water—Guy knew almost nothing about him. Trusting LeChat too much could be a deadly mistake.

Nat's face told Guy nothing.

"Tell us what you know about Jazz Babes. Anything that stands out."

"Nothin' good," Dwayne said. "And I'll give you some free advice. Stay away from the place. Underage prostitution was their thing—until they got busted. Not that it stopped them. The way I heard it, they moved that part of the business off premises."

"Where?" Nat said at once.

Dwayne shook his head. "Never bothered to find out but I probably can."

"We'll get you the information," Jack told them.

"It was the killin' that really cleaned up their act," Dwayne said. "Some girl disappeared from home. Wild kid. Parents got a tip they should look at Maison Bleue. They went. They looked. Nothin'. When they got back home the girl was in her bed, only she'd been dead some hours then tucked under the covers while her folks were gone."

"How did she die?" Guy asked.

Dwayne glanced at Celina. "Lack of breath."

"Who owns the place?"

Dwayne said, "Used to be a Giavanelli stronghold. They sold it. It's managed by a man called Felix Broussard. I'll do some diggin' there, too."

Nat stuck out his long legs and drummed his fingers

on his flat belly. "Could be time to concentrate hard on Jazz Babes. I'll go take a look. Anyone know the name Pip Sedge?"

So much for treading lightly. Guy watched Jack and Dwayne.

Dwayne unwrapped a piece of gum, folded it twice and put it between white teeth. He frowned at Jack, who leaned forward and snapped his fingers. "Used to be a high flyer. Made it in real estate."

"Wrong man," Guy said.

"Let him talk." Cyrus spread his hands. "Times change and so do fortunes."

"That Sedge?" Dwayne shook his head slowly. "Lost his shirt. Poker. He couldn't get it together afterward. He comes into Les Chats now and again. Quiet guy. No trouble. Jean-Claude, my softhearted friend, feels sorry for him."

"You don't read the papers," Nat said. "If this is the same guy, he was murdered a couple of weeks back. Shot to death."

Dwayne screwed up his eyes.

"This guy was divorced," Guy said. "His wife figured they'd be better off not married. But they were still friends."

"Sad," Celina said.

"That's him," Dwayne told them. "That's the one I was talkin' about. His ex-wife makes wedding gowns. Real high-end. He was a nice guy."

"That would be the one," Nat said. "Zinnia. She cried when she was told about Sedge. I know on account of I was the one who told her." He got up and paced. "Either Mrs. Sedge doesn't know a thing about her husband's life since she kicked him out, or she doesn't want to talk about it."

"Guy," Cyrus said. "You'll go see what you can get the lady to share with us, I guess."

Already on his feet, Guy said, "I'm on my way. Best you don't go this time, Nat."

"Ain't that the truth."

"She's grievin'," Cyrus pointed out. "What would it hurt to give her a little longer?"

"There are one or two things you don't know," Guy said. "I think there's a connection between Pip Sedge's murder and the way Caruthers Rathburn died in the yard behind All Tarted Up. That's two deaths. Way I see it, we don't know if scores are settled or if there are more to come. Time we don't have."

"You're goin' now?" Cyrus said, and stood up. "Of course you are. Okay if I tag along?"

"Probably a real good idea."

"I wish Madge could be with us," Cyrus said absently. "She's the best when it comes to puttin' people at ease."

Guy saw Celina Charbonnet's hand go to her mouth. The sad look she gave her brother said it all. She knew Cyrus and Madge were caught in a relationship only they understood.

A seven- or eight-block walk would take them to St. Ann Street, where Zinnia Sedge lived and ran her workroom. Cyrus and Guy left Nat to take Guy's car and drive to the precinct house, then crisscrossed streets on foot. They found what they were looking for on St. Ann, just around the corner from Dauphine Street.

"In the courtyard," Guy said, pointing to a board with Zinnia's Bridal and an arrow painted on it.

Tall, black iron gates stood partially open. In the center of the palm-shaded yard a fountain bubbled and flowers overflowed along surrounding galleries.

Guy frowned and said, "Do these places look lived-in to you? Apart from by flowers?"

"It's pretty quiet." Cyrus pointed to a window one story up. "This is the place, though." Zinnia's Bridal appeared again, painted across a window.

Hurrying, as if he felt he must protect the woman from Guy, Cyrus took ringing metal steps two at a time and stepped into the recessed doorway at Zinnia's. Guy caught up in time to see Cyrus try the door and find it locked.

A single gown stood in the window and Guy guessed it looked okay.

"Says she opens at ten," he said, looking past Cyrus. "She's late. Try the bell."

"I think that's for her home."

"Good." Guy pressed the bell and the two of them stood back to wait.

"There's an intercom," Cyrus pointed out. "She may have closed up shop and gone to stay with relatives."

The logic of that disappointed Guy. He had become

convinced he needed some input from Zinnia Sedge. "I'm going to have to find out who those relatives—or friends—might be."

Laborious footsteps on the noisy stairs eventually produced a lady with curlers in her gray hair and a floral apron tied over a striped housedress. She wheezed with each breath and stopped frequently to suck in air through pursed lips—before replacing her cigarette.

"I hope we haven't disturbed you," Cyrus said, and Guy wondered if being so doggone polite ever got tedious.

"You made enough noise getting up here," the woman said, talking around her bobbling cigarette. "What d'you want?"

"We're looking for Zinnia Sedge," Guy said, but he'd lost the woman's attention.

"You a priest?" she said, leaning closer to Cyrus. She produced a pair of glasses with brilliant stones set in upswept black frames, and put them on to get a better look at him. "Yes, I guess that's what you are."

"Pleased to meet you," Cyrus said. "I'm Father Cyrus Payne."

The woman's lips parted and she looked at the shop. The cigarette had burned down but lipstick-stained paper stuck the butt to her lower lip. "Did something happen to Zinnia?" she whispered, and stepped back to crane her neck and see the uppermost floor. "She dead? That would explain why I ain't seen her for a day or so."

"We have no reason to believe Mrs. Sedge has passed," Guy said. "Does she often go away?"

A shake of the head sent metal curlers swinging. "Not Zinnia. Hardest workin' woman I ever did see. Husband was no good." She snorted. "Like any of 'em are. He took off and she's been doin' her best to keep things together. She and that Pip used to own this property. All of it." She looked at the buildings surrounding the courtyard. "They had real estate all over. She never said, but if you ask me it was women and drugs—and gamblin'."

Guy stopped himself from telling her she hadn't been asked. He took out his badge and showed it to her. Not strictly kosher, but special circumstances required special measures. "Detective Gautreaux," he said. "You are?"

"The caretaker. *Miss* Trudy-Evangeline Augustine. You can call me Trudy-Evangeline."

"That's a mighty fine name," Cyrus said, and Trudy-Evangeline smiled, putting life in her pale blue eyes and dimples in her doughy face.

"Do you have a key to Mrs. Sedge's property?" Guy asked.

"Sure do." The six-or-so-inch-diameter key ring she pulled from a pocket reminded Guy of chatelaines of old. All business, Trudy-Evangeline selected a key and unlocked the shop. She stuck her head inside and yelled, "Zinnia! You here?"

She didn't wait to walk in and Guy waved Cyrus ahead of him. The tiny showroom seemed curiously quiet, and so did a much larger workroom beyond where heaps of silks and satins and bolts of lace and pearl trim lay heaped on tables with sewing machine heads protruding from them.

"It's not like Zinnia to leave a mess," Trudy-Evangeline said, returning to the showroom. She wiped her palms on her apron and looked behind curtains covering dressing rooms, whipping the fabric back each time as if expecting someone to jump out.

"We better call the po-lice," she said.

"I am the police," Guy reminded her.

Cyrus put a hand on her shoulder and said, "We'll look after you. I think we should check out Mrs. Sedge's living quarters. She may be sick."

"Oh," Trudy-Evangeline said. "Oh, you're right. What am I thinkin' about?" A door at the back of the shop wasn't locked. She went through and called Zinnia's name again.

Guy stayed close and climbed stairs to the next floor behind her. Not a thing seemed out of place in the living room, dining room, bathroom or kitchen.

Trudy-Evangeline paused.

"What is it?" Guy asked.

"I feel funny about going into her bedroom. Bedrooms are real personal if you know what I mean."

"We do," Cyrus told her. "But I think we have to do it, don't you?"

With a shrug, Trudy-Evangeline led the way to the very back of the flat and a large bedroom with white embroidered curtains that matched a coverlet on a smoothly made bed.

"If Zinnia left in a hurry, there's no sign of it," Guy said. "When do you think you last saw her?"

"I saw her the day before yesterday. She had on her yellow jacket over the black pants and shirt—she always wears black—and she said she was going shopping."

"You haven't seen her since?" Guy persisted.

"No." Trudy-Evangeline led the way from the bedroom to a closet behind the door into the shop. "Yellow coat still gone, and her purse. She always keeps her purse here when she's home."

"She could have come home and gone out again," Cyrus said mildly.

"But she hasn't." The woman's voice rang with something close to triumph. "She keeps that Vespa of hers in the courtyard. Pulled back under the gallery and chained up. She took off on it that day but I haven't seen it since—or Zinnia."

"That was the night Rathburn died," Cyrus commented.

"Rathburn?" Trudy-Evangeline said.

Guy frowned at Cyrus. "Let's get Nat." And he would figure out how to remove Jilly from the Prestons' clutches.

"Are you a real priest?" Trudy-Evangeline asked Cyrus.

"I am. My parish is in Toussaint."

She opened a window a crack and flicked out her

203

cigarette butt. "Could you hear my confession before you go, Father? It's been thirty-seven years since I made my last one."

14

Wearing a pale pink satin robe and matching slippers, Edith sat on a chaise covered with rose-patterned fabric fringed around the bottom with a skirt of dark red beads.

Heavy velvet draperies in a shade of ashes-of-roses had been drawn since Jilly arrived and she felt closed-in.

"It's getting late," she said. "You didn't touch lunch or dinner. Let me call the kitchen and ask Michael to bring you something." Mr. Preston had taken Jilly aside and asked her not to leave Edith alone while he visited some clients.

Edith sighed and rolled her face toward Jilly. "I'll eat somethin' shortly, darlin'. Just havin' you here with me is all I need to feel good."

Jilly smiled and tried not to fidget. For long periods, Edith didn't talk, only stared as if at something Jilly couldn't see. The slightest noise from outside made the woman jump.

"The tonic—or whatever it was—seemed to help you. The one Ken and Jolene made. I could get some more for you."

"Maybe. How's that nice young man of yours?"

The question took Jilly by surprise. "Guy? He's fine. What made you think of him suddenly?" They'd been in the room together for hours.

"He wants you."

The feelin' is mutual. "How do you know that?"

"When I see that darkening in a man's eyes when he looks at a woman, I know. Dark and hungry—and confused sometimes—that's how it looks to me. But only confused if the man wants somethin' more than sex from the woman."

Jilly laughed at that. "You do know men, Edith. I'd say that a man who felt somethin' more than lust for a female could be *terminally* confused."

"Did he ask you to marry him yet?"

"No!"

"Well, you don't have to sound so horrified. Marriage does have a way of followin' the other stages."

"That may never happen for Guy and me."

Edith let out a shuddering sigh. "I don't want to die. Not yet."

"Of course you don't." Jilly's heart beat uncomfortably.

"If Caruthers hadn't rescued me, I'd have died already. Bled to death. I wish he was here right now."

"He was faithful to you," Jilly said. "It meant a great deal for him to make sure you were happy."

Edith turned her eyes to Jilly's face again. "Do you know where he is?"

"Not exactly." She should know. "It's been a bit

crazy for me. I'll call Reb. She examined him at the crime scene. She'll know where he was taken after the morgue. Were you and Mr. Preston able to help them contact Caruthers's family?"

"He doesn't have a family." Edith opened her mouth wide and her eyes fixed.

"Are you okay?" Jilly asked, taking one of Edith's hands in hers. An icy hand. "Say something."

A scream started, first as a shrill and whispery sound, then gradually building until Jilly surged to her feet and leaned over to take Edith in her arms. She smoothed her hair, looked into her face and tried to talk to her.

On and on, the scream went until it cracked and became a gurgling moan.

"Please," Jilly said. "Please talk to me. Tell me what made you scream."

Edith fell back in the chaise. "When?" she said.

For a moment Jilly blinked at her, then she knew with horrifying clarity that she had just broken the news of Caruthers's death to Edith. Preston hadn't told her. Laura knew, but that poor woman was in an impossible position. She would have been warned not to tell Edith. How could Preston have forgotten to tell Jilly that Edith didn't know?

The door opened and Preston strode in. "What's goin' on in here?" he said. "What are you screamin' at, Edith? For God's sake get a hold of yourself or you'll drive Jilly away. Most people can't stand your carryin' on."

"It's nothing, Daddy," Edith said before Jilly could gather her wits to make a comment. "Just some fool child outside with a horn or somethin'. Whatever made you think I might be screamin'? Why, the very idea."

She had laced her fingers together in her lap and they turned white where she gripped so hard. But she tilted her head at Preston and smiled girlishly.

"Just children," Jilly said. She wanted to protect Edith—from Preston—although the reason was only something she felt, like a bad premonition. He treated his wife with affection most of the time and didn't hide his concern for her.

Still frowning, he went to Edith and kissed her mouth. "I understand you haven't eaten a thing all day, sugar. You won't get strong that way. I've got to go out again for an hour or so, but I've arranged for the two of you to eat in here. Jilly, make sure your mother eats. We've got to get her built up. She doesn't know it yet, but I'm plannin' a surprise."

Edith looked away, but not before Jilly saw fear in her eyes.

"I'm takin' you on a cruise," Preston said. "A long cruise. I haven't decided where for sure, not yet, but I'm narrowin' it down. Just you and me and beautiful surroundings. We'll call it a second honeymoon."

The tight feeling in the bottom of Jilly's stomach had everything to do with the way Edith breathed through her mouth and closed her eyes before she said, "That would be wonderful. Thank you." She looked at Preston and the tortured expression was gone, replaced with another smile.

"There's my beautiful, smilin' girl again," Preston said. He turned to Jilly. "I may be a bit late. When Edith's ready, would you help her get settled in the bedroom? You're next door so you won't have far to go when I get back."

Jilly wished she hadn't agreed to spend the night. "We'll be fine," she told him, wondering how she would break it that she wasn't taking the Hummer back to Toussaint.

"I want you to marry Guy," Edith said from the heavily carved bed where she and Preston slept. "Don't look at me like that. I saw how it was with you two so I'm not tellin' you to do anythin' you don't already want to do. If you don't want to get married at once, then live together."

Not one word came to Jilly. She looked at Edith, who had showered and changed into a lilac peignoir set trimmed with swansdown.

"It'll make everythin' so much easier, don't you think?"

"You're in shock about Caruthers. That's what all this is. You were asking me where he was because you expected him to come back and I thought you already knew he was dead."

"I can't talk about it yet. Daddy shouldn't have tried to protect me from the ugliness. He never did want me to see or hear anythin' ugly." She rubbed her face and

208

retied the lavender ribbon that held her hair back. "You'll only have to ask Guy to move in once and he'll be there."

"Edith," Jilly said. "I can't believe you're saying these things."

"I'm practical. I see things clearly and—"

"This isn't something you have to decide," Jilly said. "Whatever happens between Guy and me is up to us."

"I'll live in that little basement apartment you don't use for anything and look after everything for both of you. After all, you'll both be busy workin'. And when you have a baby, you'll need me to help even more. It'll be perfect."

Jilly took a large swallow of the merlot Michael had brought earlier and put the glass on a table beside her chair. The room was as masculine as the one Edith had in Toussaint was feminine.

"Jilly?" Edith's voice rose. "It will be perfect, won't it?"

She couldn't even imagine making the suggestion to Guy—or telling him the rest of Edith's idea. "You've hardly spoken since Mr. Preston left the house and now this sudden, strange outpouring."

"Hearing about Caruthers's death did shock me. I couldn't think about anythin' else afterward—until I got settled up here. I think better here."

"I assumed Mr. Preston would have told you about what happened. The police talked to him because they hoped he could help them with next of kin." She knew at once that she shouldn't have said that. "Mr. Preston must have been so shocked he's closed it up inside him."

Settle on one excuse for his behavior and stick with it, Jilly.

"Caruthers was my husband's most trusted man," Edith said. "That's why he sent him to Toussaint. Daddy worries so much about me and he likes to know I'm being looked out for."

"Of course he does," Jilly said, grateful for a reprieve from the topic of cohabiting with Guy . . . with Edith living in the basement. "You look tired. Get some sleep now. I'll curl up in this big old chair and rest."

Edith wriggled until she could prop her head and look at Jilly. "Honey, you aren't takin' me serious. It won't be any problem to explain to everyone how you and I want a chance to know each other better— so we decided to spend quality time at your place— alone."

The kind of panicky feeling Jilly remembered from being moved to yet another foster home came like a physical blow. Edith couldn't come and live with her. She didn't want her to.

"I can be useful at the bakery, too," Edith said, her voice breathy, her words rapid. "When I left Toussaint, I worked in kitchens and served up plenty of meals. I can be an asset to you."

"This is bizarre," Jilly said, sitting up straight and planting her feet on the floor. "You know Mr. Preston and the rest of them won't stand by while you move in with me. He thinks the world of you. Anyway, how would we be alone if you got your way about Guy? You're not makin' much sense."

Edith closed her eyes and tears slipped down her cheeks. "Women shouldn't be on their own. They need a man around to keep them safe. Guy would do that for us. I wouldn't intrude on the two of you."

"But *why?*" She was so grateful she'd never felt she needed a man around all the time—until Guy. Jilly smiled a little.

"I'm frightened," Edith said, wiping at her cheeks. "I don't even know if I can explain it too well, but I've got this feelin' someone's puttin' somethin' over on Daddy and one of these days—if I stay where I am—they'll hurt me."

Jilly looked at her hands, then, surreptitiously at Edith's left arm. Where she'd propped her head, the swansdown had slid to her elbow, showing skin that matched the whiteness of the soft trim. "How is your arm?" she said, not quite sure why she had decided to mention it.

A little pink flooded Edith's face. "It's gettin' better. You want to see?"

If she didn't look, Guy had better never find out the offer had been made. "Sure. Were you shaving your legs on the bed or in the shower?"

Edith peeled back a thick, white plaster and Jilly barely stopped herself from shuddering at the sight of a dark, jagged cut where a few widely spaced sutures still remained. "It's healing," she managed to say.

"Yes. It happened in the shower and I fell. That's what Caruthers heard and he rescued me. I passed out. I don't remember a thing. They told me there was blood everywhere." She wrinkled her nose. "I do know I'd had some drinks that night—Laura reminded me. And I didn't eat." Either she lied deliberately, or she didn't remember a thing and believed what someone had told her.

"The pudding you had for dinner tonight wasn't exactly a meal," Jilly pointed out gently. "We need to build you up."

"Yes," Edith said, covering the wound again. "If I'm with you I'll want to do that. Jilly, I'm wonderin' if I took my sleepin' pills before I got in that shower. That could make it hard for me to hold steady while I did my legs. Why don't I remember?"

"I guess we'll never know for sure," Jilly said. Maybe she was some kind of coward, but she couldn't say what Edith wanted her to say—not without a lot of thought and some advice from a person she trusted.

Guy. With her brother Joe away, Guy was the only one she could turn to.

Well, there was Cyrus, but he would probably go to Spike for his opinion and there could be all kinds of trouble. For Edith's sake, Jilly had to keep quiet until she'd figured things out. She glanced at Edith, whose eyes were closed again. There was Reb. Reb O'Brien Girárd knew about keeping confidences, and Jilly could ask an offhand question about losing a lot of blood possibly leading to a patient feeling persecuted and not making much sense.

Well, not exactly like that, but in a more general way.

Edith slid deeper into the bed and her breathing gradually became regular. She'd drifted asleep and Jilly let out a silent, relieved whistle.

On one side of the room French doors opened onto a gallery at the back of the three-story house. In the wall opposite the bed, four bay windows stretched from ceiling to floor. Jilly got up, turned out all but one small light in the room and peeked through the draperies covering the French doors. A blue-white moon shone bright, shading the sky with its shiny halo. She heard the trees rustling and creaking. A wind had picked up.

She'd like to go out onto the gallery but couldn't risk waking Edith. Slipping behind the curtains over one of the other windows, she stood in heavy, stifling darkness and looked down on one side of the house. A silvery car was parked there, in front of a closed building without windows. Probably a garage. Or it could be a stable, she supposed. It had a loft.

Headlights swung around from the front driveway and a dark town car slid in beside the other vehicle. Mr. Preston had returned, and as much as she wished she didn't have to see him again, at least she was closer to getting some sleep and, in the morning, leaving for home.

Once she was in her room she would call Guy. She

had turned her own cell off to make sure he didn't call her when she couldn't talk.

Preston opened the driver's door and swung his legs out. She should get away from the window before he got out. If he looked up, he might be able to see her.

He climbed out, locked the car and approached the house. But he stopped and swung around. To Jilly's horror, he held a gun and crept back toward the car. He opened the door behind the driver's seat and leaned into the back of the vehicle. Jilly couldn't hear a thing, but the man hauled someone out, someone who had evidently been hiding in the backseat.

A woman in dark clothing, small and anonymous from Jilly's viewpoint, struggled against Preston's grip. Jilly pressed a shaking fist against her mouth. Preston pocketed his weapon and shook the woman. When he let her go, she fell backward but quickly scrambled to her feet. Preston turned from her and disappeared from Jilly's view, leaving the woman where she was.

He's coming here. And he carried a gun. The woman below huddled with her arms wrapped around her. At first she moved slowly toward the front of the house, but suddenly she ran, her hair streaming behind her, until she was also out of sight.

An urge to run, too, to do some hiding of her own until she could escape the house and make it to safety, overwhelmed Jilly. Preston was sick—or, more likely, involved in something illegal. She wondered who the woman could have been, other than someone who wanted to speak to him privately. He'd soon showed her he didn't appreciate being sneaked up on.

Jilly's skin heated, but a chill attacked her shaky muscles. If she tried to leave, she was as likely to run into Preston as to get away. She returned to the chair, curled up and pretended to be dozing.

Seeing Preston with another woman shouldn't surprise her. Everything about him suggested he could be a really sexual man. But to drive to this house with that woman—even if she had hidden in the car—then send her on her way in the dark?

He was dangerous.

She closed her eyes and let her arms trail over the arms of the chair.

Preston entered the room without a sound. Jilly smelled his cologne and her stomach met her diaphragm. She was ready to "wake up" when he leaned over her. She felt his heavy presence, his proximity, and struggled to keep her breathing even.

With the pads of his fingers, he touched her face lightly and withdrew again. Jilly curled up inside but she held still. He was too close and if she moved she might collide with him.

Preston was so near his breath met her ear. He didn't move. Neither did she. *Please let him go away.* A scream started up her throat.

The faintest caress, a slight pause for an almost imperceptible squeeze, and he went from her breast to her shoulder and shook her gently. "Jilly," he whispered, "time to get ready for bed, sleepyhead."

A shudder shook her, there was no way to stop it. But rather than look up at him, she leaned forward and rubbed her face, hoping he'd mistake her reaction for something she normally did when she woke up. "Sorry I fell asleep. Edith's already drifted off." She yawned and couldn't remember ever having a stronger urge to leap to her feet and run as far and as fast as possible from a place.

Totally sure of himself, he took her by the hand and pulled her up. "C'mon, let's make sure you've got everything you need."

Short of risking a scene, possibly a loud one, she had no choice but to let him lead her from the room. Once outside, she faced him and said, "Everything's fine, thank you. You need to get to bed yourself." The thunder of her heart made her light-headed.

He inclined his head and smiled into her eyes. "You're a good daughter."

I am not your daughter, you pervert. She cleared her throat. "Look, I wasn't aware that Edith didn't know what happened to Caruthers. I'm afraid she does now."

His nostrils flared. "That's unfortunate. Edith doesn't cope well with tragedy."

"I wasn't told to keep anything from her. Anyway, I'm not sure if or when she'll mention it, but I needed to let you know she might."

"I should have told her myself," he said. "Don't give it another thought." He went to the door of her room and threw it open with a little bow.

"Thank you," Jilly said, and made to pass him.

Preston took her by the shoulders and kissed her cheek, catching the corner of her mouth as he did so. He straightened and looked down at her from beneath lowered lids. It was so hard not to swipe a hand across her lips.

"Good night," he said, and turned to walk swiftly back to his own bedroom.

15

"I can't hear you," Guy said, pressing his cell phone tight against his ear. "You're still at the Preston house?"

"Yes," Jilly whispered. "I wanted you to know I have to get out of here—now. Where are you? I'll come to you—if that's okay."

"I'll come for you."

"No, you might cause trouble for . . . Don't come. Just tell me where to meet you—I know my way around the area."

He glanced at a clock on Nat's kitchen wall. "No. Stay there. It's very late and very dark. You will not go out there alone."

He couldn't make out Jilly's response. "Get somewhere you can lock yourself in and call me back," he told her. "You're whisperin' and I can't hear you."

"You don't understand. No one's tryin' to kill me,

but I have to get out of this house now. I'm goin' to leave everything behind and make a run for it."

Nat stood only a few feet away, staring at Guy.

"Stay there. Don't go outside. Nat and I are comin' to get you. Quit worrying, we're on our way." He grabbed his piece and the keys to the Pontiac and made for the front door.

"*No!* I mean it, Guy, don't come here. I'll be gone, anyway, and I'm not takin' the Hummer."

"On foot? You're goin' to be out there runnin' around alone?"

Nat locked the house behind them, but rather than get into Guy's car he threw open the door of the cruiser parked there and slid behind the wheel. Guy's imagination went on overload but everything he came up with had Preston's face on it.

"I'll turn left out of the gate and go down as far as Washington," Jilly said. "That's well lit. From there I'll head to St. Charles Avenue."

"You will not, cher." He needed to calm her down.

"Why are you in such a stew, Guy Gautreaux? Cool it. There's nothing to worry about as long as I leave now and I have my route planned. This is makin' me think, though. I hate 'em, but maybe it's time to carry a gun."

Nat swung the cruiser onto the street in front of his house and turned to Guy with his eyebrows raised. The dash lights rippled over his face and he was one serious man.

Guy pointed and Nat took off in that direction.

There would be no discussion of Jilly carrying. "Okay," he said. "We're on the road. This won't take long." Fat raindrops marred the windshield. "It's rainin'. You don't want to go out there and get wet. We're in a cruiser and we'll pull up to the front door."

"Oh, my—no! I'm hangin' up now and headin' out. I'll go to that big church on St. Charles. What's it called?"

Nat had the wipers on and he leaned forward—probably because he had allowed his foot to get real heavy on the pedal and he figured he'd better watch carefully.

Spinning it out, Guy said, "Now, what big church would that be, cher?"

"Big church where?" Nat snapped.

"Oh, just some big church on St. Charles—down past Washington Avenue." He squeezed Nat's leg as a warning and got an elbow jab for his trouble.

"That's not funny," Nat said. Then he raised his voice. "Christ Church Cathedral, Jilly."

Guy elbowed him back and covered the phone. "I was lettin' you know I didn't want to tell her about any church. She can wait where she is." They were moving so fast they might be in a church—or church-yard—sooner than they'd expected.

He put the phone back to his ear. "We're makin' good time."

"Thanks," Jilly said. "I'll be lookin' out for you. I'm outside already. Bye."

"Jilly!" She'd hung up and he didn't dare try to call back. "Well, *hell.*"

They would drive a police car up to the Prestons' front door and pick her up? Jilly shook her head. Sometimes she was sure men didn't think ahead. Guy and Nat to the rescue. Never mind if Mr. Preston would know she'd called them. Never mind if Preston would stop her from seeing Edith again. And never mind that Guy and Nat were overreacting.

Every rustle of the wind in the trees brought her heart into her throat. If Preston discovered she'd left the house and came after her, he might do anything.

A laurel hedge rose high above iron railings surrounding the property. She poked her head out and checked the street in both directions. Didn't see a thing move. She did have her purse and looped the long strap across her body.

Keeping close to the railings, she set off at a brisk pace. A purposeful, head-held-high pace. She quickly reached a corner, Seventh Street. For some reason she'd thought Washington Avenue was the first cross street but it must still be ahead.

The rain Guy had mentioned grew heavy, and the wind threw twigs and leaves into Jilly's path. She liked wild weather—or she did most of the time.

Someone ran past her, barely missed bumping into her, a small woman with wet hair flapping. Jilly considered calling out and suggesting they go together, but that could bring all kinds of trouble.

Some yards ahead, the woman dashed to the curb, turned a pale face in Jilly's direction and scurried across the street. She bent over as if to make herself invisible, or at least even smaller.

A flashlight beam, as brilliant and directed as a searchlight, burst over the hunched figure who let out a cry Jilly heard. The beam followed its quarry when she reached the opposite sidewalk and kept running.

The woman from Preston's car? She could be.

Pulling as near to the railings and vegetation as she could, Jilly looked back and located the position of the person with the flashlight. He stood on the same side of the street as Jilly—until he hurried, the beam wavering, to the other side.

Soft-soled shoes squeaked on wet ground. The man rushed past without noticing Jilly. It would be easy to throw up right then and there. She breathed deeply through her mouth and pressed a hand over her heart as if she might slow it down.

She did what seemed best and slipped to the other sidewalk herself. A person couldn't just let a woman be chased through the night and do nothing.

She grabbed her cell phone from her purse and quickly dialed Guy's number. He answered at the first ring. "Jilly? Where are you?"

"I've got to keep my voice down. Something's going on. A man is chasing a woman. She's got a lead on him but he's faster. He's got a flashlight trained on her. Guy, I'm terrified he'll shoot her."

"And maybe he'll shoot you next. Where did you say you were?"

"Still on Prytania. Washington's farther than I thought. I can't talk and run. I just wanted you to know what I'm doing."

"You're running? Why? It's better to walk. You're less likely to draw attention to yourself."

"Look—" she knew he wouldn't like this "—she's alone and I've got to try to help if I can. I called because I knew you'd want to know."

"Stand still at once. Oh, my God, Jilly. Stop running. You're a good woman but you're . . . you can't help. I'll call for backup and we'll be right there."

Jilly hung up and switched off. She absolutely couldn't risk having her phone ring now. And if she was a fool to try to help a stranger in terrible trouble, she hoped someone else would do the same if she was ever in the same position.

The woman crossed Sixth, seemed to hesitate, then carried on. So did her pursuer, only he'd turned off the beam. Jilly watched his sneakers moving.

Taller iron railings loomed, and inside the railings the crooked shapes of old tombs caught the hazed-over glimmer from a streetlight.

Jilly swallowed, and swallowed again. Brave she might be, but any fool knew to stay away from New Orleans graveyards, especially at night. She crept across Sixth and hid herself there, out of the line of sight of those ahead.

She wanted to turn back, but the truth was that if she

didn't do something, *now,* and she read in tomorrow's paper that a woman had been murdered in that grave-yard, she would go to pieces.

Around the corner and back on Prytania Street she went—just in time to see her flashlight buddy turn right through a gate into the cemetery. She plucked at her clothes, absently pulling her sodden brown wind-breaker away from her skin.

She couldn't delay. At the entrance, she listened but heard only the rain and the whining wind. But she saw that flashlight shining again and went past the gates, using tombs to shield her from view, slipping from one to another to get closer. Her breathing grew so loud and rapid, she feared the man would hear her.

"Forgive me," a woman's voice wailed. "Forgive me. *Please.*" Then she screamed, a long, thin, high scream that faded away.

Jilly hugged herself. Goose bumps encased her body, and her hair, heavy and wet, lay on her back in an icy rope. She tiptoed forward, swiping rain from her eyes and face, and passed a massive brick tomb topped with silently howling stone dogs.

"I promise," the woman cried. "Whatever you want, I promise I will do."

Jilly persisted until only a single marble tomb stood between her and the others. Back to the wet, slick stone, she slid along with arms outstretched until she touched a corner. A sound came from above her and she glanced up. The flat slab on top of the tomb had been turned sideways, leaving the resting place open to any who cared to peer inside. The noise she had heard got louder until a black thing erupted from the crypt, shrieking an unearthly cry.

With a hand over her mouth, Jilly crumpled to the muddy ground and watched, her eyes strained wide open.

The black apparition swelled and seemed to beat the air before it rose into a murky halo of light from a streetlamp. A bird, a huge bird that swooped in Jilly's direction, a bloated worm trailing from its beak, before it flew upward and she heard the slashing of its wings against the wind before it was gone.

A male voice rumbled, but the owner kept it low and Jilly picked out, ". . . It will never happen . . . living at my pleasure. You'll die at my pleasure if—"

"Don't hit me!"

At once Jilly heard the fearsome sound of a connecting blow and rage overtook her. "You stop that right now," she yelled, and jumped into the open. The woman crouched on the ground and the man bent over her. "Stop it!"

He straightened at once and Jilly took off running. The flashlight picked her out and she ducked aside, pounded down a narrow strip between the hulks of graves. He would want to silence any witnesses. All she had to do was run fast enough to give the other woman time to get away and then get away herself. She set her mouth in a grim line. *All* she had to do. Guy could show up anytime he pleased.

She heard sneakers slap smooth, waterlogged mud.

They were too loud because they were too close. She stopped to catch her breath but the footsteps kept coming. They were to her right. No, to her left.

An owl hooted and a mouse scurried up a granite wall and inside a tomb.

How could the rain get heavier? It did and it deadened any movements.

She didn't know what made her turn back, only that she was driven to do it—to slip and slide toward the place where the woman had been. Jilly had to know if the other one was safe. Could Preston have sent someone to kill the woman?

This had been the way she came, surely this was the way.

No, the tombs weren't familiar. Or they were all the same. She tripped over a broken piece of masonry and fell hard again some railings. When she gripped the cold, slick metal and looked up, she saw a stone angel carved so it appeared ready to soar.

Hands closed on her shoulders. An agonizing grip on her hair stopped her from looking behind.

"I got lost," she said, and felt lame—and stupid.

A snicker chilled her.

Down he pushed her, down, his weight like a mountain on top of her. An engine roared and she forced her eyes open, praying for flashing lights but seeing none.

"Mind your own business," the man said, his voice muffled by whatever he held to his mouth. "Curiosity can kill."

Pain blasted through her head.

16

Cyrus sat at the table in the rectory kitchen with his arms crossed. He couldn't see or hear Madge but he could feel her, feel her confusion. Dealing with people in crisis was part of his job and he felt capable in his role. He might be sad, overwhelmed by the need to take away their pain, but he knew what to do and when.

A quietly furious woman who marched away with compressed lips at the sight of him didn't call for any of the skills he'd learned. Not that Madge hadn't been angry with him before.

He'd been late getting back from New Orleans. There was a good reason to get the cold shoulder.

Madge should already have gone home to Rosebank hours ago. Listen to him. Didn't he feel like the victimized one? Kind of like a child who hadn't realized he was breaking some rule and now that he'd been chastised, he got petulant.

A petulant boy—now, there was an attractive picture when the boy was a grown man who usually thought he'd gained some wisdom.

"Damn it all," he said, with no remorse. "I'm just a man. No man understands women."

And that was a cop-out.

On his feet again, he poured two mugs of coffee, put

cream in Madge's, then found the honey and added a spoonful. She liked it that way.

He scuffed along in his stocking feet to her office door. It stood open and she wasn't inside. She wasn't next door in his office, either.

Peering through his office window he could see the shape of her car on the parking strip, so she hadn't sneaked out without a word.

Stopping every few steps to steady the coffee—and still losing a drop here and there—he climbed the stairs and went toward the big sitting room where he entertained and saw those who came for counsel.

Madge met him in the doorway. She looked at the coffee and frowned, then took both cups from him and walked back into the room. "You don't have to make up to me, Cyrus," she said. "You've got a right to be where you want to be, when you want to be there. You don't owe me a thing—even if you do know I get worried out of my mind if I don't know where you are."

"Madge—"

"No, no, you're not at fault, not at all. I am because sometimes I expect more than I have a right to."

He sighed. "It's been too long since we took some time for ourselves and talked about what we have a right to expect—from each other."

Her dark eyes became suspiciously brilliant. "That's just it, Cyrus. I know exactly what I have a right to expect from you. You're the one who must feel he's steppin' around land mines here sometimes. I'm sorry for that."

Aghast, he took the mugs back from her and set them on the table in front of his worn green couch. "I never want to hear you apologize to me again." He smiled but couldn't quite get both corners of his mouth to cooperate at the same time. "You're givin' your life to this parish, and to me, and it's not fair."

She turned away sharply and walked to the windows. The view—if it weren't inky black outside—would be over the back gardens and down to Bayou Teche where cypress and willow trees bowed over the water. Madge stared down as if she could see. "I like havin' those old Fuglies there," she said. "Ugliest piece of so-called art I ever did see but it reminds me of that sweet, unlucky Bonnie Blue."

Homeless and down on her luck, Bonnie Blue had passed their way some years ago. Cyrus had taken her in and given her a place to live and Madge looked after her as best she could. The two-dimensional bronze of five capering figures irreverently known as the Fuglies dated back to Bonnie's tenure and remained on the lawn despite the complaints of some parishioners.

"We share a history, Madge," Cyrus said.

She nodded but didn't look at him. "Years seem to fly by," she said, and closed her mouth firmly. Those were the things she should never say to him. They weren't fair. Cyrus had told her she needed a life, a husband and children—he didn't deserve for her to salt the wounds he must carry over the friendship they shared. The "passionate, chaste relationship," he'd explained to her, offering her all he could as a man of God.

It wasn't enough. Most of the time she made do, happy just to see him, to feel his hand on her shoulder or at her waist, but the days and nights had become too raw. The tightness in her throat rarely faded completely anymore.

"Bad day?" Cyrus asked, arriving beside her.

"No. Frustrating maybe, but not bad. You taught me about that, remember? That days aren't really bad, it's the way we choose to see them."

"Did I say that?" He looped an arm across her shoulders. "Pretty stupid, huh?"

She looked up at his face.

"I have bad days," he said, staring ahead as if watching sun shine on bayou water. "A lot of them."

Sadness bathed her. "Why did you wait to tell me? I might be able to help. You know I'll do everything I can to lighten the load for you. Look, forget my meanderings, they don't mean a thing. I get crotchety sometimes is all."

Cyrus rubbed her shoulder. "Poor, dear girl," he murmured, not meaning to speak aloud. "As long as I can get away with it, I carry on—grateful to have you near me as often as possible. It's not fair. I'm the one makin' the rules."

"You have to be." She choked on the words and he caught her by the back of the neck.

"It's all a trick, don't you see?" *Lord, help me. Give me the strength to do what I must do.* "We should

229

never have met because somewhere back there, when we weren't even born, a mistake was made. They marked us for each other without noticing they'd already . . ." *I can't say it, Lord. I can't deny you, but I can't tell this woman I will abandon her if I must.*

He turned to look down into her face.

"They didn't notice they'd already given you to God. Isn't that what you were going to say?"

The hopeless love he saw in her eyes shamed him. He could have stopped this. From the day he hired her, he felt laughter in his heart at the sight of her. He'd be a liar if he pretended he hadn't longed to lie with her. But then he'd learned to discipline his reactions, in the same way he'd learned to discipline his bodily responses, his urges, since he set out on his chosen path.

"I love you, Madge."

He turned his head from her and dropped his arm. *My God, hold me, help me. Carry this woman in your hands and heal the wounds I've caused.*

"It's okay," she told him softly. "I understand. Even if I could, I wouldn't take you from your rightful place here."

"It's ironic," he told her, not caring that his voice broke, "but loving you makes me a better man. It makes me a better . . . priest."

"Thank you," she told him, finding his hand and taking it to her lips. "Loving you makes me . . . Cyrus, I understand, or I try to, but sometimes I feel I've died for wanting you."

Appalled by the knowledge that she suffered so much destroyed him.

"No," Madge said, releasing his hand. "That's ridiculous. I'm feeling a bit sorry for myself because I'm tired. Forget—"

"Neither of us can forget. You'll move on, but you won't forget completely, although you will be happy."

She could make a life and he'd be glad?

"I am happy," Madge said. "We've said enough. I stayed because I wanted to be with you when you see something."

"I'm going to ask you to leave, Madge."

Facing him, her back straight so the top of her head almost reached his chin, she studied his face and her mouth set again. Not in anger this time, but with trembling resolve. "You're firing me?"

His body began to dishonor him. He glanced away and took deep breaths. "I can't fire you."

"Then why would I go?"

"Because I can't give you what you deserve."

Her fingers, stroking the side of his face, tormented him even while he fought to keep his hands at his sides. "Women, some women are all emotion and not a whole lot of common sense," she said, smiling a little. "You've always been honest with me and I accepted the truth of what we can have a long time ago."

"If I'd been half a man, I wouldn't have bound you to me and sentenced you to only half a life."

"Cyrus." With a hand on either side of his face, she

came closer and smiled into his eyes, really smiled with the bubbly, disarming merriment he'd never seen in anyone else. "No, get rid of that sad look. I won't go. It's as simple as that. If you want me out of here you'll have to change the locks, and if I manage to sneak in, you'll have to drag me out again."

Moisture along her lower lids only added to the sparkle. So why had his throat jammed shut? "I don't think I'd be much good at dragging you out."

She made a valiant effort to keep her lips steady but she gave up. "What a pair we are. I love you so, I can't believe how lucky I am."

My God!

Standing on tiptoe, she kissed his mouth softly and immediately withdrew. "Forgive me for that. I think it was pretty chaste."

He tried to laugh and failed. Instead he reached for her, pulled her toward him so hard she all but fell. Cyrus gathered her up. For an instant nothing moved. *"No."* He knew Madge didn't hear his silent cry. He brought his lips down on hers, hard but without opening his mouth. Her body shuddered and seemed about to draw back, but she put her arms around his neck and returned his kiss desperately.

Reason hovered somewhere on the edge of his consciousness, but the consciousness had turned black and tinged with red. Red, or fire? In his belly an agony mounted. The throbbing all but brought him to his knees. He took her in his arms as he had never intended. And it was Madge who parted their lips.

Cyrus moaned and felt tears squeeze from his closed eyes. A sobbing sound came from somewhere and he knew it wasn't Madge. He couldn't let her go, even though she must feel his response to her, he could not make his arms release her.

"Cyrus," she said, so very quietly. "What have I done to you?" She found his wrists and held them while she stepped away. How many times had she promised herself she would help him avoid this awakening no matter what it cost her. She'd failed, and if they couldn't overcome the barrier they'd overstepped, then she *would* have to leave him.

With his head bowed and his arms at his sides, he visibly collected himself. He gave a small laugh and sniffed—and blood rose in his face.

"I look at you and I see love, Cyrus," she told him. "But it's a bigger love than anything you could have for me and that's okay." It wasn't okay, oh, no, it would never be okay, but she would keep on taking whatever he had to spare.

"You didn't take religious vows, sweet one," he said. "There is no reason for you to live as if you did."

Tears clogged her throat. "We have an understanding," she said. "I just violated—"

"You have violated nothing." He almost shouted. "Nothing, do you understand? This is my cross, to love you when I can't have you. But you don't have to bear that cross. How many ways can I beg you to fulfill your real purpose in life?"

Madge smiled at him and didn't give a rat's . . . She didn't care that Cyrus saw her openly crying. "I'm smiling and crying. That makes me a nut, hmm? Please, may we go back to our understanding? A passionate, celibate affair? You have given me so much tonight—I'll never be able to tell you how much. And now I'm going to behave myself."

She couldn't know how badly he wanted to forget vows and promises he'd made a part of his soul, vows to which he'd given his soul. "I can't let you hurt day in and day out."

"Send me away and I'll hurt every minute I live. There, I think we're bein' real honest so you'd better believe me." She remembered the reason she'd stayed until he got home, the original reason, or at least the one she'd come up with. "Am I fired?"

"Never." He shook his head and shots of blue showed in his black curls. "But you are not to stay when you decide you have to go."

"Right." She looked up at him from beneath her lashes. "Cyrus, I've got something you need to see and make some decisions about—if you're not too tired."

"Show me, cher."

On shaky legs, Madge went to the couch and took a thin newspaper from beneath a cushion. She shrugged, embarrassed. "I put it there because I didn't want to look at it." Sitting down suddenly, she smoothed her dark blue dress over her knees.

If he didn't notice every move she made, it might

help his peace. But she could just save them—at least for a little longer—with her sense of humor. And her love. Madge had the prettiest legs. Narrow ankles and softly curving calves and thighs—and hips.

He went back to the window. "What's the paper?"

"The *Toussaint Trumpet.*"

Cyrus swung back to her. "The old *Trumpet*? The one Lee O'Brien's trying to get going?"

"She's got it going. Cyrus, I think it's going to be a huge success."

He raised his brows. "You don't say? Good for Lee. It is good for Lee, isn't it?"

"I think her marketing plans are unusual and . . . Cyrus, you'll have parishioners lined up outside your door in the morning."

He looked heavenward. "Just what I need."

"You are never given more than you can bear," she said, and burst into laughter.

He caught her around the neck and tapped the end of her nose. "You are a cruel woman." They smiled at each other, and he let her go. "All right, let's get to it. The coffee's cold but we could be really wild and have a glass of wine."

You bet, dear friend. Madge took the coffee cups to the sink beneath the bar and emptied them, then opened the small corner cabinet where Cyrus kept his meager supply of drinks. "Red wine is good for us," she told him sagely. What she knew about wine . . . she knew nothing about it, but she had read about the positive results of drinking a little now and then.

She got out two glasses and poured until each was three-quarters full.

"Here you go," she told Cyrus, putting the glasses on the table. "Sit down, please. You'll want to go through this. I took the liberty of highlighting some of the high points." She giggled.

"What?" He frowned at her. "Well, thanks, I guess." He would like to congratulate her on her incredible ability to defuse an explosive situation. He would also like to think he wouldn't revisit this evening's events when he was alone tonight.

Once he sat beside her, she lifted a glass and gave it to him.

He smiled but didn't remark that she'd used water goblets.

The paper's name, printed boldly, included a sketch of a French horn emitting a stream of notes. "She might want to change that to a trumpet," he said absently and Madge snorted. "Now what?" he asked.

"That's the least of our worries. Reb and Marc called tonight and they said the horn was deliberate—another ploy to make people think twice."

Cyrus's scalp grew a little tighter. He looked for the price of the publication, turned from front to back of the single sheet, folded in half, searching.

"The first week is free to encourage paid circulation."

"Does that sort of thing work?"

She took the paper from his hands and turned it back to the front page. "If you can hang out some juicy worms of gossip, leaving out the punch lines, it might. Depends on the worms, I guess, and in a little town like this, gossip gets personal. Lee hasn't spared too many people."

Cyrus took the rag back again and went directly to the lead article, thoughtfully highlighted in yellow by Madge. "Massive Accident in Toussaint. Police Investigate Potential Reckless Driving."

"Shi—shoot," Cyrus said, looking at Madge. "She can't do this."

"Sure can. Freedom of the press."

"To make up lies?"

"Cyrus, Jilly went right through a stop sign and hit your car. She didn't mean to, but it happened."

"Sure, but this headline . . ."

"Boring headlines don't attract readers."

He pointed at her, let his hand drop, then pointed again.

"Yes?" she said.

"Jilly and I will have Lee print a correction. That'll be that."

"Good," Madge said, a bit too evenly. "Lil may be the first in line to see Lee, though." A sidebar drew attention to "Tryst With the Devil. The Mystery of the Missing Bingo Boards."

Cyrus tried to be very serious but failed and fell back on the couch laughing. "You don't think Lil took the boards and hid them, do you?" he asked when he could speak.

"It doesn't say it was Lil," Madge pointed out.

"It says how a woman who could gain access to the Parish Hall, a woman so angry with her preoccupied, scheme-a-day husband that she resorts to such things to get his attention was driven to deranged behavior?" He pinched the bridge of his nose. "Has to be Lil. All hell's going to break loose here."

"I think Lee would have liked to lead with this, but even she has a little anxiety about reprisals," Madge said. "There we have 'Mob Connection? Offed at All Tarted Up. Flakiest Forensic Efforts in Town.' Lee went on in detail to explain how the forensics team had gone about their business, showing their ignorance by making a big deal about paper bags being used for evidence because she 'guessed they couldn't get hold of any plastic ones.' And Lee boldly pointed out that it was obvious the victim knew his killer because he didn't draw his own gun and walked straight toward the murderer—a fact she's sure the police missed. And," Madge added, "Lee will give further insights into her crime-scene findings next week."

She frowned at Cyrus. "Is she right about all this? What about the bag thing?"

"Maybe. She's goin' to have to be protected from herself," Cyrus said. Someone should have checked what the woman was up to. "She's got most of her facts wrong. Who checks her facts for her?"

"Not sure. She probably can't afford anyone. Wally's the delivery boy and he likes it."

"It might not be a good idea for him to work there.

I'll have a word with Gator and Doll."

"You can't stand in the way of free enterprise."

"I'll think about it." Cyrus massaged the back of his neck. For years he'd put more time into bringing Wally up than his parents had. "I'll find out what Spike wants to do about all this."

"Spike can't do anything about a person's First Amendment Rights."

"I'm not suggesting he can or would." He couldn't bring himself to look at Madge. "Is that all the damage she's done?"

"Nope. Just the beginning. By the way, Lee's put in all kinds of lovely ads for free. There's one for St. Cécil's with a wonderful picture. She's got a picture of you, too." She put the picture in front of his face.

"And you," he reminded her. "We look pretty good."

They were pictured walking arm in arm out of St. Cécil's and Cyrus groaned inwardly. "She says the parish is a friendly place to be where people get to know one another really well."

"I think that's so sweet," Madge said.

His bishop had better never see it. "She didn't ask if she could put in all these ads. Look at them all. 'Homer Devol's Guzzle, Gobble, Gas and Gab'? And 'Joe Gable Gets the Goods.' My, my, that's not professional for a lawyer."

"But they're all free," Madge pointed out.

He glanced at her lovely, honest face and looked quickly away again.

"'No Job Too Small for Sheriff Spike and His

Posse.'" His mouth fell open. *"Posse?"*

"All of that's just poetic license," Madge said. "Mostly I think she's trying to make it catchy."

"Like, 'Tuck in at Rosebank Resort, Clothes Optional'?"

"Let me see that," Madge said, leaning past his shoulders. "Oh dear."

"And, 'Let Wazoo Arouse Your Deepest Potential'? 'Passionate Packages Our Speciality.'"

"Okay, it's too much. I told you it would have to be talked about. If you're really sweet to her she'll tone it down."

"Me!"

"You're the only one who can do it. Here, look in the middle."

Dutifully, he spread the sheet across his lap. "What am I looking for?"

"That." She tapped the page. "The gossip column."

"Like the rest of this isn't gossip?"

She ignored that. "'Lurking With Lavinia.'"

Cyrus closed his aching eyes. "I thought it was going to be Patti-Lou's column."

"Lee changed her mind. Listen, I'll read it to you. 'Who's lying about their whereabouts last Friday night? Did something happen behind the old laundry after the crash? Who is the redhead with the flashy fingers? Which woman should keep a watch over her man? I know who offered blood money to St. Cécil's, do you? Next question—who turned it down and why? Who's angry about not hearing from a friend?

240

Whose marriage is wobbling over a sad loss? Who wants to marry an out-of-town lady only he doesn't have the guts to ask? Why does a man give expensive gifts to a woman who isn't his wife? And why does the recipient make such a show of not wanting those gifts? Which establishment has the worst food in town? Who—' "

"Stop," Cyrus said. "This is terrible. All she'll accomplish is a lot of infighting."

" 'Who is sleeping with a handsome stranger? Who wants to sleep with a handsome stranger? And do we have a heavenly scandal on our hands?' "

Cyrus turned cold. He turned to Madge.

She closed the paper and set it on the table. "Sounds a bit like clues for a crossword puzzle . . . sorry to be flip. This could start some real problems, couldn't it?"

"Real problems if she's ruffled the wrong feathers and someone wants to shut her up."

17

"There's a flashlight movin' around," Guy said. "Over there. In Lafayette Cemetery."

Nat glanced in the direction Guy pointed. "They keep 'em lighted for safety now?"

"I'm talkin' about a flashlight and it's goin' wild, jumpin' all over the place. Now it's out. Shit. If some asshole's hurt Jilly, I'll . . ." He breathed slowly

241

through his nose. "She wouldn't go into a cemetery, would she?" He looked at Nat, who shrugged.

"Aw, get on, she wouldn't."

"I've got you two figured out," Nat said. "You fell for her because she's got guts. And she's gorgeous and sexy of course."

"If she's in there, she's mad." He peered left. "There's the light again. Let's go."

"Don't you want to know why I think she's interested in you?" Nat swerved up onto the sidewalk near an entrance into the graveyard. "I'll tell you, anyway. She's got bad taste."

Guy grinned. Another unit came toward them, lights flashing, sirens blaring. "Here comes Petit. Can't he make more noise?"

"Probably a good idea to make a minor storm," Nat said. "Should scare the bastard away."

"If it doesn't make him do something desperate before they take off. Light's gone out! He's on the move. And speakin' of storms, this is a doozy. It's going to make the going tougher."

He and Nat were out of the car and approaching the cemetery on the balls of their feet—fast.

Petit and his partner had slewed to a stop and they caught up. Guy recognized the partner, a tall, serious-faced black kid who had already showed signs of becoming a good cop.

Petit had been a middleweight boxer and he still kept in shape. "In there?" He nodded toward the tombs.

"Unfortunately," Guy told him. "Not what we expected. A male suspect chasing a female suspect and another woman following to try to help."

"Holy shit," Petit said. "Some of these people don't have the sense they were born with." Petit's Irish brogue belied the fact that he'd never been to the land of his fathers.

Guy whispered, "It's all about listening now. Fan out."

With Nat in the lead, he and Guy moved straight forward—very slowly. Nat turned and grabbed Guy. "We should have told those two not to use flashlights."

"Petit's smart—so's the kid," Guy whispered.

Along one crooked path between tombs, they went, then back along another. They'd worked together so long they didn't have to talk to make a decision. Nat stood still and Guy stood beside him. They raised their heads to listen.

Nothing but the rain and the wind.

Guy turned hard left and dodged this way and that in a jagged route, stopping in the cover of each tomb he reached.

A thud and a curse stopped him. Nat had tripped over a decorative curbstone and fallen. He had the sense to stay where he was and keep still.

Guy did hear something then. A rustling, a grunt. Could be Petit.

"Guy?"

A thick voice, Jilly's voice, reached him, and so did a string of foul language and threats. "Little fucker," a man said. "Open your mouth again and it'll be the last time. Keep still."

Nat pushed to his knees and looked up at Guy. He put a finger over his lips as if Guy might be fool enough to call out.

He turned the other way and went to the opposite end of the tomb.

"Freeze!" Petit's bass voice bellowed out. "Drop her and get down on your face."

Guy winced, and waited.

A single shot rang out with the sound of a grenade in an enclosed room. And someone screamed.

"Careful," Guy told Nat, who stood behind him again. "Could be a move to get us in the open."

"Shit," Nat said. "There he went."

Guy saw it, too, and started to run. A figure, hunched over and running about two tombs ahead. He was only visible a moment. Guy, with Nat at his heels, arrived at the point where the perp had disappeared.

A moan stopped Guy. Petit's sidekick huddled on the ground grasping his thigh, and not more than a few feet from him sat Jilly, holding her head.

"C'mon," Nat said to Petit. "You stay, Guy, I can still hear him crashing around."

The detective and the beat cop took off and Guy dashed to Jilly while part of him didn't want to leave the chase.

"He's been shot," Jilly said, pointing at the rookie. "He was trying to save me."

"How you doin'?" Guy asked the kid, scooting over

to look at the leg. "I don't think I got your name."

"Lemon," he said. "Winston Lemon. It ain't fair but I didn't get to choose. I only got a flesh wound, but you know how they like to bleed. I've got it under control."

"I like your name," Jilly said promptly. "Thank you for what you did."

Lemon snorted. "I'll probably get reprimanded for doin' somethin' wrong. But I'm glad I'm here, ma'am. How you doin'?"

"Better—except for the headache."

Guy called for the medics, then went back to crouch beside Jilly. He took out a penlight and flashed it in her eyes. Quickly over the pupil, then away again.

"Take a better look at Winston's leg," Jilly said.

"I'm doin' fine," Winston said, and Jilly saw his smile in the darkness.

"So he's Winston already?" Guy whispered. "Have a care, I'm a very jealous man."

She leaned her head on his shoulder and tried to see his face. Best not mention the blows to her head with the flashlight or he'd cart her off to a hospital. "You were quick," she told him.

"Mmm." Guy brushed her wet and matted hair away from her face. "Want to explain why you left the Preston house?"

"I shouldn't have left. I overreacted. What I've got to do now is get myself back there as quickly as I can, with some excuse they'll have to believe even if it sounds fake."

Guy's face turned stony. "Why would I let you do a damn fool thing like that?"

"First, because I think Preston had something to do with the man who went after that woman. If the man gets away he will report back to Preston that he was interrupted by someone. Preston shouldn't think it could have been me if I go back to the house and don't mention it. He thinks I trust him, so why wouldn't I tell him all about something like that?

"Second, I know how you feel about Edith, but she's sick and pathetic and my conscience says I ought to make sure I don't get cut off from her."

Standing on the front steps at the Prestons', Jilly knew she was a lucky woman to have persuaded Guy to let her come. She probably wouldn't have if Nat hadn't pointed out the good sense in what she said, in her reasons for insisting on returning.

Guy and Nat hung around outside the tall laurel hedge, and she'd been warned by he-who-would-be-obeyed that if she didn't get a call to him within half an hour, he'd be coming in after her. The horrible man had got away, leaving the officers in sullen moods. But Jilly was glad Guy and Nat were right behind her. She needed to do this, but might not have had the guts on her own.

She rang the bell. Lights shot on inside so quickly someone had to have been up and walking about.

The door opened and there stood Laura Preston in a short black evening dress that showed more than it

246

covered. "Jilly?" she whispered. "Oh, Jilly, where have you been? I went to your room to see if you were awake and you'd gone. I didn't know what I was going to tell them. Get in here and go to bed before someone else misses you."

Chilled and shaking, wet to the skin, Jilly stepped through the door and stood on a mat inside. "I'm dripping. I'd better blot myself off before I go upstairs."

"Where have you been?" Laura asked urgently. "I don't understand you."

"I'm a pretty open book. How about you? What are you doing here?"

"Wes and I went to a gallery opening in the Quarter. We went straight from Toussaint and just got back here. You didn't tell me where you've been."

"Out," Jilly said, turning her mouth down. "I'm a private person and I need my space. I had to walk on my own. Thank you for caring."

A thin shriek came from upstairs and Laura closed her eyes. "Damn it all, Jilly. That's Edith. You can bet your boots she's found out you're not in your room."

"I can't deal with this," Jilly said. "I'm not used to having every move I make watched." And the electric tension in the house messed with her resolve.

Laura went pink. "The Prestons are a tight-knit family. They don't like not knowing where to find one of us."

"What's going on down there?" Preston's voice boomed from the second floor. "Get back to bed, Edith. And stop whimperin'."

"I will not, Daddy," Edith said in a quavering voice. "I want my Jilly. Where is she? You frightened her away, didn't you?"

Laura put her hands over her ears.

"Hush," Jilly said. "It'll be okay. Mr. Preston. Edith. It's me, Jilly, and I know I'm a terrible nuisance. I'm fine, just fine, and I'm going back to bed right now." She was anything but fine. Even "terrified" wasn't that close.

"In the sitting room, all of you," Preston ordered, hurrying downstairs in a silk paisley robe. He glared at Laura and cast a disgusted glance back at Edith, who followed him slowly.

"Wes has to stay out of these things," Laura said in Jilly's ear. "He loses his temper and it's dreadful. The three of us will talk when this is over."

Preston walked into the sitting room, but Edith came to Jilly and took her by the hand. She smiled softly at her, and at Laura. "Good girls. Sweet girls. We'll be just fine."

"Look at you," Preston said the moment Jilly went into the room. "Explain yourself. As a member of this family there are standards we expect of you. You went out to meet someone, didn't you? Was it that gas jockey?"

Gas jockey? He meant Guy and the fact that he worked for Homer part-time. "I went out for a walk but I got a bit lost and wandered where I probably shouldn't have gone. It's raining and I managed to fall on some mud and bang myself up."

"Sit here," Edith said, patting the back of her own chaise.

"I need a shower," Jilly said. "I'm filthy."

"Not good enough," Preston said. "A young woman doesn't just go wanderin' around in the middle of the night. Not here."

If she was right about the woman, and the man who chased her, how long would it be before Preston found out what had happened? "I get claustrophobia. I never know when it's going to hit but it did tonight, probably because I was in new surroundings, and I went out. That's what I always do." A hired bully wouldn't want to admit he'd been tripped up by a woman, would he? Jilly's anxiety eased a little.

"Poor, dear girl," Edith said.

Time was moving along. If she didn't get upstairs on her own and make that call, her "gas jockey" would be bursting into the house. "Please. Everyone go back to bed. I'm going to get ready for bed myself and see if I can calm down. I am so sorry for upsettin' everyone." She looked at Preston, who looked back with hard eyes. The identity of the woman she'd helped wasn't a guess anymore. Jilly couldn't shake the conviction that the same woman had got out of Preston's car beside the house and that he'd sent the man after her.

"Run along, baby," Edith said. "I'll make sure you get some hot milk with somethin' in it to make you sleep. I'll have it left outside your door, so don't you worry about bein' interrupted. Come along, Daddy. Good night, Jilly, and you, Laura."

"That son of mine too drunk to put in an appearance?" Preston snapped.

"Wes works too hard," Laura said. "He's so tired he just passed out on the bed the minute we got home."

Edith steered Preston upstairs; Laura also went up but turned left toward another wing. Jilly went straight to her room, locked the door and immediately called Guy. "Jilly here," she said in a low voice. "It's okay. I'm in my room." She listened to Guy. "Don't worry, I'm too scared not to be careful. I need to take a shower, I'm a mess." She smiled. "Thank you. I'm glad someone likes me no matter how I look. I'd better go. I'll get in touch in the mornin'. I'll be away first thing."

Guy hadn't finished. "I want you to take that Hummer with you, got it? You do nothin' to make waves with those people."

"I won't, but they aren't going to do anything to me." Later she would have to tell Guy what she'd seen when Preston got home.

"You don't know that. What happened to make you run out of there?"

Oh, no, she wasn't going into that tonight. "It had more to do with some hang-ups of mine than anything," she told him. "When we can get together, I'll explain it to you. Remember, Preston will figure there are plenty of people who know I came here. He'll be cautious. I'm safe. Bye, Guy."

"You mean a lot to me, ma'am."

Her heart thudded all over again. "Thank you. The feelin's mutual."

"The house will be watched. Don't argue, it's happenin'. If the situation changes, call back. I'll be waiting."

"Thank you." She hung up and held the phone against her chest. What did he really mean when he said she meant a lot to him?

She threw her small duffel on the puffy bed and found her toiletries and a pair of pajamas. Life used to be so uncomplicated—or it had been occasionally.

One good feeling she had was that the woman in the cemetery had gotten away.

In the bathroom, she started the shower and remembered to turn on the fan. Then she locked the door and stripped off her clothes. Wet mud had found its way to her skin in places where she couldn't figure how it got there.

The shower sloped and needed no doors. She felt euphoric when hot water beat down on her. She lathered her hair and washed her body again and again. Only one thing was missing, one thing to make this a perfect shower—Guy. She touched her aching breasts and shuddered.

Once she was dry, she went through the tedious process of combing and brushing her hair before putting on her silk pajamas. She thought of Preston settling a hand—so sneakily—on her body and grimaced. She wasn't one of his "other women," and she never would be. The idea disgusted her. But more unnerving was the idea that the man had shown he could be violent.

She hurried between the sheets and attempted to relax, only to have the door open quietly, the door she thought she had locked. Swallowing a scream, she grabbed the cell phone from beneath her pillow.

"It's only us," Laura whispered, and waved Wes into the room behind her.

Jilly pulled the covers up to her chin and held on to them while she sat up. Wes turned on a light by her bed and Laura carried a mug of milk, which she gave to Jilly. The smell of liquor tickled her nose.

"I locked that door," Jilly said.

"It opened right up," Laura said, looking at Wes, who shrugged. Dressed in a tuxedo minus the jacket and with his black tie hanging loose, he was something to look at. "You have to listen to us," Laura said. "It's for your own good."

"Let's get to it," Wes said. He looked at Laura with the kind of possessiveness Jilly didn't find healthy. "Edith needs you around, Jilly."

"I intend to be around," she told him.

"But there are precautions you have to take," Laura said rapidly. "Aren't there, Wes? Like—"

"Like accepting the truth. My father has a weakness for women. A certain kind of woman."

Anger stiffened Jilly's spine. "What kind of woman would that be?"

"Weak ones. Malleable ones. Sexy ones. He has the kind of appetite that means one woman could never keep him satisfied."

A slight move made Jilly look at Laura, but the woman, still in her beautiful, beaded black dress, had made her face stony. Jilly wondered if Laura had been subjected to Mr. Preston's advances.

"Yep," Wes said. He followed the direction of Jilly's glance. "If you're thinking my daddy knows every inch of my dear wife, you're right."

Jilly gasped and Laura looked defiant.

"He's the one with the money," Wes said, crossing his arms. His narrowed eyes were on Jilly. "He calls the shots. Did you take a shower?"

Everything he said disturbed her. "Yes, why?"

"Give her somethin' to put on," Wes said.

Laura took a sheer black robe from a closet and held it out for Jilly, who slipped it on.

"Come with me. Don't turn the bathroom lights on."

"Don't, Wes," Laura said. "Why do that?"

"Because our little friend needs to know what she's up against. And she needs to know we're her friends and we'll look out for her interests." Wes turned off the light beside the bed, found Jilly's hand and led her to the bathroom, where he let her in and closed the door behind them.

Jilly sweated. She could hardly take a breath. When she tried to free her hand, Wes held it even tighter and pulled her forward. She could see the sheen on the mirrors and smell the expensive shampoo and soap she'd used.

Wes took her to the center of the wall opposite the shower, the wall where two mirrors were separated by the portrait of a woman. He took her right hand to the picture and pressed the tip of her index finger to the painted woman's eye.

Jilly jerked away, then pulled herself up to sit on the counter. She put her face against the mirror and gradually got closer to the portrait. Then she applied her finger to the eye again and felt a smooth, very slightly convex surface.

Before Wes could stop her, she knelt and put her own eye to what was clearly glass and tried to see beyond. There was only darkness.

She jumped down and hurried back to the bedroom, where Laura snapped on the light the moment Wes returned from the bathroom.

"It's a peephole," Jilly said, hugging herself.

"In a way," Wes said. "There's a lens in there. It gives Daddy a complete view of the bathroom. Doesn't have to miss a thing. Apparently you went out earlier without getting ready for bed. He must have thought he was in heaven when he got a second chance to watch you."

Jilly grabbed up her duffel, but Wes took it from her and put it back on the floor. "Get some sleep. You'll be okay—Laura and I will make sure of that. Just make sure you never stay under the same roof as my father again."

• • •

"Don't touch me," Laura said, putting distance between them.

Wes closed the door to their sitting room. "Shut up. Keep your voice down. All I want from you is cooperation."

"I've cooperated. I've done everything I can."

"Except get rid of her back at the beginning when it would have been easy," Wes said. "If you'd done as you were told you could have paid her almost nothing to get lost. Now she knows there could be a lot in it for her if she sticks around."

"Let it go," Laura said. "I told you it was impossible to broach with her. End of story."

Wes walked past her. "No, it isn't. But we can manage her. Daddy's bad habits scared her. Unlike some, she isn't going to buy her way into his pockets with sex."

Laura smiled. Why argue? What he suggested about her was true, or it had been until lately. "What are you thinking of doing?"

"Being careful," Wes said. "Keeping her out of his bank accounts and keeping him out of her pants. That's your job."

"Pig," she said. It still hurt a little that her husband was so willing to share her, but she smiled at him. "You can count on me."

18

A honeymoon couple asked if Jilly and Guy would take their picture in front of the Hummer. "Where else but New Orleans would you see a thing like this?" the man asked. Guy obliged and returned to Jilly with a sunny smile on his face.

"If I have to bail that pink pig out of hock, I'll be so embarrassed, Guy." Jilly would never get used to the folks who pointed at the Hummer and laughed. "It's taking too long to get a prognosis on the Beetle."

"Your custom vehicle will be safe outside Jack and Celina's place. Jack's gonna hang some permit or other on the mirror."

Jilly pursed her lips. "Lovely. Someone's goin' to do something illegal and one of the men supposed to uphold the law thinks that's just fine."

Guy wiggled his eyebrows. "Strictly speaking, I'm not on active duty. The permit is because they live here, I think," he said. "Don't you think Piggy's a great PR tool? Wait till you have more business than you can cope with."

Jilly stood in front of the vehicle to block her own picture.

"How come you had me meet you here rather than at Nat's place?" she asked. "I'd like to thank him for all he did."

"Well, let's say that boy prob'ly flunked house-keepin', cher. He was nervous you'd visit before he has a chance to clean up. He reckons he's havin' us over when the smoke clears."

"I like Nat," Jilly said. "So does Wazoo."

"Lord help Nat."

"I think he likes her, too."

Guy's lips parted, then snapped shut. He said, "Ready to tell me what sent you out into the bad world last night?"

"No. It's not relevant."

"It is to me," he said. "Poor old Winston Lemon probably thinks it's relevant, too."

"Two separate things. What made me want to get some fresh air, then what happened afterward. Just another night of crime in the old city. I'll make sure I visit Winston."

She could tell by the long, intense stare Guy gave her that he wasn't buying her glib explanations, but she wanted to be well away from the Preston house when she told him a watered-down version of the truth. He would need time to accept that she had no proof so he could not do anything.

"I could have interrupted a lovers' quarrel in the cemetery," she said. "But I'm glad I did because that man was mean."

"*No.* Mean? You overreact sometimes. I bet when he doesn't have his gun and he isn't beating up on a woman, he's a pussycat."

He caught her by the hand and steered close to a

257

shop window. With his free hand framing the right side of her face, he made sure she knew she had been kissed, and when he had given her time to draw in a breath, he kissed her again.

Her eyes felt slightly out of focus, but she blinked at him and said, "What was that for?"

"I've been waiting to get close to you for hours. It's a good job you got here early or I would have marched up to the Prestons' front door and kissed you right there. And kissin' isn't gonna be enough, lady. Just wait till I get you—"

"Hush up," she told him. "You can be so bad."

He played his fingertips over her mouth. "I want us to have a chance to be together without all this other stuff goin' on."

She laughed a little. "Me, too."

"It'll happen. You can't figure out if two people work when they've only been together while visions of murderers danced in their heads."

"You're funny. That's true." And the happy moment popped. She could almost see a big bright soap bubble splattering on the sidewalk. As far as Guy was concerned, she was still on trial.

He looked at her and the smile was gone.

All business, she said, "Guy, you being an ex-cop never came up with Preston. He doesn't know. Neither does Edith or the other two. I mean, we can't hide it forever, but for as long as we can might be good, unless you suddenly decide to return to active duty."

Just like always, he narrowed his eyes at the mention of whether or not he'd return to duty, but he didn't protest the idea. "You're right," he said. "Let's get over to Dwayne and Jean-Claude's place. Jack's going to meet us there. Apparently they've been doing some homework. Hey—" he put an arm around her waist and studied her face "—I'm not sure it's a good idea to take you to Les Chats."

"Why?" The bustle had started and a sidewalk portrait artist had chosen the exact spot where they stood to set up his easel. She and Guy moved a few feet. "Why wouldn't it be a good idea?"

"I think we've scratched the surface of a bog and it's going to stink real bad when we open the thing up. So far all we've got is two dead men and a mess of details I know connect up somewhere. I don't want you in danger."

He looked so sincere she could hardly bring herself to break a piece of down-home news to him. But she'd manage. "I'm already in danger—probably. I intend to look out for my own interests. Try to shut me out and I'll be like a mosquito after the sun goes down. I'll find a way to get you."

The smile he gave her was actually lazy. "I'll get me a real big fly swatter."

She shook a finger at him. "Don't you mess with me, Guy Gautreaux—or I'll have to write to my brother and his bride and tell them to get back here from that trip they planned for so long."

On a gallery above, someone had decided to water pots of lush ivy geraniums. A gush overflowed and

Jilly pulled Guy off the sidewalk.

He covered his face and shook his head. "Okay, okay, you win. But this isn't a game."

"You thought I thought it was?" She gave him a deadly serious look. "I saw Caruthers's brains spread all over my yard at All Tarted Up. Let's quit yakking and get on."

Guy held her hand firmly, jutted his chin, tipped his Stetson over his nose and marched along with enough attitude to make his boot heels ring.

She hurried to keep up.

In silence they cut through Toulouse Street, turned right on Royal, past the Court of Two Sisters and the smell of early morning baking and sauces guaranteed to make the mouth water. St. Peter's Street to Bourbon, a right turn and a few short blocks brought them to a club with totem poles on either side of dark blue double doors. Totem poles carved in the shape of dozens of cats climbing over one another. Beside the totems were the glass-covered billboards all the clubs had. They showed off photos of beautiful women dressed as cats.

"Don't look at those," Guy said, pulling her.

"Why? Because this is a strip joint? Don't be so weird."

"There you are, you lovely couple, you." Dwayne hopped down his front steps, his hair wet from the shower, and looking snappy in a khaki shirt and jeans, no socks and expensive-looking brown loafers. He glanced at a billboard and immediately insinuated himself between Jilly and the pictures. He glared at Guy. "What are you thinkin' of? Take my new young friend inside. Jack's there and so is Nat and things are jumpin'." He gave Guy a knowing sideways glance.

"On second thought, you come with Dwayne," he said, tucking Jilly's hand under his arm. "You're not a child but you've lived a sheltered life."

Oh, yeah, a really sheltered life.

"Jean-Claude is my partner and you're going to meet him. He is a lovely man, the best thing that ever happened to me."

"I'm glad for you," Jilly said.

"Now, I don't want you to take what you see in the club seriously at all," Dwayne said. "This is a dance club, not a strip club. People come here to watch the dancing. It's very exotic and the artistes are incredibly accomplished."

Jilly caught Guy's sweetly wicked smile and smiled right back. A stage dominated the place, with trapezes and tall, red-carpet-covered poles running from the boards and out of sight in the rafters.

Under the fingers of a tall, angular man with a cigarette in his lips, an upright piano that looked as if it might have been hauled off the bottom of Lake Ponchartrain, then set fire to regularly, emitted the kind of blues that turned Jilly's bones to mush.

"He is so good," she told Dwayne.

He laughed, hanging his head back and basking in the compliment. "That's my Jean-Claude. Wait till you see him dance." The serious look was back. "Some of the artistes are going to be practicing. If anything about them looks strange, just don't watch."

Jilly nodded and flashed Guy an evil glare. She stood on tiptoe and whispered in his ear. "You told Dwayne I'm a sheltered small-town girl, you creep. Wait till I get you alone."

"I'm counting on it. There's our group. Sheesh, they aren't crackin' any jokes as far as I can see."

"Mornin' all," Guy said, sliding into a seat beside Nat, who didn't bother to acknowledge his old partner. Jilly sat beside Guy with Dwayne on her other side.

Jack had somehow got there ahead of Guy and Jilly and sat with his feet on the table and a mug of coffee beside his ankles. Jean-Claude left the piano, stubbed his cigarette out in an ashtray he passed and came toward them with a loose-limbed gate. He sat with Dwayne.

Canned music blared and Dwayne yelled, "Turn it down," before a tall woman in gold, her face made up like an elegant, sequined cat, positioned herself at one of the poles, swung a leg straight above her head and did the splits standing up.

Jilly said, "That looks painful."

"You have no idea," Jean-Claude said with a smile.

Although the place was all but empty, Dwayne leaned across the table to say quietly, "I've got a friend I trust who spends time at Jazz Babes. Has for years. They always have a high-stakes poker game going there and he has the money to play until he runs out of money. Reckons he's seen some ruined men totter out of that place."

"Did he ever see Pip Sedge there?" Nat asked.

"Maybe. He's going slow with some of the information."

"That's another way of saying the guy still doesn't have enough money to please him. He wants to be paid," Jack said.

Jean-Claude sniffed and glanced at the woman on the stage, who had to be a contortionist.

"She has the most beautiful legs I've ever seen," Jilly said.

"Nice legs," Dwayne said. None of the others made a remark.

"Tell them what my friend did talk about," Jean-Claude told Dwayne.

"I like that man," Dwayne said. "He's got his principles. He doesn't like men who mess up girls. He remembers that girl we were talkin' about. The one who showed up dead at her parents' place."

"After they'd been at Jazz Babes—or Maison Bleue as it was then—lookin' for her," Jean-Claude said.

"Is this going to lead us back to Caruthers and Pip?"

"Could be," Dwayne said. "We gotta be patient. We don't even know there was a connection between Pip and the other vic."

"I'd lay odds on it," Guy said. "Keep going."

"This friend of mine said Pip got mad at the manager over there. Felix Broussard. Mad bastard. He's been there forever. Pip threatened him because he said

Felix was mistreating girls."

Jack swung his feet to the floor. "How long ago was this?"

"Not recent," Jean-Claude said. "Back around the time that girl got chopped. Several years ago now. Pip got thrown out on his ass—after Felix and one or two of his boys had a private chat with him."

Nat turned to Guy. "So Pip had an old history at Jazz Babes, a bad history. He must have been told to stay away but he went back."

"How do you know that?" Dwayne said.

Nat shrugged and said, "When Pip was offed he was on his way to Toussaint. He had a matchbook from Jazz Babes with some instructions about finding a place in Toussaint. At least, that's what we think he intended to do."

Guy said, "He never made it, but another guy was shot exactly where Pip may have been headed."

Jack stared at Guy. "Caruthers something?"

"Yeah," Nat said. "The other guy we mentioned."

"What did he have to do with Jazz Babes and Pip?" Dwayne said.

"That's the rub. Nothing. Not a blamed thing as far as we can tell." Nat took off his fedora and threw it on the table.

"There is a connection," Guy said. "There has to be because there always is."

Tentatively, Jilly said, "I think Caruthers was in the wrong place at the wrong time. I don't think the killer went there expecting to find him."

"What did he expect, then?" Guy said.

"He didn't expect a man to be delivering the ugliest vehicle on the planet and walkin' around the place just to make sure everything was okay."

"I want to know who was in your house, Jilly, and what was the point?" Guy muttered. When the questions started he waved them off. "Forget I mentioned it. I'll work on that later."

"Maybe he was lookin' for somethin' he could use against me—as some sort of blackmail," Jilly said. "And the guy who did it could also have wanted to show me I'm vulnerable, that he can get at me."

Guy stared at her thoughtfully. "You could be right. Sometimes we make things too complicated."

Jack said, "The girl who went missing all those years back, her name was Paula. She was classified as missing for several days but then her folks got a call saying she'd been seen alive and kicking and in New Orleans."

They all leaned forward and kept their voices low.

"A woman placed the call and said she'd meet the parents."

Nat got up and paced. He kept rubbing his eyes. When he got to Jack he bent down and said, "Did they meet?"

"Probably," Jack told him. "But the woman called the shots. Place, time of day. She took money from the father and took off—after she told him Paula had been pulled into a prostitution ring and was as good as a prisoner at Jazz Babes. Only trouble is that by the time the girl's parents recovered enough from finding Paula in pieces at home and talked to the cops about what the woman had said, Jazz Babes was clean. If it had ever been anything else. And no connection was ever made."

"Did they find the female informant?" Guy asked.

"Nope."

"We need to talk to the parents."

Nat grimaced. "I'd give back a month's pay, maybe more, to know why the case records never got on the computer—and why there're big chunks of simple information missing. Oliphant said the parents split up, went their separate ways. No trace of 'em." Nat dropped into a chair again. "Seems to happen that way a lot when a couple lose a child. They don't stay together. Seems a shame if you think that's when they need each other most."

"It's more complicated than that," Jilly said. "What d'you think would happen if it got around that the police have found Paula's dad and he knows who the informant was?"

She had the rapt attention of all present. "I think that if the woman exists she'd be scared shitless—I mean really scared."

Nat guffawed. "We don't have a clue where she might be, or if she's anywhere. Probably six feet under by now with the circles she moved in."

"I guess," Jilly said, but Nat's defeatism annoyed her. "But it couldn't hurt to give it a try."

"What do you think she's going to do?" Nat said.

"Come in waving a white flag?"

"Cool it," Guy said. "You need sleep, partner."

"And you don't?"

Guy ignored him. "I doubt we'll get anything from it, but we'll try, Jilly."

He was throwing her a bone, but she was sick enough of all the uncertainty to pick it up and be grateful.

Nat straightened his jacket and wiped his face with a paper napkin. "If we had a description of the woman we could put out an APB, but that's obviously out. Who's going to pay for ads in newspapers all over the country?"

"That won't be a problem," Jack said.

"I can help," Guy said, surprising Jilly.

"We'll chip in," Dwayne told them. "Anyone have TV connections?"

"We might be able to do something there," Jack said.

Several women moved around the stage now. At one point a group of them hooked their elbows together and did high kicks à la Rockettes. They were good, they also laughed a lot. Jilly stared at them, fascinated.

A second barman arrived and flipped on the TV behind the bar. He stood with his back to the room, watching.

"Nice work if you can get it," Jean-Claude sang out in a smoky voice, and got to his feet. He did a soft-shoe across the floor toward the bar and said, "Harold, we pay you to work, not watch the box."

267

The barman turned and grinned, then went back to watching his program on some Podunk station.

"I better stick around New Orleans for now," Guy said to Nat.

Jilly avoided looking at either of them but felt adrift. Where did she fit in now? she wondered. A lot of brave words on her part didn't mean Guy wouldn't shut her out.

"Eh!" Jean-Claude called, and snapped his fingers when he had their attention. "I think you want to see this." He inclined his head toward the television screen.

Jilly got up, as did the rest of the group. The bartender laughed and staggered around behind the bar slapping his knees with a dish towel.

"I hope it's that funny," Jack said. "A laugh is always a good thing."

"Turn it up, please, Harry," Jean-Claude said.

"Whooee," Nat said, starting to grin himself. "That's one familiar piece of real estate."

A reporter held a microphone for Lee O'Brien. They stood in front of All Tarted Up with a camera angle that showed off the pink front door.

"No," Jilly moaned. "What are they talking about?" She got a round of "Hush!"

"In the yard behind the café," Lee was saying. "I shouldn't give any more details about what happened. I'd really better not." She hesitated. "A man was shot to death there—in the head. His brains were everywhere. This bakery belongs to Jilly Gable. A peach.

She's an absolute peach and she's had such bad luck with love and everything else."

"Too bad." The reporter clearly wanted to get back to the case. "Lee, any idea why the killer might have chosen this particular place?"

"Jilly Gable's yard, you mean. It could be worth your while to talk to her, Danny. She's had troubles with some of the people in her life. Her last boyfriend, well, that was a while ago."

"What about her last boyfriend?"

"Let's just say he was a bad apple and he had to know a lot of bad people. So Jilly's probably met one or two of them. Could be someone came back for her but got interrupted, or not. She was there when it all went down so she could have a lot of information."

"And your paper, the *Toussaint Trumpet* . . ."

"Yes, we're finally going to get to the bottom of a lot of mysteries hidden away in this so-called sleepy town."

19

"Vivian's really upset," Spike said. "I don't expect you to make that go away, but I could use your advice."

Cyrus glanced sideways at his friend's face. They'd left the rectory to get away from the stream of visitors and phone calls complaining about the *Toussaint*

Trumpet. They made their way along the winding path above the Bayou Teche, where the occasional fish broke the surface under cloudy skies on a day so humid the air felt rationed.

"She thinks that crack in the paper about a marriage being wobbly because of a sad loss is about us."

Cyrus picked up a rock and skimmed it across the dull water. "That was the idea. To print stuff that could apply to a bunch of people, then watch the fallout. And report on it, I suppose. Lee's a decent woman. Bright, funny, but she's not cut out for small-town living and she's trying to make it exciting enough for her. Leastwise, that's how I see it. She'll ease up."

"It's not true," Spike said. He carried his Stetson, slapping it against his thigh every other step. "Vivian and I are sad, okay, but we've only gotten closer. My challenge is to knock down any thought she has about being guilty of something. The pregnancy didn't pan out and we lost . . . we lost our baby. It hurts. It damn well hurts like hell, but I'm married to the best woman in the world and I'm not having some gossiping news-paper type putting Vivian through misery."

Cyrus kept quiet. He thought it best to let Spike talk as long as he had a head of steam on.

"It's taking advantage of the kindness around here. Folks accept people, they take them in and make them welcome."

"And include them in any local information, real or otherwise," Cyrus murmured, and ducked as a bird flew up with a berry in its beak.

"Yeah," Spike said. "She may not even have been talking about us."

"Absolutely," Cyrus said.

They walked on. The sky took on a faintly green hue and Cyrus expected rain at any moment—thunder and lightning wouldn't surprise him. He cleared his throat and shortened his stride. "Spike," he said, "did Reb say you and Vivian should wait a bit before starting another pregnancy?"

Spike took a long time to say "Yes."

"But it would be all right now?" He couldn't help unless he knew what was really going on here.

Whatever Spike mumbled, Cyrus didn't hear.

"You are going to try again?" he asked. "You'll have another child?"

"Oh, yeah," Spike said, loud enough to be announcing a blue-light special. "Of course. Vivian's crazy about Wendy but it's natural for her to want a baby of her own. I want that, too. But Vivian may still be sorting out her hormones and you know that can take a bit."

"So I've heard." Now he was certain Spike was here more for help with his marriage than because he expected Cyrus to censure Lee O'Brien.

Spike sighed and Cyrus looked at him. "What is it?"

"We haven't been making love." His face reddened.

These were the deep issues a priest was supposed to alleviate with his wisdom. Briefly, Cyrus saw Madge's face, he felt her lips on his and actually

271

touched his mouth. He dropped his hand quickly. This wasn't about him. "Vivian doesn't want to make love?"

"I'm afraid to . . . I don't want to hurt her."

Cyrus draped an arm over his friend's back. "You say whatever you want to say in your own time. There's a way through all this."

"I wait till she's asleep before I go to bed." Spike kicked a rock viciously. "If she wakes up I pretend I'm already asleep. I don't want her to feel she has to do anything she doesn't want to do."

A single shard of lightning split the clouds. They'd walked quite a way and soon they'd be near Edwards Place. "Vivian needs you," Cyrus said. "Show her your love. Physical love."

"What if she turns me down?"

"You're a big boy. Work through it because she needs you more than she ever has."

Spike stopped walking. He looked toward the bayou and put on his Stetson as rain began to fall. "I love her so much."

"Then show her."

"Cyrus!" Madge's voice came from behind them and he turned to see her running along the path in the high heels she favored. He liked them, too, liked the way they showed off pretty feet and legs. She waved her hand. The yellow dress she wore had a square neck and no sleeves, and a finely pleated full skirt flipped around her knees in the breeze.

"Stop running," he called. "You'll fall."

If anything, she ran faster until she reached them. Not even breathing hard, she said, "Good morning, Spike, I didn't know you were here," and appeared agitated.

"You did," Cyrus reminded her. "You forgot is all. Let your heart be quiet, cher. Tell me what's upset you."

"I'm not upset." She shook the dark curls she'd grown almost to shoulder length in the past few months. Again she slid Spike an uncomfortable glance.

"I'd best be going," he said, thumping Cyrus on the back. "I'll think through what you said."

"No, no," Madge told him. "Don't let me chase you away. It's good for Cyrus to get out of the house and walk. He spends too much time with other people's troubles."

Cyrus didn't look at Spike. "The calls are still coming in, I suppose," he said.

"Yes, but it's Homer I want to talk to you about."

"What about Homer?" Spike snapped. "What about my father?"

"He's fine," Madge said quickly. "Just mad is all. He's really steamin' and he expects you to fix it, Cyrus."

"It?"

"He says he's been written up in 'Lurking With Lavinia.' He says Lee's talking about him and Charlotte in the bit about a man being too chicken to ask an out-of-town lady to marry him."

"Good grief," Cyrus said.

Charlotte Patin was Vivian Devol's mother and Homer's good friend. They shared a love of Wendy because when Vivian and Spike married, Charlotte couldn't wait to be a grandmother to Spike's daughter.

"Listen you two," Madge said. "You know how Homer can be. He's on a tear. He says he's not going to Rosebank again because he doesn't want to run into Charlotte."

"That's crazy," Spike said. "He loves to be there."

"Apparently not now he's being chased by a conniving woman who told lies to a gossip columnist."

"He's calling Charlotte a conniving woman?" Spike shook his head. "I reckon he may have been having some romantic notions about her or he wouldn't be so mad."

Cyrus took Madge by the arm and started back toward St. Cécil's. "I'd better go and sort this out."

"I hope you can. He's going to file for custody of Wendy."

"What?" Spike shouted.

"Well, he says he spends more time with her than you do and he's taking her back to his place."

20

The thing that got a man was knowing he was in trouble but not why. In New Orleans everything had been great with Jilly until she turned cold on him. Now they were back in Toussaint, and the prospect of a meaningful discussion hovered ahead of Guy.

When he opened Jilly's front door, he braced himself for a lick attack from Goldilocks. The dog didn't show and Guy didn't mention her. If something had happened to the interloper, he didn't want to be the one to bring it to Jilly's attention.

"Where did you get that key?" Jilly said behind him, all sharpness.

"You gave it to me. In case I needed it, was what you said. Would you like it back?"

He turned to look down at her and she tried to stare back, but gave up and averted her face. "It might be useful for you to have it. In case they manage to kill me. No, you keep it."

"Right." He wouldn't get drawn into a discussion about how likely she was to be murdered because Caruthers had died at her place. Besides, he knew she was afraid and his job was to give her some confidence.

He walked into the house.

Jilly followed. Since they had left the others in New

Orleans she had treated him like an ax murderer. Driving back one behind the other in their separate vehicles had been a blessing of sorts. At least he'd had an opportunity to calm down and try to figure out why she was mad at him—only he hadn't figured it out.

"Is it okay if I check things out before I go?" he said.

"Suit yourself." She went into the living room and he heard her making sure the windows were locked before she drew the curtains. "Come on in and be comfortable." Her tone sounded less antagonistic.

"I will after I go through the house," he told her, and heard the phone ring.

"Hello," Jilly said. "Hey, Wazoo. You're right, I am tired out. Doll Hibbs? Well, she's served enough meals at the Majestic. Sure, if she wants to make some extra money, let her help fill in. Don't forget we've got Hungry Eyes to cover till Joe and Ellie get back . . . of course you haven't forgotten. It's just me obsessing. I'll be at the shop early in the mornin' and we'll all talk."

Guy wanted to "be comfortable" with Jilly. He went from room to room and found no sign of disturbance. Upstairs the story was the same until he came to Jilly's bedroom. The disturbance there was shiny, black and rumpled. Goldilocks had turned the comforter into a swirling mess to make a cocoon. She lay in the middle, peering out at him with one eye, although her tail wagged.

"You no-good mutt," he told her, but gently. "Look what you've done to Jilly's bed."

"What has she done?" Jilly came in and stood beside him. She giggled. "This girl surely does know how to make herself at home."

Goldilocks lifted her head and got up slowly, wiggling out of the comforter. She was about to jump down from the bed when Jilly stopped her. "You're a lucky man to have a dog like this," she said to Guy. "I know you're still fightin' it, but you're good with her and she'll be your best buddy."

The best buddy he wanted wasn't a dog, although he did feel a twinge of attachment to the mutt. He wouldn't be telling Jilly about that.

Jilly put her arms around Goldilocks's neck and hugged her. "Sweet thing. Time to get down." She sat down and the dog promptly flopped and settled her head on Jilly's knees.

"I'll get her down," Guy said, moving in the dog's direction.

"Whoa," Jilly said. "Look at this."

"What?"

"Her tummy." She stroked the shaggy fur in both directions from the center.

Guy moved in closer and looked at Goldilocks's slightly pink belly. "Is it the wrong color?"

"No." Jilly rolled her eyes. "She's . . ." She rolled the dog onto her back, which Goldilocks seemed to think was the best thing that had ever happened to her. "Guy, I think this girl is pregnant."

He blinked rapidly and got a little closer. "She's a pup herself. How can she be pregnant?"

"We don't know how old she is, but she's old enough to have puppies. See how big she is here?"

Guy sighed. "That's all we need. How many months before she has 'em?"

"Weeks. Maybe eleven. Twelve." Jilly stroked Goldilocks's head and looked at Guy, who had backed off a step or two. "I'm no expert, but I don't think our Goldy girl's bikini will fit so well shortly."

"You'd better get to be an expert fast." Guy frowned so deeply his brows all but hid his eyes. "She'll need special food and care. And a vet. You'd better get her checked out by a vet quickly. With her being young like that, she could have a lot of trouble."

Jilly didn't laugh, but she wanted to. "She'll want a box and a blanket," she told him. "They like to nest when they're expecting babies. I know that much."

"How did it happen?" Guy said. He sat gingerly on the bed, at Goldilocks's other side, and held one of her feet. "Some *animal* took advantage of a poor, helpless creature. She couldn't even have known what was going on."

"Where did you grow up, Guy?"

"New Orleans. Why? What does that have to do with anythin'?"

"Nothing. I was just thinkin' how you don't sound like a farm boy."

He spared her a glance. "I don't know what you're talking about. Does a big dog like this have an easier time having pups than a little one would, huh?"

"I suppose so." She sensed he was going to be a ner-

278

vous owner—unless she lost the fight and he decided he wouldn't keep the dog. "You'll want to find another home for her." Keeping an innocent face wasn't easy. "You wouldn't want to deal with this."

"What d'you mean?"

She reached across Goldilocks and held Guy's wrist. "Don't feel guilty about it. You can't be expected to deal with a pregnant dog and puppies."

He put a hand on the back of her wrist and stroked absently. "D'you think there's one of those Dummy books on all this—on dogs having puppies?"

"I wouldn't be surprised. You'll have to disclose any defects, Guy. It's like a car—or a house—you have to come clean with any prospective new owners."

That got her another of his stares.

The hard, warm pressure of his fingers shouldn't feel so good.

"You know what I'm talking about," she told him. "If the plaster on your walls is all cracked, you can't put a curtain over it and tell buyers it isn't cracked. That's grounds for legal action. I don't know what they call it, but Joe would."

"She's not defective," he said abruptly, and leaned over to nuzzle the dog's head with his own. "You're perfect, aren't you, cher? Gonna be a mama. What a clever girl, and don't you let anyone tell you anythin' different. We'll get you the best box there is and one of those fleece blankets. Two blankets so you can squirrel around in 'em. I'll cut down the sides of the box, too. You won't want to hurt yourself gettin' in

279

and out. Then there'll be the babies with their little legs." Goldilocks slurped at his face and showed all her teeth in ecstasy. "They can't climb over much and the kids'll be wantin' to play soon enough. Maybe I'll make a box. Homer knows about that stuff. I could put somethin' soft along the edges just to be safe."

Jilly hovered between tears and laughter. This was a side of Guy she had never seen.

"Are you laughin' at me?" He looked up at her sharply, suspiciously. "Knock it off. You're ready to get rid of her just because she was taken advantage of. That's not going to happen. Once she's had her babies she'll be operated on so she doesn't have more and I'll find homes for her puppies."

He made Jilly feel good. "That's so nice of you."

"Wouldn't think of doing anything else." He scratched Goldilocks between the ears. "And this is a one-of-a-kind dog, see if I'm not right. When I've got her trained, you're going to wish you'd taken me up on my offer to give her to you."

"Probably." She kept a straight face. Suddenly he was spouting what she'd already told him about Goldilocks as if it had been all his idea in the first place.

He settled his gaze on her lips. "You've been mad at me for hours."

"Yep."

"You drive me nuts when you behave like that. Mad and proud of it." He continued to watch her mouth. "You got an old blanket?"

"Sure I do."

"Goldilocks needs it till I can get something better. It'll be easier for her at my place with everything on the same level."

Jilly got up and went into the hall, to the linen closet. She dug out a big old crocheted afghan and arranged it in a fluffy heap in one corner of the bedroom.

Guy slid his arms under the dog and lifted her up when he stood. "She doesn't weigh so much," he said. "Needs feedin' up. Isn't it true the babies take everythin' from the mother?"

"Absolutely true." Something about the way he fussed over Goldilocks made Jilly ever so slightly jealous.

The dog rested her head on his shoulder and he carried her to the afghan where he set her down and pulled the bright wool around her. She sighed hugely, got up, turned around and around and flopped down again.

Guy covered her up once more.

"You can be a sweet guy."

"Me." He pulled his brows down. "Not this man, lady. I'm one mean son of a gun. Ask anyone."

"You tried to get rid of me in New Orleans."

Shoving his hands into his pockets, he braced his feet apart. "Now we're getting to whatever your problem is. I tried to look after you in New Orleans."

"I don't need looking after." That was a wicked lie. "I need to be . . . if I'm your friend, I have to be your equal. If you look out for me, I look out for you. You were going to stay in New Orleans. You said you were."

"Uh-huh?"

"Oh, forget it." She got up and headed for the door.

Guy put an arm across her body and held her waist. Almost immediately he slid his hand up and let his arm rest on her breasts. Jilly didn't feel inclined to move away.

"When I said I ought to stay, I didn't think about you coming back here without me."

"You know I've got a business to run. Between Wazoo, Missy and Vivian, things are getting covered, but I can't expect them to carry the whole load."

He spread his thumb to press the soft side of her breast. "Maybe I'm testin'. Tryin' to find out what you'd put first if you had to make a choice."

Jilly digested that suggestion. "Are you tryin' to get out of this by sayin' you wanted me to stay in New Orleans, too?"

He looked at the floor.

"Guy?"

"Yes." He looked at her again. "Maybe I'm startin' to think of you bein' around all the time." The things he was saying rattled him. He had a self-assigned mandate, and that was to do his best for Jilly.

Guy couldn't take his eyes off her.

"That scares you, doesn't it?" she said.

"Could be. Commitment always has in a way."

With a hand spread on his chest, she tipped her face up to his. "I don't have a great history of successful relationships. But you know that."

"Yes. Neither do I. That's a good reason for us to go slow and careful together."

She started to move away from him but he stopped her. "I didn't say it was a good reason for us to stop, cher. I couldn't do that."

"How much danger do you think I'm really in? How do I fit in with this plot that's going on?"

"You got in the way. That's what I think. This isn't really about you and it'll play out well away from you as long as we're careful." Scaring her could make her more vulnerable, so he'd keep on lying. He didn't know why, but she was a player all right.

"Do you think Pip Sedge intended to come to Toussaint?"

He and Nat had already discussed this. "Why?" He'd like to hear her angle.

"I don't know, but he could have. Did you make sure it was Pip Sedge's writing on the matchbook?"

She made him smile. "Nothing definitive on that yet. It's scribbled in pencil. We'll get an answer when they make a decision. If they do. Could be difficult. But his fingerprints were sure all over it."

"Couldn't it be that someone else wrote it but Sedge picked it up? To light a cigarette or something. Dropping things like that in your pocket is automatic. Then the other person came here, anyway. On the matchbook—those could easily have been directions to All Tarted Up and Caruthers was already being set up but Sedge had nothing to do with it. Or the directions might have been to another place on the lane."

"Could be, but we don't know any of that." The location of the killing was unlikely to be random, and he hadn't forgotten her house had been broken into.

Jilly frowned at him and he leaned to rest his mouth on the crease between her brows.

"Okay, then," she said. "We'll find out somethin' definite soon. What's going to happen to Lee?"

"Nothin'. As far as I can see she hasn't actually slandered anyone. Of course, there's always malicious intent."

"I don't think Lee's got a malicious bone in her body."

"We'll see. Spike will want to talk to her, I expect."

"Think so?" she said.

He saw her throat move when she swallowed. "Reckon so," he said. "I've been in this town more than a year. That still makes me a Johnny-come-lately, but I can almost hear the wheels turnin' in people's heads around here. Half of them will be thinkin' she's writin' about them."

"She wrote about us?"

They'd picked up the paper when they got into town and read it on the street.

"Think so?"

"Don't play with me," Jilly said.

"I like playin' with you."

She turned pink and her eyes moved away from his.

Jilly felt him, felt him against her as sure as if they were naked. Humidity roasted her skin. Guy's skin

284

would be hot, too, but naked he'd feel so good in her arms.

He pulled her chin up until she raised her eyes. "What happened *behind the old laundry* was the most excitin' thing that ever came this man's way. Lady, you are a spitfire and you were mad—and sexy as hell."

If she was supposed to feel embarrassed it wasn't happening. With one hand, she unbuttoned his shirt to the waist and spread it wide enough so she could kiss his chest, lick his nipples, catch the flat buds between her teeth—and smile when he sucked in a breath.

He didn't wear a belt. She undid his pants and slid her hand inside to take hold of him. His penis leaped in her fingers and he said, "If all you want is to tell me good night, I suggest you stop right there."

Jilly parted her lips and held the end of her tongue between her teeth.

"Mmm." Guy inclined his head and touched his tongue to hers. He breathed heavily. They kissed every way Jilly had known existed, and some she'd never known about at all.

Guy paused, his cheek against hers. "I thought you were angry with me."

"I am," she whispered. "Haven't you noticed the way I prefer to cool down when I feel like rippin' you apart?"

"Just don't cool down too fast." He caught the bottom of her T-shirt but she whipped it over her head and tossed it aside before he had to do any of the work.

Jilly pressed against his chest and pushed his shirt from his shoulders. They gleamed in the low yellow light from the single lamp. She let him shuck the shirt all the way without any more of her help.

"You told me you wanted to get me alone," she said.

He ran his fingernails back and forth beneath the lace on her bra. "I kinda thought you gave me the same message."

"Your imagination makes things up." With both hands she delved into his pants again and Guy rocked gently as if they were dancing. She was aware of how her arms pressed her breasts together. He stared down at them and pushed his pants from his hips.

Guy unhooked her bra and took it off. He cupped her breasts, moved his fingers softly back and forth above her nipples.

Her legs were weak but she pushed herself harder into his hands. His teeth closed gentle on a nipple.

The denim skirt she wore rose easily to her waist and above and he put his penis inside her panties. Slick on slick they rubbed together and Guy began to move his hips. He hummed and moved her with the rhythm.

She started to pant. Pricks of fire shot from every inch he touched and she feared she'd climax right then and there. Angling her hips forward, Jilly rocked with him between her legs. She threaded her fingers through her hair and clasped her hands behind her head.

"You . . . Cher, I'm burnin' up here."

She kept her eyes closed and didn't open them even

when her feet left the floor and he sat her on the end of the bed. He impaled her and she couldn't take in all she wanted of him. Straining, scraping her feet up and down the outsides of his legs, she pumped him and heard the sounds she made.

She didn't care.

Faster and faster they came together, Guy with his hands on her breasts again, his eyes squeezed shut, his teeth clenched, Jilly fighting to keep her eyes open and watch him.

He came, his face dark and hard. "Jilly." His voice slid higher. With his eyes slitted and glittering, he looked at her while his seed spilled. "Cher, cher."

Guy didn't come out of her. He swept her on top of the bed and came down on her hard, stimulating her with his hands while he kept up his rhythm. When she climaxed, her body shuddered and kept on shuddering while the waves washed through her.

"I wanted to hate you," she murmured. "I thought you were trying to get rid of me. Send me home from New Orleans without you."

"Silly woman." With his face between her legs he used his tongue, sent it jabbing against her.

"No," Jilly said, trying to pull him away. The effort was futile. He nipped and pushed until she fell back, shrieking softly with the power of what he did to her.

"Well, hell," he muttered. "This could be inconvenient but I can't get enough of you."

Jilly rose to her elbows. They hadn't turned off the light and she gasped at the sight of his big, hard body,

287

as ready for sex as it had been only moments ago.

He looked at himself, and at her. Jilly gave him a shove and he tugged her close.

"Help!" she cried, laughing at the same time. They'd been too close to the edge of the bed and landed on the floor.

Giving her no time to decide if anything hurt, Guy sank inside her again and the lovemaking was stronger, took longer, than it had before.

She collapsed on top of him, too exhausted to get up.

"I like you right there," he said.

Very quietly she said "Ditto" into his ear. And then he kissed her.

21

Finally, after trying to nail his father all day, Spike had him. Homer walked along the dock, all the way to the end, and shaded his eyes with his right hand.

Spike looked up and down the bayou, then leaned forward to see what Homer could be concentrating on so hard. Guy had a car up on the lift and he'd rolled out to welcome Spike when he arrived. Spike kept it short and Guy was a fast learner so he went back to his business.

There was still a little sun, sure enough, but not enough for Homer to do more than squint, just the way he always did.

"Homer," Spike called. Damn the old coot, anyway, making trouble for no reason. "Hey, come on and have a word. I've got to get back to the station."

"Go on, then. Get back now. You never did have time for anythin' else."

That did it. Spike marched over the gently swaying wooden boards of the deck until he reached his father. "You got a problem?" Spike asked.

"You're the one with the problem."

"Not from where I'm lookin'."

"I'm not havin' all the flappin' lips in this town talkin' about me and tellin' lies."

"Okay, let's quit pretendin' either of us doesn't know what's goin' on. You've decided Lee O'Brien made a reference to you in the paper and now I'm supposed to pay for it." He jutted his chin, which Homer didn't see. "Don't you even think about using Wendy because you're angry."

"I'd never use that child." Homer swung around. He hadn't shaved and gray stubble outlined his lean, lined face. "Maybe we can work somethin' out without goin' into somethin' really ugly. But if I can't be at Rosebank, and I can't, then Wendy needs to spend time here with me, same as she always did."

"I don't have any plans to keep Wendy away from you. But neither am I goin' to put up with this damn fool business you're into, either. You think Lee was referring to you and Charlotte. Is it true? Do you want to marry her?"

"Upstart kid," Homer said, and for an instant

seemed about to take a swing at Spike. "What d'you know about anythin'? Can't even make that lovely woman you're married to happy."

"Shut up!" Spike whipped off his Stetson and waved it. "Don't go talkin' about things you don't understand."

"You'd be surprised what I understand." Homer wiped shaky hands on a handkerchief. "You're bein' a fool with Vivian. She's so miserable, she can hardly get out of bed of a mornin'."

"What do you know?" Spike asked, moving in close. His father didn't budge; straight back, his short gray hair sticking up in a thick crew cut, he stared back into his son's eyes. "Speak up. If someone's said something to you about Vivian and me, I want to know about it."

"Damn you young 'uns." Homer shot out the words. "Damn everyone in this fool town. A man minds his own business and expects other people to do the same. But, no, they gotta poke their noses where they're not wanted or needed."

"Homer?" Spike made no attempt to keep the threat out of his voice.

"Charlotte's worried about the two of you. Vivian's a skinny little memory of what she was. She spends every minute she can with Wendy. That little girl is too old for her age. She understands the woman she thinks of as her mama these days is unhappy. But a girl not even nine shouldn't be suffocated that way."

Spike punched the air rather than his father. "That's

290

not the way it is. Vivian's gettin' over a hard time, dammit. And so am I. We lost our baby, Pop."

Anger melted from Homer's face. Without as much as a flinch, he took Spike by the shoulders and pulled him into a bear hug. "You ain't called me Pop since you was a little'un." He gave the faintest sniff. "And I know all about what you two kids are goin' through. But it'll pass, you understand me? You and Vivian will have more babies, but you won't have 'em while you're both so wound up you can't relax. Don't have to be no specialist to figure out how babies stay away from nervous Nellie parents."

Hesitantly, Spike put his arms around his father. They hugged, brief and hard, and let go. They continued to look into each other's faces.

"I didn't mean what I said about taking Wendy away," Homer said, shamefaced. "I'm embarrassed is all. And worried. I love you all." He turned bright red.

Spike punched his shoulder and muttered, "I love you, Pop."

"Ah, we're goin' soft," Homer said, but one side of his mouth turned up. "It's only fair on Charlotte for me to stay away from Rosebank. We've become real good friends, but she'll be horrified to have our names linked in some damn fool romantic manner. We're too old for that."

"Did you ask her?"

"No!"

"Don't you think this is something two friends should talk about?"

Homer scuffed his boots on the boards and glanced toward the shop. Ozaire, the weak sun glazing his bald pate, stood in the doorway. He stared down toward them, drying a glass at slow speed and shaking his head.

"Busybodies," Homer muttered.

"You may have difficulty with this idea, but people in this town care about you. Charlotte also cares about you—a lot. But maybe you don't see her as more than Vivian's mom."

"I'll be a rat's ass, I think that woman's the best thing I ever happened on, but who am I to have feelings other than friendship for her? She's a real lady and she's kind to me is all."

Spike shook his head slowly. "Wrong. I hoped you'd come to this yourselves, but there's more there than kindness. That's all I'm sayin'. Throw it away or give it a whirl. What harm could it do to invite her to Pappy's Dancehall. You always did cut a mean two-step."

One corner of Homer's mouth jerked up and Spike almost expected him to say *Aw, shucks*. "Don't say any more about it, okay?" he said instead.

"Okay. And, for the record, Vivian and I love each other even more than we ever did. Give us a chance to get through what's happenin'."

"You got it," Homer said. "You're pretty good friends with Guy Gautreaux, aren't you?"

"Sure am. Good man."

"Yeah. Think he's plannin' to go back on the force in New Orleans?"

292

"It's always possible." Spike felt uncomfortable. "But he hasn't said so."

"Don't beat about the reeds with me, boy. I asked what you think. He loves Jilly, doesn't he?"

Sheesh, nothin' got by Homer. "Perhaps he does."

"She loves him and he could do nothin' but worse. But I gotta know if he's plannin' on cuttin' out."

"Why? As long as he's doin' a good job for us, and he is, why not let things take their course? Truth is you employed him to give him something to do because we were all worried about him bein' shut away alone all the time. You were just bein' nice."

"No such thing." Homer scowled. "I need the help for sure now. He always does more than his share, even if he does choose his own hours. But dammit, I don't like givin' a man a job when he needs one only to have him leave me flat when somethin' better comes along."

Some things never changed. "So you think you want to find out just so you can fire him before he quits? Could that be it?"

Homer puckered up his lips and shrugged. "Could be."

"Is that worth eating your insides for?"

"Old feelin's die hard."

"Times change. No one's steppin' on you these days. Give Guy some room to find out what he wants. Look, I'll come clean. I think he's crazy about Jilly and the feelin's mutual. But they've both got baggage and they're afraid of another failure."

"Man ought to be able to make up his mind if he loves a woman and do somethin' about it," Homer said through his teeth. "That's the manly thing to do. None of this creepin' around pretendin' he's too tough to need anyone."

Spike smiled. "You sound like a philosopher there." He gave Homer a poke in his hard belly. "You think there're any bits of advice you could use yourself?"

22

Snaffling Jilly from All Tarted Up in the middle of the day—on the pretext that he needed help with Goldilocks—had seemed like the perfect recipe for a long, luscious afternoon. Until the telephone rang and Jilly made him pick up.

Nat wanted to see them at Spike's office. Now.

Guy joined Jilly in the Pontiac in front of his house and slammed his doors. He turned to her immediately and started kissing her as if he had no intention of stopping.

"Mr. Gautreaux, it isn't my fault if you came roaring past my place of business and made some fool excuse for taking me home in the middle of the day."

"Needin' to check up on Goldilocks and wantin' your help to get her settled at my place was no fool excuse."

"Seems to me we just did more than get Goldilocks

settled." She kissed him back, leaned across the console, wrapped her arms around his neck and tucked her face under his chin. "I wish we didn't have anythin' to worry about but us. Even if it could only last a little while."

"Hmm." He leaned back to look at her. "I'm optimistic. Things are movin', that has to be why Nat wants us over at Spike's office."

"I'm surprised he didn't come right here."

"I'm grateful he didn't." Guy turned up one corner of his mouth. "I can't say I'm sure he was bein' thoughtful, but he may have been. Also, he intends to make sure he gets along well with the local boys. Guess it was Cyrus who came up with somethin'. He's meetin' us there, too."

"I can't think what Cyrus would know."

"Me, neither. There's somethin' goin' on with Wazoo, too. Somethin' to do with Marc Girard's sister, Amy."

He studied Jilly briefly, but not so briefly he missed the sadness that flitted across her features. Later would be soon enough to find out what that was all about.

The drive to town wasn't long unless you were in a hurry to get there.

When Guy finally pulled into the forecourt at the old station house, not far from the town square, his stomach jumped and he could see the glisten of perspiration on Jilly's brow. It wasn't that hot.

A gnarled sycamore spread its branches over the

parking lot at the single-story sheriff's building. The surface of the lot, most likely poured when the original construction was done, reminded Guy of the inside of a dormant volcano when old lava cooled into cracked veins all over. Three official units crowded under the tree in the only available shade.

A motorcycle cop roared in and parked before gathering bulging envelopes from a pannier and making his way inside. Guy had his window rolled down and he could hear the trooper's boots creak with every step.

Madge's secondhand white Toyota was there. Her previous car had given her nothing but trouble so Cyrus insisted she make a change. She must have brought him here today, and there could be no mistaking Nat's black Corvette. A nondescript van, so old it was more rust than paint, hugged a wall of the building.

"Know the van?" Guy asked.

"Uh-uh."

"We'd better get inside."

"I sure don't want to."

He squeezed her hand. "But you want this over and so do I. We'd like to catch this guy before he spatters someone else's . . . We'd like to catch him."

Jilly said, "This has sure made me realize how fragile we are."

Guy walked behind Jilly toward Spike's office at the far end of a corridor inside the building. He admired the slight sway of her hips in white cotton pants, and the way her hair glinted where it lay around her shoulders.

"Hey, you two." Deputy Lori caught up. If anything, since the birth of Baby Tippy she was slimmer than she'd ever been, and she glowed. "Word of warnin'." She pulled them aside down a corridor where the toilets were.

"What is it?" Jilly got concerned if Lori was ever anxious. She was one woman who might have invented the word *cool*.

"No biggie. Just want to fill you in a bit before you walk in there and feel ambushed. Father Cyrus and Madge are there. And Nat Archer. So is Laura Preston. I feel sorry for that woman—she just wants a simple life but she's human and can't make herself get out and leave the money behind. Leastwise, that's how I see it. Those two who live in the trailer at St. Cécil's are here, as well—waiting in another room. Reckon they've got something to get into the open. I don't know about those two, but they should probably be watched."

"Why?" Guy said.

Jilly studied his expression. He wasn't happy with current developments.

"They've got all kinds of things to say about Mrs. Edith Preston." Lori glanced at Jilly. "Sorry. I forget she's your mother."

"You don't need to be sorry," Guy said before Jilly could respond. "Mrs. Preston forgot she was Jilly's mother for years."

She saw he knew his mistake at once. He rubbed the space between his brows hard. "Sorry. That was uncalled-for."

Jilly didn't answer. He was right. "What kind of things are they saying about Edith?" she asked Lori.

Lori chewed on a fingernail. "Most of it doesn't make sense. It sorta sounds like that voodoo stuff. They're worried about her. About her life. Someone's trying to kill her and she needs protecting. That's what they're suggestin'. It was strange how they wanted to talk to Spike alone."

A cold shell encased Jilly. She worried about all kinds of nameless horrors when it came to Edith. "Thanks for warning us."

"That's it, then," Lori said, backing away. "I hope I didn't talk out of school."

"You didn't," Guy told her. "I'd just as soon not be ambushed."

"Spike's not in yet but he's on his way," Lori said. "So is Lee O'Brien. Not that she doesn't stop by most days to see what's goin' on in town. She's not so bad and I hope she makes a go of the paper. She's startin' a campaign in town to get the Christmas decorations out of the square during the year and just put 'em up at Christmas. Says it spoils the impact when you can see the wires hangin' there all year—and the blow-up Santa gradually losin' air." Lori laughed and when she was gone, Jilly and Guy regarded each other for several seconds.

"Do you get the feeling there's a lot of stuff that

doesn't mean a thing but it's muddying the waters over what's really wrong?" Jilly asked.

"I couldn't have put it better." Guy took her by the arm. "Much as I'd like to get to the Pratts now, we'd better see what's going on in Spike's office. Is that okay with you?"

When Guy showed sensitivity it didn't surprise her anymore. "I don't think we can put much stock in what they say, but thank you for askin'."

Spike's door stood open. Since his promotion he'd graduated to a larger space, just as sickeningly pea-green as the previous office and with the same bad linoleum on the floor, but with a larger desk, a bigger window and a rug on the floor. His visitors sat silently around, waiting for him.

"Get yourselves in here," Nat said. "You're holding back progress."

"We haven't stopped movin' since we left for New Orleans yesterday mornin'," Guy said.

Jilly could have sworn Nat sniggered, but his straight face suggested she'd imagined the sound.

"I don't know what this means," Cyrus said, getting up and giving a folded map to Nat. "To be honest, we don't have the faintest. But it's interesting, and given some of the recent history we've dealt with I thought I should show it to you—and Spike. Most of all Spike, since this is his stomping grounds."

"This place is starting to scare me," Laura Preston said. Today she wore all gray and gave a subdued impression. "Every place scares me. I wouldn't know where to go to try to be safe. Not New Orleans, that's for sure."

"You're okay, Laura," Jilly said, not at all certain of that.

"I'm out in that big old house on my own. Wes dropped me off in the chopper and carried on. Business, he says. Just me and the servants—and the men startin' on the new pool. I hate it. Father Cyrus must think there's something to be scared of or I wouldn't have been invited here."

"This has nothing to do with being scared," Nat said. "This is Cyrus's meeting, but he wants folks prepared, not scared."

"Prepared for what?" Laura's voice tightened. Today she seemed pale and, yes, scared, and Jilly wondered just what she'd been through since their last encounter in New Orleans.

"This isn't my meeting," Cyrus said. "I'm just sharing some information I got by accident. If Lil hadn't been cleaning out the hymnal cupboard we'd never have found it."

Spike walked in and looked around with eyebrows raised. "To what do I owe this honor?" he asked.

A trestle table stood under one of the fluorescent lights. Nat opened a map there. "This was found at the church." He gave Spike a sloppy salute, but he was another one with doom in his eyes. "It's pretty old."

Spike went directly to the table and smoothed the old map carefully. It had been so tightly folded that he weighted the creases down with empty glasses. "Quit keepin' us in suspense," he said. "What's the deal with this?"

"It's about Parish Lane," Nat said. He looked sharply at Guy. "Among other things."

A circle of blank faces looked at him.

"Tell me where the lane goes," he said.

"Will there be a test?" Guy asked. "It runs behind Main and Conch."

"Right," Nat said. "Where else?"

Jilly turned to Guy and frowned.

"Do you mean, where else does Parish Lane run?" Guy asked. "That's it, just that short strip."

"Wrong," Nat said. "Take a look at this."

They all crowded around him while he put a nail on Parish Lane and followed it on the map. "It keeps going on the other side of Main Street, not much more than an unpaved alley there, then way out here—"

"See how it curves around and heads for the bayou?" Cyrus interrupted. "That whole track above the water is Parish Lane. I called up the surveyors office and they checked it out. Sure enough. That lane makes its way past houses on the outskirts of town. The ones close to the bayou. It eventually goes by the rectory and St. Cécil's and keeps right on going. There are any number of properties on that lane."

"I always thought of it as the trail by the bayou," Jilly said. "I didn't know it had a name there."

"Interesting," Spike said, but he looked at them as if they were wasting a valuable part of his day. "Got some news for you this mornin', Cyrus. They reckon they're goin' to have that wreck of yours ready for the road in a couple of days."

A group groan went up and Madge said, "Spike Devol, you know he shouldn't drive those wheels of death again. You just add to his bad behavior and that's all it is, y'know. Bad behavior. He hangs on to the Impala just to vex me." She turned glowing red.

Spike's visitors became Madge and Cyrus's audience. Guy didn't miss how the others in the room watched them while trying to appear as if they weren't.

"Madge," Cyrus said. "They've fixed the Impala. That's good news. Why would you think I'd drive that vehicle to vex you?"

Her blue eyes were too shiny. "Of course you wouldn't. I can't imagine what I was thinkin' of to say a thing like that."

"Well I can," Jilly said. "And you're right. Men have a way of tryin' to worry people who have their best interests at heart. That Impala should have been buried years ago." She wished the body shop would give her the verdict on her Beetle.

"You do have a point about this Parish Lane thing?" Spike said. If he thought his change of topic subtle, he was mistaken.

"Point is," Nat said, his fedora on the back of his head, "until we get more feedback from forensics *and* manage to tie it to a suspect, any suspect, we don't know if the murder at Jilly's shop was something Pip Sedge knew might happen. If he did, and he'd lived, he could have intended to warn someone. But his deal could just as well have nothing to do with Rathburn. Sedge had his troubles but he was never connected to any crime."

"You didn't talk through that far with me," Guy said. Sometimes Nat presumed Guy could read his mind. "Gimme a second to work my way there. Anything else on the matchbook yet?"

"Just Pip's prints," Nat said, looking fed up. "A couple of others but no matches on record. And who knows who wrote on the thing? It doesn't help that it was raining that night and the thing got damp."

"I wonder if you ladies would mind waiting in another room," Spike said. "I understand the Pratts are somewhere around. Maybe you could join them."

Madge started to move at once, but Cyrus stopped her. Laura was slower to react.

"Sure," Jilly said, thinking how thickheaded men could be. Did Spike think she wasn't up to her neck in all of this?

"No need for you to go, Cyrus," Spike said.

"I'm not a pro here, either," Cyrus said. "I'll keep the ladies company."

Jilly's heart took a little twist. Cyrus had a way of drawing lines in the sand when it came to fair play. Surely, Spike didn't realize he was treating all the women present like poor little souls to be protected from reality—that or as if they were too stupid to keep their own counsel. But he did give that impression. Cyrus wasn't having any of that.

"Okay, okay," Spike said. "Everyone stay, but remember that what you hear is privileged information. And if you hear anything that curls your ears, ladies, don't complain to me."

Guy smiled with one side of his mouth. How nice that he was amused, Jilly thought.

"So," he said. "What you're suggestin' is that Rathburn's deal could have been random and we may still be waitin' for the main event?"

"Rathburn probably thought his event was pretty main," Jilly said.

Spike scowled at her.

Jilly gave him an innocent look. "You said I wasn't to open my trap outside this room, you didn't say I couldn't make a comment while I was here."

Both sides of Guy's mouth curved up.

Spike blinked rapidly. "Let's get on with this."

"It's possible Rathburn's death was incidental," Nat said, and added quickly, "as far as our case is concerned."

"I see what you mean," Cyrus said. "There are yards with walls or fences that back onto the lane all the way."

"Yep," Nat said. "Including Edwards Place and the Green Mansion, although that house is pretty far from the water there."

"We aren't far away," Laura said. "The wall is real close. You wanted me here because you think something terrible will happen at the house."

"No," Nat said. "We thought someone from

304

Edwards Place should be here is all. Everyone in town will have to be warned to watch out for intruders."

"This changes everything," Guy said. He bent over the map again, then looked up sharply.

When he didn't continue, Nat said, "What?"

Guy shook his head.

Spike shied his Stetson at a peg on the wall and made a clean hit. He went behind his desk, rested his elbows and covered his face, except for his eyes. Guy didn't like the way he watched first one, then the other of them.

"Look," Cyrus said. "I'm an amateur. That's an understatement. But what if it was Edwards Place Pip scribbled about on that matchbook? Rathburn could have been diverted so the perp could finish what he started. Then Rathburn was killed because he might know too much."

"Perp?" Nat sniggered. "You'll be ready for the force anytime soon. What do you mean by 'what he started'?"

"At Edwards Place," Cyrus said. "You don't think Edith had an accident, do you, Guy? I could tell you didn't when we were there."

Jilly swallowed hard. "What are you talking about?"

"You're right," Guy told Cyrus. "Although I think everyone was trying to believe she did. But it didn't make sense. The first thought I had was suicide. I may have been right."

"She was happier than she'd been for ages," Jilly said. "She kept saying so."

"Rathburn took the Hummer to Jilly's," Laura said in a shaky voice. "I knew about that because it was delivered late in the afternoon and he said he'd been told to take it over after the shop closed—so Jilly would be surprised. I'm not sure when he left because there was so much going on."

Guy frowned. "Looks like Rathburn was the intended victim—for all the reasons already mentioned. But I doubt if he was at risk before Edith was attacked—if she was."

"And the instructions on the matchbook were to Edwards Place?" Jilly said. "For someone going there to do harm."

"Like kill Edith," Laura muttered.

"I wish I'd been there that night," Nat said.

"That makes two of us," Spike muttered.

"Do you believe someone tried to kill Edith?" Cyrus asked Guy.

Madge drew in a loud breath and Jilly wished she could sit down without breaking anyone's concentration.

Guy walked to sit on the edge of Spike's desk. Every eye followed him. "Could be, if I follow Nat's reasoning, that Rathburn interrupted someone with Edith," he said. "She said he saved her, but she was told that. She was unconscious at the time. But that does make one thing clear." He pointed to the map on top of the trestle table. "At some point Rathburn left, or was told to leave and deliver the Hummer. The two events are connected. Edith's episode and Rathburn's death. Think, Laura. You were there. When's the last time you saw him?"

"I don't know." Laura sounded distracted. "He was there while I called Daddy."

"Why not 911 first?" Spike said.

She trembled visibly. "Rathburn told me to call Daddy. I never thought of doing anything else. We all rely on one another. Cook showed up while we were waiting for the chopper, but there was nothing she could do—except cry—so we sent her away. Then the house was full of people—Daddy, the medical personnel."

"It's all speculation," Jilly said. "If Rathburn was still there when Mr. Preston arrived, there wasn't a killer around, or not one who had an opportunity to touch Edith. Why would anyone try to kill her, anyway? She hasn't done anything to anyone."

Guy narrowed his eyes at her but had the sense to keep his mouth shut.

"Excuse me," Spike said, slowly standing up. "I hate to interrupt all this constructive thinking, but *what goddamn matchbook* are you talkin' about?"

23

"Helluva day," Spike said aloud, slamming the door of his unit. "Helluva night, too." How had it got to be after midnight?

And how much had he still not got done?

He hadn't managed to see the Pratts, but they'd seemed okay with that and said they'd catch up with him early tomorrow. Wonderful.

Laura Preston needed some individual attention—he wanted to be sure she didn't know anything useful—and she deserved reassurance. Not that he was convinced she didn't have a reason to be nervous. Too bad Cyrus had mentioned Parish Lane and the Pip Sedge evidence in front of her—obviously thinking she already knew. Spike guessed if Cyrus hadn't waded in he might still be in the dark himself. He closed his eyes and worked his aching jaw. Nat and Guy had pleaded that they thought they had told him everything. They had forgotten he'd been unable to make it to New Orleans with them when they talked it through with Jack Charbonnet. Maybe it was the truth but he was still mad enough to spit.

Tomorrow his first priority was to get together, alone, with Nat and Guy and make sure there wasn't something else crucial they'd forgotten to tell him. That and insist on the coroner's report on Rathburn—and anything forensics might have forthcoming.

He turned away from the big house—now a resort—at Rosebank and stared into the darkness. Vivian and her mother, Charlotte, avoided as many changes to the estate as they could. Banks of white roses, even more lush now than when the women had first taken up residence, continued to billow along every fence and wall, and the great oak-lined driveway still hadn't been lit, despite his repeated suggestions that it ought

308

to be. Guests had a way of wandering out for late-night walks, but Vivian said it was more romantic without lights interfering with people's privacy. He smiled a little at that.

A breath took in the scent of roses and the vanilla of night-scented clematis. He approached the H-shaped building that had become so popular with tourists. This wasn't the busiest time of the year but there were still a goodly number of guests. The family had their own wing, one floor of which was for long-stay boarders. Madge, Wazoo and the Savage brothers, Andre and Roche, fell into that category.

Andre and Roche were an enigmatic pair, pleasant enough in an assessing way. They had mentioned a business venture in the area but had given no information on what kind of venture, but Vivian and Charlotte liked them, and Spike guessed they were okay.

He was one edgy man tonight. Lee O'Brien, together with a Simon Menard, her new business partner evidently, had hung around the station all afternoon, questioning anyone who moved. He had avoided them, but that wouldn't last and Lee needed regular reminders about protocol, even if she ignored them.

To his right, most of the windows in the hotel were illuminated and he faintly heard music from the bar. A competent staff made it easy for Vivian and Charlotte to manage without spending twenty-four hours on the job.

On the left, where the Devols and Charlotte lived—

and the long-stay boarders—most windows were dark. He looked up at the third floor and the bedroom he shared with Vivian. That was dark, too.

He stepped lightly. No point in waking anyone, even if it would be good to talk and know whatever he said wouldn't be judged.

Inside the great hall—renovated lovingly to keep the eclectic motif Vivian's uncle had favored before he died and left the estate to his sister-in-law and niece—Spike stood with his hat in his hands. Was he hungry? Did he want to go to the kitchens and eat? Truth was, he didn't know what he felt or what he wanted any-more—other than to wring a few necks around Toussaint.

Yes, he did know what he wanted. He spread a hand over his face. Vivian was who he wanted. She could quiet his heart and mind as no other person had ever managed to do. Please, God, let him take the right steps at the right speed.

"Spike?"

He jumped, peered and saw Charlotte's small figure in the gloomy passage leading to the kitchen. "I thought everyone was in bed," he said softly. Vivian's tiny Chihuahua, Boa, shot from behind Charlotte and vaulted into his arms. He'd come to like the miniature critter. Probably because Vivian loved her—and because she was fiercely protective of the family.

"Come on," Charlotte said, inclining her head toward the kitchens. "I've been waiting up for you."

Dandy, just what I need: a chat with my mother-in-

law. That wasn't fair when she was more a mother to him than he'd ever known. He followed her and entered the big kitchens, which had been part of the working hub of the estate. The kitchens had been completely renovated for the resort.

Small with close-cropped gray hair and big eyes in a smooth face, Charlotte stood close, looking up at him and, he thought, seeing too much.

"You're mad," she said.

Dammit, can anyone look at me and know what I'm thinking? If they could he'd better work on it because it was a lousy trait in a lawman. "I'm just fine, Charlotte, thank you."

She pulled up her shoulders. "If you say so."

At first Charlotte and Homer had seemed unlikely friends, but Spike understood how they found strength in each other. He also figured his father felt protective toward Charlotte; among other things a son would rather not think about where a parent was concerned.

"You don't want to talk to me, do you, Spike?"

He wasn't getting away with a thing here. "I'm a bit tired."

"You've had a bad day—one of a lot of bad days."

Spike looked at his shoes. "Charlotte, sometimes you see too much."

"You're the best thing that ever happened to my daughter, that makes you important to me. So I guess I'm kind of in touch a bit more than I might be. Don't worry about anything. That's all I wanted to tell you."

He blew up his cheeks and took a slow stroll to the

311

butcher-block-topped island in the middle of the room. "Want to tell me what *anythin'* is?"

"Surely. Homer got a bit bent out of shape is all. Could have happened to any of us. He'll calm down and forget he was ever mad."

Spike had already decided that was true. "I think so, too."

"Thought so. That Lee O'Brien is a very nice young woman. She didn't mean anythin' bad by writin' what she did. It's just that Homer decided she'd written about us and took it in his pride a bit."

"Like you say, he'll get over it. I think I'm finally tired."

"Spike." She settled a hand on his crossed arms. "The other . . . You and Vivian are so much in love, it hurts to watch—"

"Please, Charlotte," he said, and dropped a peck on her cheek. "You're wonderful but let us try to come through this on our own."

"Yes, of course." She stepped away from him.

"I'm sorry. It's been too long since Vivian and I relaxed together. I think it's my fault. Until we get it all in the open we can't put it to rest. She's tryin' to save my feelings."

"And you're tryin' to save hers," Charlotte said. "So quit bein' so considerate, both of you." She walked out.

Spike stood there until he was sure she'd gone to her rooms—and he used the interval to consider what he was supposed to do to take the stress out of his marriage. Rage welled in him. What he and Vivian had was too special to be ruined.

Why had their baby died before he took his first breath?

And why did he keep asking himself a question when there wasn't any answer?

Carrying Boa, he left the kitchen, went through the passageway past the salon and upstairs, up the flights that took him to what had become his home with Vivian and Wendy. His girl adored Vivian, but then, Wendy had good taste, too. The dog was happy to be popped inside the little girl's room.

The door to the bedroom he shared with Vivian was closed tight. He turned the handle carefully and let himself in. Vivian hadn't closed the drapes and the light from a cloud-shrouded moon showed his wife's shape in the bed. She faced the window.

Spike bowed his head. He felt so helpless, even while his mind told him this was the one human being in the world who was always on his side.

"What's the matter?"

Startled, he took a second to say, "Hey. I thought you were sleeping."

"I haven't been sleeping too well lately."

Spike swallowed, swallowed again, but his mouth stayed dry. "Me, neither."

"Something happen today?"

"How do you read me like that?" he asked. He didn't add that her mother seemed to have pretty good instincts where his feelings were concerned, too.

"Practice," she said. "I spend a lot of time thinking about you."

His gut tightened. "I think about you, too."

"So what's happened?"

"I'm mad as hell, that's what." He told her about Guy and Nat, Cyrus and Jilly talking all around him about his case while he sat there like a fool not knowing what they meant most of the time. He explained the matchbook, then apologized. "I'm sorry, Vivian. I make a point of not bringin' my work home. It's always best that way."

She was quiet again and he undid the buttons on his uniform shirt, pulled it free of his pants and shucked it. "I bet they thought they'd told you, Spike. These cases with more than one agency involved can get confusing, can't they?"

Vivian had a clear head, almost always. He smiled to himself. "They can and you're probably right." He mentioned the Pratts, Lee O'Brien and Simon Menard.

"Ah, cher, my poor sweetheart. You're getting overrun. Do you think this Menard is a romantic interest of Lee's?"

He had sat down to pull off his boots, but he put one foot back on the floor. "Didn't look that way to me." He finished taking off the boots, then followed them with his pants.

"Wazoo has seen Amy Girard," Vivian said. "Apparently it didn't go well. Wazoo drove out to Clouds End and Amy seemed afraid when she saw her. I told

Wazoo Amy's probably still shell-shocked. She came close to being killed."

Spike snorted. "Did you remind Wazoo that while Amy was locked up in that bayou house people managed to think she'd already been buried? That was the reason for the memorial or whatever it was. So if Wazoo sang for it, Amy isn't to blame."

"Wazoo knows that but she expected Amy to welcome her, I think. She's hurt."

"She'll get over it," Spike said. "She and Amy will get things back together again."

He stripped the rest of the way and, when he was naked, fumbled in a drawer for a pair of pajamas. He hated the things but circumstances made them appropriate.

"Don't put those on," Vivian said, and he stood still. "You don't like wearing pajamas, you never did."

"No."

"You started wearing them after we lost the baby."

He scrubbed at his face and ran his fingers through his hair.

"I don't like you in pajamas, either. Come to bed, Spike."

He glanced down at himself, at his nakedness, and at his erection. He'd have to be careful not to let her be aware that he was aroused.

Moving quickly, he started for his side of the bed.

"This side," Vivian said, scooting backward and opening the covers for him. "I warmed the bed up for you."

He trembled, actually trembled. She was reaching out to him and he was too damn scared to reach back. But he did as she asked and got into bed, his back toward her and his knees bent.

"There's nothing that means as much to me as being with you," Vivian said. With her warm hands, she smoothed his back and shoulders, his arms, his sides . . . and she placed dozens of light kisses where her hands had been. "There's just one thing I want you to tell me while I make a fool of myself. Have you fallen out of love with me completely?" She tucked her thighs against the back of his.

"No! I love you more with every hour. I love you so much I'm fallin' apart with what's happenin' to us." He tried to turn toward her but she was faster. Wrapping her arms all the way around him, she flattened herself to his back.

Vivian was also naked. "It's been too long since we spooned." She laughed shortly, a husky edge in her voice. "When I hold you like this I feel as if we've melted together."

He arched his head back until his cheek rested on hers. "I don't know what to do," he murmured. "I can't bear to see you hurt again, like you were. It feels like a no-win. If what the doctor said is true and we might not start another pregnancy . . . We could, though, she said it was possible. But what if . . ."

Vivian placed her fingers over his mouth. "We don't get to make the decisions about any of it. All we can do is live our lives and take what comes. We've got

Wendy and I couldn't love her any more."

"I know and I'm grateful," he said, closing his eyes and concentrating on the way her breasts felt against his back.

"If we get pregnant again, it'll be wonderful. If we don't, I will never love you less, Spike. But you know somethin'?"

He held his breath. "What?"

"Turn over and look at me."

His control wouldn't hold out much longer but he did as she asked. All he saw in the gloom was shadows beneath the sharp bones in her face, the faint sheen in her eyes and, when he looked lower, her breasts bathed in a hint of light.

"I'm looking at you, Vivian. You didn't get ugly or undesirable and . . . I want you so much."

"What's taking you so long?"

24

From a distance, Vivian heard tapping. She rearranged herself more comfortably on Spike's chest, kissed him there sleepily and relaxed again.

Once more a tapping.

"Go away!" Spike called out so loudly that Vivian jumped. "And don't come back." He tightened his arms around Vivian.

More tapping. "Vivian, Spike," Charlotte called,

clearly miserable. "You've got company."

Spike's eyes opened at once, but he felt no inclination to leave the place where he'd prefer to stay for good. He craned his neck to look at the clock. "Company at seven?"

"Who would come so early?" Vivian muttered. She wasn't sure she could move, anyway.

"I'll make them comfortable," Charlotte said. "You come when you're ready."

They heard her footsteps recede.

"Should have asked who it is," Vivian said.

Spike grunted, stroking her back and burying his face in her hair.

"We'd better go down. Wendy will be up anytime, too."

"You're right." Spike scooted to sit up and plunked Vivian down beside him. "I feel like a new man."

She giggled. "I'm feelin' pretty good myself." And so lighthearted. "Didn't you say the Pratts were going to see you this morning?"

"I didn't invite them to come to my home and wake me up." He thought for a moment. "They are so literal, they may have assumed that's what I meant though." The growling sound he made amused Vivian.

After that they showered and dressed and went downstairs. Soft voices came from the small sitting room to the left at the bottom of the stairs. This room sported a new, exact replica of the original striped, tentlike ceiling hangings. The disappearing corners that gave a clever impression of the room being round continued to fascinate Spike.

When he followed Vivian into the room, Ken and Jolene Pratt got up at once. Their faces were as shiny and scrubbed as usual, but today Jolene didn't wear a tail at her nape to match Ken's. Instead her straight light brown hair spread around her shoulders and she wore a floral dress. She actually looked quite attractive.

"Good morning," they said in unison. "We're sorry if we got you up. We didn't think about that."

I wish you had thought about it. "The sooner we deal with your issues, the better. I wanted to get to you yesterday," Spike said.

"You had a busy day," Jolene said. She looked at Vivian. "You're beautiful. I've seen you before, but not so close."

Vivian, her face pink, said, "Thank you."

She was beautiful, Spike thought. Her shiny, straight black hair curved around her jaw and she had the greenest eyes he ever hoped to see. "You're right," he told Jolene. "My wife is beautiful—and a saint to put up with me."

Ken laughed and put an arm around Jolene's shoulders.

She turned her head toward him and said, "I'll start, if you like."

He said, "No, it's my job," and Spike guessed the niceties were over.

"Please be comfortable," Vivian said. "I'll get you some coffee—if that's okay, Spike?"

"I'd like you to stay," Jolene said quickly. "You

make me feel more relaxed."

They all sat and before they could get started Charlotte appeared with mugs of coffee on a tray and a plate of fresh, deep-fried pig's ear cakes coated in thick cane syrup and chopped nuts. The pastries were fragrant and still hot.

Spike hadn't been hungry but he was only human and had one of the twists on a plate and in front of him before he even reached for coffee.

Charlotte left at once and Ken Pratt, chewing his first bite, said, "Your mama's quite a cook," to Vivian.

She agreed, with a sense that the Pratts were grabbing at reasons to delay whatever they'd come to say—a need she'd felt herself before now.

"You're going to hear it all, anyway," Jolene blurted out. "Lee O'Brien will nose it out and make something of it—we think she may already know—so we want you to hear it from us."

"You talk, I'll listen," Spike said. They had a firm hold on his curiosity.

Vivian touched his arm. "I probably shouldn't be here."

He smiled at her. "If Jolene and Ken want you, it's fine." She knew better than to say anything during whatever was to come.

"We've been in Toussaint longer than people know," Ken said. "Maybe nobody but us knows when we got here."

Spike held back a frown and kept a smile on his face.

"We like people in Toussaint now—since we moved onto St. Cécil land—but we didn't know how much until, well, until things changed."

His tongue was going to be frayed, but Spike didn't want to prompt them.

Ken's twist lay on his plate. He'd eaten just that one bite. "We came almost two years ago," he said. "Looking for a safe place to be and a way to keep to ourselves. We arrived at night and we moved about at night. We had to."

"We'd had a business," Jolene said. "A bookstore and café."

"Like Hungry Eyes," Ken put in. "Except we also made natural remedies and sold organic vegetables at a local market. It wasn't in a good area and we had problems. The kind of people we wanted to attract came at first but they got hassled and they got fed up. In the end we had to close our doors."

"That's a shame," Vivian said. She hunched her shoulders. "Sorry."

Ken and Jolene stopped talking. They looked at each other, then at the floor.

"You'll find out, anyway," Jolene said quietly.

"Yes," Ken agreed. "This way there won't be any misunderstandings. If we don't explain, the rumors will start. We're already worried about Mrs. Edith, we don't want her upset by hearing things about us that are only partly true."

Spike's patience began to stretch. "Is this something to do with the so-called voodoo stuff?"

"No," Jolene said at once. "That's just something Wazoo says because she thinks we're competition. We're not. We aren't going to interfere with her animal therapy or anything else she does. We grow and sell vegetables and flowers and make natural remedies."

"There have been some comments made about you," Spike said, thinking of a mention that they took night-time walks in the graveyard. "Maybe all you need to do is be more open with folks so they won't have any reason to make up lies."

"We lived in the grounds at Edwards Place until the real estate people started coming around and put the estate on the market," Ken said.

Jolene crossed her arms tightly. "Then Mr. Preston bought the place. We loved it there but we knew it wouldn't last forever."

Spike stared at them and held back an urge to mention trespass. "I see."

"We weren't doing any harm. We had our trailer out of sight in some trees and we grew enough to support ourselves. We took stuff to market out of town and made any money we needed. You don't need much really."

Not when you're using someone else's property. "You wanted me to know this before someone else tells me?"

"And we want to talk to you about our fears for Mrs. Edith Preston. You weren't there after . . . after her incident. We don't believe she cut herself by accident the way she's saying."

Spike felt in his pockets for gum but found none.

Too bad someone hadn't come to him earlier, before he got taken totally by surprise. "Do you want to share your theory?" He should have been called to the Prestons' after the incident. For a moment he thought about that. No, as long as they were insisting Edith had an accident, he wouldn't be called. But someone should have told him about it afterward in case there were follow-up questions. Guy was too used to doing his own thing, and to taking charge.

"They drove her to it," Jolene said, holding a coffee mug and staring inside. "I think that Mr. Preston is cruel to her. He *is* cruel in strange ways. They may all be. She's too nervous and fragile and she's more that way than when she first came to Toussaint. We met her outside the church when she was first here and she was fine then. She came every week. Now she's gone somewhere. We tried to find out where, but we couldn't without drawing attention to ourselves."

"She's with her husband in New Orleans," Spike said. At least he knew that much.

"I hope she's safe," Ken said, and he wouldn't meet Spike's eyes. "We think she tried to take her life that night."

Spike bought time by eating more of his pastry, licking the sticky syrup from his fingers and wiping his hands on a napkin.

"Mr. Preston wouldn't want anyone else to know we think that." Ken took hold of Jolene's hand. "It might spoil the story about the way he looks after his wife. She's his prisoner."

"That's pretty harsh," Spike said. "What proof do you have of any of this?"

"We know is all," Ken said. "Some of us sense more than others. We know we were trespassing at Edwards Place but we did no harm. If we need to face charges, we're ready."

"That would be up to the prior owners," Spike said, grateful for an out. "We don't have the manpower to track them down."

A little color returned to Jolene's pale face.

Ken shook his head. "It's no good," he said to his wife. "Eventually someone will tell the whole story. You know someone must have seen us."

"Hush," Jolene said. "We've told the whole story." She choked her words out.

"Okay." Ken subsided and pushed deeper into the couch.

"Not okay," Spike said, keeping his tone even. "You've left out more than you've told me. Am I wrong?"

Jolene turned up her palms. She sighed and shook her head. "We may not have been seen at all, but now we're not sure. We used to take our sleeping bags into the house when it was cold. We lit a fire now and then because the place is so far away from any street the smoke wasn't likely to be seen. We only did it at night."

Spike said, "Thank you for telling me," but wondered why they had, unless they feared being blamed for something. He considered whether there was any reason for them to think they'd be implicated in what happened to Edith but couldn't imagine a connection.

"Have you had any complaints?" Ken's light eyes fixed on Spike and didn't falter.

"No," he said, honestly enough, although Wazoo had indeed made some suggestions about them. He had decided she was the one they spoke of, the one who might have seen them at Edwards Place. Wazoo went too many places alone and at questionable times. The woman was a pain but the whole town cared about her.

Spike drank coffee and glanced at Vivian, who had a thoughtful crease between her brows.

"What did you mean when you said Preston is cruel to Edith in strange ways?"

"Nothing really," Jolene said quickly.

"He isn't the gentleman he pretends to be in front of other people." Ken sounded determined. "I'm afraid we could get blamed for something he's doing."

"Ken, no." Jolene's voice wobbled.

"It's true. We think Mrs. Edith's being poisoned . . . no, not that exactly, but given drugs to weaken her. She is weaker."

Spike figured he had to ask a question to which he already knew the answer. "How do you know?"

Ken blushed instantly.

Misery flattened Jolene's eyes. "We've seen him do it. After the first time when he forgot himself and pushed her down in the gardens, we decided to keep watch over her. He does it when they're alone. He takes the pills from his pocket and stands over her while she takes them. She used to try not to, but now she does as she's told and seems to like it. She smiles at him."

"That's why we're here," Ken said, "so if anything happens to her, you'll know it wasn't us."

It was Spike's turn to feel thoughtful. "Thank you for telling me." Not that he could do a thing unless he had more to go on than hearsay. And the Pratts wouldn't be the first ones to come up with a supposed safety net for themselves. "I don't think you should continue going onto Preston's land." These two would have to be kept under surveillance.

Jolene wound her hands together. "I was afraid you'd say that. How can we try to watch over her?"

"You can't. She isn't even here now so snoopin' around wouldn't help her, would it? Everythin' you say may be easily explained, but leave it in my hands and stay away from Edwards Place. Better for you. And keep your own counsel."

"Yes," they said, making leave-taking motions.

"Finish your coffee and eat those pig's ears or Charlotte will be offended." He smiled and saw their relief.

The front doorbell sounded, a low boom made by a monkey perched high in a corner of the great hall. The garish plaster animal was wired and brought a leather-wrapped stick down on a drum when someone rang the bell. Vivian's uncle had brought an eclectic and whimsical taste to Rosebank.

Spike leaned forward and said, "Have you seen any

evidence of injectable drugs? Think about it and let me know later, if you like."

Ken and Jolene shook their heads no.

Murmuring from the hall quickly materialized into Charlotte leading Guy and Jilly. If he weren't so damned happy, Spike might try to seem peeved. That sounded like a stupid idea right now.

The Pratts excused themselves at once, even though both Jilly and Guy were pleasant to them.

Wendy peeked into the sitting room. Contact lenses had replaced her round pink glasses and her pretty eyes shone. A bob reached her collar but Spike still missed her pigtails. Fortunately she remained a small girl. He wasn't ready for her to grow up too much yet.

"Mornin', pumpkin," he said, and she separated herself from the doorjamb to run in and hug Vivian, Spike and Charlotte.

"Could I have a hug?" Jilly asked quietly, a soft smile on her face, and she was immediately squeezed tightly. Spike watched the way Guy observed the two. This man was going to have to do something serious about his feelings for Miz Gable.

Charlotte took Wendy to the kitchen. Jilly sat beside Vivian but Guy hovered. "We all feel bad about yesterday," he said to Spike. "You do believe it was one of those crazy things, don't you? Who knew we hadn't filled you in?"

"I did—yesterday."

Guy's black eyes moved past Spike to Vivian and Jilly on the couch. "The last thing Nat and I want is to pull your chain. You know that."

He wasn't in the mood to smooth feathers. "What else don't I know?"

Vivian pouted at him and pulled down her brows. She couldn't hold the critical expression and slowly started to smile.

Spike winked at her.

"I don't think there's anythin'," Guy said, frowning. "Nat's been busy in New Orleans, but we don't get closer to making a real connection between events there and events here."

"But you think there is one?"

"Yeah. I've never been big on coincidence. We need a break and we aren't getting one."

Charlotte returned with two more mugs of coffee and fresh pig's ear cakes. Guy fell on them and slid into a chair making noises of ecstasy. Jilly watched him and laughed.

"What d'you think it means that Rathburn was walking into Jilly's yard when he was shot?" Guy said around a mouthful of flaky dough. "Way I see it, he thought he was going to see a friend, or someone who was supposed to drive him back to Edwards Place."

Spike barely managed to hold his temper. "Maybe he didn't think he'd see anyone," he said. Still, Guy spoke about facts Spike should have been the first to know.

"He was shot at close quarters," Guy said. "He had to have seen his murderer. Single shot to the head. No sign of a struggle. One usable footprint. It isn't Rath-burn's but they don't know who it does belong to. Narrow foot."

Jilly sighed as if bored and said, "Why were the Pratts here?"

"Just stopping by," Spike said, and didn't feel guilty.

"Rathburn would always have carried a weapon," Guy said. "His kind do, but he didn't have one when he was found. He did have sticky stuff under his right index fingernail, and the thumbnail."

"Would you like to share the deductions on that?" Spike said carefully.

"Tape," Guy said. "There were tiny scraps of paper, too. Microscopic. They think he peeled off a piece of tape from somewhere."

This was unbelievable. "How do you know all this?" Spike asked, keeping his voice level.

"Nat got it from the coroner, among other people."

"Is that so? Boy, I'm relieved. And there I was thinkin' you'd been readin' the reports in my office. Haven't seen them myself."

"Cher?" Jilly said, standing up.

Guy raised his hands and let them drop. "Look—"

"You look," Spike said. "I've had it with this. I'm this close—" he held a finger and thumb a millimeter apart "—to telling you and your buddy Nat to get lost. You're in my face and I don't want you there. I want you and Nat Archer in my office by late morning. Whatever you know, I need to know."

"I'm . . . dammit," Guy said. "I didn't set out to

trample your toes. If I had, I wouldn't be talkin' to you now."

"What did you think?" Spike said. "Did you think I'd be okay with you givin' me a verbal autopsy report?"

"I assumed you would already have read the thing."

Vivian got up. "Hey, you two."

"It's okay, sweetheart." He didn't want her upset and she detested argument. "We've got to set up a workable system for communication is all. Without anyone makin' assumptions about what I know."

"You've got it," Guy said, but he didn't look happy and Spike was no novice, he knew how men like Guy liked to be in charge. He seemed to have forgotten he wasn't on active duty.

Jilly walked past them all and stood at the window. "There's a connection between that Pip Sedge and Rathburn. I'm sure of it. And I don't think this is going to be over real soon."

"No," Spike said quietly.

Vivian cleared her throat. Her eyes bored into Spike's and he knew what she wanted from him. "The Pratts spoke of suicide, that maybe Edith tried to kill herself."

Jilly made a small sound but didn't turn around.

"I know it wasn't an accident," Guy said, looking at Jilly's back.

"There's someone comin' to the house," Jilly said. "Better be careful what we say."

Guy's cell phone rang. He swore under his breath

330

and barked "What?" into the receiver. A few seconds and he said, "Sure, Cyrus. How do you know that? Of course, you did tell Miz Trudy-Evangeline where to find you. I don't want to get my hopes up too far but she could hold the key. I'll have Nat get over there right away—before someone can take her out, too."

He put the cell phone away and felt all eyes on him. The doorbell boomed again and Charlotte hurried past the sitting room.

"Pip Sedge's wife has showed up at her home," he said.

Spike pinched the bridge of his nose. "His wife?"

"Ex-wife. I'll make sure you know everything, okay? If you'd been with us in New Orleans you would have known."

"I have a district right here," Spike said. "I had other business to attend to that day. Now, fill me in on Mrs. Sedge."

"Come on in!" Charlotte said from the hallway. "I'll get Wazoo. She'll be thinking of leaving for All Tarted Up. Vivian?"

Charlotte led a woman into the sitting room, a thin woman with huge eyes and black hair sprinkled liberally with gray. The hair was cut short and brushed back from her face.

"This is—"

The woman, clutching at Charlotte's arm, cut off anything else she might have said.

Jilly had turned from the window and she smiled at the newcomer.

331

Without uttering a word, the woman looked back at Jilly. Still silent, she spun around and fled the house.

25

Jilly could tell Guy was taking his time driving from Rosebank to Toussaint. He rested his right wrist on top of the steering wheel and crept along. She turned in her seat to look at Goldilocks, who sat on a thick foam pad covered with fleece on one side and sheepskin on the other and looked through the window as if she'd spent her life being chauffeured on outings. The back window had been lowered and the dog's ears flapped in a strong current of air heavy with moisture.

"She has a water dish on the floor," Guy said, as if trying to read Jilly's thoughts. "I carry some dry food and biscuits."

"Great. You take good care of her. Are we . . . yep, we're driving in the wrong direction."

"If you don't mind, I'd like to stop by work and check in with Homer. Let him know I'll be in much later."

Uh-huh, Guy checked in when his schedule was going to be disrupted? Jilly didn't think so. "Go ahead," she said.

He smiled at her and she took a sharp breath. Gentleness wasn't what she expected to see in his eyes.

"I'm not as tough as I hope people think I am," he

said. "When I'm around you I feel anything but tough."

She swallowed and turned up the corners of her mouth. "You make a good job of hiding your feelings most of the time."

"I've had a lot of practice. I wish you and Joe had the same mother. You'd have fared better, Jilly. I don't say that because of my feelings about Edith—it's obvious is all."

"Maybe." She and Joe never discussed their past. Talking about it didn't come easy. "I always wanted to know more about my father." Her eyes prickled and she hated herself for being weak.

"I didn't really know my dad," Guy said. "My mother never said a bad word about him, but I don't think he was good to her."

"Your mother filled the gap, didn't she? The gap your father left?"

"Yes. I couldn't have had a better mother." He frowned at Jilly. "I feel guilty for saying that to you."

"Don't." She stroked his arm. "I'm glad for you. I don't know if my father is dead or alive. I don't know why he suddenly stopped payin' those people for my keep. The money came regularly before." She didn't want to say she thought the man had died.

"You'll probably never know, but I'd be wonderin', too."

"Y'know, I don't like self-pity. It's somethin' I don't admire in other people but I have some for myself sometimes. Isn't that the pits?"

"It's human." He glanced at her, his expression serious, maybe sad.

"Sometimes I'd get a little note from him. He'd put it in with the money. He never wrote much except he'd be back for me one day." Now she felt it rush in, the self-pity she loathed and fought against.

Guy's mouth set hard. His knuckles whitened on the wheel.

"Anyway, that's all long over now," Jilly said. "I don't spend time standing at windows watching for him anymore." But now and then, when she was alone, she cried for the girl she'd been and wished she could reach back and hold her, and tell her she was loved.

"Kids are precious," he said, and took her hand to the wheel where he held her fingers under his. "They need to know they're safe and important. No kid deserves to be born to people who didn't want 'em in the first place."

If you could really feel sad and happy at the same time, Jilly did. Guy Gautreaux wasn't just a quiet man, he was thoughtful, and so special.

"Jilly, this may not be the best time but I'm famous for bad timin'. We haven't had a chance to get into what upset you in New Orleans."

"We've had chances," she said. After all, honesty had a place in all things—even if she had begun to hope he'd forgotten all about the incident.

Guy released her hand and rubbed her thigh, rumpling her thin green silk skirt. Jilly shuddered, just a little, and he sighed. "If I get to choose between makin' love to you and talkin', there won't be a contest."

"We couldn't do both?"

"Depends on what we talk about. You're avoidin' the night you were with the Prestons. Why?"

Because it's over and it's not important but you'll go ballistic if I tell you. "Forget about that. I got so lucky in that graveyard. Things could have gotten bad."

"What was goin' on when you first called me?"

"Guy!" She leaned forward to look at his face. "You haven't pushed me on this until now. Why today?"

"You didn't want to talk about it so I gave you some space."

"Thanks. Don't you wonder why that woman rushed out of Rosebank this morning?"

"You're changing the subject. She left because she saw you."

"I didn't need you to say that." He was right but the experience had shocked her. "Charlotte said she's a friend of Wazoo's. I never saw her before."

"Know what?" Guy raised a brow. "I think Spike knew who she was but he's bein' bloody and keepin' it to himself. That means he's decided to get back at me by not sharing information."

"Spike isn't like that."

"He was this mornin'."

"You can't be sure of that. You two agreed to share information."

Guy smiled. "He decided he deserved at least a little

dig. Charlotte was goin' to tell us after the woman left but somethin' made her stop. Bet it was friend Spike givin' a signal."

"So who is she? I wonder," Jilly said, almost entirely to herself. "She's pretty in a way. Dramatic, but too thin."

"We'll find out."

"She may not have run away from me. Why would she? I bet she remembered somethin' important and wasn't even thinkin' about me."

He waggled his head. "I don't think so. Why did you call me in New Orleans—when you said you had to leave the house?"

"Ooh, Guy, you don't know when to leave things alone."

He drove quietly for a few minutes. The day grew darker, and hotter. A band of purplish haze crushed down on the trees with a faint green fuzz coming right behind. They'd get a storm shortly.

"I'm waiting," Guy said.

"Do you promise not to lose your temper?"

"No."

"I'm not telling you anythin'," she told him.

"I won't lose my temper."

"Yes, you will."

"Jilly, I will not lose my temper. Unless you keep on stringin' me along."

"I'm very afraid of you," she said, smiling, but his face had turned hard. "I got a funny feelin' there, okay?"

He glanced at her quickly. "Not okay. Expand."

"That house doesn't feel right. And I didn't like bein' around Mr. Preston. There, I've told you the truth, now drop it."

Guy drove his Pontiac onto a bumpy verge and under a stand of live oaks. Moss trailed onto the hood of the car and swished across the roof. "Aw, don't do this," she said. "Don't grill me. I need to get to work."

"You will as soon as you explain what you just told me. Did that man touch you?"

She would have to tiptoe around the truth. "I got ruffled because I was sittin' with Edith while she fell asleep in her bedroom and I heard a car drive beside the house. I looked out. It was Preston and I think a woman had hidden herself in the back of his car—I know she had."

Releasing his seat belt, Guy sat sideways and pulled his right ankle onto his knee. "Go on." He sounded tense—and amazed.

"He realized she was there and pulled her out. He shook her, or kind of shook her, and walked off."

"What happened to her?"

"She left. It was dark so I couldn't see much. Preston was rough with her."

"This was the woman you thought he might have sent the goon after," Guy said.

She'd had more time to go over everything. "I don't have any proof of that. I don't have any proof it was even the same woman." But she couldn't quite shake her original theory.

"Do you still think Preston's a nice man?" At least he didn't sneer.

"I don't know what to think." She didn't want to say she considered her mother's husband a perverted lecher. "I do think he cares about Edith."

"You're not lookin' at me. That's not like you. Are you afraid I'll figure out you're lyin'?"

He used a forefinger to brush back strands of her hair but she shrugged away. "I don't lie."

"Not even by avoidin' the truth?"

"Let's get back on the road, please." The first fat drops of rain hit the windshield and the moss swung more wildly. "Guy, I mean it."

"What did he do to you?"

"If you confront him and use my name, the one who will suffer is Edith. I'd never forgive myself if that happened."

He took hold of her wrist and wouldn't let go. "You're loyal. You're decent. What is it about Edith Preston that makes you want to waste your time on her?"

Wind buffeted the car. Jilly breathed through her mouth to settle her jumping stomach. "Edith is my mother. She made a lot of mistakes but she's not a strong person. I'm worried about her for a lot of reasons. You think someone tried to kill her."

"Not for sure."

She glared at him.

"Okay, yes, I do. And I'll be very careful not to make things hard for her."

"It was all nothing, anyway. He kissed my cheek when he came to take over from me with Edith. She's still recoverin'. I turned the wrong way and he caught my mouth. I hated it and I overreacted. That's all."

He shrugged. "The man's a pig. I don't want you near him. Is that why you held me as if I'd been gone a month when you saw me the next mornin'?"

"It must have been," she told him. "I didn't know I had."

"Jilly—"

"Okay, okay. But what I'm going to tell you should make you truly sorry for Edith." Jilly hoped she was making a good call. "She isn't surrounded by nice people. Preston has a way to watch people in the guest-room bathroom next to the room he shares with Edith. From their closet."

For far too long Guy blinked slowly, his eyes losing focus. Then the focus returned. "The guest room you used?"

"Yes."

"Watch what? The shower? What?"

"The whole room. He's got some sort of lens in a painting. He's just a sick man, Guy. Let it go, I intend to."

Guy's breath whistled out through his teeth. "Did he watch you in the shower?"

Oh, no, she'd been so afraid of this. "He may have."

"I'm going to kill him."

"Don't talk like that." Jilly put a hand on top of his

and encountered cold, hard fingers. "If you feel any-thin', feel pity for him."

"Because he watched you naked? Oh, yeah, I really pity him."

She threw herself against the back of the seat and crossed her arms. "You are such a *man*."

"Buckle up," he said, his mouth a thin line. Then he turned on the engine again and returned to the road. "How did you find out?"

Jilly gave herself time to think about what she said next. "Laura told me. I think it happened to her."

When he didn't respond Jilly began to feel nervous. "Please, for me, leave it alone."

"Give me some credit. I won't do anythin' to hurt Edith."

He still quietly steamed when they got to Homer's place. Ozaire gave them a thumbs-up and continued talking to several fishermen, making the kind of gestures fishermen made about the fish they didn't catch.

Jilly hopped out, pulled her seat forward and encouraged Goldilocks to join her. The dog hit the ground with the kind of joy that meant she remembered and liked her surroundings. She carried a small stuffed animal in her mouth and Jilly shook her head.

"What?" Guy all but bellowed from the other side of the car. "So I got her a stuffed puppy to practice with. She's never had pups, she needs to learn to be gentle." He rammed on his hat.

"Great idea," Jilly said, holding up both hands in submission. She didn't say she thought Goldilocks looked as if she was gaining weight too fast. Guy fed her too much.

Although they'd driven out of the rain, the haze had gobbled up any hint of sun and Guy expected more of the wet stuff at any moment. The earth smelled damp. "Where's Homer?" he called to Ozaire.

That got him one of Ozaire's knowing and infuriating grins. "You're screwin' up a good thing, boy. Reckon you've done it already. Homer's in the shop."

Jilly scowled at Ozaire, who gave her his innocent look. Guy walked away without looking back and went into the shop to the right of the house across a yellowing lawn.

"Homer?" Guy said, walking through the best convenience store he'd ever seen. If you wanted it, Homer probably had it. That included darn good sandwiches, cold drinks, beer and wine, cleaning supplies, home-repair supplies, a pair of men's shorts or a baby bottle, a book—or bait. And if Homer should come up empty-handed on a request, he'd do his darnedest to put the shortcoming right in short order.

Guy could see the older man's salt-and-pepper buzz cut moving back and forth behind the counter. And Homer could hear a fish take the bait before a fisherman knew he had something on his hook, so it was fair to say he was ignoring Guy.

"You mad at me, Homer?" He picked up a discarded washcloth from one of the tables provided for snack customers. "Hey, Homer, you got a problem?" The slap of sandals meant Jilly had come into the shop.

"No problem," Homer said. "You do good work."

That stopped Guy where he was. "Thanks. I like it here. Wanted to let you know I've got kinda caught up in Spike's case and if it's okay with you, I'll make up time later in the day."

"No problem. Seems to work for both of us."

"Tell him to water the hanging pots," Jilly said to Homer. "Those geraniums are goin' to curl up their toes shortly."

Guy grinned at her. "I'll do that, ma'am. I think we're missin' some bulbs in the fairy lights, too."

"I love this shop, Homer," Jilly said, wandering the aisles. "Where else could you buy an electric pencil sharpener or a packet of ladyfingers?"

"Nowhere, I guess," Homer said, but he had softened up with Jilly's arrival. "How about a strawberry smush? Wendy's favorite and Vivian likes one now and then, too. Strawberry pudding made part with 7-Up. Goes pop in your mouth, or so I'm told."

Jilly accepted a parfait glass filled with the pink stuff and made approving noises while she ate.

A kid came in. He wore double-wide jeans resting halfway down the crack in his butt and sported a snake tattoo around one skinny upper arm. "Chew," he said, flipping back his black hair.

Guy watched Homer assess him before sliding a pack of bubble gum across the counter. "On the house," he said. "How about a sandwich?"

The boy's ears grew red and so did the back of his neck. He gave Jilly a sick smile, put a buck on the counter and slithered out, gum in hand—not quite the chew he had in mind.

"You're a good man, Homer Devol," Jilly said.

Guy thought so, too, but wasn't about to say as much as long as Homer had a bee where it shouldn't hang out.

"Need me to move some crates or somethin' before I go?" Guy asked, looking through a window. "There's a bunch of stuff out there."

"That's Ozaire's." Homer came around the counter and stood, feet braced, a few inches from Guy. "You gonna leave?"

"Yeah, but I'll be back later."

"Don't fool around with me," Homer said, swiping a hand across the bridge of his nose. "You know what I mean. Are you about ready to move on?"

Guy couldn't look at Jilly. He struggled with this question every day. He couldn't see Jilly leaving Toussaint and living in New Orleans, not that he'd asked her. But living somewhere without her turned him cold and opened an aching place in his chest.

"Are you?" Homer prompted.

"I don't know. I'm not planning on it."

Homer shifted his weight. "When will you know?"

Guy almost felt a wall against his back. "When things work out the way they're going to," he said. "The way they're supposed to."

26

"Hey!" Lee O'Brien said. "I was hoping I'd run into you two. This is Simon Menard, my partner. He finally got to move here. Well, he's found a place to live when he is here, anyway."

Jilly offered bespectacled Simon Menard a hand and he shook it firmly. She wondered what Guy was thinking. Lee, with her unexpected partner in tow, had erupted from the backyard at All Tarted Up to greet them when they got out of the car. A delivery truck, its nose poking into Parish Lane, filled Jilly's parking space so Guy had pulled close to the wall outside.

"I'm showing Simon around," Lee said. "He got here yesterday and I showed him around the sheriff's offices. I want him to meet everyone in town before he has to duck out on me again."

Simon Menard's expression gave away nothing of what he might be thinking, but he went along with Lee pleasantly enough.

"Why don't you come on inside and have some coffee?" Jilly said. "I'm running behind with every-thin' so I'd better get to it."

"That's what I wanted to talk to you about," Lee said, glancing at Simon. "I've got a good nose and maybe I could help out with the big case."

Jilly braced for Guy's reaction but none came.

Simon's smile transformed a serious face. The glitter in his dark eyes was wicked and his wide mouth turned distinctly up at the corners. "She does have a nose," he said, his speech slow in a nice way. A quietly sexy man—the most dangerous kind. "Lee also has questionable timing. We'll take you up on that coffee, then be on our way. I am glad to meet you." Simon had spent enough time away from Louisiana to blunt his accent.

"Of course he's glad to meet you," Lee said, all bubble and grin. "And I knew you'd like him. We've known each other for *years*—since I was in college. He was teaching in the journalism school, I was a student. He was very young to be teaching. Simon's been an investigative reporter for *years*."

"Does he have a nose, too?" Guy asked mildly.

Lee scowled at him. "Okay, so I go on a bit sometimes." She swallowed and said, "I would like to mention something. Simon thinks I should before I write about it, not that I'd name names, or anything like that. I'd probably pass it on to Lavinia for her column so it wouldn't be anything more than innuendo." She had the grace to smirk.

Jilly decided she wouldn't be getting inside as soon as she'd hoped.

Simon put his hands in his pockets and wiped all expression from his face. At least he didn't push Lee to do what he thought she should.

"Let's do this," Guy said. "Wait till you decide if

you're going for public innuendo, then, if the answer's yes, talk to me first."

"I think I'm going for it," Lee said at once. "On two counts."

"Two?" Simon said. "What's the other one?"

"Jilly's Beetle." Lee pulled herself up very straight. "But that may be something she'd rather I left alone."

"What about my Beetle?" Jilly asked. "It's not fixed yet. The body shop isn't sure how long it'll take."

Guy's hand came down on the back of her neck and he gave a definite squeeze. Not that she knew what the signal meant.

"I got this, this *thing*," Lee said. "A thought, a little niggle like you're not sure, but you might have a rock in your shoe. You know what I mean."

"Maybe."

"I knew you would." Lee delved into the bottom of an oversize canvas tote and pulled out a notebook. She flipped through several pages, frowning and squinting as she read her own writing. "Yes, I think I'll start with the car. I wasn't actually there when you ran the stop sign, but I got to the scene quickly. One of my strengths is that—believe it or not—I can listen well. There were skid marks—I heard that, and saw 'em—but folks didn't say anything about you slipping on something."

"The idea that she slid was only mentioned as a possibility," Guy said.

"It was that rock in my shoe," Lee said. "I went on the Internet and looked around and I was right. The brake hoses need to be checked regularly."

Jilly shuffled her feet and waited for one of the men to say the obvious.

"Any car's brakes should be checked regularly," Simon said mildly.

"Yes, well, I decided it was worth special attention, just in case, so I called the shop. They said they hadn't gotten to it yet and they sounded a bit peeved."

"You called and they talked to you about my car," Jilly said, feeling irritable herself.

"I said I was you." Lee didn't sound contrite. "Anyway, I went over there when the place was closed and found your green Beetle. I did some poking around myself. The Internet's amazing, you know. You can get anything there. See this diagram of the brake system in your car?" She flapped a piece of paper in front of Jilly's face and jabbed at it. "It wasn't easy with this but I found what I was looking for. Whoever did it didn't cut the hose, or anything. They just pinched it hard—like with a big wrench or something."

"You shouldn't have been there at all," Guy said. "If you felt you had something useful, Spike was the one to talk to—or anyone at the sheriff's office."

Lee smiled sweetly. "They don't talk to me there. D'you know what it says about those hoses? They're in layers, and if they get damaged inside the fluid leaks through and it's real dangerous. I don't think Jilly's accident was an accident. I think someone wanted her to get hurt badly."

"If the brakes had been tampered with," Guy said, "the body shop would have contacted Spike as well as Jilly." He should not have been too preoccupied to follow up on the car. Hell, what was the matter with him—he hadn't even thought about the VW since the accident.

"They might if they'd looked at the car." Lee's blue eyes sparkled with enthusiasm. "It was way out back. Do you see any reason why I shouldn't tell Lavinia to kind of *think* about why a body shop might not bother to check out a customer's car? She wouldn't use Mortie's name, of course."

"Don't," Guy said and heard Simon and Jilly echo him. "You've told me about it and I'll mention what you've said to Spike. I'm askin' you not to splash this theory in the *Trumpet*."

"Okay, I won't."

So why didn't she sound disappointed? Guy thought. And why hadn't the body shop gotten to Jilly's car yet? He considered Lee's meddling just that, meddling, but there was no avoiding the fact that Mortie's ought to have given a report by now.

"The Pratts have been in the graveyard again," Lee said.

"You already wrote your innuendo on that one," Jilly said promptly. "They're honest people, I'm convinced of it. Why not leave them alone?"

"It's Lavinia who writes the innuendos," Lee said. "It's not a good idea for them to be wandering around there at night. You never know what kind of crazy could decide to follow them."

Guy muttered, "Isn't that the truth?" but if Lee heard him, she didn't react.

"Lee," Simon said. "Let's get in and have that coffee—if we're still welcome." He glanced from Guy to Jilly.

"You're always welcome," she told him.

"But you wouldn't have a problem if Lavinia brought up the Pratts' graveyard shifts again?" Lee said.

"Yes, I would," Guy said. "But we both know you can print what you like. You can also get sued."

27

"I don't see how you can leave All Tarted Up to the likes of Doll Hibbs," Guy said, grudgingly making conversation after an hour of deliberately keeping his mouth shut.

They had left Toussaint for New Orleans because Guy didn't figure he could wait any longer to visit Zinnia Sedge. By the time he got to the Quarter, Nat was likely to be waiting.

"Doll has Wazoo supervising—and Vivian checking in," Jilly said. "We're covering my place and Ellie's very well, thanks. The Majestic may not be the Ritz but Doll and Gator have made a living there and it's hard to make a go of a twelve-room hotel in a place like Toussaint. It's not like having Rosebank where people go just to be at the place. Doll and Gator live from day to day on whoever shows up."

"Okay," Guy said. "You're right."

"And I don't see how you can leave Toussaint when you promised Homer you'd go back there and get some work done." Jilly had Goldilocks on her lap and it was a wonder the woman could breathe.

Wishing again he could have persuaded Jilly out of going to New Orleans with him, Guy ignored the comment, snatched up his cell phone and dialed Homer's number. After so many rings he almost hung up, then he heard Homer's voice saying a gruff "Yeah?"

"It's Guy. Can I take you into my confidence?" The man hardly talked at all and he certainly didn't gossip. "I know I can."

"If you want to. When you comin' in?"

"That's part of why I'm callin'. Looks like we may be makin' progress with that Parish Lane killin'."

"You mean at Jilly's place. Why not say so?"

"You're right. I need to go into New Orleans to meet up with my old partner. You talked to him. Nat Archer."

"The one Wazoo keeps yakkin' on about," Homer said. "Sure I talked to him."

Guy's feelings about Wazoo might not be too logical, but he didn't want Nat getting tangled up with her. Inspiration hit. "I'm steppin' in it with both the Devol men." He forced a chuckle. "Spike expects me in his office, you expect me at work. I want to be both places but I've got to do this, Homer. Can you understand that?"

Long pause. "I can understand wantin' to do what you can to keep people safe. Can't fault you for that. Could fault you if you break Jilly's heart, though."

Guy looked steadfastly ahead at the highway. What the critics didn't think about was that in the end Jilly might decide she didn't want him—if he messed up enough. "I don't intend to do that. Would you track Spike down and tell him where I'm goin'? Tell him I've got to get back tonight and I'll be in touch then. Cyrus knows what's up so he could talk to him about the details if he likes."

Homer agreed to take care of things and seemed pleased to become Guy's confidant.

When he switched off, he felt Jilly looking at him. He didn't turn his head but he reached out to pat her hand, missed because Goldilocks was in the way, and patted Jilly's leg instead. The dog—who got thicker by the day—licked Guy's fingers. "Everythin's on the up-and-up with Homer. I need to work on includin' the people I trust a bit more. That way they won't think I'm deliberately keepin' them in the dark."

She covered his hand on her thigh. "There's hope for you. I think you're learnin'. It wasn't so hard to let me come with you after all, was it?"

"Yes, ma'am. I didn't want you here. Still don't. If somethin' turns nasty I don't need someone who can't look after herself."

Crossing her arms, Jilly rested her head back. He glanced at her again and felt irritable that she didn't appear upset by the put-down. His lady was too clever for her own good. She knew how to ring his chimes.

His lady?

Was she?

He guessed so. When this case was finished, one way or the other, he'd have to decide what he intended to do with the rest of his life, including whether he wanted to ask Jilly to share it with him.

The same old answer took him by the gut. He didn't like the idea of not having her around.

"I've been thinkin' about your Beetle," he said. "I'll make sure it gets a thorough going-over but I'm thinkin' Lee's imagination got away from her. Even with her printout from the computer, what does she know about cars? For all we know she wasn't even looking at the brakes."

"You're probably right. But they were a bit mushy."

"That could have been coming on slowly."

Jilly nodded. "I'm sure it had been. I'm bad about taking care of necessities."

His hand still rested on her thigh, on top of that sexy green silk that wouldn't look so appealing if her skin weren't coffee-gold and sleek. Inch by inch he slid the skirt higher.

She didn't make a move to stop him.

His little finger came to rest on another piece of silk and he felt her heat through her panties.

"Is this a good time to be foolin' around?" Jilly said.

She liked every moment of feeling him touch her, but there was always a time and place. A small smile settled in. So far they hadn't always been particularly appropriate in this area.

"You want to fool around?" he asked.

He said something like that and might as well have punched her diaphragm. The air didn't want to go into her lungs.

"Jilly?" He met her eyes and the question was very serious. "I think I need to hold you. You give me strength."

"Minutes ago you told me you didn't want me with you. And you're as tough as tacks—you don't need me to make you stronger."

"There's more than one kind of strength. One feeds off the other. Could I hold you?"

"You're drivin'." She felt disoriented.

Guy searched the road ahead, saw what he was looking for and drove onto a gravel strip. A track led through trees then petered out. Several heaps of gravel dotted a turnaround. He drove between two gravel stacks and farther into the trees. When he stopped and turned off the engine, Jilly looked back and realized they'd driven downhill. She couldn't see the gravel anymore.

They sat there, staring ahead.

Goldilocks licked Jilly's face.

"Over you go," Guy told the dog, and helped her carefully into the backseat where he rumpled up a blanket on top of Goldilocks's foam bed so the dog had her favorite thing—a nest. "Now, go to sleep," he said.

"I thought you were in a hurry," Jilly said. He confounded her again and again.

"Time's tight, but not so tight I shouldn't spend some of it on something that's really important to me."

Men needed sex, not that women didn't. But she believed he would be able to move on if the mood took him. Move on and leave her behind. She didn't want to be a convenience, surely not in this way.

"Is this too calculated for you?" he asked, putting his hand on the keys. "It is. I'm sorry, Jilly, it's just that I need you—in a lot of ways."

"You can turn your feelings on and off," she told him. "You put the case in one compartment and your needs in another. And when the needs get strong you open the appropriate compartment."

He turned toward her so abruptly, she flinched. "It's not like that," he said, his mouth a straight line. "I'm not going to debate the nature of the male, but I've got feelings other than the animal ones. By the way, there's nothin' wrong with animal feelings, they're damn good. I—"

Jilly took his face in her hands, pulled him to her and kissed his lips so hard she made her neck ache. When she took a breath, he didn't say anything, just waited for her to continue.

She continued.

Kissing him again, she undid his shirt and slipped

her hands inside to rake through the hair on his chest. He shuddered and she teased him more. The top of her dress was a backless halter, belted and with a crossover front. Guy's hands heated the bare skin on her back and he held her tighter as he forgot to let her take the lead. Gradually he returned her kisses with enough pressure to lean her backward.

Cradling the back of her neck in one large hand, Guy studied her. His every touch made her tremble and he had aroused her until she felt blood pulsing beneath her skin.

Guy kissed her neck, the dips behind her collarbones, the skin exposed by the deep neckline of her dress. She spread his shirt wider and nuzzled his slightly salty skin. He jumped at each touch.

For a moment he held her upper arms and stared at her chest.

"What?" she said, wriggling to sit up.

She didn't think he noticed her struggle. He just held her right where she was.

"Guy! Why are you staring at me like that?"

"There's no back on your dress."

"No."

A lazy grin spread on his face. "You're not wearing a bra. Just silk to cover the good bits."

"Good bits?" She giggled. "You say the strangest things."

"Well, you're not, are you?"

"No—well, more or less no."

That earned her a quick kiss on the nose before he

parted the front of her dress. He took a deep breath and, she thought, turned a little pale. The idea made her feel powerful although she was a tiny bit uncomfortable knowing what he was really looking at.

"You have beautiful breasts."

Now she was embarrassed. "Thank you. Your body turns me on whenever I'm near you. And when I'm not near you but I think about it."

His grin let her know he enjoyed the sexy compliments. He feathered his fingers over her breasts. "Why use these things?" He ran a fingernail back and forth on the peach-colored silk pasties she wore over her nipples.

Ignoring the sensation his fingernail produced was impossible but she still blushed. "They're only because I'm not wearing a bra."

"They're a turn-on. Where are the tassels?"

"Don't," she whispered. "I'm embarrassed."

"You're sexy—naturally sexy." Carefully, he peeled off first one pastie, then the other. After a long-enough perusal to make her squirm, he used the tip of his tongue to make circles around her nipples before taking one in his mouth and sucking, nipping, until she arched up toward him.

"Okay," she managed to say. "We held each other. We kissed. We *connected,* but we'd better get on the road."

"You're kidding," he said, his eyelids heavy and half lowered. "Help me get your panties off."

Jilly turned so hot she burned. "Not here." But she

slipped her hands beneath her skirt and got her thumbs under the elastic of the silk-and-lace thong. Supposedly helping, Guy took her bottom in his hands and got in her way.

Laughing, she smacked him off and swallowed when he wrenched his belt undone and unzipped his jeans.

She had barely taken one foot from her underwear when Guy picked her up by the waist and sat her, facing him, in his lap—with his penis deep inside her. For a moment he rocked her back and forth. Jilly held his shoulders and moaned. Her arms pushed her naked breasts together and she felt wanton and wonderful—and desperate.

Guy held on to the cheeks of her bottom and began exercising his hips at a heart-bumping pace. "Oh" was all she managed to say before the top of her head hit the car roof and she bent over him, tucked her face into his neck. Their bare skin rubbed together, her aching nipples against the silky hair on his chest.

Jilly heard a keening sound from her own throat, and an answering stream of meaningless words from Guy.

Too soon she climaxed explosively and straightened her arms between them while ripples of intense sensation hit again and again. She felt his release, hot and wet, and didn't want to let him come out of her.

"Hold me," he murmured, pulling her into his arms and hugging her so tight she felt he might crush her bones. "Jilly, we need each other. We fit . . . match."

He knew what he said and meant it. Let the damn chips fall wherever.

Nat stood on the curb outside the building on St. Ann, just around the corner from Dauphine. He bounced on his heels, flapping his toes up and down over the gutter. He turned up his collar against a cool wind that whipped scattered raindrops down the narrow street, and checked his watch. A sweat turned cold on his skin and he felt sick. Guy should be here by now.

A lot was coming down—fast. In the last two days he'd made some headway gathering information on the girl who was murdered after being seen at Jazz Babes. Her name had been Paula Hemp and she'd been whacked around the time when Detective Fleet had been up to his ears with the club. Unfortunately organization was Fleet's weak point and so far Nat had turned up only a fraction of what should exist on the case.

Nat contemplated his headache. He'd spent last night at the Sump Pump off Jackson Square, doing what he'd been trying not to do for a couple of years. He had drunk himself off a stool at the bar, then taken two packs of Jax and a bottle of rum home. He'd sunk himself into a stupor and started his day at ten in the morning with raw eggs in vinegar, his grandpappy's "cure." Only he still wasn't over the thumping behind his eyes and at the back of his head and the "cure" had made him throw up. Maybe that was the idea.

Where the fuck was Guy, dammit?

When he could, Nat intended to spend some time with Wazoo in Toussaint. Maybe he'd bring her up here for a few days. If she'd come. She let him know she enjoyed being with him and she made him feel good like he hadn't in too long. He needed someone around him, someone he liked.

"At last," he muttered. Guy's Pontiac slowed at the corner before turning onto St. Ann's. He pulled in so close to the curb he took Nat by surprise and he forgot to step back in time. His unceremonious fall to the concrete didn't help his head, or his mood. "Goddammit!" he shouted, just in time for Jilly to be out of the car and offering him her hand.

Sheepishly, Nat accepted the hand although he sprang to his feet under his own steam. "Sorry about the language," he said. "I'm not having a good day and I'm feelin' sorry for myself."

"Don't worry about it," she said.

From the other side of the car Guy said, "Didn't your mother tell you to stay back from the street?" and laughed.

"I'm goin' to *fry* your balls," Nat said, glowering. "You drive like a friggin' maniac."

"Love you, too," Guy said. He crossed his arms and stared at Nat. "You've got a headache," he announced. "I can see it in your eyes."

"Great," Nat said. "Now you're psychic or somethin'."

"Long night?"

"My nights are my own business," he told Guy, but

359

felt mad as hell at himself for the bender. "Let's get to it. I waited for you so we wouldn't be repeatin' ourselves. Miz Trudy-Evangeline Augustine don't have a lot of patience—or so Cyrus told me. Doesn't sound like we can get to Miz Sedge without going through the caretaker."

Guy tangled his fingers in Jilly's thick hair and looked down into her face with the kind of smile Nat recognized. Possessive. Nat liked to see it but worried Guy would do something to mess up a good thing—he had before.

"Cher, it would be less confusin' for the lady we need to see if you weren't there. I know you understand."

"No, I don't."

"This is police business."

Nat winced at the official tone.

"Ooh," Jilly said. "I'm so impressed. And I'm not stayin' out here worryin' about what's goin' on in there. I'm good with people and women usually feel more comfortable with other women around. You've heard that, haven't you, Nat?"

He didn't want to be in the middle, no sir. "I'm not sure."

"You'll do what you want to, anyway," Guy said with a wry grin, and he led the way through the black iron gates. The fountain bubbled away and despite the overcast day, the flowers in the courtyard were brilliant.

"Trudy-Evangeline told Cyrus that Zinnia had come

back," Guy commented. "Let's hope she hasn't left again." Immediately he saw the Vespa and felt relieved.

He met Nat's eyes and they silently acknowledged seeing the scooter.

Nat worried Guy. The man looked hellish. His clothes had obviously been slept in and today he wore an old brown fedora—its brim turned up all around—jammed straight down on his head and touching his eyebrows. The skin on his face shone and Guy reckoned Nat must be clammy about now. The wild drinking bouts used to be routine until he'd lost his brother in a traffic accident involving booze. That stopped Nat.

"What are we waiting for?" Jilly asked when they'd paused at the bottom of the steps to Zinnia's place.

"I guess we're waitin' for Trudy-Evangeline to jump out at us," Guy said. "Let's go."

A different wedding dress stood in the window of the shop. Jilly said, "That's really beautiful," and Guy glanced at her face. She was entranced and the idea scared him to death.

Why should it, you clown?

"Ready?" Nat said, and turned the door handle without waiting for a response. The door opened and he went in. Guy followed with Jilly behind him.

Overhead a cane-bladed fan revolved noisily. A radio played the Huckberry Ramblers singing "Frankie and Johnny." An old-fashioned ledger lay open on a glass countertop and a land phone had been

361

set down on top. The receiver was off the hook.

Guy whistled and ran his eyes over boxes of shoes—little white satin numbers, he imagined—a case filled with beaded things for the head, a display of veils. On a round table beside a comfortable-looking chair stood several piles of large books. He went closer and discovered they were filled with sample wedding invitations, thank-you cards and the like.

"Full-service shop," he muttered.

"Nice," Jilly said, then, "Hello?" She raised her voice and tried to see into the open workroom.

"Mrs. Sedge?" Nat added.

Something slammed in the direction of the woman's living quarters. "Here she comes," Guy said. He turned to Jilly. "From Trudy-Evangeline's description it sounds as if this is a reticent person. Private. Best to be low-key."

"Don't worry about me," Jilly said.

Minutes passed with no sign of Zinnia Sedge.

Nat started to pace and Guy said, "I wonder if there's a back way out of here."

"Why would she run out?"

Guy stared at the phone receiver, then picked it up. A recorded voice asked him to hang up, a beep followed and the message was repeated before the line went silent.

"I think she's taken a powder," he said. "She could have plenty of reasons not to talk to us."

He knocked on the door leading to the flat and

opened it at once. "New Orleans Police Department," he shouted. "Zinnia Sedge?"

"There's water running," Nat said, frowning and looking up the stairs. His expression cleared. "She's takin' a shower."

"After leavin' the phone off the hook?" Jilly said. "Like she was talkin' to someone and went to check somethin'?"

"She could have forgotten the phone," Guy pointed out. He went upstairs to the bedroom door and knocked again. Nat was right, the shower was on. "She's not gonna be happy if we walk in on her."

"She'd probably have a heart attack," Jilly said. "Let's wait in the shop."

Nat, who had joined Guy, lifted a foot and they all looked down. The boot had made a soggy popping noise. Blue fitted carpet had turned dark outside the bedroom door.

"It's flooding," Jilly said. Water slipped under the door, visible now, spreading through the carpet while they watched.

Nat said, "I think it might be a good idea for you to go check on that dog, Jilly."

Her response was to push past and go into the bedroom. Guy caught her by the arm but she narrowed her eyes at him and said, "If it was me, I'd rather a woman helped me."

How did you explain to a layman that after years on the force, trouble was something you smelled?

His nose could be off today. Guy let Jilly go but he

363

dodged around her and paddled through a thin layer of water running from the bathroom over wood and carpet.

"Let me just take a look, huh?" he said to Jilly.

She had stopped moving. Her face had turned a chalky white. She felt trouble, too, now.

Nat squelched over the floor, his mouth set and his nostrils flaring.

"Did she know you were coming?" Jilly asked quietly.

Nat shook his head but said, "Maybe. If Miss Trudy-Evangeline told her."

"Stay put, Jilly," Guy said, and he made sure she heard that he meant it.

He nudged open the door and moved inside fast.

"Shit," Nat said, drawing his gun as he joined him.

Deep pink water bubbled over the side of a white tub. The shower curtain had been closed. The water ran over the floor like thin red ink.

Guy ripped back the curtain. "Found," he said, dimly realizing how stupid that sounded. Going to his knees, he stared down into the water. "Turn it off," he told Nat. "Try to preserve what you can."

Nat did as he was asked and stood over Guy. "I knew we were getting close to sensitive parts," he said. "No one's answerin' any questions. Everyone I've talked to suddenly got amnesia." He flipped on his radio and talked rapidly. This place would be overrun soon.

"Cruel bastards," Guy said. "I want to take her out

of the water." Automatically he felt for a pulse. Not a flutter.

"But you won't get her out," Nat said. "No point. You don't get any deader than this lady. The boys will want to see all this just the way it is."

"You've got to find who did this," Jilly said.

Guy looked over his shoulder, hating that she was there. "They're gone," he said, drawing his own weapon, "but take a look around, anyway, Nat. And be careful. We don't want anyone pointing out we don't have a warrant."

"Sure." Nat patted Jilly's shoulder and went back into the bedroom.

"They made sure she wouldn't talk to you," Jilly said.

In the tub, dark hair fanned from a small woman's head. Her throat had been cut, but the wound seemed a pointless afterthought. Her teeth showed between parted lips and a bloody lump trailed by a thread of flesh from the corner of her mouth.

"They cut out her tongue," Jilly whispered.

28

It had been a long night and it wasn't over.

Each time Guy spoke to Nat he got a one-word answer—not a reassuring sign. Nat refused to make eye contact—a lousy sign.

"Okay, enough of this," Guy said, hauling exhausted Nat to a stop at the back of the squad room at NOPD.

"This is a shortcut to the chief's office," Nat said.

Guy formed an expletive but bit it off. "I know my way around here as well as you do. I'm not talking about routes. Why are you behaving like a jerk and why do I suddenly have to talk to the chief?"

"Jilly seemed as anxious to leave town as you were to have her go," Nat said.

Guy hadn't seen things that way, not at all, but he let it go. "I asked you a question."

Nat turned tired eyes on him. "The media will likely go after this one. The chief just wants to get up to speed in case he has to go on camera. Sound bites. You know the routine."

"Like he isn't already up to speed? That would be a first. If he needs anything else he can get it from you."

"You're more articulate than I am."

That was a new one. "I'm not even supposed to be here."

"You thought that meant he didn't know you were?"

"I'm just helpin' out because you asked me to," Guy told him. "I could step away at any time."

Nat snorted. "Sure you could. You don't have any personal interest in the case, do you?"

"Smart-ass. I'm in on this one now but we still haven't tied the Sedge killing to Toussaint, and I sure don't see a connection to Jilly. One matchbook with some scribble on it doesn't make the case."

"Maybe not," Nat said. "But it probably will and

you think so, too. Pip Sedge knew something was going to happen in Toussaint—in Parish Lane."

"He could have picked up the matchbook by mistake. Maybe he never knew anything was written on it."

Nat pushed through a double door. "Sure. And his ex died in a random murder? None of this is linked?"

"Damn it," Guy said. He leaned against a wall. "I think a lot of things and most of them make me edgy. I've got nothing to learn in here. It's all out there." He made a vague gesture to the Quarter outside. "Except for the rest of what Fleet turned up. Get that and we could really have somethin'."

"Agreed," Nat said, scuffing his boots back and forth and leaving black marks on the floor. "There's an unofficial, official instruction that nobody goes near his ex-wife. Don't ask me why. I wanted to ask her if he said anything useful about what he was doing around the time Paula Hemp died. Mentioned it to the chief and he about took my head off. Said he's seen his share of cop divorces but Fleet and his missus's story was about the saddest ever. Off-limits, that's what he said. And he reckons the couple's biggest problem was Fleet's work—big surprise—and they had an agreement that Fleet never mentioned his work."

Guy shrugged away from the wall. "He's right. She wouldn't know anything. If she did she'd have told us by now." Their eyes met and each of them gave a half smile. Nothing was ever for sure.

"Okay, friend," Nat said as they reached the big boss's door. "I'll be leavin' you here. You'll find me in our office. I'm gonna try givin' Wazoo a call."

Guy started to say something, but closed his mouth. He wasn't Nat Archer's mother. For a few seconds he watched the other man walk away, his shoulders back, swinging confidently again. One stop-'em-in-their-tracks dude going to "our" office. Damn but some decisions left ugly fallout no matter which way you chose to go.

He knocked on the door and opened it when Chief Carson growled "Yeah" from inside the room. Carson saw Guy and pulled his bushy gray brows low over his eyes. "Oh, it's you." The man's seamed face looked ready to be immortalized on some canyon wall. Yellow from too much time inside, too much hooch and too much nicotine, one feature hadn't lost any light; his eyes were the color of gray agates in the sun. If they didn't see through you, they were lying. He didn't like wasting time getting his hair cut and tight gray curls often looked as if he'd whacked a few off himself.

"I got a message you wanted to see me while I'm visitin', Chief," Guy said, emphasizing "visiting." The sooner he made his situation clear, the better. On the other hand it had struck him that Carson might have been looking for an opportunity to kick his AWOL detective's ass out of the department permanently and he, Guy, had just given him the perfect excuse.

"Did I contact you and ask you to work on the Sedge

killin'—killin's?" Carson asked. He stubbed a cigarette out in an overflowing tin ashtray and immediately lit up again. Little piles of ash lay on his gray-painted metal desk where admirers had left sweet notes, like "Fuck you, dumb-ass" and "They say you good to you' mama. When you gone, I be good to her, too."

"Well?" Carson snapped.

"No, sir," Guy said, wondering how it would go over if he sat down. "You didn't ask me to do that. Can I pour you a cup of coffee?" he said, suddenly inspired. He wanted to sit down and Carson would have to ask him if they had coffee.

"There's nuthin' but mud in that pot," Carson said, opening the right bottom drawer in his desk and removing a brown sack. From this he took a steel flask covered with greasy smears. He unscrewed the cap, filled it with whatever and tipped it straight down his throat. He poured a second capful and held it silently out to Guy.

Turning down the chief's hooch would not be smart. Guy tossed it back, felt good Scotch burn a blissful path into his veins and gave back the cap. "Thanks," he said.

"Siddown," Carson told him. "Not over there. Pull a chair up here. I prefer to keep my voice down on sensitive issues."

Sensitive issues. Now, there was a comment to curl a man's nose hairs. But he dragged a metal folding chair close to the other side of Carson's desk and flopped into it.

"Archer's been through three partners since you left—I mean since you left for a mental health break or whatever the hell you said you needed."

"Yeah? I didn't know that."

"You do now. That boy hasn't been the same since you went sunbathin'. Doesn't want to work with anyone but you, so he says. I've offered him some of the best and brightest we got but he turns 'em down."

In other words, Guy was chopped liver. "That's too bad."

"I can't afford men who rile things up around here. Other officers don't like it when Archer treats 'em like piles of dog shit."

"Nat isn't the kind of man who—"

"He gives 'em the silent treatment then goes off on his own. They never know what's goin' down. But you do, don't you, Gautreaux? You two are pals. In a hot moment he told me he's keepin' your seat warm as well as his own. He's workin' with you on the Sedge cases."

Lying wouldn't ease whatever pain was coming. "Yes, sir."

"How's it going?"

Guy looked at the rangy man suspiciously. He knew softening-up tactics when he heard them. "Frustratin' case but some parts are starting to wave at one another. We feel real bad about Mrs. Zinnia Sedge."

"We all feel real bad about it, too," Carson said, his eyebrows shielding his eyes again. "The whole force feels bad. I feel bad. My boss feels bad. I can't help but wonder if it could have been avoided if this case wasn't being dealt with piecemeal. Maybe I need a whole new team on the case, a team where everyone works full-time for the department and can be where they're needed in ten minutes rather than a couple of hours."

"Understood," Guy said. The old crust wasn't getting a rise out of him.

"A big mouth managed to let me know Nat fell off the wagon couple of nights ago," Carson said. "I thought he didn't do that anymore. Bad sign. Word has it he's not reliable when the booze is in."

"Shit," Guy said with feeling. He'd like to know who squealed to Carson. "Nat's overtired, is all. He didn't realize he'd gone too far until it was too late."

"Bullshit. He's trying to do two men's work because he's makin' sure he keeps your space open." He glared at Guy. "And I don't want you suggestin' I've been ridin' him, because I haven't."

"He's anticipating you will," Guy said quietly.

"We'll get back to that. I've read through everything we've got on the case so far. Maybe it's more than it looks. I sure as hell hope so."

Guy tipped onto the back two legs of his chair. How he hated the sick-colored walls in this place. "I don't want to sound like a fool, but I feel like it's going to take one good, solid piece of information to put us over the top. We haven't had any luck finding what it is that glues the events together, but it's there, take it from me."

371

Carson looked up through his beetling brows. "You may be right, but from the rate we're losin' citizens we can't sit back and wait. This Zinnia Sedge murder will be front page. Quiet little woman like that getting her tongue cut out." He shook his head and Guy figured his own desire to snicker was hysteria.

"I agree with you one hundred per cent," Guy said. "I'd better get back to it." He longed to ask Carson's permission to approach Fleet's ex-wife but figured he better not push too far.

"Guy—" Carson stubbed out a butt that had burned all the way down between his fingers "—we gotta get some things straight. You know we can't go on like this forever."

Guy's throat tightened. His forehead turned moist. He knew what was coming.

"It's been more than a year since we agreed you needed some time away from the force."

"Yes, sir."

"I never expected it to be this long before you decided to come back. Are you back now?"

Nat was falling apart and Carson blamed him. They had a big, showy case on their hands and he was needed full-time. And to boil it all down, Carson was about to tell him to put up or shut up. Damn, he was too tired for this now and he wanted to check on Jilly.

And there was his curse and his blessing. Jilly. He wasn't sure how he felt about the force. In a way he was a natural detective and he enjoyed the work when it wasn't making him spitting mad. But he wanted more out of life. He wanted Jilly and now he had to make a choice. He could ask her to give up everything for him, but that would be an ultimatum: *show me how much I mean to you. All or nothing.* Unless she did the unimaginable and convinced him she'd been born to play second fiddle to the law, that she wanted a man in her life whose career was his mistress, not on the side but right out in the open. Some chance.

"Gautreaux, I asked you somethin'."

"And I can't answer you except to say I'm definitely not ready to make a final decision yet. With your permission, I would like to work on this case with Nat."

Carson lit another cigarette from a smouldering butt in the ashtray. "I'm on the ropes, Guy."

The first name rattled him. "I'm sorry to hear that, sir."

"I'm being asked questions. They want answers. We can't afford to keep an inactive body on the roll."

"Afford? You aren't paying me."

Carson's only reaction was to reach for his flask again. "I gotta have a return date."

Should he come right out and say he was quitting? Guy wondered.

"How about one more month to be sure?" Carson said. "Sometimes we need a time frame to make us concentrate on making a decision."

A month. Sweat slithered between his shoulder blades. "Gimme another six." He took the whiskey-filled cap from Carson again and drank the stuff down.

"Sorry," Carson said. "If it was up to me you'd get

it, but I've got people breathing down my neck. A month, Guy. Then I'd like you to come back here and tell me your decision. I hope it's to stay with the force. You're a good man. We need you."

Time was running out. But so what, all he had to do was make a decision that would make or break the rest of his life.

29

In gathering darkness, Jilly stood in front of All Tarted Up. Through the windows she could see Wazoo sitting at a table with a dark-haired woman. The lights were low but Jilly was certain this was the person who had left Rosebank so hastily that morning.

She breathed through her mouth. The horror wouldn't leave her, or the sense of evil everywhere—and helplessness. In her mind she carried a vivid picture of the woman in the bathtub. Guy said the autopsy would give an estimated time of death. Jilly wanted to know the second when Zinnia Sedge died. She wanted to know that she and the men had not stood in the shop while a woman was brutally murdered a few yards away.

Wazoo's phone request for her to come to the shop on her way home sounded like an invitation to another drama. Jilly had been in more than her share of drama for one day.

Cyrus and Madge had driven to New Orleans to bring Jilly home. Guy would stay, at least for a day or two, he'd told her. And this time he'd made it clear she would help him by leaving the Quarter.

Madge Pollard got out of her car and joined Jilly. "Is that Amy Girard?" Madge said. "I knew she was back, but this is the first time I've seen her. I never did really meet her but she fits her description."

Cyrus stood behind them. The women inside the shop hadn't noticed company approaching and he eased Madge and Jilly to one side. "It has to be Amy," he said. "Why would Wazoo insist you come here to meet her? It's getting late."

Amy Girard? Marc's sister? She could want to explain her earlier behavior, Jilly thought, but she didn't mention that incident to Cyrus and Madge.

Madge touched Jilly's shoulder. "You don't have to do anything now," she said. "Why don't I go in there and tell Wazoo this will have to wait?"

"There's no point in putting it off. Wazoo made it sound important." Jilly had no idea why she would have any connection to Amy Girard.

"Wazoo has a rather dramatic approach to all things," Cyrus said. "I agree with Madge. Give yourself a break. Get some rest first."

"Thanks, but I don't feel like going home and being alone yet, anyway."

"I won't let you do that," Madge said quickly. "I'll take you back to Rosebank with me. You know you're welcome there anytime."

"Or you can have a room at the rectory," Cyrus told her. "There's no reason for you to be on your own. When this mess gets cleared up it'll be different."

Jilly looked at the Hummer parked in front. Even in the darkness it seemed to shine. She giggled and felt out of control. "I've got to get rid of that thing. I'm using it like a billboard till I do and only driving it when I have to. I'll talk to Mortie at the body shop tomorrow, tell him to get a move on fixing my Beetle." Guy had said chances were that Lee wouldn't know a brake hose from an alternator, any more than Jilly would, but she'd make sure the brakes were checked out.

"Your Beetle should be done by now," Cyrus remarked. "The Impala was in worse shape and they put that back together."

"Thank you for coming to get me," Jilly said. "I'll take it from here." She stood by the door, picking absently at the first signs of flaking paint. It would have to be painted, the whole place would.

"If you don't mind," Cyrus told her, "I'd like to wait in Madge's car until you let us know everything's okay. Normally I'd insist on comin' in but I don't think I will right now." He looked at the women in the shop. "No, Wazoo would only set the meeting up this way if she was lookin' for privacy."

Madge smiled up at him and said, "The truth, Father, is that you're not in the mood to be hailed as *God Man* by Wazoo." She touched his chest and laughed.

"Thanks," Jilly said, and watched them go back to

Madge's Camry before pushing on the door. It was locked and she opened her purse to find her keys.

Movement made her look up. Wazoo rushed toward her in a cloud of flying black-and-purple lace. She whipped open the door and pulled Jilly inside. "I never was so glad to see a body," she said in a low voice. "Now, you got to use all that tact you got, the tact you forget most of the time. This is Amy Girard, Marc's sister. She's not in good shape. Not herself. You understand?"

"Okay," Jilly said quietly. She wanted, more than anything, to be with Guy. Even having her arms around Goldilocks would be comforting. The dog had stayed with her master, who had stopped talking about not wanting her.

Wazoo peered into her face. "You okay, sexy woman?"

"Yes," Jilly said, shaking her head. *Appropriate* wasn't a word in Wazoo's vocabulary. "What's going on?"

"I'll get some coffee for all of us. I need it if you don't. Hoo mama, this has been a bad day."

"Trouble balancing everything I've heaped on you?" Jilly asked, very aware of the woman sitting alone.

"That's no sweat, no, ma'am, no sweat atall. But you and me is livin' in one unhinged town. I know more than a bit about psychology—from all of my work with animals, even if they are sharper than humans—and we got folks who belong in institutions walkin' around here."

Jilly saw no reason to argue.

"Homer Devol's up in arms because Ozaire pulled a fast one on him. Said he needed to store some crates for a few days, but he didn't tell Homer those crates was filled with exercise stuff he wanted to store in the boilin' plant out there. Ozaire and his gym, y'know. He's not givin' up on the idea, but he doesn't have a place for it. Homer says if he doesn't move them machines out of there in twenty-four hours they'll be rustin' on the bottom of the bayou."

"Wazoo," Jilly said, trying to be patient. "I'm real tired. Could we do what you wanted me here for, and talk about these other things tomorrow—or some other time?" She didn't care about Ozaire's latest and ongoing get-rich schemes.

Her cell phone rang and she smiled. Guy had said he'd call to check up on her. Only the caller's number was restricted. "Hi," she said, propping an elbow on a forearm.

"Where are you?" Laura Preston asked. "Do you know how much trouble you've caused? Ducking out in New Orleans the way you did, then giving us the silent treatment?"

"This isn't a good time," Jilly said. "I'm sorry if I've made things tough but I didn't intend to. You know why I left."

"You didn't need to sneak off," Laura said. Either she had a cold or she had been crying. "We said we'd look after you. If you'd told Daddy you had to leave you could have made it easy on us. He's furious. He's blind to his own faults, or pretends to be."

Jilly sighed. "Then it's past time one of you set him straight."

"You don't know anything. He'd make our lives hell."

So get out on your own, you and Wes, and live your own lives. Jilly knew why they didn't and there was no point in antagonizing Laura. "I'm sorry."

"Edith keeps asking me when you're coming back—and she's gone into her adoring-wife mode. She's useless."

"I've been very busy," Jilly said. She'd seen more than she cared to see of what Laura and Wes were prepared to do for Preston's money. Just being polite took discipline.

"You've made it so tough on us," Laura said. "Daddy's doing a Godzilla act and blamin' all of us because you left."

Laura had started repeating herself. Weariness weighted Jilly down. "I'm seein' to some business now. Where are you? Can I call you back?"

"We'll be in Toussaint tomorrow but don't come to Edwards Place."

Jilly frowned. "Why?" Wazoo busied herself making coffee and Amy Girard ripped a napkin into small pieces as if she'd forgotten she wasn't alone.

"Wes and I both told you to stay away from Daddy once you left the New Orleans house," Laura said. "We're concerned for your safety. We've seen him when he's obsessed with someone before. He can't leave it alone even if he wants to. I think he knows sniffin' at you isn't right but he's gonna do it, anyway. When I talk about safety, I don't mean I think he'd hurt you, but he could make you pretty miserable."

"The way he has you? Wes doesn't pretend Mr. Preston hasn't come on to you." *And neither do you.*

Laura took a while to respond. "That's history. I don't want you to go through it, too."

Jilly didn't bother to say she'd heard Laura agree to seduce her father-in-law. "I will come over tomorrow," she said firmly. "Staying away could do more harm than good." And, there were some things she'd like to check out if she could get away on her own there.

"Why don't you consider getting out of Toussaint?" Laura sounded intense. "Go somewhere and don't say where you are. Just till things blow over."

"*No.* Runnin' doesn't work. Quit worryin' and I'll see you tomorrow."

Laura said a reluctant goodbye and they hung up.

Wazoo had returned to her friend and watched Jilly anxiously as she approached.

"I didn't even guess you two hadn't met," Wazoo said. "I should have. You wouldn't have known each other before. Amy just told me."

The woman turned to look at Jilly, the same woman who had rushed out of Rosebank that morning, all right. She swallowed at the sight of Jilly, and blinked rapidly. Then she held out a hand. "Amy Girard," she said. "Sorry I behaved like an ass this morning. I know it must have looked like it was something to do with you but it wasn't."

"Um, Amy—"

"I'll do just fine explaining myself," Amy told Wazoo. "It'll be good for me."

Wazoo frowned and sat down. Jilly sat next to her and accepted a mug of coffee already heavily laced with cream the way she liked it.

"You're Jilly Gable and your brother is Joe," Amy said. "He's a lawyer."

"Yes. And you must be the . . . You're Marc Girard's sister."

"The woman who almost got murdered on the bayou a few years ago?" Amy said. "Is that what you were going to ask? The answer is, yes." She looked away and studied her folded hands on top of the table. She had squashed the pieces of napkin into a ball.

"Wazoo, what did you mean the other day when you said you sang at Amy's first—" Jilly winced, then kept her mouth closed.

Laughing in her abandoned way, Wazoo said, "I said I sang at your first funeral, Amy, but that's not quite true since you haven't had a funeral yet. I guess I could say I sang in your memory."

An unhappy and deep crease sank into the skin between Amy's brows. "What did you sing?"

Jilly decided against drinking the coffee. She didn't need to get more jumpy than she was already.

Wazoo actually blushed, something Jilly didn't recall seeing before. "Well, remember I'd been told a false story about you being dead. I sang, 'Dem bones, dem bones, them d-ry . . . bones.'" Her voice trailed away. "I was bein' respectful, Amy, because I thought my friend had died. We knew each other quite a while."

Amy tried not to smile but failed. "Sounds like a lovely affair." Her eyes settled on Jilly again. "You didn't send me running this morning. It was being inside Rosebank for the first time since I was a girl."

A slight movement caused Jilly to look sharply at Wazoo. The other woman's mouth hung open.

"It's okay, Wazzy," Amy said. "I'm all right. I can talk about this now, especially when I've got you to make me strong. Jilly, I don't want Marc and Reb to know we've talked. With the baby due, they've got enough on their minds without worrying about me. You won't say anything, will you? Or you, Wazoo?"

Jilly was tempted to point out she had no idea what she wasn't supposed to talk about, but let it go. "Don't worry," she said, and Wazoo murmured the same thing.

"I was feeling bad because I hadn't got in touch with Wazoo." Amy smiled at her and Jilly got another glimpse of a pretty woman behind the usually sad and prematurely aged face. "That's why I went over to Rosebank, to try to see her before she went to work. I'm sorry, Wazoo. I've been on my own a lot for a long time and sometimes I forget there are people who care about me."

Wazoo grinned. "We used to argue," she said

bluntly. "You called me Dirty Darlene because you didn't like my clothes, or much else about me."

"No!" Amy shook her head emphatically. "It was just a sort of nickname is all. Your clothes suit you. I'm glad you got rid of the Darlene. Never did like that. L'Oiseau de Nuit is pretty."

"You're a fashion plate now, aren't you?" Jilly said to Wazoo, and winked. "Never mind us, Amy. You're more interesting."

"I'm not interesting," Amy said. "Not interesting at all. Just ask anyone who ever knew me. I ran out this morning because I hadn't been inside Rosebank since my daddy died. I was a girl back then, a teenager. Daddy played cribbage with the Mr. Patin who used to own Rosebank. Vivian Devol's uncle. I guess I walked through that door and into the sitting room where I'd seen Daddy sitting so often and I freaked out. You know how I used to go there with my daddy, Wazoo? Sorry about that."

A faintly strangled sound escaped Wazoo but she nodded.

Amy listened only to herself. "I'm agoraphobic, you know. It's hard for me to leave home. I panic. There was that this morning, too. Yes, agoraphobia. And some post-traumatic stress syndrome. I get nervous when I'm with other people, especially strangers."

The woman didn't seem to notice that she was babbling, or giving a laundry list of excuses for her behavior of the morning.

"I'm not good in crowds," Amy said, and smiled.

She laced her fingers in her lap.

"I'm not great at that, either," Jilly said.

"Then there's me," Wazoo said. Worry darkened her eyes even more. "Put me in front of a crowd and I love it. You can't stop me from talkin' and sayin' things I regret later."

"You won't do that about me, will you?" Amy said, reaching to hold Wazoo's hands tightly on the table. "Wazoo, say you won't."

"I won't." Wazoo's eyes got bigger.

"Please forget it happened," Amy said, looking at Wazoo, then Jilly. "It didn't happen. I always find it easy if I put something down to my imagination."

"That's right," Wazoo said quietly.

"Don't mention I was at Rosebank," Amy said. Her thin hands moved continually. "Tell the others, too. From this morning. Tell them what happened to me and why. Then ask them to forget all about it."

"Okay," Jilly said, trying to still Amy's hands. "It's forgotten."

"I loved being at Rosebank with Daddy. Wazoo knows. Thank you. I want to go home."

They all got up and went toward the door.

Amy turned back. "You won't tell anyone?" she said, tears slipping from her eyes. "I don't want to frighten you, but if anyone finds out about me, they'll kill me. They tried before."

Jilly grew still and cold. "I promise you I'll make sure no one talks about you being upset, or anything." If she hadn't been a witness at a murder scene today she might find it easy to laugh off Amy's remark.

"Don't talk about me at all," Amy said, breathless, her body stiff. "Not to anyone."

"We're going to make sure," Wazoo said. "Let's get you home and see if you can go back inside without being seen." She glanced at Jilly. "We came in my van. I know Amy doesn't want Reb and Marc askin' where you've been."

Amy walked through the door and Wazoo shot out a hand to pull Jilly close. "She said she had to tell you something, then she must have changed her mind," she said. "I never heard any of that other stuff before. Jilly, I met Amy in New Orleans when she was almost thirty. I never knew her when she was a child and I never met her daddy or saw her with him. I think she's makin' it all up. She's scared out of her mind."

"She needs more time to heal," Jilly said.

30

"Oliphant and Fleet were partners," Nat said, as if he were giving Guy a piece of news. "Why aren't we askin' Oliphant about Fleet's missing notes?"

"There's more missing than notes," Guy pointed out. "We're not askin' because he's not offerin'. He knows we're lookin' at one of their old cases but he hasn't said word one."

"I don't think Oliphant had a lot to do with it," Nat

said. "There's somethin' about the way he reacts when I mention Paula Hemp or Jazz Babes. As if—aw, I can't read him."

"As if he doesn't know much about it, maybe?" Guy said. "And it rankles?"

Nat pushed his beige straw fedora way back on his head and pointed a long forefinger at Guy. "Exactly," he said, jabbing the air. In flickering light from a candle on the table, animation sharpened his angular face. "You were always so good at workin' out that type of stuff, the finer stuff. The feely stuff."

Jack Charbonnet laughed. Together with Dwayne LeChat, the four of them sat at a table at Les Chats and talked fairly freely because the audience approval of the review on the stage whited out any other noise. Candles provided all the light in the club apart from spotlights on the stage. A smoky pall hung, gray-white, over the finger-snapping, hooting onlookers. Perfume made a questionable companion for the celebrated down-home Cajun food Les Chats served.

"You won't get any complaints about feely stuff from me," Dwayne said, his grin more gleeful than wicked. "What happened to Fleet?"

"Heart attack," Nat said.

Guy thought about it. "He went out on a call and never came back."

"Was Oliphant with him?"

Nat frowned. "Nope, don't think so. Like I said before, Fleet was into doing his own thing a good bit of the time. Oliphant was Fleet's faithful dog. Smart, detail-oriented. Took the death hard."

The music turned slinky and slow. Jack snapped his fingers and closed his eyes. The piano player had him by the soul. A server slapped a heaped platter of soft-shell crabs in the middle of the table, slid plates and silverware in front of each man, and Jack's eyelids didn't even flicker.

"On the other hand," Guy said, "Oliphant could know something he doesn't want us to know. What if he's protectin' Fleet's reputation?"

Nat stared at him for seconds before saying, "Either way he wouldn't be rushin' to help us out."

They forked crabs onto their plates. Guy put a small one in his mouth whole and dropped his fork. "Ho-hot," he complained, grabbing for water. "But so damn good."

"Thank you, thank you," Dwayne said. "What happened to Zinnia Sedge is horrible. What's your take, Guy? Did she die so she couldn't talk to you and Mr. Mouthy here? Or for some other reason?"

For once Nat didn't grin at a derogatory reference.

"I don't know," Guy said. Neither of them had laughed much since they found Zinnia. "It's easy to jump to conclusions and think we were the cause, but until we find the building caretaker I'm not going to know."

"Come again?" Dwayne said.

"The caretaker of the building where Zinnia lived. Cyrus and I met her the first time we tried to find Zinnia. Miz Trudy-Evangeline Augustine. The lady wasn't there today, but yesterday morning she called Cyrus and told him Zinnia was back if we still wanted to see her. Question is, did she let someone else know Zinnia was likely to have cops coming around?"

"No one deserves what happened to her," Dwayne said.

Jack dropped sugar cubes into a tall mug of coffee. Slowly, rhythmically, the cubes plopped as if he'd forgotten what he was doing, but he stopped at last and started stirring. Guy watched, fascinated, while the other man filled the bowl of the spoon with melted sugar and ate it. He grimaced and shook his head.

Nat said, "Who knows if the lady talked to someone other than Zinnia? Who's psychic?"

A glossy picture came sliding across the table from Jack. "I'm hoping this helps," he said. "At least it puts a face to a name. And there are some out there who would like to forget both. It'll get their attention."

The photograph looked like the kind they took for high school yearbooks. A girl with a round face, young-looking, braces on her teeth. Mouse-brown hair flipped carefully back with a curling iron and lipstick applied with too heavy a hand. A white net stole was supposed to make the subject look starry-eyed and sexy. This girl just seemed like a child posing as a grown-up. Nice smile. Nice brown eyes that tipped up a bit at the outer corners. Clear olive skin. Not quite ready to be a swan.

"That was Paula Hemp, the girl who was seen at

Jazz Babes, then found dead," Jack said. "Got it from a friend."

"You have a lot of friends," Guy said neutrally. He stared at the girl with fresh interest and Nat leaned closer to see.

"I think she was sixteen there," Jack said. "From what little I can find out—and I've got a nasty feelin' the word's out someone's askin' questions again—but that's probably when she was around sixteen. She was dead before she made eighteen. We're going to publish the shot and ask for the original informer to make contact. If you still think that's what you want. There'll be a reward."

Guy thought about it and nodded. "Yeah, that's what we want."

"Yeah," Nat echoed. "There's a good chance someone involved at the time could be scared into making a mistake."

"Good," Jack said. "It's set for tomorrow and it'll be seen in major cities and a bunch of small ones here in Louisiana. I figure other small-time rags will pick it up. It won't take the media long to trace the ads to a little public relations firm where they're experts at discretion. The media will want interviews. How do we handle that?"

"You stay out of sight." Dwayne waved his fork. "You don't know if some leftover Giavanelli soldier is still lookin' for an opportunity to take you down. I could go on as a spokesperson and give 'em a line about Paula having been the daughter of a friend who isn't in any shape to deal with any of it but wants to find the person who contacted him right before the kid died."

"The kid would have been around twenty-eight now," Guy pointed out. He raised his eyebrows at Jack, asking for his reaction to Dwayne's suggestion.

Jack nodded slowly. "Dwayne should have gone on the stage, anyway. He'll be convincin' and he'll sure put my wife's mind at rest. *And* he's not exactly lyin', except we don't even know if there's really a parent who still gives a damn about Paula Hemp. Small detail."

Guy thought it a big detail and felt the stir of shock at the idea that he still wasn't hardened enough not to care that a young girl died and someone had gotten away with the crime so far.

"That's settled then," Dwayne said. "Any calls get referred to me."

"Let us know if someone gets in touch," Guy said. "We should run through our message. We should do that, anyway."

"You gotta admit they're convincin'," Nat said, his face turned away. "Beautiful, even. If you met one of them anywhere else you'd probably put the make on her . . . him."

"What are you talkin' about?" Guy asked.

Nat indicated the stage.

Guy looked at the accomplished lip-synching cast dancing and striking poses. "I'd call them amazin'," he said, and barely touched the contents of his glass to his lips. Sobriety wasn't a choice tonight. "But I know what a woman smells like, even in the dark."

"They're transvestites," Nat commented. "I guess that just means gay in women's clothes."

Guy inclined his head and watched an Asian performer produce a strand of pearls, apparently from a place that shouldn't exist.

Tapping a single fingernail on the table, Dwayne said, "As you can see, there are gay and heterosexual transvestites. Mostly gay but not all. Just folks who like to dress up and make it an art form. Are you enjoying the show?"

Guy shrugged. "That was quite a party trick. She's a knockout."

A storm of hoots and applause made it impossible to respond. A creature with a flawless face, wearing white feathers and crystals, swung on a trapeze. Guy noticed her expression never changed, as if the performer wore an incredible plaster mask that didn't move.

"Is she wearing a mask?" Guy said when the noise died down a bit.

"No mask," Dwayne said. "The makeup, the preparation, can take hours. It's a discipline for those who are the best. Some are smilers, but facial expressions can spoil the perfection."

Guy turned from the stage and leaned toward Dwayne. Nat did the same. "Sounds like you heard all the details about Zinnia?" Guy said.

Dwayne nodded. "Evil bastards. Jack and I have

been busy. Brick walls everywhere but we're not giving up. This woman's murder is a blow."

"It was a blow to us, too," Nat said. "I'm kicking myself for waiting too long to go into her shop. Preliminary reports suggest she died before we arrived there. But I think the killer almost certainly heard us and he got out fast. A window was open to a fire escape."

Guy nodded slowly. "If there's anything useful, the lab will find it. You should have seen the ton of brown sacks going out of her place. Photographers did a good job."

"Makes me wish we'd taken a look around the first time we were there," Nat said.

"Just what we'd need," Guy said. "Unlawful search, and don't think they wouldn't have traced it back to us."

"Wouldn't be the first time we took a little heat, partner," Nat said.

Guy made sure what he was feeling didn't show on his face. The thumbscrews were getting too tight. Nat was special, and he trusted Guy—and held on to the hope he'd come back in the fold permanently. No matter the direction Guy's decisions took him, someone got hurt—including Guy Gautreaux.

"Listen up," Jack Charbonnet said. "Felix Broussard manages Jazz Babes. Has for as long as I can remember. There's no love lost but we go back a long way."

"Felix has been there a long time," Dwayne said.

"That club is his baby and he'd get nasty if he thought it was threatened." He seemed ready to say more but met Jack's eyes and changed his mind.

"Dwayne already mentioned the Giavanelli connection," Jack said.

Guy nodded. A lot of people not only knew the name Giavanelli, they had reason to remember it with fear. Guy couldn't get past the bizarre notion of Jack having been connected to the Family, even if only through his dead father.

"The club in question was theirs. It'd be easy to put two and two together and come up with five, but those people were out before this started. And they didn't have enough to reorganize with after we had that little war. Sure, there are some diehards with grudges, but forget them in our current equation. Felix may not even know who he works for, but it surely isn't for any of the relatives. In my opinion, we aren't goin' anywhere fast till we get a line on the owners who took over after the Giavanellis. And Felix is a follower, not a mastermind."

"They still got the big poker games there?" Guy asked.

"You bet. Deep pockets come and go and they aren't hangin' out in the bars." Dwayne nibbled the legs off a soft-shelled crab. "Hell, of course they're still playin'. Look, Pip owned that whole building where Zinnia still lived in a few rooms. I couldn't prove it, but someone could—he lost the lot. Not all at once, but just steady. Word had it someone was fond enough of Zinnia to set her up in part of the place after Pip was out."

"As in, she had a thing with someone who could do that?" Guy asked.

Jack's face hardened. "Maybe. Stay away from Jazz Babes, Guy. You, too, Nat. Rely on Dwayne and me. We've got people we can trust to go in, people who won't be recognized. Even if Felix Broussard didn't recognize either of you, he's been in the business long enough to get a rash if a cop comes within a mile."

"We'll be goin' in, anyway." Guy put his hands flat on the table. He felt as if he were running in deep water and he needed to get somewhere fast. "Just friendly drop-ins and we'll help keep Felix's mind busy enough he may be less likely to notice anyone else lookin' around. What I'm dreamin' about is one of Paula Hemp's parents showin' up—and some other phone contacts, of course. The very least we need out of this publicity is the ID of the informer. Meanwhile, my friend here and I will keep busy."

He and Nat avoided eye contact. They knew what they had to do. Oliphant knew something, even if it was only that Fleet kept the Hemp case to himself.

Nat got up and walked quickly outside.

"What's that about?" Dwayne asked.

"He's got a call coming in," Guy murmured. "If we need another meeting like this, I'll let you know where. We all understand not to hesitate to get in touch if there's any news?"

"Uh-huh."

Wearing the kind of wide-awake expression Guy recognized, Nat returned and dropped into his chair.

"What you got?" Guy asked, knowing that at the least Nat had a useful crumb.

"They took casts from some tire tracks the night Jilly tried to help that woman in the Garden District. In the graveyard. Guess the woman had a good reason for going in there. That's where she'd hidden her transportation. Perfect match, including soil samples."

Guy spread his fingers on the table, ready to push to his feet.

"The tracks are from Zinnia Sedge's scooter."

31

Miz Trudy-Evangeline Augustine made a slow circle around the statue of the Fuglies on the back lawn at St. Cécil's rectory.

The sun wasn't completely up and gray mist still hung close to the ground.

"Why's she out there?" Guy said. He'd just entered the kitchens with Goldilocks and had seen the woman through the windows. "Shit, someone's going to see her."

"She went out to smoke—said that's the only way she can think," Cyrus said, starting for the back door. "Is that a problem?"

Guy passed by Cyrus and strode outside with

Goldilocks lolloping along as if expecting some great game.

"Miz Trudy-Evangeline," Guy said, bearing down on her. "I must ask you to come inside at once."

She squinted at him through cigarette smoke. "Keep your wig on, you. What's the hurry?"

"I thought I heard you came here for protection, ma'am," he said when he reached her. "Not a whole lot of protection out here."

She shrugged, but looked all around and hugged her ample arms across herself. "You got a point there." Trudy-Evangeline stubbed out her cigarette on one of the Fuglies—with visible relish—and plodded uphill toward the house. Cyrus stood ready to usher her inside and Guy closed and locked the door behind him.

"How did you get here?" he asked the woman.

"By bus. Late last night. I been visitin' my sister, but when I got back I saw all the action, the TV cameras and such. And someone told me it was poor Zinnia who got murdered in that flat of hers. All alone and killed by some maniac."

Guy rested a hand on her shoulder and felt her tremble. "That had to be a terrible shock for you."

"Yessir. Particularly when . . . well, I imagine someone wanted somethin' from Zinnia."

Guy smiled but didn't interrupt.

"I wasn't goin' to interfere, not me," Trudy-Evangeline said, and swallowed loudly. "I already had my bag with me, so I took off. Father Cyrus was the only good person I could think of to head to. I need to be hidden just till they get that killer."

"Do you know why Zinnia Sedge was killed?" Sometimes the shock approach worked.

She frowned. "Could be. I got to have time to think what I want to do."

"You think the killer wants you, too?" Guy said, catching Cyrus's outraged eye.

"Well, could be." She looked terrified. "But I want that killer punished for what he did to Zinnia. If I gotta take a risk, I'll do it. Makes sense to be careful, though, so I got more thinkin' to do."

He heard footsteps behind him and looked over his shoulder. Jilly approached looking as angry as Cyrus. Well, they'd just have to disapprove of his interrogation methods. They didn't understand he had a job to do and this lady might be right, she could be in deep trouble. How did they know for sure that she wasn't? He did admire her guts.

Goldilocks, whose midsection had grown even heavier, descended gleefully on Jilly, who bent to scratch the dog between the ears. Promptly, Goldilocks kissed her face, whimpering with joy while she doled out a good face wash.

"You must be the lady from New Orleans," Jilly said to the newcomer. "I'm Jilly Gable. Cyrus let me know you'd be coming. I'm afraid I fell back asleep."

Trudy-Evangeline wasn't too scared to look from Jilly to Cyrus with deep suspicion. "You live here?" she asked Jilly. "Under the same roof with a priest."

Cyrus shook his head.

"Cyrus is an angel," Jilly said. "He and his house-keeper make sure there's always a room or two made up for strays in need. I was there when Zinnia was found and last night I was in need so I was allowed to stay here." She looked directly at Guy and he knew he didn't imagine that she was troubled.

"You poor girl," Trudy-Evangeline said. "I need to look into burying Zinnia, too. I don't think there's a family, or not any she ever mentioned."

"We'll help," Cyrus said, then he added with some urgency, "Lil will be coming. I'd better put her off today given the circumstances."

"Shall I make the call?" Jilly asked. "Lil won't have left yet. Madge can get back to her when she arrives."

"Lil and Madge?" Trudy-Evangeline said, her eyes screwed up.

"Cyrus's housekeeper and assistant," Guy said.

"A call to Lil would be a good idea," Cyrus told Jilly. "Will you fill Madge in when she gets here?"

"Surely will," Jilly said, leaving the room with Goldilocks.

"Excuse me for a few," Guy said, following. He caught up with Jilly and went with her to Madge's office, where he stood by and listened to her tell Lil she had the day off and no, Cyrus hadn't said why, only that Madge would be in touch later.

"Good job Cyrus remembered about Lil," Guy said when Jilly hung up. "All we need is Lil and Ozaire Dupre talking about a visitor from New Orleans.

Whatever it takes, we're going to make sure no one else finds out she's here. She's got information we need."

Jilly studied Guy's tense features. He was all business. "How do you know she's got useful information?" she asked.

"Why else would she be afraid enough to look for a place to hide?"

"Could be she's just shaken up by a murder happening in her building."

"Not when she's hinted at knowing why Zinnia died. Looks like she's the only lead we have, or she may be."

"You deliberately made her more frightened than she already was," Jilly said. "I suppose you're used to doing those things so you didn't care if she's quite old and probably can't take too much more."

"Sometimes we do what we have to at the moment," Guy said. "I'm in a tough business. We prefer to be kind but we're not employed to hold hands."

Jilly felt he'd put her in her place. Her face stung. "So you probably wouldn't care if she was murdered, too, as long as you got your information first."

He turned away from her and shoved his hands in his pockets. His shoulders rose and fell with the deep breath he took.

"I just overstepped myself," she said. "I'm sorry for that, but you sounded so cold."

"I haven't been to bed since the night before last and this case is breaking. These are tough times. I'm not up for coddling people's feelings."

Certainly not mine. "I understand," she said. "Why don't you get back to your work? I'll wait here for Madge."

Without answering her, he walked out and she listened until the sound of his boots faded.

Guy would go back to the force.

Jilly couldn't swallow. Her hands felt clammy and they shook. He was in his element doing what he'd been trained to do. He cared for her, maybe even loved her in a way—he'd said he did—but he loved being a homicide detective more.

Cyrus put a cup of coffee in front of his guest, and a plate of toast. When she didn't look interested, he said, "Eat up. You need to look after yourself."

She smiled at him, a wobbly smile, but sipped at the coffee.

"Now we can get back to it," Guy said, coming into the kitchen.

Whatever had passed between him and Jilly hadn't made him a happy man, Cyrus thought. Guy seemed on autopilot, plowing ahead with no thought for anyone's feelings, only the issue of getting information he wanted.

Trudy-Evangeline spread marmalade on her toast and took a bite. She chewed slowly and looked straight ahead.

Guy's mouth became a thin line. He turned to Cyrus and said, "There's a match to one of Zinnia Sedge's scooter tires. They found it in that graveyard. In the Garden District."

"You mean where—"

"No, no," Guy said quickly, stopping Cyrus from mentioning how Jilly had followed someone into a graveyard. "I wonder why she would park in there and what she was doing in that area at night." He avoided looking at Trudy-Evangeline.

She had stopped eating and sat with her hands in her lap, her eyes large and turned on Guy. "When did they find it?" she asked.

"A few nights ago."

"I don't know why she'd be there unless she was seeing a client. She did go to a bride's house sometimes if they wanted to pay the price."

"Why would she park in a graveyard?" Guy said. "To avoid paid parking?"

"You're not amusin' me," Trudy-Evangeline said. "If you want me scared, be happy 'cause I am. But don't treat me like a fool."

Cyrus hid a smile.

Guy seemed unfazed. "Have more of your coffee. I think I'll pour myself a cup." When he looked at Cyrus his eyes were expressionless.

With a mug of coffee in hand he went to sit across from Trudy-Evangeline at the table. Cyrus decided to remain standing.

"Damn, I'm tired," Guy said, rubbing his eyes.

"You young ones think you don't need any sleep," Trudy-Evangeline said. "This is the way it is, so listen up. If someone thinks I know somethin' they don't want me to, they'll figure a way to get rid of me. And it'll be on your head."

Guy didn't try to defend himself. "How many people know you're here?"

"Not a one far as I know," she said. "Ain't even let my sister know and don't intend to. She's got a big mouth. Father Payne here says he'll hide me."

Cyrus frowned. "I'm going to give you sanctuary," he told the woman.

"Did you know Pip Sedge?" Guy asked. He'd produced a notebook and pen.

"Of course I did," the woman said. "I used to work for him—till he lost everythin' with his gamblin' and schemes and things. He owned the building I live in, the one where Zinnia lives—lived. And other properties. I'll tell you one thing, he really loved Zinnia. There wouldn't have been no divorce if he'd had his way."

Guy and Cyrus glanced at each other.

"Did Zinnia own the flat she was in?"

"I don't think so. She didn't spell it out but I got the impression there was some arrangement about it with the new owners."

"Who are they?"

"I don't know. And it was a lot of years ago so I don't expect to find out now."

Guy drummed his fingers and Cyrus prepared to step in if he got carried away again.

"I'll tell you one thing I thought was a real shame,"

Trudy-Evangeline said. "There was a really nice man who was good to Zinnia—Bob Fleet. He was a policeman, too. They met when he was looking into that terrible thing that happened to Zinnia's daughter. Some people never have any luck. Zinnia and Pip were separated. So were the Fleets. But that Bob Fleet died before they could work things out."

Guy leaned across the table. "Bob Fleet? You're sure?"

"I don't forget names. See, Zinnia's daughter, Paula, was murdered, too. It was horrible."

"Paula Hemp," Guy said quietly.

"That's right," Trudy-Evangeline said. "Hemp was Zinnia's name before she married Pip."

32

Her house felt familiar again and, with Guy there, Jilly was glad to be home.

She was even happy, if she didn't think about how long she had with him before he told her he had to return to his old life.

He stood in front of the sitting room window, his cell phone to his ear, talking to Nat Archer. "We should probably get in to see him as soon as possible," he said. "I don't have any idea what to expect, do you?"

Evidently Nat said he didn't. "That's what I

thought," Guy said. "We do have one advantage—if he does know about Bob Fleet and Zinnia and we drop it on him cold, he'll react in some way."

So, with no sleep in two days, a head of frustration making him short-tempered and in a downpour beginning to resemble a monsoon, Guy intended to get back in his car and drive to New Orleans.

Jilly made up her mind and picked up her phone. She called Edwards Place and Laura answered in the middle of the first ring. "Laura Preston."

"It's Jilly. If I make it over today it won't be until late, possibly real late. Let me talk to Edith."

"She's resting. I'll tell her."

"I want to tell her myself. I know you're used to looking after her, but maybe she needs to stand on her own feet a bit more. It's not healthy for her to let other people take away her control."

Silence followed and Jilly recognized that she had been more honest than might have been a good idea. "I didn't mean that the way it sounded, Laura. It's just that I worry about her. I worry about you, too. You spend more of your life looking after Edith than you do with anything else."

"You're saying that because you've seen the way Wes treats me sometimes," Laura snapped. "Well, he's given you the wrong impression. He gives everyone the wrong impression. We're very tight, in every possible way."

"Of course you are, I—"

"I hear Edith moving around now. She's coming

downstairs so you can talk to her yourself."

"Don't be angry," Jilly said. There was nothing to gain from being on bad terms with Laura.

"Let's forget it. Here's Edith."

Jilly heard Laura say, "This is Jilly for you, Edith. I'll be in the salon reading."

"Hello, darlin'," Edith said. "I'm so excited to talk to you. Everything's going to be wonderful. We'll put all the doubts behind us—Sam said so."

"Good," Jilly said while goose bumps shot out on her skin. What else could she say? "I'm not sure I can get over today. If I do make it I'll be late. Forgive me."

"Why, I'd forgive you anythin', cher—except if you don't come at all. Just come when you can, doesn't matter how late."

Jilly gritted her teeth. "If I can, I will." She had decided what she wanted to do, and when, for too long to accept limitations now. "I'm goin' into New Orleans. I'll see how I feel when I get back."

"Of course, dear, but I've just got to tell you somethin'. I can't wait a minute longer. Daddy and I had a lovely talk. Sometimes I marvel that little old ordinary me caught the attention of a man like him. He's good through and through, Jilly. Good to the heart and bone."

"That's nice." She made a face and looked at Guy. He wasn't on the phone anymore and sat on the couch with Goldilocks sprawled at his feet.

"Guess what Daddy's goin' to do," Edith said.

"I can't."

"Oh, get on. Try."

Jilly met Guy's dark eyes and took a deep breath. What was he thinking? "You're just going to have to tell me, Edith, because I'm no good at guessing."

"He's going to make you a member of the family! There, what do you think of that?"

Jilly's attention was divided. Guy stared at her, a half smile on his lips. *A member of the family.* "What family?" she said.

"*Our* family, you goose. The papers are goin' to be drawn up. Oh, Jilly, I've never been so happy in my life. You never had a real father. I know, I know, that man was your father in the biblical sense but never as a man. My dear Daddy is goin' to be that for you. We'll all be one big happy family."

"Er." Jilly sat down in the nearest chair and rubbed her temple, trying to come up with a response that wouldn't cut Edith to the quick.

"I want you to enjoy thinkin' about it for a while," Edith said, her voice giggly. "Jilly, darlin', you're goin' to be in the will! Oh, I can hardly believe it. Daddy *insists* you become his daughter in every way. And he's goin' to make a settlement on you right now so you don't have to want for anythin' ever again. Can't you come over right now? Please?"

She covered the mouthpiece and whispered, "They've gone mad over there. They want to adopt me."

Guy grinned.

Jilly frowned and shook her head.

Guy frowned and shook his head, too, only the grin kept coming back.

"Edith," Jilly said, removing her hand. "We've got a lot to talk about and I wish I could come now but I can't. Like I said, I'm going to New Orleans."

Guy's grin disappeared and stayed gone. He had finally registered that she might mean what she said.

"Wonderful," Jilly said. "Yes, Edith. You have a good day and we'll visit soon. Bye." She hung up fast.

"You're not going to New Orleans," Guy said.

"Excuse me while I make another call." And while she gave herself time to think before she spoke. Being sweet to him would get her further than telling him she'd do what she pleased. Too many rings later someone picked up the phone at Mortie's Body Shop. "Yeah?"

She asked about the Beetle.

"What color would that car be, ma'am?"

"Is Mortie there?" she said, out of patience already.

Mortie came on the phone. "That you, Jilly Gable? It's nice to hear your voice again. I need to hear a lovely lady's voice at least once a day. What can I do for you now?"

Guy took his hat and started to get up. The slimeball intended to get away while she was busy. "I'm hoping my Beetle is ready to be picked up, Mortie." She tented her fingers in the middle of Guy's chest and jabbed. When it didn't bother him—even if he made a horrible face—she jabbed again, hard, and again, until he raised his palms and flopped down again.

Mortie wasn't saying anything.

Guy made extravagant hand signals, indicating the dog, pointing at her, then at Jilly. She had no idea what he meant but she shook her head no.

"Mortie, you still there?"

"Yes, ma'am. I'm afraid you changed your mind too late. Your friend called. The car was stripped and picked up for scrap yesterday—just like he said you wanted. It'll be metal mush by now."

33

Sam Preston held very still and lowered his eyelids, pretending to sleep. He didn't like the house in Toussaint but it served its purpose by giving him a place to stash Edith and keep her out of his way when he had important business to attend to. He felt warm inside. Important business came in a variety of shapes and sizes, it even came in meetings with the people he sold fine, fabulously expensive antiques to, or loaned money to, and in the army that worked for him.

Yessir, he had plenty of business to attend to. Wasn't that what had made him one of the wealthiest men in America, attending to business? But part of the reward was getting his pick of women in their various shapes and sizes, all of them particularly succulent.

Laura had come into the upstairs study he'd designated for his own private use, apparently unaware that he was there. Bitch. She'd played hard to get for months, ever since the lovely Jilly had come on the scene. He and Laura had enjoyed their own particular entertainments before that and he missed them.

He heard rustling and opened his eyes a fraction. She had her back to him and was replacing a book in one of the cases that lined every wall in the room.

"Laura," he whispered, and got pleasure out of seeing he'd startled her.

She twirled around with a hand on her breasts. "Daddy. I didn't see you there."

"What were you reading?"

"Just a little somethin' to broaden my knowledge of things that interest me. You do have quite the collection in here."

"And who does this room belong to, and these books?"

"You, of course." She smiled and dimples appeared in her cheeks. "Am I in trouble for comin' in here without an invitation?"

Don't be too eager.

"Maybe not. Do you have a few moments to talk?" When she said she did, he told her to close the door. She did, and locked it.

He pretended not to notice that she'd shut them in but his privates hardened. Could be just habit so he'd better keep his head.

"What d'you want to talk about?" She looked serious. It was midmorning but she wasn't dressed. Her brilliant hair had been brushed until it glowed and she wore makeup, or at least a coat of shiny lipstick, but a red silk robe with green dragons, one opening its mouth over each breast, and a third curling over her back, parted occasionally and just enough to show bare legs. He wondered what, if anything, she had on under the robe.

"Edith and I have been talkin'," he said. "I want to be the one to tell you what's been decided, and to put your mind at rest that it doesn't change a thing for you."

She walked a little closer, her backless, high-heeled mules slapping the bottoms of her feet with each step. "Daddy," she said seriously. "You have always been considerate to me and I'm grateful. I don't think I'm as good to you as I should be. At least not lately. I guess I've been in a mood and I hope you'll forgive me."

Well, well, how very nice. He shifted in an attempt to relieve the pressure building against his zipper. "There's nothin' to forgive you for, baby girl. Never could be. You're about the best thing that ever happened to this family." Wes had told him Laura was the perfect wife: kinky as hell but scared enough about losing what she'd got to keep her mouth shut when her husband had other fish to fry. Sam could have told Wes a thing or two about Laura's talents.

"We both know Jilly has made an impact on our household," he said, pleased with himself for taking an almost honest approach. "But she's only part of our lives because she's Edith's daughter and I like my

410

wife to be happy. Jilly makes her happy. I don't have to tell you that girl is a pale shadow of you. Why, she disappears if the two of you are in the same room."

Laura arranged herself gracefully on a black damask chaise. She made the thing look as if it had been made for her. Kicking off her shoes, she stretched out her legs, folded the robe demurely over them, but promptly bent the knee closest to the back of the chaise. She wore tap pants the same color as the dragons on the robe.

"I'm sorry if I've been preoccupied with business," he told her.

"I'm sorry, too, Daddy. Sorry because I've missed you." She propped an elbow and cradled her head so she could look into his face. "Let's not drift apart again."

His cock leaped and he rocked his hips to one side. He burned.

"Let's not," he told her.

She lowered her eyelashes. "I know what you like, what you've always liked. But maybe you're not in the mood."

"Try me." He had only so much control.

Laura ran one fingernail from her knee to her groin, parting the robe all the way to her waist. The pants were nothing more than a green scrap that didn't quite cover her pubic hair. "Relax," she told him. "I like to do everything. You know that."

And he liked her to do everything—especially when everything was enough to leave him exhausted but ready for more. "I know that," he told her gruffly. "I'm your slave, ma'am. What you want, you get."

She ran her pointed tongue around her shiny lips and smiled softly. Then she blew him a kiss and slipped the robe sash undone. One side slid away at once. So she'd had a little boob help from a good doctor, the result squeezed his balls. The breast revealed overflowed a matching green bra made to be a platform not a cover. Her big nipple perched in full view. Laura looked down and tweaked the tip between finger and thumb.

Sam's hips lifted from his chair and he readjusted his crotch.

Laura arched her back over the arm of the chaise and pulled on both of her nipples until she tossed her head from side to side.

This ability to pleasure herself as if she were alone shortened his breathing and turned his body rock hard. She made him feel young, not that he was old. He was in great shape and could keep up with any woman.

Sam got up and walked to stand by Laura. Her flat belly sucked in deep and she pressed her legs together tight. Carefully, he bent over and licked her fingers away from a nipple before sucking it into his mouth. Laura smiled almost sleepily up at him but she didn't give him long before she swung around him and knelt on the floor. She pointed to the chair he'd vacated and Sam returned there, even if it did hurt him to sit down again.

Kneeling up, her back still slightly arched, Laura let

the robe drop away. She moved closer to him and pushed three fingers of her right hand between his lips. When they were wet, she slid them down her stomach, under the pants and between her legs. She parted her knees and flexed her thighs.

"Do it," he told her. He'd swear she hadn't been getting enough. Everything about her cried out for release.

Laura went to work, stroking back and forth, dipping inside herself for more lubrication, rubbing harder and faster until her body jerked and her mouth hung open. She paused to tear off her bra and watch her breasts when they jounced with the violent racking, with the bouncing of her bottom up and down on her heels.

She screamed, but kept pumping her hips for a long time. Then, slowly, she fell back onto the carpet, moaning and rocking her drawn-up knees.

"Sam," she whispered. "That was good, but not good enough. Could I sit on Daddy's lap?"

She turned her head to see his face and he held his arms out to her. It had been much too long.

Laura came to him, undressed him, licked and nibbled his body and groaned with pleasure. She was the best of them all.

Astride his lap, she still wore her tap pants. A big diamond on a diamond-studded chain slipped back and forth between her breasts. He took the chain and hooked it around one of her breasts. "Daddy always gives you the best, darlin'. That's some sparkler." He leaned forward to suck her deep in his mouth. When he let her plop out he said, "I wasn't talkin' about the diamond, but I do have something for you. I've been keepin' it till we were together like this."

She kissed his lips, darted her tongue in and out of his mouth, and whispered, "You don't have to spoil me. I just want to be with you."

He pulled open a drawer in the table beside him and removed a square white box. Inside, coiled around and around on itself, lay a long, deep yellow gold chain decorated with ruby dangles.

"This belonged to a princess," he said. "It's three hundred years old." Quickly, before he blew it—literally—he fastened the fabulous piece around her waist. "I want you to wear it all the time, for me."

She fingered the gems. "I will," she breathed. "But I don't deserve it."

"No, you don't, do you?" He slapped her rump hard and she pressed his face between her breasts.

The pants tore, leaving her open to him.

"Make sure I learn my lesson," she said.

Sam made sure. She took him deep inside, raised herself up and drove down again, and each time she lifted up her sweet rear, he slapped it, and she shrieked.

34

When Guy walked into the old office, Nat sat there with his feet on the desk, staring as if he'd been waiting for him to arrive. Which he probably had.

"Who tied your guts in a knot?" Nat said. "You look like hell—mad as hell."

"Shut the fuck up," Guy told him. "I'm not in the mood for your smart-ass remarks."

"I think I just told you I'd noticed that." He slapped his boots on the floor, pulled a notebook toward him and took up a pen. "If you feel like communicatin', I'm here for you, brother."

"I don't have any brothers and if I did, they wouldn't look like you."

Nat knew when Guy was pulling out all the stops to make his old partner mad. He didn't rise to the bait.

"This place is a sty," Guy said. "No wonder everythin's missin' around here—it's probably all in these shit heaps."

"The case file on the Hemp killing isn't," he said mildly. "I don't think that thing is in the buildin' anymore, if it ever was. And I've searched the online system again. Nothin', Guy. And you know material must have been entered. One or two have even mentioned knowing Fleet worked on it. Gone. Wiped out. Now we know about Fleet and Zinnia, I wonder how much was ever there. The stuff I brought to you after Sedge died came out of a cardboard box in a store-room. I could tell it wasn't everything but I thought it was a start. Man, it wasn't even that."

"What we're both not saying is we think Fleet may have gotten rid of a lot of stuff," Guy said. "Hell, I'm sorry for bein' a prick, Nat." He meant it. He felt like a moron for going off at Nat. "I'm havin' a *really* bad day."

"We've had several of those."

"This is worse. I gotta think what I'm doin' here. Oliphant has to be dealt with just so or he'll clam up— not that he's likely to run off at the mouth. My mind isn't focused. Instead I'm worryin' about Jilly. She raised the worst hell you ever heard and wouldn't let me drive back here myself." He felt stupid and blushed—and felt more stupid. "No sleep, over-worked, on and on she went about all the reasons why I was a danger on the road to myself and anyone else. Oh, then there was the rain and the slippery roads."

Nat watched Guy's face and he saw a lot more than he presumed Guy wanted him to see. The man had a really bad case. He loved Jilly Gable and he still didn't know how to handle that. "It's a good thing when someone cares about you," he said. "Be grateful. You like her, too."

Guy stuck out his jaw. "Yes, I do. A lot. But I've got a job to do here and she's out there in the Quarter on her own. I told her to go see Jack and Celina, but she won't do it, I just know it."

"Thousands of people are out there alone. Jilly's a smart woman. She can look after herself."

"Can you promise me there's no one in the area who would think it a good move to do something to her? Even if it was only rough her up? That might just make me back off the case, mightn't it? Don't bother to say anythin', I know the answer and I didn't need the extra grief today."

"Crap happens in any city. She's as safe here as anywhere."

Guy's nerves sang in his ears. "You might want to take that suggestion back. She found out her car was mysteriously scrapped—without her permission, although the guy at the yard insists he got instructions from a man who said he was her friend. Lee O'Brien reckoned someone fiddled with the brakes—not that she's a reliable witness to that. But it's as likely as not that Jilly was set up to get hurt—or worse—and the car was gotten rid of so there wouldn't be any evidence."

"Um—" Nat cleared his throat a few times "—you thought about givin' Jilly somethin' meaningful?"

"Meaningful? Like what?"

Nat shrugged. "Anythin' that she could have to remind her you care about her."

Guy frowned, then got an odd look in his eyes. "Don't go there, Nat. That's not funny."

"It wasn't meant to be. I remember you sayin' you'd learned somethin' from Billie, bless her soul."

Guy made a fist and Nat braced himself. The fist

relaxed slowly. Billie Knight had been Guy's girl for a long time—before she got taken out by a crazy while she was looking at a little antique diamond ring she had her heart set on. Guy kicked himself for that. He'd known about the ring but didn't think he was ready for commitment. When it was too late he would have given anything to buy Billie that ring.

"I shouldn't have mentioned any of that," Nat said, and felt lousy. "It's none of my business what you do."

"Let's go for Oliphant," Guy said, but the lines fanning from his eyes looked deeper and a white line surrounded his tight mouth.

"Guy—"

"You had every right to say it. I needed to hear it. You gonna do anything about Wazoo? I know you've been seein' her now and then."

"We really aren't near anythin' like that," Nat said. "We may never be, but I do enjoy that woman."

A faint smile softened Guy's features. He and Nat left the office and set out for Oliphant's cave. They all called it a cave because it had no windows and rather than use the fluorescent lights overhead, the detective kept on a low-wattage desk lamp.

A short, wiry man with close-cropped dark hair and a mustache, Oliphant hammered away at a keyboard, scrolling through lineup shots and checking with a mug shot blown up on the right side of his screen.

"Pretty boy," Guy said, tapping the door frame on the way in. He looked closer at the screen. "I've seen him before. Pimp. Can't remember his name."

"Otto Reeb," Oliphant said. "We think he got bored and decided to make sure we thought he was important. Killed one of his girls. Beat her to death with a tire iron. Real original disposal of the body. He put her in a Dumpster."

"So why are you botherin' with further identification?"

"A witness fingered someone else. The witness is one of Otto's girls, by the way."

"Convenient," Nat said. His edginess showed. "Got some time for us?"

Oliphant swung his chair around and scooted it on its wheels to the part of his desk that faced Guy and Nat. The man didn't look so good. "Always got time for you two charmers," he said, jerking up one side of his mouth. He had sad eyes that had lost their life, like so many in Homicide. "Shut the door and pull up a pew. I got something you two might enjoy."

Guy dealt with the door while Nat pulled forward two chairs with padded plastic seats from which dirty gray stuffing spilled.

Oliphant went to a metal cabinet against a wall, shook open the sticky door and carefully transported three crystal highball glasses to his desk. He returned with a bottle of Courvoisier.

"Beats my Rémy Martin," Guy said. "Ever wonder why so many Homicide types are brandy men?"

"Nope," Oliphant said, dumping a couple of fine gold fingers in each glass. "We see the worst, the scum and the horror. Gives us an appreciation for fine

419

things. You'd hardly expect us to go for blended whiskey."

Nat and Guy murmured an emphatic "No," although they'd both drunk their share of whatever was handy on occasion.

They sipped the brandy and fell into a moment of appreciative silence. Guy ran his eyes over the office. The amazing bulletin boards ought to fall from the walls. He'd swear every piece of paper ever pinned or taped up there had been left for posterity. The effect resembled a couple of dirty rag rugs stretched out like funky artwork. Nat had found the picture of Pip Sedge at Jazz Babes in that lot. Guy applauded the man's perseverance.

A second desk, the one Fleet had used, was bare except for a computer on one side, a couple of wire baskets with In and Out written in black marker and stapled to the front—very few pieces of paper in either one—and a framed picture of severed heads in bell jars.

"Nice," Guy said. "Who's your partner these days?"

Oliphant laced his fingers behind his neck and rocked back in his chair. He squinted at the ceiling. "You don't really want to know but he's Len Fuzzo— I'm not makin' that up—a dickhead they've shipped from cop shop to cop shop because he manages to freak everyone out, especially female staff. He's okay by me. Comes on time, leaves on time, and all that—" he waved at the grisly photo "—is an act. He doesn't have the guts of a chicken—excuse the pun."

"Not much like Bob Fleet," Guy said, arms crossed and fingers crossed.

"Hah." Oliphant gave his full attention to the Courvoisier again. "They don't make Bob Fleets anymore. Why do the best always die young?"

Guy felt short on wisdom.

"Seems like the deck's stacked against 'em," Nat said, his expression serious. "Only the good die young, huh?"

Guy was impressed. What Nat said didn't mean diddly but it sounded sage.

Evidently Oliphant thought it brilliant. "Still, I had one terrific partner. I can't complain." He looked from Nat to Guy. "Good to see you two back as a team. Chief Carson said it was happenin' finally."

Guy swallowed an announcement that he still had slightly under a month to make up his mind about teamwork around here. He didn't comment on what Oliphant had said, despite feeling Nat's scrutiny.

"Too bad about Fleet and Zinnia Sedge," Guy said, and prepared to watch the show.

Oliphant disappointed him. The man raised heavy brows, looked as innocent as a Cub Scout and pushed his head forward in a "come again" attitude.

"He had to have put the Paula Hemp case into the system but it's sure not there now," Nat said, cleaning his fingernails. "Any idea where he might have kept a backup?"

"What backup?" Oliphant said. "You know we don't do that. I'm not even sure we could if we wanted to. It's all central."

Nat got to his feet, leaned over Oliphant's desk and pointed to a slot in the man's computer. "Time you caught up with the times and used CDs," Nat said.

"Bob didn't like computers," Oliphant told them. "He pretty much stuck with a paper trail."

Guy gave the bulletin boards a meaningful glance. "So I've heard. He's been gone quite a few years."

"I'm comfortable," Oliphant said. He could have sounded belligerent, but didn't. "I like my habits and I like being in familiar surroundings. Fuzzo threatened to clear off the boards, but he only mentioned it once." Oliphant let his meaning hang there.

"Kevin." Few people knew Oliphant's first name, let alone used it. Guy had decided this was the time for intimacy. "You'd have done anything for Bob and I reckon you still would if you thought there was a reason."

Oliphant finished his brandy and poured more. He didn't offer the bottle to his visitors. He also didn't give Guy an answer.

"It must have shocked you when you found out he was involved with Zinnia. But, I can understand it. She'd had a rough time and he was an empathetic guy. Also, his marriage was in name only by then and Zinnia was beautiful and on her own. I'm glad they found some happiness together."

Oliphant kept his mouth shut.

"I expect you heard Zinnia was murdered yesterday."

Oliphant jerked upright and stared. "For God's sake,

no." He got up and paced around the room. "I was out sick with stomach flu. Only been in an hour today. When did she die? How?"

"In the bathtub off her bedroom in that flat where she lived. He put her in the bathtub and slit her throat—turned on the water—for effect, I suppose. She was underwater when we got in there." Guy thought a minute. He glanced at Nat, who nodded. "Her tongue was cut out. Since someone may have found out we were on our way to talk to her, we figure the tongue was a message to us."

Oliphant pulled his lips back from his teeth. He turned his back. "So it's over now," he said. "The girl, Zinnia, the ex-husband and Bob. Put to bed, God help them all."

"How can you say that?" Guy asked. "Someone was responsible for each of those deaths except Bob's. And you could make an argument that he may have died as a result of what some crazy set out to do to the others. Did he love Zinnia?"

Oliphant leaned forward to study his shoes. "What harm can it do now? They loved each other. Bob wasn't the kind of man to spread himself around. He suffered a lot emotionally. That probably helped kill him. He still cared for Mary, his wife, but she never forgave him for bein' a cop—even though that's what he was when they married—and she gradually froze him out. I liked Mary but she didn't know when to quit. She convinced herself she could persuade him to get out of the force, but it was the only work he knew, the only job he wanted to do. He felt he was making a difference."

"Bob was a good cop," Guy said. "I did his scut work some years ago and he was fair. Help us, Kevin. Give us any information you've got. The chief told us not to go near Mary Fleet, but there could be something she knows that would help."

Oliphant thought about that. "I think he removed every reference to Zinnia, and to Paula Hemp because he wanted to keep them out of something he knew damn well was dangerous and real nasty. The girl got pulled into some sex ring where rich men from overseas came here and bought young girls. Somehow Paula got away, but the finks had to make sure she didn't talk out of school, so they killed her. Zinnia and Pip Sedge found her in her own bed. Stone cold and with parts of her body severed but laid where they should have been. No parent should have to see that."

Guy already knew a good deal of this even if there were a couple of inconsistencies, but he let Oliphant get it off his chest. "Poor devils," he said. "So pointless."

"Did Mary Fleet marry again?" Guy asked.

"Nah. Mary's a one-man woman and for her, that was Bob Fleet." He produced a tissue and blotted his mustache. "Bob didn't meet Zinnia until after Paula was killed and he was on the case—he'd want to be sure you knew that. It wasn't talked about but Zinnia and Pip were already separated. Mary lives in the house she and Bob shared and she does okay. I check

424

up on her from time to time and make sure she doesn't go short of anything."

This announcement surprised Guy but he kept his mouth shut.

"Help us out, will you, Kevin?" Nat asked, his face troubled. "We need all the help we can get, but only from someone in the know. If you came with us to Mary's, she'd be more likely to relax with us."

"Look," Oliphant said. "I don't think you're going to get anything out of her, but I guess you need to try. Here's the deal. If she starts to close up, or gets upset, you lay off."

"Well—"

"Those are my terms," he said. "And she shouldn't be rushed."

"Whatever you say," Guy said, and hoped he'd be able to stick with the promise. "I'd like it if you were there with us."

Oliphant didn't looked too enthusiastic, but he nodded. He bowed his head. "I tried to get him to open up to the chief about the case. Killin' that girl didn't make any sense. It seemed to be a warnin'. Bob wanted to be the Lone Ranger on this one. I'll do what I can—but I won't stand by while anyone drags Bob's reputation in the mud. He was a fine detective."

"I know he was," Guy said sincerely. He didn't add that he'd already caught Oliphant in a lie, even if it wasn't a big one. It was true that Bob Fleet liked to keep a hard copy of everything, but Bob Fleet had been the one everyone came to when they had computer problems. He'd been more comfortable with change than most of the officers.

Nat said, "Bob sure was a damn good detective. We could use him now but you get the duty instead, Kevin."

One of the clerks from reception raced into the office, landing a perfunctory rap on the door as she passed. " 'Scuse me, Oliphant. Don't miss this, Nat," she said, turning on the dusty-screened TV, and flipping through channels. She pulled a sleeve over one hand and swiped at the screen. "They said something about a report on a killing in the Quarter yesterday. They went to a break, then it'll be on. A Mrs. Zinnia Sedge who made fabulous wedding dresses. Her daughter was murdered some years back. There are appeals for new information all over the papers and on TV today. It's what you're working on now, isn't it?"

She tossed an open copy of the *Times* on Oliphant's desk and a full-page ad showed Paula's high school photo.

He shifted to the front of his chair and braced his hands on his knees. A news anchor gave the information on Paula's death and asked the informant who came forward to help again. The anchor quickly switched to the killing of Zinnia Sedge.

"Cross your fingers they didn't get their fingers on the stuff we don't want broadcast yet," Nat said.

Guy grunted. He always got a sense of unreality looking at a familiar scene on television. The police tape flapped and people milled around St. Ann Street.

A cameraman managed to get himself into the building courtyard and a voice, deliberately low, gave a monotone commentary. "First the daughter, then the husband, now the wife," the reporter droned. "Somewhere out there is someone who can help the police. This city is used to horror, but if you know anything, call NOPD at the number on your screen. We can't know who this freak's next victim will be."

Nat rolled his eyes. "If the publicity works, fine, but that boy surely wants to be on the stage."

"He is," Oliphant pointed out.

"Apparently the police were already expecting trouble," the reporter continued. "They may even have been on the premises when the killing occurred."

"Oh, bloody wonderful," Guy said. "That's something we wanted the world to know."

"Looks like they're bringing out evidence." Members of the forensics and evidence teams carried brown paper sacks down the stairs from Zinnia's boutique and put them into a white van backed into the courtyard. Uniforms were everywhere.

"That's Detective Nat Archer," the reporter said. "He was one of the first on the scene. The tall man is Detective Guy Gautreaux and the woman beside him with her back to us is Jilly Gable of Toussaint. There are rumors of a tie to Toussaint. Evidently a man was shot to death there recently." A heavy pause set Guy's heart pounding.

"Shit," Nat muttered. "Did they show this yesterday, too?"

"The victim's name was Caruthers Rathburn and he was killed in the yard behind Jilly Gable's café and bakery—All Tarted Up—on Main Street. The victim might have been linked to Pip Sedge, Zinnia Sedge's ex-husband. Attempts are being made to contact Miz Gable for an interview."

Guy leaped to his feet. "Why not just paint a target on Jilly's back? Where did he get all that—he couldn't have had time to do all the research?"

"Does Lee O'Brien ring a bell?" Nat asked through his teeth. "She'll be furious she didn't get a mention, not that it matters because I'm goin' to wring her neck when I catch up with her."

"Lee O'Brien of the *Toussaint Trumpet* said the folks in the town are pretty shaken up," the TV reporter said.

Oliphant snickered and Guy bowed his head. "It's the little things you can't control that get you every time," he said.

The phone on Oliphant's desk rang and he snatched it up. "Yeah. Yeah. Yeah, I'll tell him. Anything else? Okay. Do something for us, will you? Keep the woman's mouth shut until we tell you otherwise. Yeah. Well, regard that as a suggestion not an order." He hung up. "A Simon something. The lady reporter's partner? He managed to track you down, Guy, and wanted to apologize if Lee O'Brien's comments may have caused any problems. He saw the reports on TV same as we did. Reckon he's in Nashville."

"Nashville?" Guy groaned. "Damn, that woman's

determined to get the name of her paper out."

Nat laughed. "Can you blame her? Think about it. She and Simon bought a defunct rag and they're already turning it into something people want to read."

"Shouldn't be at someone else's expense," Guy said.

"It's the nature of the media to peddle trouble. People want to know about it," Nat said. He got up to turn off the box but paused and glanced at Guy over his shoulder. "Nice shot of Jilly."

Guy looked at a close-up of Jilly on the steps from Zinnia's place and cursed. "I've got to get her off the street."

35

Cyrus approached Edwards Place but pulled the Impala up short of the security gate.

"Are you havin' second thoughts?" Madge asked. She sounded nervous.

"In a way. What right do I have to call on a woman who hasn't asked me to come? My excuse for droppin' in here is that I thought I'd make sure she's doin' well—since we haven't seen her lately—and offer her the sacraments, of course, but it's only an excuse."

Madge sat straighter. "You wouldn't come if you didn't want to do the right thing," she said.

He smiled. Madge would probably back him up if he decided to rob a bank. "That's true." More or less. He had something quite different on his mind and it seemed important enough to follow up, even if through subterfuge.

When the Impala was close enough he rolled down his window and waited until a sensor produced a voice on the intercom. "Yes?" Rain slashed into the car.

"Father Cyrus Payne and Madge Pollard to see Mrs. Edith Preston."

There was a pause before the voice said, "Please come in," and the gate swung inward.

"I don't like this place," Madge said when the gate closed behind the car. "I know they've done all sorts of things to make it beautiful again but it still feels unused."

"I think I know what you mean," Cyrus told her. He absolutely did know and he might also have said there was an unhealthy feeling about Edwards Place. "I guess the chopper's in use," he said, driving up the winding driveway. The empty pad sat at a distance and a man mowed the grass there—even though the rain still hadn't let up and the sky had only grown darker.

"They could all be out," Madge said, with more than a little hope in her voice. She touched Cyrus's arm and smiled at him. "It wouldn't matter, we could come back another time."

"Someone answered the intercom," Cyrus pointed out.

"Did I tell you Lil's been fishin' because she thinks

we're not tellin' her about something?" Madge said.

"Like Miz Trudy-Evangeline?"

Madge bent forward and chuckled. "Lil said she was certain she saw someone at one of the upstairs windows at the rectory. She said the person stepped away quickly."

"Lil is supposed to be on that vacation I gave her," Cyrus said, grinning. "That woman is incorrigible."

"Cyrus." Madge looked at him with tears of laughter in her eyes. "Lil said she went to look up from under the window—just doin' her duty, she said—and she found cigarette butts." Madge's body quaked as she tried to control herself. "I said she must have imagined it but . . . but, she had the butts! She collected them and . . . showed them to me. She's going to show you. Talked about a ghost but I told her ghosts don't smoke—as far as I know."

"As far as you know," Cyrus said. "What if it's a ghost posin' as Miz Trudy-Evangeline?" Cyrus pulled up before the front door, which opened at once. Edith herself appeared looking chic in narrow turquoise silk pants and a matching short top with buttons of knotted silk down one side. Her heavy hair looked much as Jilly's did sometimes; drawn back and tied with a length of ribbon. The difference was that rather than blond streaks, gray showed in Edith's. Madge thought the gray was dramatic.

"She's good-looking," Madge said, collecting herself, "and so much like Jilly."

Cyrus got out of the station wagon. "Good afternoon, Mrs. Preston," he called. "Get in out of the rain." He ran around to open Madge's door and she popped out at once, raising an umbrella as she did so. She stretched an arm to hold it over Cyrus, too, and they hurried together into the house.

"My, it's a wild day," Edith said when they were all inside. "I can't tell you how glad I am to see you. I was feelin' a little lonely."

Thunder hammered through the heavens, beating on and on while the three of them stood still. Lightning followed, the kind that lit up the sky in bursts. Cyrus could see it through the fanlight above the front door.

The blond man Cyrus had seen the last time he came emerged from the back of the house. As before he wore light, well-pressed blue jeans and a white V-neck sweater. "Let me take your umbrella," he said, and also waited for Madge's red windbreaker. "Will your guests be having lunch, Mrs. Preston?"

"Of course, Michael," Edith said.

"I don't think so," Cyrus said quickly. Then, when he saw Edith's disappointment, added, "But Madge and I would enjoy something to drink, wouldn't we? I think I'd like coffee."

"So would I," Madge said, smiling at Edith. The blond man moved smoothly away on almost silent white tennis shoes.

"Can I tell you a secret?" Edith asked. She gave an impish smile. "I don't like that big old salon. You just about need megaphones to talk to one another in there. There's a sweet little sitting room back this way and it's much more comfortable. Would that suit, d'you think?"

"It sounds lovely," Madge said. "This is an interestin' house."

"I suppose it is," Edith said. "I'm still not used to it but I do love bein' close to my Jilly. I'm not fond of bein' here on my own, though."

Madge turned up the corners of her mouth politely. She doubted there was anyone in Toussaint who didn't know Edith Preston had left her baby girl with a difficult father in order to find herself a more interesting life.

"Are you all alone here, Mrs. Preston?" Cyrus asked, feeling edgy and dishonest.

"Jilly couldn't come over like she was supposed to," Edith said. "Wes doesn't really like it here so he spreads out his visits, and Laura went into New Orleans with Daddy. I don't know what I'd do without Laura but that girl does like to shop." She giggled. "Of course she does, what pretty woman doesn't? Anyway, I like to see her and Daddy getting along so well. Daddy said the biggest canary diamond you ever saw came in with a lot for auction. You'll have to visit the shop sometime. Anyway, Daddy said the stone is perfect—set in a ring. Of course, Laura's eyes lit up so she's going to see it."

Madge made an agreeable noise. They followed her along a corridor to a pretty room done in shades of daffodil yellow and cream. Cyrus wondered how Mr. Preston felt about such a cozy, unpretentious room.

Edith looked girlish when she said, "I'll expect to see that ring when Laura comes back." She laughed. "One of the benefits of the antiques business is that the most beautiful jewelry passes through our hands and Daddy likes to decorate his ladies. Come on, make yourselves comfortable. Michael will find us with the coffee. He knows I like it in here."

Cyrus frowned. "I wonder if you'd mind if I used a bathroom?" he said, not daring to look at Madge, who would know he was up to something.

"Please," Edith said. "It's probably quickest to return to the hall. Take the corridor toward the salon. Second door on your right."

Cyrus muttered his thanks and moved with unseemly haste in the direction he'd been told to go. Fortunately it was the way he needed to take, anyway.

In the hall he looked around and upward, making sure no one watched him from above. He didn't see anyone and moved swiftly to the beautiful Dresden vase he remembered from the evening he visited Edith—after her accident.

His heart met his throat and he felt almost weak.

He scarcely believed his good fortune. At the bottom of the vase lay a ball of paper. Cyrus held the vase steady and shot in his hand. His fingers closed on the now-solid gum in its paper wrapper. He'd forgotten about Wes Preston coming in that night and tossing his gum into the vase—until he'd gone over the events of the evening just that morning, trying to think of something useful to the case. He hadn't met Wes until later

434

and by then he'd been thinking of other things.

With the gum in his pocket, he carried on to the bathroom, waited a reasonable time and returned to the sitting room. He had looked at the little wad of paper but hadn't attempted to unwrap it. That was something the police needed to do, not that it was likely to be anything other than Wes's discarded gum. He did note that the paper wasn't a gum wrapper but rather white with green lines on it.

Coffee had arrived in the sitting room and Michael had poured. He gave Cyrus a sidelong stare as he left the room. Apparently he didn't appreciate waiting on impoverished clergymen.

"I thought everyone was staying in Toussaint today, but they left," Edith said, sounding petulant. "We have so much to celebrate, and I'm going to tell you all about it just as soon as I can."

"That'll be very nice." Cyrus ached to get off the premises and bear his little and probably useless package to Spike.

"There's a question I've got to ask you," Edith said, raising her shoulders girlishly. "I think there's somethin' deep between Jilly and that nice Guy Gautreaux, don't you?"

Madge bit her lip and seemed disinclined to help Cyrus out.

"Well—" He wished Jilly and Guy would give him some idea whether they planned a future together. "Well, I do think they like each other considerably," he said, and felt like a wimp.

Edith shook a finger at him. "You, Father, are bein' evasive. Shame on you, but I understand. Eat one of Cook's pear fritters. They are her pride and joy and she'll be offended if we don't have any of them."

"Pear fritters?" Cyrus said. He picked one up at once and bit into a tender, brown-sugar-coated crust. Sweet, fresh pear, thinly sliced in its own thickened juice, filled his mouth and he closed his eyes. The rest of the fritter disappeared down his throat and he reached for another from the plate. "Madge, you've got to have one of these," he said.

"I've had two," she told him. "The deep-fried biscuits on the other plate have lime custard in the middle."

He winked at her. She knew very well that sweets, especially beautifully made sweet desserts, were his downfall.

"Oh dear," Cyrus said, dusting sugar from his hands and wiping his mouth on a napkin. "I came to bring you communion. Since you haven't been well enough to get to mass."

Edith smiled and bowed her head. "You are the sweetest man to think of me," she said. "I'd like to receive, Father."

"Perhaps you'd wait outside, Madge," he said, and she withdrew. "Now, is there anythin' you'd like to tell me about, dear lady?"

Edith frowned. She sat on a couch and Cyrus sat down there, too, turning to face her. "I get jealous, Father. Of my daughter-in-law, Laura. Sometimes I think she and my husband are too close. It's just silliness, I know it is, but I can't seem to help it. Then there're all the thoughts I had about my accident. It's wrong but I think about it when I lie down to sleep. Dear Caruthers rescued me, you know."

"He was a good man," Cyrus said. "You must miss him. Don't worry about a little jealousy. Remember how you said you liked Laura being close to your husband? You're a generous woman."

She leaned close to Cyrus and whispered, "That night. I don't remember much, but I get these sort of dreams. Shapes moving around me. One shape. A voice muttering. And I was pushed—*manhandled*. Then I think I fell." Edith looked directly at him. "I didn't have an accident tryin' to shave my legs." She colored.

"Are you sure?"

"I get my legs waxed at the spa. I didn't try to take my life, either, Father. I'm sure folks have wondered. Please believe me. I didn't do that. I value life."

"But you were depressed?"

Her eyes filled with tears. "Yes. But I didn't try to take my own life."

He leaned close. "What then, Edith? Your wrist was cut."

"I think someone wanted me dead."

So did Cyrus but he wouldn't speak of that to Edith. "You're going to be all right," he told her. "I'll tell everyone how well you're doing here, how good it is for you. But there's work to be done. You can't live like this."

"In a gilded cage, you mean?"

Why lie? "Yes, a gilded cage. Shut away and a bit frightened, I think."

"I do get frightened," she whispered.

"You aren't the mistress here. The staff don't treat you well. Neither do some members of your family. Do you want to do something about that?"

She nodded slowly. After giving Edith communion and a few thoughtful moments, Cyrus went to bring Madge back in and she sat to listen to what they had to say.

Cyrus knew he had to get to Spike now. "I've got to run an errand. Could I leave you two ladies here to visit? I'll be back shortly, Madge."

She didn't look happy, but immediately said it was fine with her if it was fine with Edith.

Almost as quickly as he'd hoped, Cyrus was on the road and headed for the sheriff's offices. The windshield wipers hadn't been replaced and he was forced to lean forward and peer through a more-or-less clear arc on the steamy windshield. Lightning shot earthward and seemed to hit the road in front of his vehicle.

In minutes he arrived and parked under the sycamore tree in front of the dilapidated building. Thoughts of Madge made him hesitate to get out of the Impala. Every day he prayed she would find a man she really loved—and he, Cyrus, would give her the most beautiful wedding ever. He thought about her too much but he guessed love was like that. Instantly he got a headache. The sooner Madge was involved with another man, the better, as long as he was worthy of her.

Out he hopped, not bothering to lock the vehicle, and he ran with his head down.

The parking lot was fuller than usual and people came and went from the building. Inside he stood in a line, dripping, and waiting to ask a clerk for Spike, but Deputy Lori spied him and hurried to take him aside.

"Is Spike in?" he asked.

"He sure is. You know you don't have to stand there like that and wait." She smiled at him. "Go on back. He'll be glad to see you."

"How's that sweet babe of yours?" Cyrus asked.

"Just beautiful," Lori said, beaming. "We'll be along to talk about baptizing her soon."

Cyrus accepted and returned Lori's impulsive hug and set off to find Spike.

His office resembled command central for some battle. It also wasn't a place Cyrus would want someone squeamish to wander into without warning.

Photographs of Caruthers Rathburn, alive and dead, decorated one wall together with shots of objects Cyrus presumed were evidence, charts and lists of measurements—at least, he thought they were mea-surements. Several flip charts, scribbled on in a variety of colors, stood on easels. Pieces of paper were pinned on boards. Chairs stood at odd angles where people had come and gone. And Spike sat behind his desk with his hand driven, very Spike-like, into his hair.

"Sorry to interrupt," Cyrus said.

Spike looked up at once and grinned. "I was hopin' someone would interrupt me. Interruptions are the procrastinator's dream."

"That sounds like a Vivianism," Cyrus said, and Spike nodded. "We're going to find the link," Spike said. "Little pieces have started to fall into place. We'll get the rest soon."

Cyrus drew in a breath and let it out. "I know. That's why I came."

A commotion in the corridor outside the office materialized into Wazoo with Lee O'Brien, and Deputy Lori half-seriously trying to intercept the two women.

"It's okay, Lori," Spike said. "We could use a little light relief around here."

That was when Cyrus noticed another wall of photos, this time of Zinnia and Pip Sedge. He glanced at the two women who hurried into the room, Wazoo opening and shutting a fancy purple umbrella with black lace around the rim and black streamers on top. She shook water everywhere.

"Every little thing is so hard around here," she said. "We try to come back here and have a word with a friend—" she looked sideways at Cyrus "—didn't expect to see you, God Man. But all we wanted was a few words with Spike, and Lori chases us down like criminals. Phooey, what a lot of commotion."

Lee stood quietly by but had the grace to keep her eyes down.

Wazoo saw the pictures of Caruthers. "See," she said to Lee. "Just like I told you. Brains all over. I made a mistake that night, though. I was thinkin' he'd probably eaten cake with his own hair and brain in it but that couldn't be. It'd be someone else who got his hair in a cake. Messes with a person's mind, I can tell you, then kills 'em. At least . . . yes, that's it." She drummed her fingers on her jaw. "No. I was right in the first place."

Spike shook his head. "I'm havin' a busy day, ladies. So unless there's somethin'—"

"Somethin'?" Wazoo said, her voice unusually high-pitched. "I'd say there's somethin'. You think people like Lee and me got time to burn? You men aren't the only busy ones." She shook out mauve skirts with points that dipped to the floor. The bodice was close-fitting, showing off a nice figure, and despite the humidity, Wazoo wore a black lace shawl.

Lee, in a white shirt and jeans with her blond hair in a single pigtail down her back, seemed all business.

"Would you like me to leave while you talk?" Cyrus asked.

"Yes," Wazoo said.

Lee poked her. "Of course not, Father. This won't take long and there's probably nothing useful in what I've got."

"It's going to break the case," Wazoo said with conviction. She swung her slightly damp skirts and hummed. "It's been too long since I went to a good dance," she said. "We got Pappy's Dancehall right up the road a ways and does anyone ever ask me to go and dance? Uh-uh." She sprung into a two-step with variations that involved slapping the feet down hard and twirling her hands above her head.

"I bet that nice Nat Archer would take you," Lee said. Cyrus liked her because she took everyone seriously.

Lee went to the wall where Rathburn's pictures were displayed. She studied them carefully while Cyrus waited for Spike to warn her off. He didn't. Then she moved to the shots of Zinnia, and Cyrus saw Lee's hand go to her throat.

"She was beautiful," Lee said. "You can see it even here."

"Look at that one up there," Spike said, pointing.

Lee followed the direction of his finger and said, "Oh, my." The photo was of a very alive and smiling Zinnia.

She turned to Spike. "I know I've overstepped myself a few times but I'm hoping you'll forgive me if I can help out."

"I've already forgiven you," Spike said. "I reckon you've got a job to do."

"Did I hear that Mr. Rathburn had pieces of sticky tape under his fingernails?" she asked.

Spike frowned.

Cyrus figured Lee was about to have her forgiveness revoked.

"How do you know that?" Spike asked.

"The truth will set you free," Wazoo sang.

Lee puffed at trailing strands of hair. "I asked questions," she said. "I went to the morgue and one of the assistants didn't seem to mind talking to me."

"Could be that was the case," Spike said, leaning back in his chair. "About the tape."

From a purse Lee wore with its long strap across her chest, she took out an envelope.

Wazoo, apparently out of patience, whirled to take the envelope from Lee and shove it in front of Spike. "Be careful with what's in there. It's fragile. Here—" she produced tweezers from her pocket "—I sterilized 'em first."

Dutifully, Spike accepted the tweezers, opened the envelope and peered inside. He removed a tricolored scrap, or rather a two-colored scrap, with a bit of tape on it.

"See," Wazoo said. "Sticky tape. And it's got a flake of pink paint and a fragment of paper on it."

Spike turned it this way and that and looked closer. Then he looked at Cyrus. "What does this look like to you?"

Cyrus went closer and shook his head.

Wazoo put a hand over her mouth and jumped up and down while Lee bit her lip to stop from grinning. "Think about *pink paint*," she said.

"Paint from the door of All Tarted Up, tape and some paper," Cyrus said at once. "Can't think of any-where else you'd find paint that color."

"Whoo-hoo," Wazoo said, twirling again. "God Man got it right and I think Spike knew, too. They may not be as dumb as they look."

"Wazoo," Lee said, almost managing to sound

shocked. "It was by chance I found it. I noticed some flakes missing above the letter slot in the door and a tiny remnant of tape. Then I saw this bit stuck on lower down. It must have fallen there and whoever was picking at the tape didn't notice."

Spike and Cyrus looked at the exhibit, then at the two women. Spike cleared his throat. "Well, thank you, ladies. I'll have this put in the evidence room."

Lee crossed her arms. "You don't have the faintest idea what that could mean, do you?"

"Someone stuck somethin' to Jilly's door then scraped it off again and dropped a bit," Wazoo said. "I reckon it was a note."

"And Caruthers had tape under his nails," Lee said. "Like he was the one who scraped it off, maybe?"

"Logical," Spike said. "I'll look into it. Did your source happen to tell you if Caruthers also had pink paint under his nails?"

Lee looked crestfallen. "I asked. He didn't."

"So this could have been a different piece of tape from a different incident?"

"Yes," Lee said.

"Maybe we should ask Jilly about it."

Cyrus bent over the desk to peer at the "evidence." And his heart started to beat faster. There was a faint suggestion of a green line at the edge of the torn snippet of paper. He took the gum wad from his pocket and felt embarrassed not to have made any attempt to keep it clean.

"What's that?" Spike said.

"Sometimes I take vagueness too far," Cyrus said. "Help me make sure I don't mess this up even more than I already have. It could have fingerprints on it."

"Surrounded by criminologists," Spike said. He put a clean piece of paper in front of Cyrus. "Put it on there—whatever it is."

"It's gum wrapped in a bit of paper," Cyrus told him. "I saw someone throw it away the night Caruthers Rathburn was murdered. The paper has lines on it like that." He pointed to the faint green line on Lee's evidence. He wasn't about to mention Wes Preston's name if this was all as ridiculous and unimportant as he thought it might be.

Spike opened his mouth, then closed it again. Probably because he'd been about to ask who the gum chewer had been but changed his mind with Lee and Wazoo there. He picked up the phone and arranged for the samples to go to the lab. "They say they can get some preliminary results pretty quickly," he said when he'd finished his conversation.

"Spike!" Deputy Lori abandoned her customary plod to rush into the office. "There's somethin' comin' on TV you'd better watch. And I don't suppose you've seen this." She slid a copy of the *Toussaint Trumpet* in front of him and turned on the television.

While Lori fiddled with the reception, Spike scanned the paper, which now had a single extra sheet inserted in the middle. He looked up at Cyrus. "A man of the cloth in the business of hiding fugitives? That you?"

Cyrus took a second to put the comment together with Miz Trudy-Evangeline. "No," he said honestly. He hadn't thought of mentioning the lady to Spike, but even if he wanted to now, he thought he'd have to get Nat and Guy's approval.

A familiar location appeared on the television screen: All Tarted Up. Again Lee O'Brien stood in front of the door being interviewed by a reporter. "Yes," she said. "This is Miz Gable's shop. Rathburn's killing took place in the yard behind. There's speculation in the local newspaper, the *Toussaint Trumpet*, about a possible connection to a wider crime scene in New Orleans."

When the piece finished, Spike turned off the set and drummed his fingertips on his desk. "When was that?" he asked Lee, who looked miserable.

"A few hours ago," she said. "They keep askin' for interviews."

"Okay," Spike said. "I'd better get over there and talk to Jilly. She should probably be moved somewhere safe until we're sure she's not in danger."

Lee sank into a chair and propped her forehead on her fists. "She's not there," she mumbled.

"Jilly's not at work?" He picked up the phone and punched in numbers. No one picked up at the other end. "And she's not at home," he said.

Lee shook her head.

Wazoo dropped her hands to her sides and looked stricken.

Spike tried another number and waited, then

another—and had a short conversation—before putting the phone down quietly again. "Guy's not at his place and Homer says he's not there, either."

This time the phone rang and Spike snatched it up. "Spike Devol." He listened for some time before he said, "She's probably wanderin' around the Quarter, Guy. If you've got people lookin' for her, she'll show up okay. We've got a couple of pieces of new evidence at this end. I should have reports before too long. I'll call you. Thanks."

He scribbled down a number and hung up. "Guy's in New Orleans. Jilly drove him in then went off on her own. Apparently there was a piece on TV there, too—naming Jilly and showing her picture. They've got people on the street lookin' for her but so far, no news."

"This is all my fault," Lee said. "I had no right—well, I was wrong to try to take advantage of something bad just for my own personal gain. It seemed a once-in-a-lifetime opportunity and . . ." She hung her head.

Madge had left the rectory as soon as Cyrus drove her back from Edwards Place. She made some excuse about running errands but Cyrus knew her too well. She had gone off to be quiet and try to deal with her concern for Jilly.

He had spent time inside St. Cécil's but hadn't found it easy to quiet his mind and pray. The open air called him and he walked between tombs on soft, wet grass.

There would be more rain but for now it had stopped. As he liked to do, he stopped now and then to read the inscription on a stone. So many of the tombs had turned dark with age and it was hard to make out what had been chiseled there, especially if there were also clumps of thick moss growing.

Perhaps it wasn't too soon to call Spike and ask if there was any news of Jilly. He continued on to the corner of the church farthest from the rectory and turned for home.

On the other side of a fenced-in family memorial, by the outer wall, he saw two crouched figures. They wore green jackets with hoods and it was surprising he'd noticed them.

Hurriedly, Cyrus made his way toward the people. They seemed still, and as he drew close he saw they kneeled side by side on the soaked ground. Fresh earth stood in two small mounds.

He ran, suddenly convinced something was very wrong.

They didn't hear him coming. Leaning shoulder to shoulder, they cradled a little metal lunch box and Cyrus heard them crying. One man, one woman. Ken and Jolene Pratt.

With a throat that closed and ached, Cyrus walked carefully, slowly, around until he faced the Pratts. "Ken," he said, "Jolene. What's happening?"

Both looked up at him. "We're so sorry," Jolene said. "It seemed the best thing to do at the time but now we can't visit anymore—like we used to at night—so we're moving our baby."

Cyrus closed his eyes. "Why didn't you come to me?"

"We buried her ourselves because we didn't know if you would let her be here. God forgive us."

"Tell me about all this," Cyrus said, looking at the smallness of the box. "You miscarried a little girl?"

Ken and Jolene nodded. "I soldered the box. It's tight shut," Ken said.

"We're not Catholic, Father," Jolene said. "We're not anything. But we came to you for help and you gave it to us. We wanted her here."

"But you tithe," Cyrus said, bemused.

"We give back for all you've given us," Jolene said.

Looking at the heavy sky, in his mind Cyrus had a quiet word with God. And he considered what it meant to be truly good. "Let's put this little one back for her nap," he said, getting down and instantly feeling the knees of his pants grow wet. He put a hand under each of theirs and guided the burial.

Cyrus placed dirt in each of their palms and when they had thrown it on the box, it was Cyrus who replaced the rest of the earth, and the sod that had been peeled back. And he blessed the baby.

From a pocket, Ken took what looked like a laminated bookmark. It said, Baby Mary, nothing more, and he slid it into a crack made by cutting the sod, slid it sideways into the ground until it wasn't visible. He got up, pulling Jolene with him.

"Is it all right?" Jolene asked.

Cyrus got to his feet and put an arm around each of them. "It's all right," he said.

36

"Good afternoon, ma'am." The man who approached Jilly pushed back a very white cuff to look at his Rolex.

She said, "Good afternoon," hating the way her stomach turned. "This is a wonderful shop. I've heard a lot about it but I've never been in before."

"Prestons is a New Orleans institution among antique connoisseurs. I'm Russell Smith, the manager." He offered his hand and Jilly shook it. She didn't miss the faint flicker of his blue eyes taking in her casual shirt and pants. "Did you have something special in mind?"

Run, run, run. Now, that would be stupid behavior for an adult woman. "I came in hopin' that Mr. Preston might be here. Mr. Sam Preston. I'm a friend of his." Since she had no idea whether the Prestons were talking about Edith's long-lost daughter, she had decided not to mention the relationship.

The change in the man's demeanor wasn't subtle. He inclined his narrow head and gave her his full attention. "Is he expecting you, Miss . . ."

"I'm Jilly Gable. No, he's not expectin' me but I'm sure he'll see me if he has a few moments to spare."

And then she would tell him what she'd been rehearsing while she drank too many cups of coffee in a nearby café.

Not a strand of Russell Smith's blond hair was out of place. He had a light, even tan that made the best of unremarkable but pleasant features.

His lengthy silence gave him away. Russell wasn't sure what to do about Jilly.

"Look," she said. "Perhaps I've come at a bad time. If he is in today, or if he's comin' in, please tell him I stopped by. I think he'll be pleased I was interested in the shop." The place was deep and she could see one room leading to another. A hush hung in lemon-scented air.

"Please don't rush away," the man said. "Mr. Preston did mention dropping by today. He spends more of his time at auction than he does here, much more, but I know he won't be at any of the houses today or tomorrow. Do let me make you comfortable while I try to find out when he might arrive."

"That's a lot of trouble." And she'd completely changed her mind about the wisdom of a heart-to-heart with her mother's husband.

"Jilly? I'll be—is that you, Jilly Gable?"

At the sound of a familiar male voice, she turned sharply, just in time to be engulfed in a crushing hug from Wes Preston. His smile was a thousand watts and he chuckled delightedly. "Of all the people I didn't expect to see in here, you're probably it. Welcome. If you'd let us know you could have come on the chopper. Has Russell been looking after you?"

She stiffened in his arms. "He certainly has."

"Miss Gable was hoping to find your father here," Russell said. "I was just going to ascertain if he plans to be in New Orleans today."

"I'll save you the trouble. He does. But he's busy for an hour or so, which gives us time for a late lunch, Jilly." He frowned slightly. "Tell me you haven't already eaten."

"I haven't." She didn't want to go anywhere with him. "But I'm not really hungry."

"Of course you are." He tucked her hand under his arm and started toward the door. "When Mr. Preston comes in, ask him to call me," he said without looking back. To Jilly, he said, "Edith called and said Laura was comin' into town with Daddy. Apparently there's some ring he wants to show her—as if she didn't already have enough. My father loves to give presents."

"I know," Jilly said. "I believe he's a very generous man with a basically good heart." Suddenly she was desperate to squelch any idea that she felt close to Wes, or that they shared some sort of secret.

"Really?" He raised his dark eyebrows.

Outside, he opened the passenger door of a black Mercedes coupe and helped Jilly inside. The moment he was behind the wheel, he grinned at her and started the car. "This is great," he said, and entered the flow of traffic. "I've got a favorite place for lunch and they're already expectin' me. They'll be more than happy when I show up with you."

"I'm not dressed for—"

"You look great," Wes said. "This is a very different place but I'm not tellin' you another word about it. I want you to be surprised. How come you decided to go lookin' for Daddy?" Some of the good humor left him.

"I wanted to talk to him," she said. There was no reason to avoid the truth. "You know things have been strained between us. I can't follow your advice and just stay away because that would mean stayin' away from Edith."

"Edith stayed away from you for most of your life," Wes said. "I don't want to salt the wound but it's true. Why do you care about her now?"

She couldn't begin to tell him how complicated her feelings were for Edith. "She wants to make up for lost time. If I can help her get over the guilt she feels—and she does feel guilty—then why not? I know all about the past but it is past and I believe in moving on."

"St. Jillian."

She ignored the dig but wished she hadn't let him talk her into coming with him.

"So what do you intend to say to Daddy?"

"I'll know when I talk to him."

Wes gave a short laugh. "In other words, back off?"

"Somethin' like that," Jilly agreed. "You've been kind to me, more kind than you had to be. Let's not argue about something we disagree about."

Wes shot her one of his brilliant smiles. "You're a wise woman."

He had driven down a one-way backstreet. Jilly had been too engrossed in their conversation to notice the route they'd taken, but they were still in the Quarter. "I don't recall this street," she said.

Wes reached a wrought-iron gate on the right-hand side and stopped. "I don't know what it's called," he said, watching while a man appeared inside the gate and swung it wide open. "I've been coming here so long, I've forgotten, but that's ridiculous. I'll ask."

He drove into a courtyard built up on three sides and without landscaping. Jilly looked back in time to see the man who let them in close himself outside the gate and leave.

Wes hit an overhead button and a garage opened. He drove inside and got out of the car and Jilly did the same before he could open her door. Why would he have controls to a garage at some restaurant? She pushed her hands behind her back so he wouldn't see them tremble.

"I've been comin' here since I was a kid," he said. "Daddy and the owner are old friends. You're going to croak when you see the way the place is set up."

They were closed inside the garage now—with several other expensive cars—and Wes went directly to punch a button for an elevator. They stood there, faces raised, listening to the car descend.

She shouldn't have gone to the antiques shop, but above all she shouldn't have come here. It didn't feel right and she was plain scared.

"After you," Wes said, when stainless-steel doors opened.

In they went and up they went, coming to a smooth halt and stepping into a bamboo-paneled hallway with fitted green carpet on the floor. Wes took her by the arm and walked purposefully to stained-glass doors where tropical flowers were scattered between fern fronds and palm leaves. The doors hung on runners and Wes pushed one aside. "Come on in and make yourself comfortable."

This was no restaurant.

Jilly kept an appreciative smile on her face and walked into an oblong room where wide silk streamers in bright hues looped the ceiling. Divans of carved dark wood, upholstered in silk to blend with the streamers, surrounded the room, a circle of them with nothing in the middle but a continuation of the green carpet.

"They haven't set up," Wes said, and Jilly thought his expression fixed. "They didn't know when I'd show and it only takes a moment. Try one of the divans. You won't believe how comfortable they are. I'll get things under way." He looked at her a moment. "You'll be okay here on your own?"

She chuckled. "I'm a big girl, Wes. Of course I will."

For the first time she was aware of him sizing her up, and the look in his eyes couldn't be mistaken for anything but sexual interest. "Right," he said. "I'll be back shortly."

She gave him sixty seconds by her watch, then trod quickly and quietly toward the door. First she listened and when she heard no voices or movement, dared a peek outside. The corridor was empty.

Even a country girl could sense danger and there was something very wrong in this place. This could be her only chance to get away.

Hitching the strap of her purse high on her shoulder she slipped swiftly out of the room and to the elevator, where she pressed the button. Her best hope was to go out by the route she'd come in—at least she knew it. She prayed she'd be able to open the garage door, and the gate out of the courtyard.

A sound from above almost weakened her knees with relief. The elevator was coming. Jilly looked around but she was still safely alone and very little time had passed since Wes left her.

The slightest of bumps came and the door slid open. Her head felt light and her stomach burned.

Jilly almost stepped inside. Before her second foot joined the first, two strong hands took her by the arms and spun her out of the elevator. Dangling above the floor, she looked back at Wes Preston, who regarded her with no particular expression.

The corners of his mouth turned down. "Why are you trying to leave?"

"I . . . I don't have as much time as I thought I did. I was going to get your cell number from Edith and call you just as soon as I could."

"Liar." He sneered and without putting her down

took her back to the room with the divans. She landed on one of them with enough force to jar her back. "Don't move from there."

Her heart beat so loud she could scarcely hear. Wes took hold of her purse strap and pulled it from her. She fought to hold on but was no match for him.

Jilly tried to stand up but he made sure she stayed where she was, this time by slapping the side of her head and grinning as she fell.

From her purse he took her cell phone. This he slipped into one of his own pockets. He searched through her possessions and, apparently satisfied they were no threat to him, tossed the purse down on top of her.

Why didn't I think to call Guy?

"Listen to me very carefully," Wes said. "Do as you're told and nothing will happen to you. I wouldn't have done what I just did if you hadn't made me mad by behaving as if you were afraid of this place and of me."

I am.

"Daddy's on his way here," Wes said. "He can entertain you while I make a few necessary arrangements. One or two warnings— In Daddy's eyes I can do no wrong. It could go badly for you if you start lyin' and suggestin' I told you to get away from him. He's so touched you wanted to meet up with him, he'll be very generous to you and to all of us." His expression darkened. "If you know what's good for you, you'll keep your mouth shut and do whatever Daddy tells you to."

37

Wazoo and Lee were still in Spike's office. Lee jumped at every footstep and every ring of the phone. Spike was on the phone now but he felt her eyes on his face.

"Guy says they can't find Jilly," Spike said once he had hung up. "If I didn't know him I'd say he was holding up real well."

"But he's fallin' apart," Wazoo said. "He got Nat with him, though, and that's the man you want when things look bad."

Cyrus walked in. "I can't stand not knowing what's happening," he said, and Spike filled him in.

"In other words things haven't really changed," Lee said. "We just don't know anything." Her knuckles would be raw later.

Each one of them tried to give the impression they were in no way overly concerned for Jilly. Spike figured "terrified" about summed up what they were really feeling. If Cyrus's checking his fingernails repeatedly was supposed to look nonchalant, he needed to practice his acting skills.

The door shot open, yet again, and Vivian Devol came in with Charlotte and Homer. "Somethin' awful's goin' on, isn't it?" she said, looking at Lee O'Brien. "Seein' your interview, then findin' out everyone's lookin' for Jilly's put us all on edge. I tried to call you but they were keeping all your lines free. What's goin' on? And don't you try coddlin' my feelings, Spike Devol, or you'll be in big trouble."

Spike saw his father struggle not to grin.

Wazoo had not sat down since she arrived and that had been several hours earlier. She faced the room and said, "Lee was just doin' her job. She wouldn't hurt Jilly for anythin'."

"It wouldn't have been so bad if you hadn't said that thing about Jilly and her NOPD friends lookin' for a link between the murder at All Tarted Up and organized crime in New Orleans. That's more or less what you said." Vivian's voice shook, and if they'd been alone, Spike would have found a way to calm his wife down. "What would make you do a thing like that? You must have called the TV people yourself."

"I'm not going to spell it all out but I have sources," Lee said in a shaky voice. "Simon for one, and newspapers from a good few years. That murder at Jilly's didn't make any sense—it didn't fit. And how often has a crazy in this town caused a car accident to get rid of someone?"

"You don't know that's what happened," Cyrus said. "Whatever was wrong with Jilly's car probably happened during the accident."

"Sure it did," Lee said. "That's why someone told Mortie to scrap the car—right at the time when we just found out about the brakes."

"Okay." Spike raised his voice a notch and stood up.

"I know Jilly will be touched when she finds out how you were all so concerned for her, but you can't do her any good hangin' around here arguin'."

"Charlotte!" Wazoo said. "You show me that finger of yours."

"Oh, this isn't a good time," Charlotte said. "We'll talk about it another time."

Wazoo marched over and took Charlotte's left hand in her own. "Look at this. Hoo mama, this is *some* ring." She looked over Charlotte's head at Homer, who had stuck his hands in his pockets and turned his attention to the pictures on the walls.

The others crowded around to ooh and aah over a very white heart-shaped diamond set in a pavé-diamond band. Spike took a peek and said, "Whoa, how many millions of green stamps did that take?"

"Green stamps?" Homer swung around and loped over to join the group. Then he caught his son's eye and chuckled. "You always did like to get a rise out of me."

"When did this happen?" Spike asked.

Cyrus reached around to squeeze his arm, but Spike intended to make the best of the moment.

"Happen," Charlotte said, her bright eyes twinkling. "You make it sound like a train wreck. Homer picked this ring out on his own. He got my ring size from my sneaky daughter and brought it to me this mornin'. Isn't it a lovely friendship ring?"

The entire assembly laughed and more than one wiped away tears. "That's a friendship ring?" Cyrus asked. "Why would—"

"We're engaged," Homer said, frowning at the toes of his boots. "I don't know how I got so lucky. Can't think how a woman like Charlotte could forget herself for long enough to say yes to an old grump like me, but that's the way of it."

"I only called it a friendship ring in case you weren't ready to announce anythin', Homer," Charlotte said. "But I'm proud to shout it outside if it's okay with you."

"Er, later," Homer said. "When we've got a few other problems sorted out around here."

The two of them accepted congratulations and Spike didn't remember seeing his old man so euphoric.

But no joy would be without a cloud until he heard Jilly was safe. He'd already taken a step he'd never hoped to take and sent a wire to Joe and Ellie Gable's hotel in Venice, where they were expected late today or tomorrow. He had to inform Jilly's brother but he only hoped he'd be able to say she'd been found by the time Joe called.

The intercom buzzed and he returned to his desk.

Lori said, "The lab guy's back. He's on his way to your office."

The instant the man walked through the door Spike snapped, "I've been waiting for a report. How come someone didn't call?"

The man looked stricken. "Dr. Barnes must have forgotten. It's pretty busy over there. Here's what you need."

A semicircle formed at a discreet distance from the

461

desk. Spike opened the manila envelope and pulled out a couple of typewritten sheets. On the top sheet, the findings had been boiled down to simple terms.

Spike read through the information twice and picked up a pen to make some notes.

"Okay," Vivian said. "What is all that about?"

He looked up. "Sorry." The job of deciding how to proceed had captured all of his attention. He looked at the still-hovering technician. "This means I need to deal directly with NOPD. Detectives Gautreaux and Archer were probably right to think what happened here is connected to incidents in New Orleans."

"Dr. Barnes tried to contact Detective Gautreaux and his partner but couldn't reach them," the technician said. "He left a message for them to call him back."

"Fair enough," Spike said, with every intention of tracking Guy down himself. "Will you thank Dr. Barnes for me? And thank you for getting back here."

Once the man had left, the edgy silence of those who remained spurred Spike on to explain.

"Lee and Wazoo, you were right about what you found. The tape was used to stick a note to Jilly's shop door. Someone pulled the note off, apart from the bit that slipped down and some scraps of tape that remained on the door."

Lee crossed her arms tightly. She didn't look happy. "Well, I hope it helps get this thing solved. I haven't done anything else right."

"The bigger point—" he looked at Cyrus "—is that

the gum you found in a vase at Edwards Place was wrapped in a note. Evidently the lab didn't have much difficulty separating the paper from the gum. The scrap Lee found fits into a part of the note and one end of the tape is a perfect match. Caruthers Rathburn took the note off the front door and carried it around to Parish Lane—like it told him to do."

He looked around and got the feeling they were all holding their breath.

"The note told Rathburn—who had just delivered Jilly's Hummer—that his ride back to Edwards Place was waiting in the yard behind Jilly's place."

"Why wouldn't someone wait right there in front to give him a ride?" Vivian said.

"Because he was going to be murdered and they didn't want to do it where they might be seen. Rathburn did as he was told, handed over the note and Wes Preston shot him between the eyes."

Several heads bowed.

"Wes Preston?" Vivian said.

"I should have gone after the gum at once," Cyrus told Spike, and to the others he said, "I was at Edwards Place the night Rathburn was killed. I saw Wes come into the house, wrap the gum he'd had in his mouth and toss it in the vase. And I just didn't think anything of it. I am so sorry."

"It'll be okay," Vivian said. "They'll get Wes. And Jilly's going to show up, too. I bet she's shopping— she doesn't go into New Orleans very often."

"I'm going to find Guy," Spike said, looking up the

cell phone number. "You might be right, Vivian, if a few things hadn't changed. Lee did suggest—for everyone to see—that Jilly might have a lot more information on the killing than she was talking about. No one seems to know where Wes is—except that he's probably in New Orleans. And now it looks as if Wes could have a strong reason for wanting Jilly out of the way."

Homer fanned himself with his hat and screwed up his eyes. His mouth turned down. "Seems to me the first thing you gotta find out, the key to it all, is why Wes Preston wanted this Rathburn guy dead."

38

Guy felt as if bugs were crawling under his skin. Sweat stuck his shirt to his back and made dark spots on the front. His palms were clammy. If he didn't respect Marc Girard and his judgment, leaving the search for Jilly to meet up with Marc and his sister, Amy, would have been out of the question.

He still didn't get why they couldn't come into the precinct but at least they'd come pretty close. Guy drove the navy blue Ford he'd been issued into a parking lot for St. Louis Cathedral, only blocks away from the office. The chief had suggested the different vehicle in case Guy's Pontiac was too hot for the moment.

On the end of the first row of slots, with the passenger side of the vehicle next to a red croton hedge, stood Marc Girard's new, dark green Land Rover. Guy swung in and stopped in the next slot. He saw Marc behind the wheel and gave him a sloppy salute, which Marc returned. There was no sign of Amy.

Guy went to Marc's door and waited for the other man to roll down the window. "Get in," Marc said. "In the back. It'll make it easier for you and Amy to talk. I'm just the driver."

Immediately, Guy opened the back door and climbed in. With her feet pulled up beneath her, and a wide-brimmed black straw hat hiding most of her face, Amy Girard sat close to the other door. She looked into Guy's face and shook her head.

"Hello, Amy," Guy said. He could see Marc's good looks in his sister. She looked better than when Guy had last seen her, her skin showing a tan now and her eyes brighter. A striking-looking woman in her way.

"I shouldn't have waited to come to you," she said, "but I was so scared, I couldn't think straight. The very first time I saw Jilly Gable, that was the time to find out who she was and—and find out if there was reason for me to go hide."

Guy nodded, and waited.

"The night I met Jilly at her café I was goin' to tell her why I'd reacted to her the way I had at Rosebank but I couldn't bring myself to do it. I believe I could get killed if the wrong people find out where I am, but now there's Jilly and I have to step forward. If those bastards figure she could injure them in some way, she's toast. It was the piece on TV that made me ask Marc to bring me to you. That and the ads for someone to come forward about Paula Hemp.

"I called the number in the paper—didn't give my name but I spoke to a really nice man who called himself DL and told me he thought I ought to come to you at once. He said it wouldn't put me in any danger. And he told me to put myself in Marc's hands, that he'd deal with everything. He also said he'd be checking up on me himself. He made me think I could beat this thing."

Thank God for Dwayne LeChat. Guy realized he'd been holding his breath. He sighed and sat up straighter. "That man was right. You're perfectly safe and we'll keep you that way. I'll appreciate any help you can give us."

"I was the one who called Zinnia about Paula," Amy said. "That was back when Paula was missing from home."

He took a moment to absorb that. "You did? Do you know Zinnia? You call her by her first name."

Amy's eyes filled with tears and she looked away. "I knew her for a number of years—even since before she met Pip Sedge and while they were married, and after that. I know what's happened to her. She never had any luck. The choices she made were no good and people took advantage of her—but she was a smart woman in so many ways. I couldn't understand it.

"Zinnia and Pip had separated and young Paula

wasn't getting along too well with her mother so she was acting out. That's why she went to the club and fooled around, only it's dangerous to do that. I found out they had plans for her. She'd be going away and not coming back. That happened to girls regularly, but they were usually runaways who didn't have anyone looking for them. Paula was holed up at the club. Afterward I wished I hadn't told Zinnia I saw her girl there."

Guy already knew why and could easily imagine how Amy had suffered ever since Paula was murdered.

"Paula died while Pip and Zinnia were at Jazz Babes asking about her. That maniac had egged her on. I knew he was sleeping with her—an underage kid. But he was grooming her." Amy raised her eyes to Guy's. "How could he do that then kill her and cut her up? What makes some people like animals?"

"I don't have the answers," Guy told her. He met Marc's eyes in the rearview mirror and saw how troubled the other man was. "Who was this man, the one who killed Paula?"

Amy let out a cry and Marc turned in his seat. "If any of them find out I was the one who told what happened, you know what they'll do," she said.

Marc reached and held his sister's hand.

"They won't do anything," Guy said. "We're going to play our cards right and they'll all be put away."

"A man called Wes Preston murdered young Paula. I saw him carrying her to the elevator but I thought he was taking her somewhere to . . . *Pip and Zinnia were down in the bar asking questions at that very moment.* I had to stay out of the way so people wouldn't know I was in touch with Zinnia. Even though they were separated and getting a divorce, Pip always showed if she needed him.

"I didn't know what Wes was really going to do. Then I read about the death in the paper."

"It's okay," Marc said to her. He turned farther around to see Guy. "There isn't any time to waste, is there?"

"No." Guy felt breathless. He had no reason to believe Jilly was anywhere near Wes, but he wouldn't relax until he found her. Dammit, he'd put her in a cell if that's what it took to keep her safe.

"Zinnia was Sam Preston's girl—Wes's dad. For years, I think." Amy flopped against the seat, her lips pale. "Sam treated her badly. He would put her down in front of people, call her a whore. That's how I know so much. She confided in me and I never repeated a word until now . . . now she's dead."

She stopped talking and looked out of the window.

"Amy's been through a lot," Marc said.

She made a snorting sound. "Because I made bad choices. One after the other, if there was a right or a wrong way to go, I went the wrong way."

"That's over now, sis," Mark said. "Remember all the things Reb has told you. She knows what she's talkin' about, you know. She's a darn good doctor."

"She's the best," Amy said. "She never gets angry

with me—only explains things and helps me. The big mystery is why she married you, brother, when she could have had anyone."

"She's got you there," Guy said, and managed to smile.

Marc reached to rub his sister's cheek. "You're doing great," he said.

"Sam Preston owns Jazz Babes," Amy said. "At least, that's what Zinnia and I decided. But he's got the ownership hidden somehow because it's never mentioned. According to him his business is antiques and that's it. The shop on Royal is real successful."

"It may take a bit, but we have people who live to trail money." Guy got lost in his own thoughts. The Prestons had been incredibly cagey. Dwayne, Jack, Jean-Claude, Nat—as far as Guy knew not a soul was following Sam Preston's tracks. "Tell me anything else you know," he said to Amy.

"Zinnia had about had it with Sam when she met Pip and he asked her to marry him. He was wealthy—in real estate—and he wouldn't take no for an answer. They married and I never saw Sam so mad. He had something on me," she said quietly, "so he liked to smack me around when he needed a punching bag."

Her voice sounded tired and Guy feared she might not finish her story. "You are helping us so much," he said honestly.

"After a bit Sam put on this show of patching things up with Zinnia," she said. "He'd invite the Sedges to dinner, and he started socializing with Pip. He pulled him into a private card game and Pip was like a baby being fed steak. He choked. Night after night he played and from Sam's braggin', night after night Pip lost. Eventually, when Pip was so deep in debt he couldn't even make payments, Sam took Pip's business. He even took the real estate Pip owned himself and there was loads of it. Sam let him know the alternative was having someone drop by every week for payments—that meant he'd be beaten up—or getting rubbed out."

"And he got away with it," Guy said. "Somewhere along the line these guys make a mistake and someone blows the whistle, but not this time. Or not until now."

"Paula's body was a gift from Wes to his father. It was to make sure the Sedges didn't try to get back at Sam. Wes let them know they'd be next if they didn't keep their mouths shut about everything and put up with it. He's jealous of anyone his father takes an interest in. He enjoyed making Zinnia suffer."

Guy had to force himself to stay where he was. It would follow that Wes must be madly jealous of Jilly—not that there was any reason to think she was with the man, he reminded himself. "Thank you, Amy," he said. "You've given us more than you know." He paused, running through what she'd told him. "You never said why you reacted to Jilly the way you did."

"Because she reminded me of someone," Amy said. "I worked with a girl called Edith. Never knew much about her except she was ambitious. She wanted Sam Preston and eventually she got him. Jilly looks so much like her—or the way I remember her—I thought I'd faint. Then I realized I was being stupid, but old fears die hard. I had Wazoo set up a meeting between us but I couldn't even make myself ask if there was another Edith in Jilly's family.

"Now I know Edith is Jilly's mother." Amy leaned forward and crossed her forearms on her knees. "She never said she had a little kid. How could a woman leave her own baby?"

Guy rubbed her back. His nerves jumped around and he checked his phone in case he'd missed an incoming call. Nat had promised to call the moment he heard anything.

"I thought about going to see Edith in that house where she's living. These days I'd like to—"

"Don't go there," Guy snapped.

"She won't," Marc said. "She knows all the reasons why."

"I kept in touch with Zinnia," Amy said quietly. "That's how I know everything. She trusted me. Just days ago she told Sam if he didn't wipe out Pip's debts, she'd go to the police."

"Omigod," Guy said. "She did that without trying to protect herself?"

"She didn't think Sam would do anything to her—for old time's sake. She never knew it was Wes who offed Paula and I never said anything because I was afraid she'd go after Wes herself."

Guy steeled himself to deal with coming to the end of Amy's testimony. So far it was all hearsay—he believed every word, but she hadn't given him proof. "When was the last time you spoke with Zinnia?"

Amy produced a handkerchief and pressed it over her eyes. "The day she died."

Guy's heart slammed against his ribs. "Did Zinnia try to confront Sam?" He already knew the answer.

"Yes, Zinnia decided to have a showdown with Sam. She waited for an opportunity while he was with some woman, and hid in the back of his car."

"And confronted him when he parked at his house on Prytania Street," Guy said. He had tried to find a link between Zinnia and the woman Jilly saw, but unless Zinnia hung around there for a long time it didn't work.

"You knew that?" Amy said.

"Yeah. She didn't leave those grounds right away, did she?"

"No." Amy looked puzzled. "She waited in the gardens deciding whether or not to ring the bell at the house. Some goon who took a turn around the grounds—probably some sort of security—shone a flashlight right on Zinnia and she took off. He followed and tried to kill her. She'd parked her scooter in Lafayette Cemetery and he caught her in there. It was pure luck but someone else came along and the guy ran away. She said he was going to shoot her. He told her he wouldn't let her cause trouble for Laura Preston. That's Wes's wife. Does that seem funny?"

Guy thought about it. "Zinnia wouldn't identify him? She didn't mention anything, not even his coloring?"

"It was real dark. All she said was she saw blond hair. And he was muscular."

"And she got away on her bike?"

"Yes," Amy said. "I wish I'd gone and stayed with her so she wouldn't be alone."

With difficulty, Guy stopped himself from suggesting that Amy might have died with Zinnia. He thought about a blond man who was concerned for Laura Preston. "Excuse me. I need to make a call."

Spike picked up on the first ring and Guy said, "I think we've found our graveyard basher. Find out if Michael—don't know his last name—the guy who works for the Prestons. Find out if he's at Edwards Place. If he is, pick him up. He could be dangerous to Edith. You can keep it friendly till I get something solid."

Spike didn't argue. He said, "Nat's got something for you," and hung up.

The immediate sound of his phone made Guy jump. "Yeah?"

"Nat," said the voice at the other end. "We've got something from Spike. Solid evidence and your Father Cyrus is a witness." Nat talked about bits of torn paper and a match to the tape under Rathburn's nails—and a ball of gum thrown away in the piece of paper the other bits came from. A note. Paint chips were in there, too, paint chips from Jilly's door at the café where they were certain the note had been stuck for Rathburn to read.

"Hang on," Nat said. "Another call coming in." He clicked off and Guy made sure his face showed nothing of what he was feeling.

Minutes passed and Marc said, "You doin' okay, Guy? This is takin' a long time."

"I'm okay," Guy said, and he lied.

Nat came back on the line. "Holy hell," he said. "We've got trouble. A detective went into Prestons—that's—"

"I know it's an antiques shop. They're going to keep that place clean, Nat. Preston can't afford to blow his cover."

"You're right, but like always, somethin' gets away from you. The manager said he'd met Jilly earlier this afternoon. She was lookin' for Sam Preston. Russell Smith, that's the manager, obviously doesn't have a clue Sam Preston isn't exactly who he thinks he is. He said how perfect Wes Preston's timing was. He arrived while Jilly was there and took her out to a late lunch."

Guy looked at Amy, who had just told him Wes Preston cut a girl up and put her pieces back in her bed. At that time Wes couldn't have been more than around twenty to twenty-two. He'd had a lot of time to get real proficient at his craft. "Nat. Please tell me he mentioned the restaurant."

"He didn't. Russell said he talked about having a special place where he goes a lot."

Guy raked at his hair. "I'm comin' in. You mentioned Cyrus as a witness. What did you mean by that?"

"He saw the wad of gum thrown away with the note wrapped around it. That was the night the two of you were at Edwards Place because Edith Preston had an accident. Father Cyrus went out on the landing to take a call and he saw Wes Preston come in. The guy wrapped up the gum and tossed it in a vase. The note on the paper was to Rathburn. Wes must have offed him."

39

If she lay where she'd fallen and didn't move, she had a chance they'd think she was dead.

Fingers pressed into Jilly's neck. "Stunned, that's all," Wes said. "The less blood the better. We're not going to be traced to this, you understand?"

"Yes," Laura said. "How the hell did this go so far? Who would have expected her to go into Prestons like that?"

Jilly heard a slap, and Laura's cry. "Don't touch me again," the woman said, her fury forcing the words through her teeth. "This time it's you and me together—not another soul to help us out, so control yourself."

"The way you always have?" Wes said. "If you'd done what I told you to do at the beginning, this wouldn't be happening. She'd be long gone by now."

"Oh, yeah. Was there somethin' I didn't notice? The fool wouldn't hear the warnings she was given. She wouldn't back off from Edith."

Wes was quiet before he said, "You think Edith was the only reason she hung around?"

"Don't you, asshole? Do you think she fell in love with the rest of us? You know she didn't. She felt some sort of duty toward the mother who threw her away. That's the kind of thing that separates the tough from the soft fools. You know which variety this one is."

"You never thought Daddy would get close enough for it to cost us money?" Wes said. "I know you didn't. He started giving gifts the moment he set eyes on her. And there's somethin' you don't know—"

"That Daddy was having her written into the will?" Laura laughed. "Sure I did. Edith told me because she thought I'd be so tickled. Damn, why do the idiots end up with all the power?"

The sound of another slap jarred Jilly and she almost cried out. One of her eyes was swollen shut, her nose still bled and her head pounded at the slightest vibration.

"What did I tell you?" Laura yelled, and Jilly heard running footsteps.

Wes laughed. Cloth tore. Heavy breathing and panting followed.

Jilly tried not to listen to them having sex while they thought she had passed out. They'd do it even if she was looking right at them, she realized, and loathed them.

"That helped," Wes said. "It always does, babe. Yeah, I like it when you take care of all the details afterward. Watch it with the zipper. We're okay. Just ready for some peace, and that's comin' real soon."

"Yes." Laura sighed. "Her nine lives are over. Wes?"

"Uh-huh?"

"I'm sorry I flubbed it with Edith."

"The only way you flubbed it was by not telling me what you were going to do. It was a brilliant idea. Daddy would have showed up and made sure everything got taken care of." He laughed. "He did that, anyway."

Laura tutted. "Yes, but she wasn't dead. I wanted to surprise you after I'd done it, but it all went wrong. She'd still have died if Rathburn hadn't ridden to the rescue. He knew she hadn't cut her own wrist and he'd have told Daddy. If you hadn't come at that moment and sent him to deliver the stupid Hummer while Michael took over from Rathburn, it would have been all over once Daddy got there with his medical people."

"I still say we make a helluva team," Wes said. "And we're going to have it all but we have to be very careful."

A hand in her hair yanked Jilly's head back so painfully she couldn't stop herself from crying out.

"Huh," Laura said, and pulled Jilly's face around until she could see it. "Don't mess with me. You're awake. Get up now." She kicked Jilly's ribs.

"Just tell us who you've talked to about this and we'll let you go," Wes said.

Fighting for breath, Jilly tried to see him better. He had to know she wouldn't buy his lies.

"Speak up," Laura said. "We're not hearing you."

Blood spattered what was left of the front of her shirt. Jilly raised a hand to try and cover herself better but Laura slapped her hand away. "No one's lining up to look at anythin' you've got," she said. "Answer the question."

"There isn't anyone," Jilly said. She held Guy in her head and heart. She would not do a thing that might get him hurt, too.

She saw Wes move behind her but didn't dare look.

A blow, a solid kick behind her knees landed her on the carpeted floor. Laura laughed and punched her ear. Ringing went on and on.

"I'll just bet you'd like to lie down on one of those cozy divans," Wes said. "We could find a blanket to tuck around you, maybe wash your face with cool water. Give you somethin' to drink. Just tell us who you've talked to and it's all yours."

"I haven't," Jilly said. "Why would I when I didn't know anything? Laura, help me."

Laura shrieked with laughter. "You found out about Wes and me and you were going to Daddy to tell tales. You thought that was the way to get everything. You thought Daddy would cut us out of his will." She shot out her right hand where an unbelievable large canary diamond shot prisms in all directions. "You don't get gifts like this just for bein' a daughter-in-law. Oh, no. You've got to be a whole lot more. Daddy would never believe you over me."

Jilly glanced at Wes, praying he'd turn on Laura, giving Jilly a chance to make a break for it. Once Laura had arrived, Wes had sent everyone off the floor so the chances of getting away were better—just a little better.

"Michael knew you'd followed him when he went after Zinnia in the graveyard. I bet you never guessed that. He enjoyed hurting you. Just like he enjoyed messing up the brakes on that stupid little car of yours."

She didn't see the blow coming, but she felt it connect, Wes's entwined fists descending on her collarbone. She heard it snap and couldn't breathe for the pain.

"What's mine is my father's," he said. "Including Laura. It's always been like that between us. I saw the pity in your eyes. Pity! You're dyin' bit by bit and you pity me?"

Jilly hit his face, and paid for the effort with pain. She tried to run past him but Laura stopped her with a fist to the belly. "Killer instincts?" Laura yelled. "You're getting 'em a little late."

Wes threw up his joined fists and slammed them down just below her shoulder.

"What have I ever done to you?" Jilly managed to say as blackness moved in around her one open eye.

The arm he'd hit burned like fire, then turned ice cold. She tried to move it but it hung, heavy and excruciating, by her side.

Wes and Laura's faces faded.

Once more steely hands connected, with her hip this time. Her feet left the floor. The wall moved toward her, crushed her.

40

Edith Preston held the arm Spike offered her. He felt her tremble and felt how warm and clammy her hand was on his skin. "Are you sick, Mrs. Preston?" he asked.

"Please call me Edith. No, I was a little shocked to see you, that's all. I thought you were going to give me some terrible news. Are—"

"No, Edith, I'm not."

A blond man hovered in the hall at Edwards Place and the looks he aimed at Spike were not welcoming.

"Would you like something to eat?" Edith asked. "I know how you busy men forget to stop for lunch. Some sandwiches?"

"I just ate lunch," Spike said. "But thank you. Could we have a little chat somewhere?"

"Thank you, Michael," Edith said to the other man in a surprisingly strong voice. "Come along." She took Spike to a sitting room with a view over a rose garden and they sat down in matching yellow arm-chairs. Two deputies were poised to take Michael in once Spike had time to settle with Edith.

"I don't suppose Mr. Preston is here?" Spike said. "Or any other family members?" He wanted to rush but knew he'd only baffle her if he did.

"No," she said. "My husband took my daughter-in-law to New Orleans. He'll go on to Chicago for a meeting and Laura will return to Toussaint with Wes."

No useful information, except that he wouldn't be interrupted by the Prestons.

With his hands hanging between his knees, he rotated his hat by the brim. "Darn, I guess people see what they want to see," he said. "Someone in town said they thought they'd seen your husband and Jilly together first thing this mornin'. I was hopin' if I found him, I'd find her."

Edith moved to the edge of her chair. "Jilly will be at her café. She's always real busy right now."

"She's not there," Spike said. "Wazoo's been helpin' her out while Missy Durand holds things together at Hungry Eyes. I came from the café and Wazoo's worried. She hasn't heard a word from Jilly today."

"I'll call her house," Edith said.

"She's not there. She's . . . look, I owe it to you to be straightforward. Guy's in New Orleans and I called him. He told me she'd mentioned meeting up with Mr. Preston but he didn't know where. She said Mr. Preston wanted to discuss some things with her in private and then they were going on somewhere.

Maybe for a meal. I was hopin' they were here. Too bad." He put a hand on an arm of the chair to get up.

"Don't go," Edith said. "I should be able to find out where Jilly is easier than you—and quicker." She took out a handkerchief and ran it over her mouth. Beads of sweat popped on her forehead. "Oh, my Jilly. She's the best thing I ever accomplished in my life and I ran away and left her behind. Please don't let her be punished for what I did."

"Hush," Spike said, wishing he'd taken Cyrus up on his offer to come with him—well, almost. Deputy Lori was good at these things but Spike decided she'd be more useful dealing with Michael.

"I can't imagine why Daddy would arrange a meeting with Jilly—unless he wants to be the one to tell her some marvelous news on his own. I will be so cross with that man if he ruins what I have in mind. I even have a cake. . . . No, I know that man of mine and I can figure out exactly what he's cooked up."

"You can?" Spike wanted her to just get it all out. Now.

"I surely can. I just bet he arranged for them to rendezvous at Prestons—that's our antiques store, very famous."

Spike nodded. Time was passing and who knew how much they had left? "So he and Laura were going to get together with Jilly in New Orleans."

"Well—" Edith frowned "—let's just say he probably wanted to talk to Laura first—just to make sure she understood a few things. She's a lovely woman and I know she'll be as excited as I am. But you men . . . Forgive me, I should have said that sometimes men don't understand women as well as we understand ourselves. I'd like to contact the shop if that's agreeable to you."

He hadn't expected this. If Preston was there, more harm than good might be done, but what was he supposed to do, tell Edith not to call her own husband?

She had taken a cell phone from a drawer in the table beside her chair. Odd, Spike thought, since there was a regular phone on top of the table. Edith hit a single number and waited. Spike wouldn't have pegged her as a woman who programmed numbers into her phone.

"Is that you, Russell?" Edith said. "Yes, it's Edith Preston. I'm tryin' to track down that family of mine." She giggled. "I know they always want me to know where they are and that's why I called you. Is Mr. Preston in?"

She slumped a little. "Well, if that isn't the worst luck. He's already gone to Chicago? That means I'll be lucky to hook up with him before tomorrow. Russell, would you do me a favor?"

Edith listened, a satisfied smile hovering. "No wonder Mr. Preston thinks so much of you. You are just so accommodatin'." She listened again, for several minutes and with the smile still on her face. "Why thank you. I'm glad of the information." She hung up and sat there with a faraway look in her eyes. "All I ever hoped for was a close family. Now I've got it and it gives me such joy."

That's just peachy. "By the look of you, you got some good news," he said.

Edith gave a little squeal. "Jilly did go to the shop. That dear girl, she wanted to show interest in the shop—that's how our manager, Russell Smith, saw it. She was disappointed Daddy wasn't there, but before Russell could try to track him down, guess what happened?"

Spike inclined his head. "I never was the best at guessing games, ma'am."

"Why, Wes arrived and Russell said he'd never seen him more happy than he was when he saw Jilly." She sighed. "I know Wes has been tryin' to let Jilly know she's welcome in the family."

"That's nice." Spike felt his blood pressure climb.

"Do you know what that Wes did?" Edith didn't wait for a reply. "He took Jilly right out of that shop and they were going out to eat together. When Daddy and Laura arrived a bit later, Daddy did a little bit of business and sent Laura off to join Wes and Jilly. Oh, listen to me babble. It's just that I've prayed for this. How I wish I could have been with them."

Spike stood up. He had to talk to Guy and Nat. "All's well that ends well," he said with a building sense of horror at the thought of Jilly being with Wes Preston. "I bet Wes knows all the best restaurants in town. Did they go to Emeril's?"

Edith frowned. "Silly me, I should have asked. All

Wes said was he was goin' to his favorite place. Some-where he goes all the time."

"You're makin' a mistake."

"I'm fresh out of choices, dammit, Nat. If Russell Smith arrives with a team of lawyers and his con-gressman—make that, senator—I won't have to worry about whether or not to work here. But he's our only hope. He was the last one to see Jilly."

Nat pushed a forefinger into the corner of each eye. "What makes you think he'll tell you more than he told Edith? He's not going to know where that creep took her."

Guy was grateful for the information Spike had got but he wished it could have been just a little bit more.

A brief tap on the office door stopped Guy. He stood up, past sweating or shaking and now so mad at his own helplessness, he hated himself.

A uniformed officer ushered a smooth-looking blond man ahead of him. "This is Mr. Russell Smith, sir," the officer said, and withdrew.

"First time I was in a police car," Russell said, and smiled. "Interesting experience. Now I know why crooks like to pull hoods over their heads when they get a ride on the city."

Guy didn't care.

"Why is that, Mr. Smith?" Nat asked hastily.

Smith gave a short laugh. "People peer in to see who you are. I felt as if I must have done something wrong."

"You were told you could drive your own car, I believe," Guy said. "You're the one doing us a favor." A muscle twitched by his mouth.

"Yes." Smith gave Guy a hard look. "I could also have walked, the way I'll walk back, but I wanted the experience. What's on your mind, or is subtle intimidation part of your job description?"

Laughter, Nat's, wiped the tension out of the moment. "Pull up a chair, Mr. Smith. My partner is one of those serious men who never learned to relax. He's known around here as Smiley."

Guy did smile at that. "Yes, please sit down," he said. "I thought it would be easier to talk here than at the shop. This is very private. Russell—may I call you Russell?"

"Of course." The man sat on a folding metal chair. "I admit I'm nervous as well as curious."

"Mr. Sam Preston is the owner of the antiques shop you manage?"

"Yes. I've worked there for eight years. I like it. Mr. Preston puts a great deal of trust in me. It wouldn't work if he couldn't because he's quite rarely there."

"Did you see him today?" Guy made himself sit down again.

"In the middle of the afternoon. He came in with his daughter-in-law, Mrs. Laura Preston."

He couldn't, Guy told himself, ask too many obvious questions, but he had to go for broke somehow because without Jilly he didn't give a damn what happened to him.

"Well, that's good news," he said, showing his teeth—he hoped, in a smile. "He'll be able to tell me where I need to look and I can clear up this little matter. I wish I'd known, I could have saved your time."

"He's already left town," Russell said. "He's a very busy man."

Guy swallowed. He needed inspiration. "Does he often bring Laura with him? I expect she gets bored bein' around the house."

"Oh, no," Russell said. "She's a busy woman. And she ought to be a happy one today." He lowered his voice. "I shouldn't say this but today she became the owner of a very important diamond. A canary dia- mond—they're yellow. Mr. Preston got it at auction and he loves his family so much. He's always giving the ladies fabulous gifts. He put it in her hand like it was a potato chip." He laughed at the picture in his own mind. "She popped that beauty on right away and waved Mr. Preston off. She was so happy."

"Nice," Guy said, thinking that Preston should reserve his gift-giving for his wife.

"They only missed Mr. Wes and his friend, Jilly, by less than an hour but Laura wasn't bothered. She said she knew just where they'd be and she'd catch up with them."

Exactly eight minutes later, with Russell Smith already on his way back to Prestons Antiques, Guy slipped out of a side door at the station and broke into a run.

He didn't stop for the traffic that honked or the cab-drivers who hung out of windows and cursed him.

He had just talked to Amy. She called back because she'd forgotten to tell him about the place Sam and Wes used as their private pleasure club. If Amy was right, Wes Preston liked to eat where there were no other customers: in a back room on the third floor of Jazz Babes.

41

Guy had sat on plenty of bar stools in his time. In his line of work, bars, where there were a lot of men and women looking for a friend with open ears, were the places to find the answers he needed. Sometimes.

Okay, so it didn't happen nearly often enough.

Concentrate, dammit. While he was organizing, looking for entrances and exits, restrooms, stairs, closed doors, Jilly might be dying.

Jazz Babes hadn't showed up on his radar until after Pip Sedge died—not in any way that had left a big impression. Nat knew the place from some petty stuff that came up before he and Guy became partners.

Guy made circles on the lacquered wood countertop with the bottom of his glass. He touched the beer to his mouth from time to time. The lights were low, the music loud, the decor opulent, the clientele well heeled. Most men came in alone and were met by some of the most beautiful women Guy had ever seen—women dressed to advertise, to suggest.

A male bartender swiped a cloth in arcs down the length of the bar. He wore a Hawaiian shirt in pink and green—hibiscus and palm fronds. A heavy gold cross nestled in graying chest hair and three more crosses dangled from his left ear. He nodded and turned up the corners of his mouth at Guy. "Drinkin' an early dinner?" he said, and sniggered. "Ain't very hungry, are you?"

"Drinkin' is the one thing I do slowly," Guy said. "You worked here long?"

"Long enough. Pay's good, no one messes with me, hours like clockwork. What's not to like?"

Guy puffed up his cheeks and slowly expelled the air. "How'd you get so lucky? Jockey I work for is a pig. All he wants is all you've got—for nuthin'." Fortunately Mr. Lucky didn't ask what Guy did.

The bartender moved off in response to a yelling customer. He'd go to the men's room, Guy decided—then "get lost" and see how he could get himself to the third floor.

Long fingernails ran along the side of his neck.

Guy looked sideways into a pair of green eyes that would do a cat proud. Red hair, too, long and sleek—and white skin, lots of it. The woman looked at him over the shoulder of a man in a business suit, and she winked. He raised his eyebrows.

Seated on almost touching stools, the female had her legs open and resting on the man's thighs. She fluttered those fingernails at Guy, who sipped his beer. The man turned his head and discovered the love of his life eyeing Guy.

She treated her companion to a big, wet, sucking kiss while he took his wallet out of his inside jacket pocket. Licking Red's neck, he pulled out several hundreds and fluttered the bills in front of her eyes. She made a playful grab for the money, then pouted when he held it out of her reach.

A white satin halter and tiny matching shorts made for a picture Guy might have watched if he'd had time. He stood up, lifted a finger to the bartender and pointed at his still half-full glass. As an afterthought, he gulped down more before he settled his hat low over his eyes.

Red caught the tip of her tongue between her teeth. Evidently she thought she was too much woman for one man. And, whooee, maybe she was at that. The man of the moment let her have the bills, and while she kissed them, he gripped the bottom of the halter and hauled it above considerable breasts. A cheer went up and she smiled fatuously all around, supporting herself proudly with her hands, caressing her skin with greenbacks.

"Twenty a kiss," the jokester yelled, pointing at nipples the size of russet-colored saucers. "Come on up."

Several customers rushed forward waving their twenties and Guy used the diversion to make his way to the men's room. He didn't want to think of Jilly being in this place. A backward glance gave him a view of several of the house ladies collecting money for those little kisses. Laughter climbed. Red's man stuck a hand inside her shorts and gave her a lower-back massage.

The sideshow could be the most useful thing that ever happened to Guy. He pushed through red-and-gold-striped draperies that covered an archway. Everywhere he looked he saw more sumptuous fabrics. The low lights probably helped the way the place looked. They obviously sprayed the place with perfume, but it didn't mix so well with the scent of booze.

Stairs at the front of the building rose a short flight and made a turn to another. A sign pointed where he supposedly wanted to go and he turned that way. He was jumpy again and desperation started a panicky sweat along his backbone. He used his wide-eyed, vacant look and stumbled a couple of times on the way. All he wanted to find was an elevator.

He went into the men's room and stood in front of a urinal. You could always rely on beer at such moments.

The door opened again and he flexed the muscles in his back.

The new arrival stood next to him. Then followed him to the sinks. Guy looked at Nat in the mirror and barely stopped himself from landing a punch. They knew him here, he'd said as much.

"I've been followin' you," Nat said, as if he'd never spoken to Guy before. "I saw you puttin' the rush on my strawberry. That girl's expensive. You owe me."

491

"I didn't touch her." And she hadn't seemed like a cokie who did it for cocaine to him.

"She touched you, man. You give her what she wanted, huh? You make plans to see her later?"

Guy barely caught the movement of Nat's beckoning left forefinger. That meant they would scuffle and get close enough to pass a message. You couldn't trust an inch of a place like this. Chances were bugs and cameras were permanent design features.

He made to walk past Nat, who grabbed him around the neck and landed a not-so-light punch in his gut. They went down and rolled. "Elevator. Turn right out of here. Around first corner. Mess up my face a bit."

Guy frowned and gave Nat's nose a swipe. Blood appeared on cue. "Asshole," he ground out.

"Fucker," Nat snapped back, then, "I'll be around," very softly.

Guy struggled to his feet, gave Nat a kick and left.

Those cameras could be out here, too. Pretending to be dazed, he started back toward the bar, stopped, shook his head, and went in the opposite direction. If he was being watched, he'd have company before he ever reached his goal.

An elevator with stainless-steel doors was exactly where Nat had said. Guy peered closely at it, swayed and pressed a button. "I'm comin', honey," he said, hitching at his jeans.

The elevator opened and he fell inside. He pressed a button again and in a second the car rose swiftly, silently upward. Out of habit, Guy adjusted the left side of his jeans jacket. The Sauer was right where it should be.

All the way to the third floor in one smooth ride and the doors opened again. He stepped far enough forward to cut off the sensor and keep the door open, then he glanced left.

"I won't do your dirty work anymore." A woman's voice, not so loud but high and breaking, came from a room on the opposite side of the corridor and to the right. Exactly where Amy had said Wes liked to have his special lunches.

"I'll help you with her. Then I'll get what we need and meet you where we said." Guy recognized Wes's voice. He also swallowed hard, twice. He could figure what they were talking about.

Black rage welled in him. If Jilly had died, so would they. It would be all the justice she got—experience had taught him that.

Placing heel and toe carefully, he blessed the soft carpet and approached the room. Once inside, the balloon would go up. He'd have a second, maybe two or three to size up what he faced.

Jilly dead.

Guy reached the open glass doors, flattened his back to the wall outside and pulled his gun. He crooked his arm, held the weapon at shoulder height and rolled forward.

Wes and Laura Preston stood toe to toe with Laura where she couldn't see Guy. Wes had his back to him.

Guy took in the scene rapidly. Divans heaped with

cushions. The only thing missing was a tent.

Blood smeared one wall, dragged down in a wide swath.

"I know I have to be the one to get what we need," Wes said, shaking his wife. "We're wasting time we don't have. When we're out, I'm shutting and locking this room until we can clean it up."

"I'm not transporting a body," Laura said.

Guy cocked his gun and swung into the room—and saw Jilly. On the floor, facing the bloodstained wall, her body was at a strange angle. The arm he could see hung behind her and blood soaked her shredded blouse. He couldn't see her face.

"Look," Wes said. "I'll make it worth your while. What do you want?"

Laura didn't laugh, didn't scoff and didn't ask him for anything.

"Anything you want is yours, sweetheart. Anything."

"Anything?"

Guy jumped Wes and took them both down under his weight. Laura screamed and she yelled "Daddy!" She disgusted him.

Striking again and again with the hand that held the gun, Guy worked on autopilot. He wouldn't let himself look at Jilly, only at the two who would pay.

He saw the moment when Wes went for a shoulder holster. The man hadn't done it often enough to be smooth and Guy disarmed him. He threw the gun behind a divan.

Laura sprawled on the carpet, bleeding from her nose and mouth, and whimpering. She got to her hands and knees and started to crawl. Guy pulled her hands behind her back and slapped on handcuffs. She moaned and pleaded with him, but he shut her out.

Gasping to get his breath, Wes huddled against a divan, curled over as if his gut was broken. Guy reached for a second pair of handcuffs and the man launched his body at him. Guy took the blow in his chest and belly and it was his turn to fight for breath and hold his seared diaphragm.

Reaching for Guy's Sauer, Wes straddled him. He spread himself out, clamping Guy to the floor.

He got a hand on the gun wrist and Guy held on. He locked his fingers and they rolled over and over with Wes slamming Guy's hand down at every opportunity.

"Wes." Laura gave a warning shout—too late.

A shot blasted out and Guy recoiled before Wes fell on top of him. A loose, leaden weight.

Guy pulled his head back to look at his opponent. A line of blood drizzled from his mouth. He looked puzzled and opened his mouth to speak. He choked on blood that rushed out of his mouth now.

The wail Guy heard was Laura's. "Daddy, Daddy, help me."

He'd like to take her by the throat and shake her, but it wouldn't help anything.

With a shove he pushed Wes away until he lay on his back. Blood had flowed from his mouth to spread a bright red stain on his shirt. He attempted to speak again and could only gurgle.

"My son," Sam Preston said, a weapon hanging loosely at his side. "My only son. He never believed I loved him. He kept trying to prove I should. Jilly, Jilly." He looked at Guy with puzzled recognition.

"We need an ambulance," Guy said quietly. "Call 911 and make it quick."

He scrambled across the room and dropped down beside Jilly. He stroked her wildly mussed hair and said, "I love you, cher. I'll always love you. They broke your arm," he whispered. "So much pain."

"Just as well Sam Preston isn't in the mood to shoot you," Nat said, but Guy didn't look at him. "Help's on the way, my friend. Hold on."

The eye Guy could see was hugely swollen shut with dried blood caking the lashes together. Garish colors had already formed. Dreading it, he leaned to see what he could of the rest of her face. The other eye was slightly open, blood from her nose smeared her face. He glanced down and where her blouse was torn away, he could see the point of a fractured collarbone extending through the skin.

"He beat her," he said to Nat. "She's a little thing. She couldn't hurt anyone. This was torture. Why?"

"She wanted what wasn't hers," Laura said. "And Daddy was going to put her in the will. She'd have had an allowance and she's nobody. She's white trash like Edith. I'd rather be a smart black than white trash."

Nat ignored the insult. "Stay where you are," he said, throwing Sam on a divan, facedown, before he cuffed him. "I've called for backup. We'll be taking you in."

"But I stopped my son from killing . . . him."

"Save it."

Guy huddled over Jilly. He should have been able to protect her. A generous woman, full of life and fun—and so much love.

He brought himself to feel for a pulse. Nat tapped him on the shoulder and pointed. Guy looked and saw the lashes on Jilly's good eye blink. And her pulse beat beneath his fingers. She tried to see him better, and she cried, mixing blood with tears. Guy couldn't speak at all, only stare at her, and kiss her cheek gently.

A furor broke out in the corridor. "Medics," a man said loudly. "Where are you?"

Nat went to the doorway and said, "Hi, guys. This way."

Police arrived with the medics and Nat took charge. A medic came to Jilly at once. "Hey, you," he said, kneeling and opening a bag. He listened to her heart and said, "Still beating. Did you take a blow to the head—other than the obvious ones?"

"Yes," she whispered. "At the back but I feel okay."

"No, you don't," he said. "You feel like something a tank ran over."

She mumbled and he leaned close. "I promise you it wasn't a Hummer."

He looked puzzled. "Can you tell me your name, please?"

"Jilly Gable from Toussaint. I run a bakery there." She whimpered with each shallow breath.

"I think her arm's broken," Guy said. "You can see her collarbone, too."

"Nice people you hang out with." The medic examined the arm and every time he moved it a fraction, Jilly wept. His strong, practiced fingers felt gently around her shoulder. "It's probably a dislocation," the medic said. "I don't want to risk a reduction with the clavicle like that on the same side. We need to get her to Emergency."

"This one's gone," another medic said, working over Wes. "The other two need to be taken in."

Guy turned toward Laura. "Did Wes break in at Jilly's house?"

She gave him a drooling leer. "Scared her, didn't he?"

"This one needs to go in, too," the medic with Jilly said.

"I'm all right," she said, almost breathless. "I'll drive home carefully and come back in the morning."

"Her brain got knocked loose," Guy said.

The medic smiled. "Nothing wrong with your brain, huh, Jilly? You want out of here because you're a smart woman. You ought to be screamin' by the way." Arthur, as his name tag read, sat back on his heels and filled a syringe, then he flicked it with finger and thumb. "This is just to make you comfortable." He gave the shot inside the elbow of Jilly's good arm and assembled his equipment. "Try to keep her still. I'll be right back with a gurney."

Wes lay where he'd died. His father and Laura were already on their way downstairs. Nat sat on the couch and Guy held Jilly as if she were a sand sculpture.

She opened her eye and looked at him, managed a little smile, bringing an amazing twinkle to that eye.

"What's funny?"

With his heart still beating too hard, he waited.

"You look strange," she said, forming each word carefully and as if it hurt her mouth.

"You gave me a scare. I'm still scared. Jilly, Amy Girard and Edith helped us find you in time."

Jilly nodded, and winced. "Something to say to you. Got to. I love you, Guy. I've got to say these things now. Something could drop me and what I think would never be known."

"That's right."

"Thank you."

Again he didn't know what to say.

"For telling me you love me and you always will."

"We're going to have things to do," Guy said seriously. "You'll marry me, right? Do you like diamonds? I've been told I must give you something meaningful for you to remember me by."

If Nat were a gentleman, he'd leave the room. Instead he leaned farther and farther forward, listening.

"I won't forget you," Jilly said. "Not ever."

"We'll get out and choose a ring," Guy said.

"Later," Jilly said. "We don't need to rush it."

"Yes, we do." He raised his voice.

Nat laughed and said, "It's okay, Jilly. Leave it to Guy. You need to rest now. They'll immobilize that arm before you go."

Leave it to Guy? Did that mean he was supposed to buy a ring for Jilly all on his own?

Arthur returned with another man. They carried a gurney and set it up close to Jilly. "Let's make sure we've got you comfortable and we'll take you to the hospital to get checked out."

"May I ride along?" Guy said.

The medics looked at each other and nodded. "That'll be fine."

"I'll follow," Nat said.

Jilly looked up at Guy. "I think we're going to be a threesome." She winced and the corner of her mouth bled again.

"No, no," Nat said. "I'm not coming in the ambulance."

Jilly frowned. "I meant Guy, Goldilocks and me." Her words grew thicker. "I love you so much, Guy."

The professionals did their work and transferred her smoothly to the gurney. They covered her with a blanket and headed out.

"Too bad people mess up so badly," a cop commented while they rode the elevator down. "That Mrs. Preston loved her creep of a husband."

Jilly grimaced and her other eye closed.

"She insisted on telling him something," the man said. "What she really wanted, she told him, just like he was listening, was to have their baby."

Epilogue

Two weeks later

At least she'd persuaded Guy out of renting a hospital bed, and out of insisting she be at his house because it was all on one floor.

There was nothing wrong with her legs, apart from a few almost faded bruises.

After two weeks she still hurt, but she wasn't an invalid, never had been.

Guy scuffed quietly into her dark bedroom and peered down at her. "You asleep?" he whispered.

To lie or not to lie? He checked on her all night every night—and he refused to as much as sit on her bed in case he hurt her. "Awake," she said. It wasn't that she was mad at him, just that she wanted him between the sheets with her, and with her arm brace, wound dressings, slowly healing ribs and black eyes. Well, the eyes were only green now.

"You're not sleepin' enough," Guy said, and turned on a lamp. He pulled his chair as close as he could get to her, sat and did a close facial examination. "Any pain?"

"I'm as good as well, Guy."

He raised his brows. "That's good to hear. Wonderful. The reception's going to be at Rosebank. Reb's all riled up because she wanted it at Clouds End, but with her due date so close . . ." He shrugged.

"What reception?" Jilly asked. "When?"

"In about three weeks. You have a reception after a wedding."

"Ooh." She sat up, wished she'd moved more slowly, but shot out her good arm and pulled him, almost nose to nose, by the lapel of the old bathrobe he wore. He wore it every night, over nothing. She knew because she'd found ways to check.

Guy rested his lips on hers.

Jilly smiled and put an inch or so between their mouths. "You're incorrigible. You've arranged a wedding for three weeks' time. What am I going to wear— green and yellow to match whatever color my baggy eyes are by then?"

"I love you in green. Or yellow."

She punched his shoulder. "Change of subject before I explode. Wally Hibbs called again."

"To ask if the puppies are born? I hope he remembered to ask how you are."

"He did."

"The way things are goin' we may not have enough pups to go round. We're keepin' one."

Jilly shook her head. "I used to make decisions."

"You still make all the decisions," Guy said. "I didn't want another oyster casserole for dinner, but did I say so? Nope, I ate it because you wanted it."

He watched her face, loving the mock resignation in her eyes, and the curve of her lips. "We'll have a girl."

Her eyebrows shot up.

"A girl puppy. The one we'll keep."

"The one we keep," she said. "Of course, I must have forgotten discussing that."

"Funny woman. Just a minute." He went quickly to the other bedroom where he slept, and where Goldilocks sat in her upscale whelping box. Her eyes followed every move he made. He gave her a good scratch between the ears and stroked her bulging sides.

Back to Jilly. He couldn't stand not being with her.

"Edith came while you were at Homer's today," she said in a small voice.

"Why didn't you say so before?"

"I guess I avoid talkin' about any of it. Amy and Wazoo came with her."

"That's too many people. I'll—"

"You won't do anythin' about it. Edith moved out of Edwards Place. She's stayin' with the Hibbs at the Majestic. And she's just about taken over at All Tarted Up. She's sad about that man but I think she's relieved he's not a danger to her anymore, too. She's not sad they got Michael."

"Good." He surely hoped he'd manage to warm up to Edith Preston. Not only was she going to be his mother-in-law but she showed no signs of leaving Toussaint. "We're never goin' to know more about the matchbook, but we found out from Preston that Pip had come to him asking for money back. He won't admit to anythin' about the killin' but it happened the same night Pip made his demands."

She looked at him for too long.

"What?" he said, with an unpleasant feeling he'd flubbed something. "Tell me, Jilly."

"Same old thing. I don't think you should leave the department. You're still talkin' about 'we' and meanin' you and Nat. You belong there. And maybe you owe Nat, too."

He didn't entirely disagree, but pretty much. "I won't be losin' touch with Nat. Hell, he'll probably be hangin' around Wazoo so much we'll think he lives in Toussaint. You're wrong about the rest. I want to be here with you, and all the rest of the crazies who live in the town. Homer's helpin' me come up with ideas for a career change."

"Homer? You haven't said a thing about it to me."

"I haven't wanted you worrying your pretty head."

"Guy Gautreaux, do you have a death wish?"

"Um, did I tell you they've made progress tracing ownership of Jazz Babes? Some glorified accountant, or maybe it's a lawyer, anyway, he's enjoyin' hangin' around in the Caymans and diggin' around for bankin' records."

"I didn't think you could get them there."

"We'll see, but everyone's an expert in somethin'."

She held his hand and took it to her mouth. Holding it there, she said, "Be grateful I'm incapacitated. I'd be doin' one of my 'behind the laundry' numbers otherwise."

Guy shifted on his chair. The woman could talk him into serious sexual frustration anytime she felt like it. "You're gettin' better every day, cher."

Whump, whump, whump. Goldilocks swayed into the room, walked a slow circle, stood to be stroked and swayed out again.

"She likes to check on her people," Guy said. He frowned. "Preston's a coward. People who do what he did usually are. Greedy, pampered and scared. He and Laura are goin' to be household faces. They already are, but wait till the trials start."

"Yes." Jilly looked at the ceiling. "I'm glad Edith's out of that."

Growling and telling her not to waste her sympathy would not be a great idea. "She's better off," he said.

They were quiet after that but Guy figured Jilly was back in the realm of her horror and wished he could wipe that out for her.

He needed to do something he'd been putting off. "Just a minute," he said, and got up.

Jilly's eyes focused on him and she smiled. "You're just the best dog dad."

Trouble was, they weren't sure when the dog got pregnant, but he had something else on his mind, and when he returned from his room again, he felt like a fool. His hands trembled and he kept them in his pockets. *Please don't let me flub this.*

"I did what I was told to do," he said. "I wanted to do it, too."

"You did?" From Jilly's expression he had her full attention.

"If you don't like it, back it goes. I have a couple of other things for you to see, just in case."

Her smile started slow, but spread as wide as he'd ever seen it. "This should be good," she said.

He pulled his hands from his pockets, a small box in one palm, and crossed his arms. "A comment like that could be grounds for an annulment."

She burst into laughter. "We aren't married and we couldn't anul one if we were—not without a bunch of explanations."

"Good," he said, and felt so very good—until he thought about the box again. "Okay, this is different so you may not like it. Made in Spain by an old jewelry family. Do you like colored glass?"

Jilly's lips parted and remained that way.

"Not the gems," he said hurriedly. "I have such a renegade mouth. Stupid, stupid. Enamel and glass or something like that. I like it but you probably won't."

She sighed.

"It's kind of like a red sunrise. There're diamonds along the straight edges and rays go up from the sun. The lines between the stuff are eighteen karat. The rest of the ring's eighteen karat—except for the glass, I mean the enamel glass."

"Sounds like a fruit salad," Jilly said, and fell back on her pillows laughing. "Guy, I love you more than my life but you worry about the small stuff too much."

He almost told her there was nothing small about this *stuff.* Instead he opened the box with an unsteady hand and held it over her face where she could see the ring.

It fell on her face.

"Ow." She sat up again and picked up the glowing thing. "Oh. I've never seen anything like this. I don't put it on my own finger. You do."

Of course he did. "I know that." He took back the ring and slid it onto the ring finger of her left hand. He cleared his throat. "Will you please marry me?"

"Yes." She turned her hand this way and that. "I've wanted to marry you for so long it's a wonder I haven't grown mold waitin'."

"I tried not to love you," he said. "Didn't work. You forced my hand."

He thought she turned a little pink but she said, "You bet I did. What a ring. I feel like a greedy kid, but I can hardly take my eyes off it. It's incredible."

Guy expanded his chest. "I knew you would—no, I didn't know you'd love it but I'm glad you do. Nat said you would."

Once more her lips parted and she blinked. "Nat helped you choose my ring."

"No! He nagged till I showed it to him—after I bought it. Nouveau 1910."

"Huh?"

"That's the name of the collection."

"You did your homework. Guy, would you do something for me?"

"Anythin', you know that."

"Take off your robe and climb carefully into this bed. Just to be beside me."

Hoo mama, he knew he was a weak man in some areas and he should refuse. Guy got up and dropped the robe. And now, fool that he was, he stood there naked. He'd forgotten that.

Jilly whistled and he edged slowly into her bed. "Don't move," he said. "Don't touch anythin'."

"You can touch anythin' you like."

No, he couldn't, but she drove him nuts. Putting an arm over her, he kissed her neck and settled his chin on top of her good shoulder. "Ah, cher, this feels so good. Won't be long before the collarbone will be completely healed and the sling can go. You'll still have to be careful, but . . ." He decided she could make up the end of his sentence herself.

A different sound, definitely from Goldilocks, froze him. The dog thumped her way into the room, whimpering between sad, pained little noises.

Guy lay still.

Jilly found his hand and squeezed it. "Do you think it's time?"

He left the bed and ran to his bedroom again, to return with a thermometer. Goldilocks struggled at first but gave up and let him take her temperature. Guy read it and squared his shoulders. "It's dropped significantly, just like my book says. This is it. Clever girl.

We love you. We love your beautiful babies." He crooned to her, put his face close to hers, and didn't take offence when she walked away from him.

"I'm going to try to keep her in my room," he said. "She'll need to keep walkin' so I'll pull my bed out from the wall so she can make bigger circles."

Jilly swung her feet to the floor and reached for her robe.

"Back in bed," Guy said. "Now."

"Help me with this." She pushed her arm into a sleeve and struggled to drape the rest of the robe around her shoulders.

"Hardheaded woman." Guy finished the job for her and fastened one button at the neck. "All you do is watch."

"That's about all I can do." She sounded disappointed, but she followed Guy next door, ogling her ring every few steps.

Guy examined Goldilocks like a man who had been dealing with pregnant dogs forever. "She's been in labor longer than we've known about. She's bulging and there's fluid."

"I'll call Reb," Jilly said with a panicky feeling in her tummy.

"Put that down," Guy said when she picked up the phone. "Even if Reb were a vet, she's in no shape to come out here in the middle of the night." He held a towel at the ready.

What felt like only minutes passed before Guy gently wiggled a black blob free of Goldilocks. With a soft towel, he rubbed the sac away from the puppy and cut the cord. "Wow," he said. "Number one and we've just begun. That's it, I like the way you sound, pup. Jilly, all you have to do is help me keep 'em warm and keep Goldilocks from accidentally stompin' on them. Rub this one gently."

"Is that all?" she said, taking the firstborn and tucking a piece of fleece around it. Already its mouth opened hungrily. "Healthy puppy here."

"Cyrus wants to marry us and I've told him it'll work."

Jilly felt disoriented. "You did what?"

"Puppy two comin' to you."

On autopilot, Jilly dealt with another newborn. "We're both fallen-away Catholics, more or less. I thought we'd have a justice of the peace."

"And ruin Cyrus's life?"

"Oh, get *on*."

"He's comin' to start talkin' to us tomorrow. Don't worry, they don't say you gotta bring the kids up Catholic anymore."

She realized Guy was on an overload, but this was too much. "Did you also find out if we have to give up birth control?"

"No. And I'm not going to. We'll have to give it up till we get pregnant, but we'll make our own decisions about things like that."

"Pregnant?" she cried. If her hands weren't full, she'd throw something at him. "When did you think we'd get around to talkin' about that? You take the cake, Guy Gautreaux. You're gettin' carried away with this birth thing."

He pushed a third pup into her lap and returned at once to Goldilocks. "She's delivering fast," he said.

Jilly started rubbing again, but she managed to smile at her ring while she did so. "Sounds like you've got good plans. I wouldn't want to hurt Cyrus—or you."

Center Point Publishing
600 Brooks Road ● PO Box 1
Thorndike ME 04986-0001 USA

(207) 568-3717

US & Canada:
1 800 929-9108

DISCARD